STANDING IN THE
EYE OF THE STORM

STANDING IN THE
EYE OF THE STORM

Copyright © 2013 by . Teresa L. Arrowood

Published by Titan Inkorp.
Cover by Titan Inkorp

Dedication

To all of those that have suffered through the shame and guilt of abuse, this book is dedicated to those who were courageous enough to make to the other side of that terror. God bless those who were brave in the sight of danger to help and protect those who were unable to protect themselves.

Acknowledgements

Thank you to my sweet husband who essentially gave up his wife for the year it took to get this book in print. Thank you for becoming the house husband so that I could devote my time to this project. I love you.

To my parents and my children who supported me during this adventure. It means more than you can ever imagine.

Most of all I want to thank God for giving me this story to share with you.

Psalm 119: 105
Thy word is a lamp unto my feet, and a light unto my path.

CHAPTER 1

I didn't know it, but today was about to be the changing point in my life.

I guess if you looked at it, I was treading water and eventually would come up to take a gulp of air on occasion. At the age of twenty-one, I thought my life was set, having the same thoughts as any other person at that time of my life, of having a husband and family. I had my own career, and I had really pushed for it. Being an only child, I felt that I needed to excel in whatever I did.

None of my father's side of the family had more than a high school education, and there were few of the nieces and nephews that went on to college. My mother's side was about the same although her side of the family was smaller.

Small towns at that time of life spent most of their time on making a living than education, especially when the families were large.

I stood at the window gazing out onto my front lawn, mostly thinking of having to come home after my shift to clean house, but Lily had asked for me to meet her after work. Oh, the things she had gotten me into, blind dates were often her forte, she always felt that I had to have a man in my life. Ryan was the last one, and that had been approximately one year ago. We had tried to make a go of it, but there were just so many roadblocks we just couldn't make a connection. I had known him for a long time, going to school with him for more than six years.

It was closing in on two in the afternoon, and I was due to start my shift at three; I sure wasn't looking forward to it. At least I was going to be meeting Lily after work, which was not typical but it was better than going home to an empty apartment.

Walking on the ward, I was greeted quickly with a

ready smile from

Carol, the hospital's clerk and my right hand at times. "Hello, Bella, ready for an exciting night in the never-ending soap opera of trauma?" She gave a smirk and a bit of sarcasm.

I looked at her equally as thrilled. "It never ceases to amaze me how people can manage to inflict pain on themselves or from the aid of others." I turned to go into trauma 1, and she stopped me abruptly, stepping in front of me. I looked at her, bewildered.

"Bella, you really don't want to take that patient. You want to take care of trauma 2, Marilyn has trauma 1."

"Okay, I'll bite. Why do I want to take care of trauma 2?" I looked at her now with a down-turned look as if I was trying to look through her.

"Marilyn started trauma 1, but believe me, she missed the boat and did you a tremendous favor." She said this with a light in her eyes and a sheepish grin. I started to feel a cold, unforgiving tremor through me. What had they set me up for this time? I cocked my head to the side and looked at her warily.

"Okay, Carol, what are you and the rest of the team set me up on this time?"

Carol looked at me and shook her head. "Oh, Bella, no setup, just dumb luck on your part. Wish I had such luck. I mean as patients come, you hit the jackpot."

"Okay, now you have me scared." I pushed my hair behind my ears and threw my stethoscope around my neck, preparing for battle.

"Bella, no kidding, you have the best of the best, you have Carter Blake, the most eligible bachelor that I know of in this area of the country." She started to flush, and the smile on her face was from ear to ear, it almost looked painful. I lifted an eye brow to comment, and I felt my face contort to a small grin.

"You mean the Carter Blake, the die-for-a-date-never-seen-with-anyone Carter Blake?"

"That's the one, Bella, maybe you're the one to melt him." She fanned herself as if she was going to faint, reminding me of Scarlett O'Hara.

"Come on, Carol, if this is for sure him, why would you think that? I mean, he must have women everywhere. He's no lack of looks by any means, and I really do not need to be set up."

"Bella, don't look at it like that, besides if I had the chance, I would take it. He's gorgeous, not to mention he is filthy rich."

"His father is filthy rich. From what I have heard, he doesn't have much to do with his father's company."

"I bet he does. Guys like that don't just give up and leave a family fortune.

If they do, they're nuts."

"Well, I better get started or I'll never get out of here tonight."

Carol gave me a wink and started to turn back to her desk. "Maybe you won't want to once you meet him."

I walked into trauma 2 cautiously. Dr. Reed met me with a very blank appearance, one that didn't give an ounce of information away. He was stern and decisive in his look, his eyes were dark and without emotion. He handed me the Mac as we stood at the foot of Blake's bed. He looked as though he was totally drained of his thoughts and had no more drive in him.

"Isabella, I want you to stay with him for a while, it's not likely that there will be further complications. For sure, he has a concussion. The first twenty-four hours will be the tell-tale of Mr. Blake. The car he was driving was pretty banged up. Lucky for him he had a seat belt on, or it would have been much worse. He could have gone through the windshield. As it is, he still hit the windshield pretty hard, the air bag did not deploy. I look for him to have a pretty bad headache when he awakes, he also hit the steering wheel.

You might want to watch his heart a little closer. Nothing showing now, but you never know. I would rather watch for problems as not."

I started to look through the chart, taking a deep breath then looking to Dr. Reed questionably. "So what caused the accident?"

Dr. Reed gave me a rather-quizzical look and appeared to be sorting out facts to himself. "Well, we aren't sure, the police report seems to guide to the road conditions, and the fact that speed may have been a factor, we aren't really sure. He hit a tree taking a curve too quickly, it's a wonder he is alive.

So far, there doesn't appear to be any major issues, but we will know more when he wakes up. Just stay with him, I'll see that he is the only one you have for now."

Dr. Reed turned and walked from the room slowly after looking at Carter Blake and the heart monitor in which he was now attached. I shrugged and thought to myself, *This is going to be a long night.*

Walking closer up to the head of the bed I saw that he most certainly had taken a beating. His eyes were closed, red, and swollen, his face covered with dirt and multiple cuts and scratches. He still had traces of glass in his dark unruly hair and cloth tape on his forehead where the ambulance had secured him to a backboard. I quickly assessed him, looking at the heart monitor determining that his rhythm and rate were good and blood pressure was on the low side. Not altogether a bad sign, it depended on what was normal for him and what this accident might have done to him. He felt cool to touch.

Walking over to the blanket warmer, I heard a few words uttered. Turning around, he was lying very still while his eyes remained closed. The words spoken were not comprehensible, so I continued with my duties and placed a blanket over him. To get a better view of the cuts and scratches, I got a washcloth and washed his face gently. They did not appear too bad, but the one over his right eye wanted to bleed, so I quickly tended to it. Looking to his chest, there didn't appear to be any cuts, but there were some red marks from the seat belt, I was sure it would eventually leave a large bruise.

It took me at least a half hour to clean up all the trash and dirt from around him. I could now see his face, he was very handsome indeed. Carol wasn't kidding; his eyelashes should have belonged to a girl. They were long and fanned out against his cheek now bruised and red. He almost had the face of a child, innocence if you will. My thoughts drifted on me, *you must have someone somewhere that is worried about you.*

Starting to speak to him, I knew from what I had been taught that no matter how far-out you might think your patients are, it is proven that they can hear you. Reaching down, I took his hand and clasped it in mine; there was never a stir from him. His hands were warm against mine. On examining them, there were no cuts, scrapes, or bruising. He did have an indention on his ring finger reflecting the presence of a past ring or wedding band that was no longer there.

"Mr. Blake, can you hear me? I am Isabella, your nurse. You're in North Dale Trauma Medical Center, you had a car accident earlier this evening. If you can hear me, I want you to squeeze my hand." I waited patiently for his response, but none came. So I tried another approach.

"Carter, I'm Isabella, I'm your nurse. You had an accident earlier, but you are safe now, can you squeeze my hand?" I waited, and finally I felt a little twitch from his fingers.

"It's okay, Carter, you're fine. I'm going to be with you, I'm not leaving.

I'll be watching you just rest now." Breathing a sigh of relief, I hadn't noticed that I had been holding my breath all this time. I started to take my hand away, and he gripped it enough for me to know not to leave him, and a strange sinking feeling filled me when I saw a lone tear slide down the side of his face. I sat down on the stool beside him and wiped his cheek. I left my hand in his in assurance that I was not leaving him.

Marilyn Strike, one of the main trauma nurses that pretty much got what she wanted, walked into trauma 2 and made a crude remark, slithering in as she approached me. How this woman ever became a nurse was beyond me, she had no compassion and absolutely had no tact. She spoke with venom most of the time. She was slender and sinfully beautiful with her auburn hair and jade-colored eyes. Having the build of any man's dream, she could have anyone she wanted and most often did whatever she had to get them.

"So you got the lottery tonight, you better enjoy it while you can. Too bad he came in after they brought me a patient or I would have had him. Maybe I will ask for reassignment." She stared daggers through me. Tilting my head to the side I looked at her sternly.

"Marilyn, don't you have work to do?"

"Yes, but I would much rather hang out with Mr. Blake. You know, Isabella. I pretty much get what I want and when I want it."

Looking at her, my look became frosted. "Marilyn, don't you have a broom you're going to miss?"

She curled her lip and started to turn away but stopped. "Sticks and stones honey, just remember I always get what I want." She walked off easily, and I took a deep breath, hoping that she would not appear for the rest of the night. But then again, it's almost too good to be true. I looked at the clock, and it was nine in the evening. It had been a long night. Bringing my chair closer to the bed, I placed the Mac in my lap to look at the reports and the description of the accident. We still didn't have a contact number for family.

I started to look through some of the things he had with him and found a number with a girl's name on it. It's the only number I have to a family or friend, so I decided to take a shot and hope that it was someone that was in some kinship to him. Dialing the phone, I soon heard it ring, and then I heard a distressed voice on the other end.

"Hello." The voice was shaky and small.

"Hello, this is Isabella at North Dale University Hospital. Is Beth

Andrews there please?"

The voice was hesitant and cracking with a small held-back sob. "This is Beth Andrews," she squeaked.

I approached this cautiously as I could. It wasn't easy when you didn't know the person on the other end. "Beth, this is Isabella. I'm a nurse at North Dale Trauma Medical Center. Would you by any chance know a Mr. Carter Blake?" She answered quickly, "Oh my god, that's my brother. Is he okay?

What happened to him?" Her voice was shaking and she began to cry.

"Beth, I have Carter here with me, I'm taking care of him. He was in a car accident earlier this evening. I'm sorry no one had contacted you. I just found this number among his belongings and took a shot someone would know where to find his family."

"Oh, please take care of him, he is all the family I have." She hesitated, and I heard a sniffle on the other end. "He was probably trying to get to me.

Please tell him I'm okay, that I'm with Molly. He's awake, isn't he?"

I choked and began to talk to Beth again, hoping to calm her, but I didn't know how she would handle just finding out her brother had been in a major car accident. "Beth, Carter has been in a pretty bad collision, he hit a tree.

12

The doctor has been in to see him and says he sees no problem right now, but he is unconscious and has a concussion as a result of hitting the windshield.

We will know more when he wakes up."

"Can I see him?"

"I don't see any reason that you can't, but he isn't awake to talk. He does respond, so that's a good sign."

"Tell him I'm coming and will be there soon as I can. Oh, tell him I'm okay and that I love him."

I assured Beth that I would tell her brother and hung up the telephone.

Stepping back to Carter, I took his hand again and looked at his face and spoke softly to him.

"Carter, it's Isabella. I just got in touch with Beth. She said to tell you she was okay, she's with Molly. She will be here to see you soon. Don't worry, she's fine. She said to tell you she loves you."

He tried to open his eyes, but he just couldn't seem to manage it. He grasped my hand with his and gave it a little squeeze. Leaning in, I pushed the hair away from his eyes. His skin was starting to warm and felt velvet soft, my heart sank to my feet. I didn't understand this feeling, it was foreign to me. Swallowing hard, I left my fingertips lightly against his temple. I felt eyes on me, and I never turned to see who it was, hearing footsteps as they clicked against the tile floor.

"Isabella, are you going to take a break?" It's Carol's voice behind me, and I tried to regain a little of my composure. I delayed in my answer as I looked at his face and studied it so that it was ingrained into my brain. "Isabella, are you okay?" I felt my breath as it stuck in my throat. I didn't move or turn to Carol to speak.

"No, um, I think I am going to stick around a while."

I heard Carol shift behind me, and I managed to get out a few more words to her. "Carol, do me a favor and call

Lilly, tell her I can't make it. I'll call her tomorrow." I finally managed to turn to her, and she looked at me in alarm.

"You okay? You look like you've seen a ghost."

"I'm fine." I lifted my fingers to my lips being unsure of my own reaction.

I felt like I had known this man all my life. It sent shivers through me, it's unnerving. I got this unbelievable pull, and I knew I couldn't leave him.

Turning back to him, I placed my hand in his, rubbing the top of his hand gently. I felt his hand relax at the touch of mine.

"Oh, I see." Carol stilled momentarily. "It's almost quitting time. Do you want me to stay with him until you change?" I continued to gaze at him.

"Ah, no, I think I will just stay here with him."

"Okay. I'll talk to you later."

"Sure," I answered almost silently. I sat down next to him and held his hand in mine. I sat silently by him, a stranger, listening to the hypnotic sound of the heart monitor. I thought back to a time when I really thought there was such a thing as love at first sight, which had long dissipated. Now I wasn't so sure. Why was I so enraptured by him?

I awoke to find my head lying on his hand, my hand still clasping his.

The light from early day cast a shadow over the sheets, and I slowly raised my head and looked up at him. His face was unstressed and calm, his lips slightly parted, his eyes closed, and his lashes fanned over his cheeks. He looked so peaceful. I stood and walked to the window and looked out onto the new day.

Seeing people walking quickly here and there, cars trying to get away from the rush, I wondered what was so important that they were in such a hurry. I was soon startled by footsteps entering the room.

"Isabella?" Dr. Reed said with a surprised voice. I turned to see him standing at the foot of Carter's bed.

"Dr. Reed." I tried to push my hair back out of my face and wiped it with the back of my hand.

He clasped his hands together and asked, "Well, how's the patient?"

I stepped closer to the bed and put my hand on Carter's. "He responds, but he hasn't opened his eyes yet."

"Well, like I said earlier, he is lucky to be alive. If he doesn't wake up soon, I'll send him for another CAT scan. I don't think we are going to find anything. I'm sure he has a lot of swelling since the air bag did not deploy.

The car was pretty beat-up from what I understand, it might be in the best interest of all to send him."

"He did squeeze my hand earlier. I was hoping he would have opened his eyes by now."

Dr. Reed walked up to the top of the bed and spoke his name and checked his pupil response as he did. "Mr. Blake, it's Dr. Reed. Can you move your arms or legs?" He put his pen light back into his pocket and stepped back. He then took Carter's hands in each of his. "Mr. Blake, can you squeeze my hands?" There was no effort. He released his hands and laid them back down on the bed and walked to the foot and checked his reflexes.

"Isabella, there is a reaction, his reflexes and his pupil reaction is good, but he isn't following simple commands yet."

I looked at him and lifted my hand to him. "Please, just a minute." I walked back to his hand and took it in mine as before. "Carter, it's Isabella, can you squeeze my hand?" Dr. Reed watched intently as Carter slowly squeezed my hand.

"Well, Ms. Cameron, you must have the touch. I think we will go ahead and send him for a CAT scan just to make sure. By the way, I thought your shift was over hours ago."

"It was, but I was kind of waiting for his sister to come in. She was coming in after I talked to her, but so far she hasn't arrived."

"Oh, okay, I suggest after that you go home and get some rest."

"I will, but for now I think I will stay a while. I am on vacation now anyway."

"Do you know this patient, Isabella?" He looked at me, bewildered.

"No, I don't." I didn't realize how strange this sounded until now.

"Well, I hope if I ever end up in here, I have you for a nurse. At least you care about what happens to your patients." He smiled and walked off.

I sat with my hand in his and looked into his face, his handsome beautiful face. I rubbed the back of his hand gently and raised my other hand to his bruised cheek and rubbed it softly, barely making contact with his face. "Carter, can you open your eyes?" I waited for a moment, and there was nothing. No response to my request. "Carter, please wake up."

The radiology crew had come in behind me to take him for a CAT scan.

They quickly loaded him and took him away. "Please, be careful with him,"

I pleaded. They covered him with a blanket and were soon gone from the room. While he was gone, I went to the locker room to take a shower and change my clothes. The warm water felt refreshing washing down over me. I quickly dressed and returned to still find his room empty. I straightened his room while I could, and sat down in front of the window looking out onto the lawn and fountain that shot water lively into the air. Voices distracted me from my view as two people walked into the room. A young man with curly blond hair and hazel eyes walked into the room followed closely by a very pregnant raven-haired, blue-eyed beauty. They stopped with a start, and she put her hand to her mouth. Standing, I walked to her. She looked at me strangely, and the young man put his arm around her shoulder as to support her. "We're here to see Carter Blake, are we in the right place?"

"Oh yes, of course. I'm Isabella Cameron, you must be Beth." I reached out to shake her hand and guided her to the chair to sit down. She strode across the room supported by the young man. She sat down and looked intently at me. The young man looked at me and introduced himself.

"Hi, I'm Landon Mason, and this is Beth Andrews. How is Carter?"

I swallowed as my mouth went dry, but I got down on Beth's level and reached out for her. I clasped her hand. "Beth, we just sent him down to CAT scan just to make sure there is nothing more going on. He does respond by squeezing my hand when I ask him, but he hasn't opened his eyes yet. I was hoping that would have happened by now. He does hear us, so be especially careful of what you say in front of him. He may not be able to respond to you as normal, but I have to think that he understands. Right now, all we can do is talk to him and pray. Sometimes that is all we have to hang on to. He needs you to stay calm and patient with him." I looked up at Landon as Beth said nothing. She just sat quietly and looked at me as if she was totally stunned. Looking at me like she had seen a ghost, her darker complexion paled.

I looked to Landon then back to her, and she began to speak. "Andrea, she looks and talks like Andrea."

I looked to Landon, and he was very matter-of-fact, shocked, as he studied me. "You look like Andrea."

I started to feel chills go down my back as I heard myself ask. "Who is Andrea?" I wasn't sure I wanted to hear that answer.

"Andrea was Carter's wife." He hesitated then continued on. "She died close to two years ago from cancer." I knew this wasn't good.

"Oh, I'm so sorry."

Landon looked at me with great respect and gratitude. "Don't be, Isabella, he loved her very much, and she was my sister." At that time, they rolled Carter back into the room and put his bed back into place. Beth started to stand, and I assisted her up to the head where she could see her brother. She placed her hand against his face and choked back tears as she spoke."

"Carter, it's Beth, I'm here, I'm okay. Landon is here with me." She reached back for him to come up with her, and I stepped back. Tears flowed down her cheeks unbidden. Landon reached for his hand and gave it a squeeze.

"I'm here, buddy. Beth's okay, she's with me and Molly. Molly is safe, you don't have to worry. We have to get you well enough to get out of here. It won't be long before your nephew makes his appearance."

Carter never made an offer to move. Walking up to the other side of the bed I took Carter's hand as Landon and Beth looked at him intently, wanting him to move or open his eyes. I pulled the chair up next to the bed and put my other hand on top of his, hoping that he would make an effort for them.

I didn't even speak, and he grasped my hand quickly. Landon picked up on it immediately.

"Beth, look." She was astonished as her brother tried to open his eyes.

"Isabella, say something to him, he responds to you. Maybe he will wake up."

I too was surprised at his reaction. He's squeezing my hand, not attempting to let go. I was in no way expecting this. I placed a hand against his face, and he turned his head to my palm. "Carter, it's Isabella, I'm here." I could feel tears behind my eyes burning. "Carter, can you open your eyes?"

18

A small gasp was released from him, and he opened his mouth and spoke in a soft, muffled voice, "Andrea."

Beth shook her head in grief for him. Taking hold of his hand, I got a little closer to his face and could feel his breath on my cheek.

"Carter, it's Isabella, I'm your nurse. You're getting better, you were in a car crash last night. Beth and Landon are here with you." I waited for a response.

"Bella," he replied, and I let out a sigh, not realizing I was holding my breath.

"Carter, can you open your eyes?"

There was no response, he had slipped back to sleep. I rubbed a lone tear from his face and looked to Beth and Landon for their response. Beth was shaking and raised her hand to her lips and kissed it, softly placing it back onto his face.

It was afternoon before Dr. Reed walked back into the room. Beth and

Landon had left for something to eat and for Beth to rest. It seemed I had been sitting here for years waiting for some news to as how Carter was going to recover. The thought returned to me as why was he different from any other patient I had had, nothing really made sense.

"Isabella, haven't you been home?"

I shifted in my seat uncomfortably. "No, I haven't. I have been waiting to hear what he has in store."

Dr. Reed looked at me questionably and ran his finger along his jaw and rested his chin on his thumb. He had this cool appeal to him as nothing got to him. He took a few steps toward me and looked at me attentively "Why is this patient so important to you?" He blinked and waved his hand as to dismiss what he just said. "Never mind, it's none of my business."

I stilled and looked at him worriedly. He set a small grin on his face and stepped a little closer. He took a deep breath and let it out through a long exaggerated one. "I have the test results back. Has his sister made it here?"

I looked down to my hands, slowly wringing them as to comfort myself, feeling a bit uncomfortable at Dr. Reed's stare.

"They have been here and will return soon."

"Well, it doesn't look like there is any reason for him not to recover well.

Of course, there is a lot of swelling, but it should subside in time. I'm not sure what effects, if any, he will have when he does wake fully. We'll just have to wait and hope for the best. Of course you know the effects of what a concussion can do, from severe headaches, nausea, vomiting, to vision difficulties and balance issues. It's important to keep him calm and that he gets plenty of rest."

"Oh, well, that's good. I'm glad to hear that. He's been out for a long time. I am just a little concerned that he hasn't opened his eyes yet."

"It will come in time, Isabella. He hit pretty hard, his brain is bruised and swollen. I was more concerned about his heart. The mark across his chest is from the seat belt, but he also has multiple areas across his chest where there are signs he hit the steering wheel. So far I haven't seen any issues with that."

"Good, I am glad to hear it. The sooner he opens his eyes, the better." I looked to him feeling lost. Helplessness was not a feeling I liked having, and right now I felt about as helpless as I could get.

"Well, Ms. Cameron, I will be around here for a while if you need me.

If Mr. Blake wakes up, please let me know." He turned and walked away, stalling and turning back to look at us again. He then continued to walk away with a grin on his face. Dr. Joseph Reed, a thirty-two-year-old surgeon, tall, thin with tousled brown hair and wire-framed glasses. The stereotypical of a surgeon, intelligent and most of the time no-nonsense persona, fit him perfectly.

Geez, what *is it with me? Why am I still here? I don't even know this man, yet I am drawn to him.* What was it about him that made me want to stay? I wasn't sure. There was something about him that I just couldn't resist, and I could not leave. As I sat there beside him, I started to put my hand on his face and then to gently stroke his hair. As a nurse, I began to look for signs of the cut above his eye for bleeding and noticed that the bruise on his cheek was larger and a black streak was below his right eye.

I had a deep longing just to hear his voice; this was unreal for me to be this attached to him, a stranger. I couldn't help but wonder where this was coming from. I knew nothing about him, and he knew nothing about me.

Certainly, there was a reason for this mysterious attraction. What was this attraction for him, seeing that he knew nothing of me? His sister spoke of his wife that had passed away around two years prior, and I wondered how closely I did resemble Andrea. Was my voice so close to hers and that's the reason he responded to me so quickly? For any reason, I guess it didn't matter right now. All that mattered was that he opened his eyes and spoke to us for the first time in over twelve hours. I soon heard footsteps coming in the door, never looking back assuming that it was his sister and Landon.

"Has he opened his eyes yet?" Beth asked in a shaking voice. Landon, following close behind her, walked up behind me.

"Not yet I'm afraid." I sighed. "I really should leave and go home and do a few things."

"I know I don't have the right to ask you to stay, but I wish that you would. My brother seems to be rather attached to you, and at least he responds to you. The only reason I can come up with is that you sound so much like Andrea. Maybe that's what it's going to take to bring him out of this."

"I don't mind staying if it doesn't bother you. I feel

like I'm intruding on your family."

Beth looked at me, assuring me. "Of course not, if it means Carter is going to be helped by you being here, I want you here. It's not many my brother attaches himself to. Andrea was the light of his life. Unfortunately, she died a couple years ago from cancer. It's been a very difficult time for him.

He has kind of shut himself off from the world since then, not allowing many people to get close to him. I love my brother. I'll do anything I can to help his recovery."

I looked to Beth and saw that she looked quite tired and very heavy with child. "Beth, do you and Landon have a place to stay while you're here?"

"No, we really hadn't thought of anywhere to stay. I really don't want to leave Carter."

I looked at her with concern and asked her about her unborn child. "How much longer do you have to go before you deliver?"

She looked down at her swollen stomach and rubbed it gently. "The doctor says it's going to be at least another three weeks. That, I'm not too sure about. I have had a difficult time recently. It's quite a long story. I'm sure that this is what caused Carter's accident yesterday."

Landon moved in behind her and placed his hands on her shoulders, more of comfort to her it seemed. She didn't elaborate on her statement, so I left it at that. Carter started to stir, first moving away then slightly moving his arms. Beth walked up to the head of the bed on the opposite side as Landon walked up behind her. She looked at me as an assurance to speak to him.

"Carter, it's me, Isabella. Beth and Landon are here with me." I took his hand in mine and placed it against my cheek. The sound of Dr. Reed's footsteps entered the door as I talked to Carter and coaxed him once more to open his eyes.

"Carter, it's okay, we are all here with you. Can you

open your eyes and look at us?"

He made a small sigh, and his eyes started to flutter. Feeling a great sense of relief, I looked into his face, willing him to open his eyes to me, to speak to me, anything.

"Carter, open your eyes and look at us." He began to squint, making a noise as if the light hurt his eyes. As he attempted to open his eyes, Dr.

Reed walked over to the window and shut the blinds and lowered the light.

He blinked his eyes several times before he managed to get them open. We waited as we anticipated his first words to us.

He swallowed hard and looked straight ahead. "Bella." I relaxed immediately when I heard his voice.

"Yes, I'm here. Beth and Landon are here too." He turned his head and tried to look around the room, blinking his eyes on occasion.

"Beth, are you okay?"

In a tearful voice, Beth answered him, "Yes, Carter, I'm okay. I stayed with Molly last night, and Landon brought me here today. He's going to be staying with me. He'll protect me, you don't have to worry."

There was something wrong, I could feel it. He wasn't really focusing on any one person in the room. I started to move my hand, and he clasped it harder, I'm sure, more than he intended. There was unsettling fear in his face, and I knew I was not the only one that was noticing it. He reached over with his other hand to clasp mine, laying it over the one he already had hold of tightly.

"Bella." He turned his head toward me, the fear was evident in his face.

"Yes, Carter, I'm here."

He, in a hushed voice, looked toward me with what looked like a plea for help. I squeezed his hand in assurance that I was with him.

23

"Bella, I can't see you."

CHAPTER 2

Dr. Reed stepped closer to the bed and introduced himself to Carter.

"Mr. Blake, I'm Dr. Joseph Reed. I've been managing your case since you arrived. You had a pretty serious accident last night. Do you remember anything about it?"

Carter closed his eyes and blinked several times, reopening them in attempt to focus. "I don't remember much of anything. The last thing I remember is getting a call from Beth. How long have I been here?"

"You came in yesterday about two o'clock in the afternoon. From what

I can gather from the police report, you were traveling at a fairly high speed and hit a tree. You were lucky. Your seat belt probably saved your life. The air bag in the car never deployed, causing you to hit your head on the windshield and your chest on the steering wheel."

Carter looked toward Dr. Reed's voice. "So why can't I see?"

There was little or no concern in Dr. Reed's face or his voice as he drew an explanation to him. "There is some swelling caused by bruising. The impact caused your brain to rattle around in your skull. When the swelling reduces, you will regain your sight. I will keep a watch on you. I don't think there's anything to be concerned about right now. All your scans come back normal. There doesn't seem to be any bleeding anywhere, all your lab work is normal, I don't expect any complications. Like I said, you're lucky you're alive, it could've been a lot worse. I know it seems difficult right now, but you will improve over time."

Carter's face went blank. Dr. Reed tried to reassure him. "This isn't going to be an easy road, but you will recover, and recover fully. I don't want you doing a lot of strenuous activity even after you regain your sight and are released from the hospital, at least for six weeks. If there are no seizures following this, there's no reason why you can't drive and be able to do the things you have always normally done. I don't look for that to happen. If such things were going to happen, they would've by now. But I want you to rest and try to relax. I know that's not going to be easy. But you have a good support system with your sister, and you've got plenty to look forward to from what I can see. You need to concentrate on getting better." Carter was in agreement as if he was waving the doctor off.

"Isabella knows where she can find me if you need me."

"Thank you, Dr. Reed." Beth smiled in gratitude.

As I stood, Carter looked to me. "Isabella, please don't leave me, there's something about you and I can't let you go. I feel like if I do, I've lost my lifeline."

Landon and Beth looked at me in amazement; they couldn't believe what they were hearing. I wasn't sure if I understood.

Taking my seat beside him once again, I took his hand. "Carter, you don't even know me."

"I know you kept me alive. You could have gone home, but you didn't, you chose to stay. I know you were here, I heard your voice. I tried to talk to you, and you knew even if I didn't have a voice. I may not be able to see now, but I sure saw a lot before I was conscious. There is a purpose for you being here. I saw my wife." He choked back tears. "Andrea has been gone for over two years." He tried to calm himself. Raising his hand, he ran his fingers through his hair as a tear ran down his cheek. "She was the love of my life, I could almost touch her. She told me to go back, it wasn't my time." He said this with a heavy sigh, as if his heart was broken. "I know she wants you to be here, she sent you here to be with me. She told me Bella."

I sat in amazement at his statement, and he stilled at

26

the fact that there was no answer from any of us. His face became tense and his jaw tightened.

"Please say something."

I was taken aback by his confession, not that this sort of thing had not happened before, but for some reason, this left me speechless.

"I don't think you understand what you are saying, this is the effects from the accident. Andrea could have not possibly put me here. I never knew her, she never knew me, you didn't know me until you came here." I started to open my mouth again and quickly decided to keep my thoughts to myself.

He looked toward my voice and continued to hold my hand, looking into my face fervently. "Isabella, God puts us in circumstances when he sees fit, not when we want them. Good situations or bad ones, it's our decision on what we do with them."

I patted his hand gently. "I'm here, and I'm not going anywhere. I'll stay with you as long as you need me. Now, you need to rest, doctor's orders."

He grinned and lay back, closed his eyes and looked very relaxed. "Yes, Nurse Ratchet." Beth giggled at him and kissed him on the cheek.

"That's my brother, the comedian."

"I love you, sis," he managed a few words before he drifted off. "Landon, you will take care of her?"

Landon laid his hand on Carter's shoulder. "Of course I will. Don't worry about her, she'll be okay. She and the little monster will be well cared for," he said with a cool grin.

"Why don't you take Beth home? She needs to rest."

Silently, Carter drifted off to sleep.

Landon put his arm around Beth and comforted her as she drew her hands to her face, sobbing softly. Getting closer to her he bent down telling her earnestly, "We need to go. You need to rest, and so does he." He tried to reassure her by squeezing her shoulder and had her tilt her head to his chest.

"He'll be fine." He tilted her face up to his by putting his fingers under her chin. He looked into her eyes and smiled. "He'll be fine. We'll come back later, okay?" He looked over at me, appreciative. "Thank you." And he walked off with Beth next to him.

I sat and looked up at the ceiling and wondered what in the world had I got myself into. I hadn't planned on this. My life was already complicated enough. I had tried to distance myself from men having a difficult time with relationships. I had thought of meeting someone and eventually getting married, when the time was right of course. The thing of it was that I never seemed to allow myself to get close enough. There were way too many issues from the past, actions and situations that had affected me for me to let that happen. I had never shared that with anyone to even allow them to help me.

I never thought I would ever find anyone that would understand. Now I sit by a man that seemed to think that I was brought into his life for some divine reason.

It never occurred to me that I was in a certain place at a certain time for any other reason than I knew where I was going to be, either because of work or something that had to be done. I leaned over the bed and caressed Carter's bruised face and pushed his unruly dark hair back away from his eyes. All that I could hope for was when he awoke was that he would be able to see again. As he lay there asleep, I listened to his gentle breathing and laid my hand against his chest that was just barely covered with the white sheet. I felt his heart beating softly beneath my hand and the heat from his body.

Bringing my hand back to my lap, I tried to shake off the feeling that was so unsettling to me.

Sitting back in the chair, I started to feel the time

that I had spent here.

My legs felt like rubber bands and my eyes were heavy. I rubbed my eyes and yawned. As tired as I was, I was comfortable here sitting next to him. What was I doing here?

Reaching over, I clasped his hand and squeezed it gently and whispered to him softly as not to wake him, "Carter, why am I still here with you? This is not me. This kind of thing never happens to me." I stroked his arm and laid my head on the bed beside him, holding his hand. I drifted off thinking of him.

I woke to a hand stroking my hair. Turning my head, I saw that he was awake. He was quietly running his long fingers through my hair. I grinned up at him as he was looking down at me. His eyes shined and sparkled at me with a shy boyish grin on his face. For a moment, he didn't speak, he just looked at me. I was starting to wonder what's going on behind that smile.

"Hi." He barely talked above a whisper. "I didn't want to wake you. You were sleeping so well." He pushed my hair behind my ear.

Looking up at him sleepily I wondered what was going through his mind.

My eyes were barely open when I saw a soft, sweet smile upon his face. His dark blue eyes shined as he looked at me. I couldn't believe I was here with him. If I ever told anyone about this, they would never believe it. This kind of thing just never happened. It's unbelievable, miraculous really, to think that he was actually looking at me like he could see right through me.

"Hi," I said in a whisper. "You look better."

He looked at me sweetly and then answered with a bright smile.

"I feel much better thanks to you."

He raised his arm across his body toward my face and traced my cheek and jawline, sending a delightful

shiver down my back. "And you, Bella, look heavenly."
His words of affection had stunned me. After a beat, I
realized he's able to see me. My breaths shortened as I
raised my head, he followed my gaze. My eyes never left
his.

"You . . . you can see me?"

I knew it was written all over my face. The shock
and the relief of him being able to see me instilled fear in
me. This was the first time he had laid eyes on me, and I
knew he's thinking of Andrea. If it weren't for his sister, I
wouldn't know of the extent of how much I looked and
sounded so much like her. He must see her; I couldn't
imagine what that must feel like. This could go either way,
and I wasn't sure if I was going to like where this would
lead.

Hearing my voice shake, I asked, "How long have
you been . . . ?" I couldn't finish a sentence. It had actually
left me speechless. I felt fear rising in me and my stomach
clenching.

"I've been awake a while, watching you."

He paused for a moment, and I started to see some
concern in his face.

"Don't panic, you don't snore." He chuckled and
appeared to be very carefree at the moment. I realized the
astonished look I must have on my face, and began to
laugh.

"Well, that's good."

He sat up in the bed and started to reach over for
both my hands and clasped them in his. "I was glad to wake
up and see you still here, I know you must be exhausted."
His charmed response made me uncomfortable.

"Wow, what a wonderful thing to wake up to."

I felt my face burn, no doubt I was blushing. "I
really don't feel too bad.

As a matter fact, I think I slept pretty well. Probably
the best I have slept for a long time." It wasn't long before

we were interrupted by the darkness and menacing of Nurse Strike. She strode in uninvited into the room like she owned the place. With an unpleasant grin and her face tight, she sauntered into the room, making her way up to Carter and eyeing him greedily.

"Well, Mr. Blake, how nice, you have your own private nurse." She sneered at me. If looks could kill, I would be dead a thousand times over right now. Of course, there was no love lost here. We never did get along, and that was okay with me, just so she stayed out of my way. This for sure did not look too promising. Taking a deep breath in an attempt to control my temper, my jaw hardened and my teeth became clenched. Her presence here was like someone dragging their fingernails down a chalkboard.

"Marilyn, it's really none of your business." She shrugged and looked over her shoulder, giving me a smug look, and then she turned back to Carter.

This woman was a tyrant, and I wished I had no association with her at all but I did have to work with her. She's the type of person that no matter what it was, if she wanted it, she'd get it, good or bad. It really made no difference to her what she did or who she did it to. She was the kind of person that would stab you and step back and watch you bleed to death and enjoy every second of it.

"Is there anything I can do for you, Mr. Blake?"

Carter wasn't sure what to say to her, she appeared like a vulture after a kill. Her intent was very clear, leave it to her to be after her next prey and it looked like it's going to be him. This wasn't going to happen if I could help it.

Suddenly feeling empowered, I stood and glared at her.

"Marilyn, if you don't leave now, I will turn you in for harassment and misconduct. If I have to, I will have you fired, do you understand that, honey?" Throwing her own words back at her, I could feel my adrenaline rise.

I knew I was in for a fight, and one I was intending to win.

She looked at me with those jade green eyes of hers, and fire appeared to shoot from them. "You don't know who you're dealing with, Ms. Prim and Proper. I don't scare easy."

"Why don't you go soak your head in the cauldron?"

"That, Ms. Cameron, is insubordination."

I raised my finger to her and showed her the way out. "I'm the customer now, not the nurse on duty, and you're stepping over the line. Leave, before I have you thrown out."

"Fine, have it your way," she said very dryly and gave Carter a wink before she left the room.

Carter looked at me, shocked. "Wow, a woman that knows what she wants."

I turned back to look at him. "Well, yeah, you could say that, she's ruthless. She thinks she can get by with anything she likes."

"I guess you told her, I don't think she will be coming back for a while."

He gave me a playful look. I enjoyed his company; being in his presence seemed to alarm me. I couldn't really call this a normal relationship, but it's the closest I had ever come since my two-year relationship with Ryan, and it ended badly. It didn't matter that the feeling was still there, and I knew he sensed it.

"She infuriates me." I took a deep breath in and sharply blew it out.

Turning, I went to sit down beside him again. He looked inviting and raised his hands toward me, pumping his hands like a child. I reached for him and grasped his hands, and he pulled me toward him. Sitting on the edge of the bed I felt the warmth from his hands as they lay in mine.

He looked at me adoringly and smirked. He was really enjoying this moment. That little turned-up grin of his caused my heart to drop to my feet. I tried to collect my thoughts and my feelings, attempting to keep them under control.

"What?" I said nervously and started to squirm.

He turned to look at me, never letting go of my hands. "You're a little protective of me, aren't you?" He teased me from the outburst I just had. He didn't quite understand how to take it. I wasn't sure that I did, being a little too transparent for my own good. I turned my face away from him, knowing he was reading me way too well.

I could hear him move behind me as he reached for my jawline with his cupped hand under my face; turning my face toward him. "It's okay Bella, you're human, and I kind of like that," he said shyly. He sat a little straighter and closer to me when I didn't respond, his former expression gone and now filled with concern. "Bella, it's okay." It was hard to talk to him, especially when his chest was now bare from the sheet that covered him.

"Carter, I'm not used to this, I don't know how to explain it."

"It's going to be fine. You don't have to explain anything. We're just friends, new ones at that, relax." His eyes shined with affection, and I knew if I didn't leave him, I was going to kiss him. Gently I pulled back, knowing he was thinking the same. Releasing his hand, I stood to leave, my feelings being evident. I just met him, and he had already gotten under my skin. My hands were shaking, and I knew if I had noticed it, so had he.

"Carter, um, I think I better go." Dropping my head and placing my hands in the pockets of my jeans, I stepped back. Regaining a little of my composure I returned my gaze upon him. I felt the full focus of his eyes on me. He looked hurt, almost to abandonment.

"Bella, I didn't mean for you to leave." He was far

too able to read what I was thinking, and it scared me to death. He acted as though he was upset with himself and ran his fingers through his hair in frustration. I closed my eyes and shook my head, I couldn't believe it. I could feel the burning from behind my eyes of tears that were unshed and threatening. *You've done it again,* Bella, I heard my subconscious telling me, standing on trembling legs.

"I'm sorry, It's time . . ." I couldn't finish a sentence now in front of him.

"I'm sorry."

He was struggling, struggling to find the right words to say or do. His lips were now tightened in a thin line. Looking rejected, he watched me intently, questioning my reaction. This was torture for us both.

"Can I at least call you? I would like to take you out, just to say thank-you," he stammered.

Raising my hand, I rested my fingers against my mouth. I felt a tear slowly slide down and away, knowing I was going to cry. Not wanting to cry in front of him, I closed my eyes and turned to leave, hearing him call my name as I walked out the door. I managed to make it outside the room and leaned against the wall and slowly slid down it. The coldness of the tile floor only added to the lost, empty feeling. I couldn't let him get close to me, I'd end up hurting him as I had everyone else that's ever been around me.

Tears ran down my cheeks and into my hands, unbidden. There were too many things in my past for me to ever consider a serious relationship with anyone. He would never understand the agony I was still experiencing, no one ever had. I was broken inside with no hope of ever being whole. Well, it was obvious he had feelings for me that I certainly didn't understand. There were things that no man could begin to understand. He would never get past it, to want me, to love me. I wasn't going to let that happen, he would be sure to leave me if he knew. It was over and done, all the promises of wonderful things to come were gone.

In my self-pity and loathing, I felt hands on my shoulders. Someone was standing in front of me in an attempt to soothe my desolate soul. Opening my eyes, I saw him. He was on one knee in front of me, and I shuddered. The touch frightened me, and I jerked. Carter looked at me, confused as to my reaction.

"Bella, it's okay, it's me. I'm not going to hurt you. Why did you jerk away?" I was hesitant to answer his question, I knew why. But I wasn't ready to share anything with what I did know about my past, and there was a lot that I couldn't remember. Maybe it was better that I didn't, but what I did know was too painful. I couldn't imagine what else my subconscious had buried.

"Carter, you don't understand and I don't expect you to." He placed both of his hands alongside my face and took his thumbs and pushed away the tears. He never said a word for a moment, he's not really sure what to make of me, and sometimes I didn't either.

"I don't know why you're turning away from me, but I intend on doing everything I can to prove to you that you can trust me." Assisting me back to my feet, he led me back to his room. He turned sharply and immediately called for the nursing staff to bring him his belongings and then contacted Landon. "Landon . . . Okay, much better . . . Can you pick me up? Yes, I'm fine . . . No . . . On my own . . . Landon, just pick me up, and Ms. Cameron will be coming with me. Yes . . . Okay, I'll see you there." Laying the phone down, he turned toward me and asked me very sternly, it wasn't a request,

"Don't leave, I'm just going to finish dressing." And he walked back into the bathroom and soon reappeared. He walked back in the room looking sharp in his white linen shirt and jeans. Carrying a blue blazer over his arm that he soon deposited on the chair beside him, he

35

quickly finished buttoning the sleeves on his shirt as he waited for his other belongings. It surprised me when a security guard walked in carrying a shoulder holster and a handgun.

"Please sign here, Mr. Blake." Carter quickly signed the form and the officer handed him over his handgun and holster. He slipped the holster on over his shoulder and quickly put the gun in its place and reached for his jacket and put it on. Taking a couple of steps toward me, he reached out his hand and saw the surprise in my face. I was fearful, and he saw it. If it weren't bad enough that I had these feelings, I now didn't know what to do, the man packed a gun. He grinned and then let out a chuckle.

"It never occurred to me that wearing a gun was so intimidating, Bella, it's okay. I'm not going to hurt you. I am a homicide detective, I carry a gun all the time."

He continued to hold his hand out for me, and I slowly took it. "Come on, let's go. Landon is waiting for us in the parking lot."

His hand never released mine as we walked to Landon's truck. I was sure most of the staff got an eyeful as Carter proceeded to escort me out of the hospital in this fashion. He was being a gentleman in keeping me under a watchful eye. Opening the door he assisted me in and followed close behind me. Landon flipped off the music and looked over at Carter then back to the road, then again back at Carter.

"Man, are you sure you're okay to go? You just come out of a major car wreck." Landon was sounding a little critical as he put both hands on the steering wheel. After some short-lived silence, I could tell that both were a little uncomfortable. Looking over toward Carter, Landon shook his head and grinned. Carter gestured to Landon by raising his hand and pointed ahead of him. "Drive, Landon, I'm fine. Don't worry, I haven't lost my mind, not yet anyway."

"You could've fooled me, brother." Carter let out a laugh, and Landon reached to start the truck.

"Okay, where are we going?"

"Home, I'm going home."

"Okay, you're the boss."

I sat next to him stiffly, and Carter placed his hand over mine, putting it over his knee and giving my hand a little squeeze. "Relax," he said. "You're fine, I'll take care of you." His voice was barely above a whisper, soft and soothing. I couldn't believe this. What had I gotten myself into? Just because he's a cop didn't make this a safe decision. How did I allow him to divert me? I was going home, alone, to cry, maybe all night. Here I was, sitting next to this incredibly handsome man that I couldn't take my eyes off. I guess I should be fearful, but I wasn't. I was calm and assured of his protection. How crazy was that? The shadows of the oncoming car lights showed a soft light against his face. He looked at me, and I could see him trying to read every thought.

"Are you okay?" he asked with that alluring voice that made me melt at the sound of it. Without much expression on my face, I shook my head yes.

"Okay? You're certainly quiet, you sure you're okay?" I turned my hand over so that our palms now met and squeezed his hand and looked up at him, assuring him I was fine.

"Yes, I'm okay, just a little confused." He dipped his head down and looked at me squarely in the face.

"Confused, about what?"

"It doesn't matter, it wasn't important." He put on that boyish grin, and I could feel myself sinking into the seat.

"You're sure? You can talk to me now. I'm a pretty good listener."

"No, I'm fine." Truth was, I didn't exactly want to discuss how I felt. I wasn't sure myself, and I was with a man I had just met around twenty-four hours ago and I was going home with him. God knows why and I really didn't want to discuss it in front of a second man that was also a stranger. It really didn't help either that I was going to this man's home. I had no idea what he expected or why I took the first step to leave with him. The unknown of what was happening frightened me, and for the life of me, I couldn't relax. This definitely was not my kind of thing to be doing, I was never this reckless.

I was sure Lily wouldn't object. She was used to this; she was always being pursued by gorgeous men, but then again, she was pretty incredible herself.

She had stunning long blond hair that gave her the appearance of a halo around her and bright, piercing blue eyes. Men fell at her feet most of the time, and she never realized really how eye-catching she was.

That was really neither here nor there; I know she would glory from this.

I wasn't sure I was even going to mention it to her; then again, she would ask me what happened to me and why I didn't meet her. How was I going to explain that?

It wasn't long before Landon turned onto a residential street and came to a stop out front of a small cottage. It looked like something that women dream of. You know, the little house with the white picket fence, flowers in the yard, and well-manicured lawn. The only thing that was missing was the 2.2 kids and a dog.

Carter opened the door and assisted me out. I heard the door slam on the other side of the truck as Landon was getting out. He walked me to the door, followed closely by Landon. Walking in the house his home was well-managed and it smelled wonderful. Someone had been cooking, you could smell the scent of fresh sugar cookies in the house. Who could had been here doing such things? Landon made sure that we were in and we were well settled before he made his leave. Carter had still never let loose of my hand,

and I had no intention of taking it from him. His fingers were perfectly laced through mine as he guided me into the kitchen, "Would you like something to drink? I pretty much just keep soda, water, juice, and milk here. I'm not much of a drinking man. I have to stay sober anyway, I never know when I will be called out on a case."

"A glass of ice water would be fine."

"A glass of ice water it is. I think I'll have one too."

With all of the time that he had held my hand, he had now let it go, collecting the glasses and filling them. He handed me one and then reached for my hand once more and led me to the living area of his home. I felt like I'd known this man for a million years. He sat down on the couch and pulled me down next to him.

"Are you going to tell me what you're thinking, or am I going to have to guess?"

I guess the best way to answer this was just to come out and say what was on my mind, but I was trying to find the words so that it didn't sound so awkward. Tilting my head to the side, I looked over at him feeling myself blush.

"Ah, you're blushing. I like that. I don't think I've ever had that effect on anybody before."

"I guess I'm really not sure what I'm thinking. There are a lot of things going through my mind, mostly it's a jumbled mess. I certainly wasn't expecting to be here with you. I'm a little embarrassed, I guess. I'm not sure of what really you were expecting."

"Well, I wouldn't want you to get the wrong idea. I was concerned about you when you broke down at the hospital. I didn't think it was right of me to let you go home by yourself in the shape that you were in. So I brought you here where I could take care of you. I really can't say that I expect anything. I felt that we had a connection, one that I don't understand. I had the feeling it was there for you to. Correct me if I'm wrong."

Looking down at my feet I took a deep breath. He

knew me better than

I knew myself and that in its self was not exactly settling. "I have to agree that there is certainly a connection between us, and I'm not sure what it is either. I'm grateful that you want to take care of me, I haven't had that for some time. I'm not one to let anyone get very close to me. Let's just say that I've had a lot of issues that have never been resolved. I'm not one to disclose a lot of things about myself or how I feel. My friends, as long as they have been around me, still don't know me very well. Sometimes I don't understand myself; therefore, I can't expect others to understand me. How did you know I was alone, how did you know I wasn't married or had a boyfriend?"

"People do talk, Isabella. You just have to know when to listen."

While talking, we have finished our water, and Carter took the glass from my hand and placed it on the table beside us. From the table, he pulled a remote that turned on the stereo system and another that turned on the fireplace in front of us. Soft, sweet music filled the air, standing he offered his hand to me.

"It's early yet, how about a dance?" I smiled shyly at him and took his hand. He pulled me close to him and placed his hand at the small my back, and the other he cupped his over mine, placing it on his chest. I could once again feel the soft beating of his heart; his cheek rested against my head.

Closing my eyes, I was lost to him. "This is nice," he whispered. "I haven't done this in years." I had to admit to myself that this felt pretty incredible to me. I hadn't allowed anyone to be this close to me physically or emotionally for some time. Ryan had tried but was never able to break through the barrier I had built between us. Why was he different? Why was Carter different?

The music softly came to a still. Carter drew back and looked down at me with that beautiful smile of his. I didn't want to leave from where I was at, it felt surprisingly safe. I was glad he came after me.

"Well, Ms. Cameron. I think it's about time we call it a night, don't you?

I'll show you where you will be sleeping tonight."

Releasing me from his hold, he continued to hold my hand and led me through the house to what I assumed was his bedroom and turned on the light. Starting to get chills, I didn't know if it's because it was cool in here or because of just being in this room with him.

"This is my room, you'll be sleeping here tonight. I'm sorry I don't have any of Andrea's old things still left here, but I have some shirts in the closet that I'm sure you can wear, and there are T-shirts in the drawer if you want to change out of your clothes. I'll be in the living room on the couch, if you need me."

"I can't do that, I don't want to throw you out of your own room."

"I'll be perfectly fine on my couch, I've done it before. Don't worry about it. I'm so tired right now I could go to sleep standing up." Laying the back side of his hand against my face, he caressed it softly, then let his hand fall to his side. "I'll see you in the morning, get some sleep." He winked at me as he left.

Looking around, I noticed that there was a door off to the right of the bed. Walking over to it, I opened the door to find a large dark room. Turning on the light I found the bathroom, it was large with an oversized garden tub. To the left was a vanity with a large mirror. Gazing into it, I pushed my hair behind my ears, thinking to myself I looked worse than I thought.

No wonder he was looking at me so attentively. I decided before going to bed, I would take a bath. It sounded like the best thing to calm my frazzled nerves. Stepping over to the tub, I turned the water on and slowly filled it with warm water. On the ledge, there was shampoo and shower gel. Also among the other assorted bottles were some sweet-smelling oils. Pouring some into the tub, the warm water hit the oils and it quickly filled the room with the sweet smell of lavender. Stepping in, I let the warm water wash over me. It felt heavenly. I sat back in the tub and leaned my head against the edge and closed my eyes, soaking in the wonderful aroma of the warm water.

My thoughts wandered, thinking of nothing but him. What was he thinking about? Was he thinking of me? I couldn't come to grips with what was going on in my head. I felt safe here, like I had a guardian, a bodyguard. I could fantasize about him all night; the one thing that came to mind was it would be nice to be able to feel like this all the time.

I soon finished my bath, but my thoughts wandered back to Carter. Was he already asleep? Wrapping myself in the towel that was hanging by the tub I stopped at the mirror. Pulling a ribbon from my purse, and pulled my hair away from my face. I could see where I hadn't slept. I certainly was not at my best, I had dark circles under my eyes, and looked very tired. I continued on and found the closet, finding there were several long-sleeved shirts hanging in there close together. Picking the blue one hanging on the door, I quickly put it on and relished in the scent that still lingered on his shirt. It had the smell of aftershave on it, and his own scent gave me a warm, protected feeling I hadn't ever had.

Before going to bed, I decided to walk back to the kitchen to get a drink when I was suddenly stopped short because of a voice I heard. It's the beautiful voice of Carter Blake. Talking softly, I realized it's a prayer. I strained my eyes to see what was still left in the light given from the fireplace and saw him on his knees before the couch, his head was bowed and his hands were folded before him.

"Thank you for the many blessings that you have given me today and the security of my family. And, God, please give Bella peace of mind and in her heart. I'm not sure what she's dealing with, but I can tell that she needs your assistance. She doesn't know me well enough to trust me. I know that you can give her the ability to trust. I may not know what she is dealing with, but you do. Give me the boldness to do as you ask, I want to be used of you, I want to be a mighty man of God. Thank you, God, for so many things. Thank you for the love that you have shown me. Thank you Lord that my salvation is in you, and that's all I need. Amen."

Okay, now I see why he's different. I felt as though I was intruding, but I couldn't get over the fact. I was so amazed that no more than what he knew of me, he felt the need to pray for me. It's heart-warming enough that I could have fallen at his feet without any problem. Surely, this was what love was meant to be. I didn't understand, we're strangers, but yet he had enough feelings to pray for me. He started to stand and noticed that I was in the room.

"Bella, are you okay? I didn't know you were in the room."

"Yes, I'm fine. I'm sorry I didn't mean to intrude. I was just going to the kitchen to get a glass of water."

"There's no need for an apology, you're more than welcome to roam the house as you please. You're my guest, I want you to feel comfortable here."

Walking a little closer to him, I saw him shake his head and look down at the floor; then he turned his head and looked up at me with a sheepish grin.

"What?" I was surprised by his reaction; I couldn't imagine why he looked away.

"I think you look better in that than I do."

I'd forgotten all I had on was one of his long-sleeved shirts, and my bare legs were hanging below it. I blushed and looked away. "I'm sorry, I didn't even think."

"It's fine, Bella. You're decent. I . . . ," he hesitated, "haven't had a lady in my home for a long time, other than

43

my sister."

"I guess we're even then. I'm not used to having gentlemen around me.

I don't date much, I don't normally have anybody in my home, especially overnight, unless it's family or Lily."

"Continue, Ms. Cameron, I think I'm going to go lie down on the couch, I could use some sleep."

I continued into the kitchen and picked up the glass that I had used earlier and filled it with water and carried it back to the room, taking small sips as I went. Looking over at the couch, Carter had already lain down and had covered up with a small throw, the light reflecting from the fireplace onto him.

"Good night, Carter."

"Good night, Bella."

I continued into the bedroom and shut the door, leaving a crack in it. I couldn't help thinking that this was very odd. Anyone staying at the home of the opposite sex and they didn't make a pass at you seemed strange. It didn't matter how well they knew you, I knew this from experience. Some of the girls and most of the guys that I worked with had different men and women at their home almost every night, none of them knowing the other person very well. Although this was not how I was raised, it seemed to be more accepted, more of a given thing. For this to happen to me even though I wasn't ready for it, it still shocked me to think there were some people out there who didn't live like that.

After setting the glass down on the table beside the bed, I pulled the comforter down and got in underneath it and turned off the light. It wasn't long once my head hit the pillow that I was fast asleep.

I awakened to the soft voice of Carter speaking, "Hey, Tink, where are you? Tinker Bell."

I looked over beside me, feeling the weight on my arm, and saw a little moppet with long dark hair curled up beside me sound asleep. I had to smile because I realized this must be Molly. Looking at her, I would say she was probably around three years old. Lying there, she had blanket in hand and thumb in mouth. Trying not to wake her, I called for Carter. He soon opened the door and walked in to find Molly curled up beside me, sound asleep. He walked around to the edge of the bed and sat down in front of her. I noticed as he sat down, he smiled down at his sleeping daughter and started to play in her long dark hair.

"I'm so sorry, Bella, she usually comes in and gets in bed with me when she has a nightmare. I didn't hear her get up last night."

I smiled up at him, seeing the love in his face for this little girl.

"Can I assume that this is Molly, your daughter?"

"Yes, but how did you know about Molly?"

"When your sister talked to me in the hospital, she told me to tell you not to worry, that she was with Molly. She didn't tell me that Molly was your daughter."

"Does that bother you?"

"Of course not."

"Molly on occasion has nightmares, and she normally wakes me up when she does. Sometimes a little story is all it takes, other times it takes me singing to her. Her mother used to do that a lot. It seems that she's comfortable with you, or she would've woken you up. Instead she decided to crawl into bed and go back to sleep. I am kind of shocked at my little girl, she doesn't take to very many people."

"Well, Mr. Blake. I am honored by the presence of your daughter."

He looked down at me adoringly, lovingly at his daughter. He certainly could not hide the smile on his face. The one thing that crossed my mind was this was what it would be like to have a family of my own.

"Why don't you go ahead and get dressed and come

in the kitchen and we'll have breakfast together? Just leave Molly there, she's fine. Let her sleep.

She will be up all too soon."

"Okay, just give me a minute, I'll be in soon."

He stroked his daughter's hair and slowly got up and watched her as he moved to the end of the bed and then turned and walked out the door, shutting it behind him.

CHAPTER 3

As we finished breakfast, I saw Molly walking toward the kitchen, holding her blanket and rubbing her eyes. She was a lovely little girl with long dark hair, and she's so cute in her little footed pajamas.

"Daddy?" she said in her sleepy little voice.

"I'm in the kitchen Tink, come over and give Daddy a hug." Her little footsteps quickened, and I watched her pad her way over to her daddy. She dropped the blanket she had in her hand and reached up for her daddy and wrapped her arms around his neck. Carter picked her up and gave her a squeeze and a little kiss on the cheek.

"Hey, Tink, did you have another nightmare?" She continued to rub her eyes and shook her head. Carter looked at her questionably them back at me, then back to his daughter. "Why did you get in my bed?"

Molly looked at her daddy and pointedly said, "Mommy." Carter was floored. "Baby, that's not Mommy."

"Me knows, Daddy."

"What about Mommy, Molly?"

"She come to see me, she come to see me when you are sick. Then I see her last night. She tell me that Daddy by himself and lady needs help. She tell me to go get in bed with lady, she cries."

Carter looked at me, astonished, and chills ran through me. "Mommy said it would be 'kay."

"It's okay, Tink." She looked up at him with her big beautiful blue eyes.

"Did I do good, Daddy?"

"Yes. Tink, you did fine."

He tenderly hugged his daughter and patted her lovingly on the back.

"Daddy, Mommy say tell you she wuvs you." He stroked her tiny face; the look he bared was tortured and painful to see.

"You miss her, don't you, Tink?" Molly shook her head yes. "Okay, why don't you go in and turn on cartoons, I'll bring in your breakfast." He gave her a squeeze and kissed her before he sat her down on the floor. Molly trotted off to the living room with her long dark hair flying as she went.

Carter turned pale and put his hands on the counter in front of him, supporting himself. Stepping around the bar, I made my way over to him, putting my hand on his shoulder. Keeping one hand on the bar and his head down, he reached his hand to cover mine.

"Are you okay? You look pale."

He took a deep breath. "I think I better sit down."

"Sure, here, let me help you." Assisting him to the stool, he began to run his hand across his unshaven face and then through his hair, coming to rest on the back of his neck. Using his hand to rest his head against, he kept his eyes closed. I could feel his body shudder beneath my touch. Molly's little revelation had shaken him to the core.

"She has never talked about her mother like this. She wouldn't have been old enough to have any memories of her. There is a picture of Andrea in her room and she knows who she is, but she has never really talked about her that much. I thought when she got older, I would tell her more about her mother.

I thought she was too young to understand what happened to Andrea. I just never brought it up, I don't know if I thought it was too painful for her or me."

"Maybe she dreamt it. You know how children are."

"No, I don't think so. She doesn't have those kinds of dreams. That's the first that she has told me her mother talks to her. Molly was Andrea's life, she fought to stay with her as long as she could, and they always had a connection. Andrea came close to losing Molly when she was carrying her. She would sit on the bed at night and rock, crying and praying for that baby. It wasn't that I did not have any feelings for Molly, I did. But there is a connection that a mother has with her child that a father never does. I don't know if I'll ever understand that. I used to read to Molly when Andrea was still carrying her, you know, just so that she could hear my voice. Andrea was a big believer in talking to Molly before she was born and quite often read and played music to her."

"That doesn't make any sense that means she would have seen a ghost."

Carter looked at me, shaken, with his eyes widened, and I knew that he believed in what he was about to say. "Or an angel," Carter replied. "I know you don't know me well, but I need you to know that my life is not that of a normal everyday person. I don't know where you stand on religion, or faith, but it has become a big part of my life. It wasn't always like that. I'm not proud of the life that I led before I came to God. It's in the past, and I don't talk about it often, but it's led me to where I am now." I was amazed at to how open he was being with me, not that I understood it. It wasn't that I'd never been in church or that I'd never been introduced to any of this, I just never believed it. As a child, my grandmother used to take me to church every Sunday morning. Being that young, you're easily influenced, but then again, you don't always take things seriously. I always had seen God as, I guess, a fictional-type person. Now he's telling me of what appeared to be some supernatural being that I didn't understand.

Pulling the barstool out beside him and I sat down continuing to listen and hung on every word he said. It's true, there was something different about him. I just was not sure how he got to be that way, maybe it's good and maybe it wasn't. My hand never left his shoulder as I continued to support him.

"I'm sorry, I can understand if this is a little too much to take in. This is not what I intended at all. I said a prayer last night for God to show me what to do next in my life. Maybe this is his way of telling me it's time to let go. I thought I had, obviously I hadn't. I guess I thought I was protecting Molly."

"Maybe you're not ready to let go of her. It hasn't been that long, has it?"

"Andrea has been gone almost two years, and it has been two years of healing. The way I live my life now is not how I lived it when Andrea was sick. When she first told me, I did everything but accept what was going on.

I ran. I vowed before she died it would never happen again. I would never run from that kind of thing again, and I would never run from God.

"The week before Andrea died, I attended a church service because I literally was at the end of my rope. It wasn't an easy thing for me to think of, raising my daughter alone. Andrea was the one that shared her faith with me, and she always wanted me to live my life in a way that God would be pleased.

I tried to honor her dying wish so that our daughter would be brought up in a godly home.

"God has changed my life dramatically, you would not have liked me if you had met me six years ago. My life, my work, and my family were in chaos most of the time. I know that before Andrea died, she prayed for me and had been praying for me for some time. Last night, I prayed to be able to carry out my life as a man of God, to raise my daughter the way he saw fit, and to build a life for my daughter and myself.

"One of Andrea's main concerns before she died was that I lived my life to the fullest and raise our daughter in a loving home, that I would not live my life alone, without the love of a good woman. I'm not sure what God has in store, but I know it will be in his time and it will be a wonderful blessing for me and my daughter."

"How can you know that? How can you know that

this God of yours can do these kinds of things? I mean, it is not something you can see, hear, feel, and touch."

Carter turned to me on the stool he was sitting on and took my hands and placed them on his knee. Being very serious and straightforward, he started to explain. "Okay, this is what I understand of God. We as people are finite, God is omnificent. God never gives us more than we can handle.

He gives us an example in everyday life of his glory, the very presence of his being, and everything we see is created by him. Everything we have belongs to him, we are nothing without him. God is faithful, it's not something that you can see or something you can touch, and it's not something that you can feel. Faith is the hope of things that are not seen. God loved us so much that he gave his son to die on the cross for sins that he did not commit but to cover the ones that you and I have committed. We are all born into sin, and the blood that was shed by God's son covers that, if we accept him as our Lord and Savior. Nothing else can save us from an eternal hell or of eternal suffering other than the son of God.

"God is the best thing that has happened to me and my family, and I want to do the right thing. I want to live my life according to God's plan, not according to my own."

I looked to him, puzzled at the revelation he had told me. I had a lot of thoughts running through my head, and none of them made any sense. I tried to change the subject, but I knew he was sincere in what he was telling me. He believed it, and I could see myself that he was different from anyone else I had met.

Carter rubbed his hand across his face and stood moving away from the bar to get Molly her breakfast. I was really quite stunned leaving me not knowing what to say. He didn't say much more but continued to finish filling a bowl of cereal and pouring a glass of chocolate milk. When he had it ready, he carried it in to Molly who was sitting in front of the television watching cartoons by now. He set the bowl down on the table in front of her, and she started eating her breakfast. There was no further comment of God, church, or Andrea at the time, although I knew that Carter was still pondering this.

"Well, I have some things planned today with Molly. You're welcome to join us if you like." His earlier conversation seemed to have been forgotten. "I promised her I would take her on a picnic. It looks like it's going to be a nice day, so I thought I would take her to the park. I don't get a lot of opportunity to spend time with my daughter, and I know she enjoys going. We could take you past your apartment if you would like to change clothes. I would enjoy your company, if you don't mind."

"That sounds like fun, I think I would enjoy that. I do need to go past the apartment and change clothes and try to call Lily. She expected me to meet her and I turned her down."

"Lily? If you don't mind me asking, who is Lily?"

"Lily is a college friend of mine. I was going to meet her after work the night you came in. I'm not one to do that kind of thing, but I really didn't want to go back to the apartment by myself."

"Oh, I see. You gave up going out with Lily to stay with me?" He actually seemed rather amused at this.

"Hey, it was our first date. I hadn't been on a date for at least a year, I thought I'd better enjoy it."

He laughed at the thought. "I guess I wasn't going to go anywhere. One thing about it, I didn't have to go out looking for a pretty lady. I had one with me all the time." I felt my face get warm up into my ears, and I knew I was blushing. "You know you're pretty cute when you blush. I like it."

He reached over and picked up my hand and kissed the back of it. "I intend on getting to know you very well. I hope you don't mind that? I'm kind of old-fashioned. I enjoy courting the young ladies instead of just taking them out. Don't be surprised if I pamper you. I believe in treating the ladies well."

"Well, Mr. Blake, I think I might enjoy being pampered. I can't remember the last time I was taken out and treated well. I look forward to being courted by you."

"I'll just finish up here and get Molly ready. I'll pack a lunch, and we'll leave for your apartment, sound okay?"

I felt like a little crazed schoolgirl looking up at him through my eyelashes, barely giving him an answer. "Okay."

As Carter finished what he was doing for the picnic and for Molly,

I spent time in the bathroom fixing my hair and putting on my clothes.

Turning my head over and brushing my hair briskly, then turning my head from side to side, I looked in the mirror. My brown hair fell down over my shoulders in long waves. My heart was racing; I hadn't felt this good in a very long time. *You deserve this time,* enjoy *it while you can,* I told myself. I quickly finished and walked back out into the main living area where Carter was just finishing with his packing. He was placing the last few things into a basket with Molly jumping up and down in front of him.

"Daddy, will you push me on the swing, oh, please?"

"You'll get to swing, I promise."

Molly heard my footsteps enter the room and turned to look at me. The next thing I knew, she's running at me. Her little arms wrapped around my legs, and then she looked up at me with a big smile on her face. I bent down to pick her up, and she wrapped her arms around my neck and kissed me on the cheek.

"You name is Bella, me glad you here." She put her tiny hands on both sides of my face and leaned in as close as she could without hitting my face with her nose. She whispered a little message to me. "Mommy say I tud wuv you. I tan give you wots of kisses and wots of hugs." She continued to kiss me, hugged me, and started patting me with her small hand. I looked over her shoulder to see Carter standing at the arch of the kitchen, holding a picnic basket and a blanket. My reaction did not go hidden, my feelings apparent.

Carter was standing there looking at us, and I studied his reaction and his appearance. He looked glorious dressed for a day in the park. He was still a magnificent sight in his faded jeans and blue button-down. His sleeves were rolled up neatly, and the top two buttons of his shirt opened casually.

I continued my gaze and realized I was staring at him, and then I noticed the shirt. The shirt he had on was the one that I wore last night. He picked up on that readily that I had finally noticed what he was wearing. I instinctively raised my hand to cover my mouth in shock, still clinging on to Molly.

He cocked his head to the side and grinned at me sheepishly. "I still think you looked better in it. The smell of your perfume doesn't hurt either." His deep blue eyes looked through me, and I couldn't help but laugh. "I love the way you laugh." He paused and walked toward me. "I told you I enjoyed your company. This way I can keep you next to my heart." He stunned me, and I had difficulty saying anything in front of him. "Well, speechless, I've never been able to do that before." He held out his arm to me, and I slid my arm through his as Molly continued to hug my neck. Shall we go, ladies?"

It didn't take long before we're outside my apartment. Carter had decided to stay in the car until I collected my things, changed my clothes and gave Lilly a call. I quickly changed into a pair of soft denim jeans, and my favorite pink shirt. As I was headed for the door I quickly grabbed my cell and called Lily to let her know that I was okay.

"Hi, it's Lily's phone. You know what to do. Bye."

"Hey, Lily, it's Bella. Look, I've a lot to tell you, I'll call you back later.

I'm going out, you wouldn't believe it if I told you. We'll talk about it when I come home. Later."

I turned off my cell, and heard the door shut behind me, and I jumped with a start.

Turning, I see a disheveled man with dark green eyes. As the picture came in clearer, I noticed that it's Carter holding Molly in his arms. I couldn't hide the ill-at-ease feeling that I had.

"Bella, Molly had to come in, she needs to go to the bathroom."

I rubbed my face, and it's noticed by him that I had went pale and visibly shaking. "Oh, okay. I'll take her." I walked a little closer to them and Molly reached out for me and I took her from him. Quickly attending to Molly, I soon had her ready to go and took her back into the living area where Carter was standing.

"Are you sure you're okay?"

"Don't you think I should be asking that? I mean, you're the one that's been in the accident recently. Not me."

"You don't have to be defensive. I didn't mean anything by it. I just thought you looked a bit shaken when we walked in. I didn't mean to startle you."

"It's okay. I'm just jumpy sometimes." Trying to lighten the mood I smiled at him.

"Shall we go have some fun?"

He bowed and then pointed the way to the door. "After you."

It's a fine fall day out. The leaves were starting to turn, and the temperature was still warm but the smell of fall was in the air. I just wanted to enjoy the time that I had with him and his daughter. I had these types of episodes before, and I didn't want it to happen today. Something was definitely haunting me.

Arriving at the park, we saw a beautiful green area framed with a wrought iron fence with the last of the summer flowers still gracing it. As soon as we were in the enclosure Carter allowed Molly to get down, immediately she ran to the sandbox. He's keeping an eye on her very closely. He looked toward me, trying to be casual with his conversation. I knew I was not going to be able to hide much from him, after all, he was used to investigating.

"Why don't we sit here? I'll spread the blanket out and put the picnic basket on top of it. It'll be close to Molly where we can see her."

"Okay, maybe we can go swing with her after a while." I teased him, but I had to admit it sounded like a good idea, even if I was way past my time for such things.

He looked down toward the ground and chuckled a little and then back up at me. "Yeah, I think we can do that." We sat down in the shade of the tree, and I was not sure if it's me or him, but the silence between us was unsettling. He began to set out the picnic foods that he had brought.

"I'm not much of a cook, but Molly does enjoy some of these things. I thought maybe you might too." He set out sandwiches of peanut butter and jelly and some cheese sandwiches along with some chips and sodas.

A smile passed my face, and he knew I was accepting. "I can make a pretty mean peanut butter and jelly sandwich. We better eat now or will never get her to sit down. I shook my head in response. He stood to call her over from the sandbox. "Molly, come on, baby, let's eat." She quickly jumped to her feet and ran to her dad, giggling as she came. Carter dropped to a knee to grab her, and she swung her arms around him as she arrived.

"Sit down here with us, Tink, and eat your lunch

then we can play." She sat down, and he handed her a sandwich, chips and a lidded cup. She seemed to be perfectly contented. With a jelly smile, she looked at him and said,

"Good, Daddy."

"Good, maybe some of it will make it to your belly." He laughed.

"You funny, Daddy."

It wasn't long before lunch was completed and she was ready to run and play. "What a bundle of energy she is."

"She has always been that way," Carter exclaimed. "She has always been a live wire. Sometimes I have a hard time keeping up with her." Standing up, I reached my hand out to him. "Come on, let's not let her have all the fun.

Let's go play." He stood and took my hand, and as we started toward Molly, she started squealing with glee. "Tum on, Daddy, wet's play."

We spent a day going down the slide and swinging her. I watched him as he played with his daughter. What a beautiful sight, he adored that little girl, and she loved him. I couldn't remember ever having a better time with anyone. He's a wonderful daddy and a very loving and kind man. When I thought of who I was and what had happened to me, I couldn't imagine him wanting me. There were things I would just soon forget. What I did remember was damaging enough for me and anyone around me. It cost me a relationship with Ryan, the very one that would more than likely would have understood, and I couldn't get past it then. Why should I think it would be any different now? I was soon awakened from my thoughts when Molly raced over to hug me as she came off the slide with her dad.

"Did you see me? Did you?" she asked excitedly.

"Of course I did, you were wonderful . . . Are you having fun?"

"Yes, wots." Her eyes gleamed.

Carter took her into an embrace and tickled her as she giggled hysterically.

"More, Daddy," she pleaded.

"Maybe later, Tink. Why don't you go play in the sand for a little while, it's about time to go home."

"Kay, Daddy." She ran toward the sandbox with her hair bouncing on her shoulders. She plopped down into the sand and started to sift it through her hands. Carter placed his knees on the blanket and crawled up to where I sat, with my back to the shade tree that had become a haven for us. He looked tired.

"She's a firecracker."

He smiled. "Yeah, she is something. She doesn't slow down easy."

"You look tired."

"I guess I am a little, I wasn't as ready for this as I thought. I hated to disappoint her." He was lying on the blanket on his side leaning on his arm to watch Molly.

Being rather brave, I looked down at him. "You could lay your head in my lap. I don't mind."

"I'm okay," he said in a low voice.

"Mr. Blake, this is your nurse talking. Please humor me."

"Okay, Nurse Cameron. I haven't had a better offer in some time." He scooted on the blanket until he was on his back and his head was lying on my lap looking up at me. Holding his gaze for what seemed an eternity, he grinned at me and I continued to study his beautiful face, attempting to embed it into my memory. His unruly dark hair, piercing dark blue eyes that seemed to look through to my soul, the strong square curve of his face, and the late-afternoon stubble of his beard was a breath-taking sight to me. *Lord, he is gorgeous,* for *this tiny moment in time,* he's *mine.*

"What are you thinking, Ms. Cameron?" he said, teasing me and smiling broadly at me. "I can see the wheels turning in your mind."

I felt my mouth and throat go dry. Oh, I'd been caught. I didn't hide my feelings well. It was no secret I had feelings for him. He knew it, and so did I. I was drawn to him from the first time I saw him. Suddenly I felt like I was back in high school and it was my first crush. I felt myself flush at his question. *How do I answer this? I am admiring you,* I *would love to kiss you.* I couldn't say that.

His expression turned serious, and he looked to me for an answer. "Bella, I'm not the only one that feels this way, am I? You feel it too, don't you? I have felt it from the time you picked up my hand. It's powerful."

"Yes, I do. I am not sure what I am feeling. It frightens me."

"Me too, but I don't think it is supposed to. Just go with it, Bella, we'll take our time. There is no reason to push it."

He closed his eyes and took a deep breath and relaxed quickly under my touch. Running my fingers gently through his soft dark hair I continued to drink in his handsome good looks glancing on occasion watching Molly. This had become a perfect day; it could never get better than it was now. I could feel the soft breath from him against my arm that circled his face. I ran the back of my hand down the bruise on his cheek and the cut area above his eye.

"Carter."

"Hmm," he said dreamily.

"Have you had a headache today?"

He opened his eyes barely. "Maybe a little one, it's not too bad."

"What about your vision?"

"Bella, I'm fine. You fret too much. Relax, angel."

"I'm sorry. You just had such a bad accident, it could have killed you."

"It could have, but it didn't. I'm blessed, Bella.

Besides I met you out of a bad situation. I told you, God places us where he wants us. There was a reason for this, I believe that."

I tried to take a deep breath and relax, but I could feel the anxiety rise in me, the sense of impending disaster was dreadful. Where was it coming from? I sat, trying to calm myself. Continuing to run my fingers through his hair I glanced to Molly, seeing a man walking toward her, the same scruffy green-eyed man I had seen earlier. Molly stood and walked toward him. I screamed at her in terror, "Molly, no!"

Carter jumped, and it freed me to run toward her. Picking her up I clasped her to my chest. "No, you can't have her. I won't let you do that to her.

Get away from us, leave us alone!" I started smacking at him, screaming at him." I could hear Carter running toward us.

"Bella," he yelled. "Bella." It wasn't long before he was with me and Molly.

"Bella." He reached out to touch me, and I stepped away. "Bella, it's me. It's Carter. It's okay. Give Molly to me." I looked up and saw that the man I thought I had seen earlier was not the fearsome man I thought, but Landon.

I sank to my knees in front of them, crying hysterically. Carter handed Molly over to Landon and came down on his knees in front of me. I could feel my chest heaving, my heart racing, and I was wringing wet from perspiration.

Carter was face-to-face with me, and I knew my eyes were large and I was shivering uncontrollably. He slowly reached out to touch me and put his hands on either side of my face.

"I'm so sorry, I'm so sorry. Carter, I'm so sorry." The tears were streaming down my face, uninhibited.

"It's okay, Bella, she's fine. Molly's okay."

"I scared her. Carter, I scared that baby."

"Bella, she's okay." He reached to embrace me. "Can I put my arms around you?" Watching my face, he was looking for permission. I shook my head, and he enveloped me. "Bella, I'm sorry, I think I understand. Come on, we're all going home." When he finally got me to my feet, he kept his arm around my waist and Molly was crying and reaching for me from Landon's arms.

"Mommy, Mommy."

He didn't bother to correct her. I looked to him for acceptance to take her, and he brought her over to me. She wrapped her arms around my neck tightly. "It's okay, Molly. I'm okay. Daddy will take care of me. Don't cry, baby." I wiped her face with my hand and she continued to hold on to me tight and I patted her gently. "You're okay, don't cry. Daddy will take care of us." Carter gave me a squeeze, and Landon looked at Carter strangely.

We walked toward the car, and Landon followed us. It never occurred to me why he was there. Carter put Molly in her car seat and buckled her in then assisted me. Rounding the car he got in and started it. I felt numb. He didn't say another word, he just put his hand down on my knee and remained silent. The tears remained but they had slowed. What he must think by now.

I really didn't want to talk about it. I was restless and tired, the events of the day had drained me of everything that I had. I could hear him take a deep breath, and I knew eventually he was going to break the silence. Seeing the look on his face, I know he's worried. I couldn't tell him because I was not sure myself what had happened to me. I was sure that what had happened had been blocked out and I'd done it myself. I could guess a lot of things, but from what I did see and remember, I didn't want to know.

"Are you going to talk to me? I know there's something wrong, please just talk to me."

"I can't. I don't know for sure myself. I've done this before a long time ago. I'm not sure what it means." My words were barely above a whisper. "I would rather not talk about it, if you don't mind." My fingers were clasped together and lay in my lap. I couldn't look at him, this had cost me many relationships, I really didn't want it to cost this one. It's too high a price.

"You know, eventually you will have to talk to someone. I would hope that you would trust me enough that you could come to me. I'll be here for you whenever you need me." I knew he was being genuine, and I wished I could say something but I just couldn't. This was the kind of thing that drove Ryan and me apart. I won't let it happen again.

We remained in silence until we pulled up into the drive in front of his home. He went to the driver side rear door to collect Molly; then came to my door to receive me. She was sound asleep in Carter's arms as he took me by the hand and led me into his home. Once inside, he released me in the living area and continued back to Molly's bedroom and deposited her in her bed.

On his return, I could see that he was solemn and quiet. He walked closer and stopped short just in front of me. He placed his hands in the pockets of his jeans. His eyes appeared to be filled with pain. Pain that I was assuming I had put there. Already I didn't like this. "I know you don't want to, but we need to sit down and talk about this. It's been going on longer than you're letting on, hasn't it?" My body stilled before him, almost rigid. He knew. He knew I had been through something traumatic. Maybe he knew more than I did.

He reached his hand out to me, expecting me to take it. I hesitated, but then reached and took his hand and he led me over to the couch. Sitting down, he sat facing me with his arm over the back of the couch and his other arm on the end. I sat with my eyes lowered, my hands in my lap, very still.

"Bella, you need to talk to someone it might as well

be me. I'm here, and I'm not going anywhere, Molly is asleep and no one's going to disturb us." He leaned in toward me carefully and raised my chin with his fingers.

"I'm not going to let you go anywhere until you talk to me. What you tell me stays here. I promise I won't discuss it with anyone."

"I . . . I don't know really." I let out a little sigh. "I don't know how to explain it. This is going to cause problems, I know it. It has before. It costs me a very good, loving man a little over a year ago. He couldn't get past it, and I couldn't help him. I don't want that to happen with you. I don't know you that well, but I know we have a connection. I can't explain how I feel because it's so unreal to me. I shouldn't feel this way about someone I barely know. I know enough that I don't want to say something or do something that is eventually going to drive a wedge between us."

"I promise you it won't happen."

"Yeah, I have been told that before."

"Bella, I didn't have a choice but to trust you when I needed it. I had to trust you with my life because you are an expert at what you are doing. I want you to be able to totally trust me with what you're going through. I can help you, I know what to do."

I shifted on the couch, my eyes were closed. I wanted to talk to him, but I was so bone-shaking frightened. I couldn't look at him, and this was just way too painful.

"Bella, do you trust me?"

I shook my head. "Good, I want you to tell me what you saw or heard that made you think that Molly was in danger. Don't leave anything out. I'm right here, nothing is going to hurt you."

The tears came again, unbidden, tracing down my cheeks. "I saw a man, a man that is older and scruffy. He has emerald green eyes that look right through me. He

63

walks toward me, and I know his aim is to hurt me. I'm not always the age I am now. I've had nightmares about this man chasing me." I felt as though I was going to hyperventilate. "I can see him standing in front of me. He has a rope in his hand, and he reaches out for me. I managed to get away, and I'm roaming this building, a brick building. I go to turn around and he's behind me and he tries to put the rope around my neck. It's all I can remember for now, it's all I've ever been able to remember. I saw him today in the park. He was calling to Molly, and she ran to him, only it ended up being Landon.

"My relationships with men, which have been few, are always destroyed by this memory. I've never been able to let anyone get close to me. No one, no one has ever touched me since. I know whatever this is, happened." I was starting to sob, and I was frightened terribly. I knew he would be gone when he heard what I had to tell him. He reached for me, and I recoiled, which was not my intent. Taking a deep breath, I finally opened my eyes and looked at him. He's sitting, looking at me with his index finger against his lips. "Carter, I'm not untouched. I don't know by who or when, but I know I am not untouched." Taking a momentary pause, I tried to see what reaction he had to what I'd told him.

"Bella, don't you think I know the signs? I've seen this before.

Unfortunately, I've seen it many times. What you're describing is from an assault, an assault on you more than likely when you were a child. It's not your fault." He started to reach out for me. He cocked his head to the side and looked at me dotingly. "Do you mind if I hold you?" I scooted closer to him, and he opened his arms wide, inviting me to him. I slowly laid my head against him, resting my hand against his sculpted chest. Being soothed by the slow and steady rhythm of his heart, he gently and tenderly put his arms around me, pulling me close to him, resting his cheek against my head.

His body was warm and firm and I felt secure next to him. Knowing that he hadn't turned and run was a huge surprise.

I could hear him sigh; his arms were wrapped around me tightly, assuring me that he was not leaving. I still felt the anxiety and tension that had risen in me. I didn't ever remember it being this bad. I felt like I had run a long-distance marathon, my heart still pounding hard in my chest. I tried to concentrate on the fact that I was not alone and enjoyed this captivating man that had been brought into my life.

"You don't have to be frightened. I want you to feel safe here, we'll work through this. We'll take things slowly. You won't be fearful all your life. I promise you that." He never moved from his position. I continued to rest where I was and closed my eyes and drifted off sweetly.

I was once again in a large brick building, it's dark and damp. I could see the light outside was getting dim. I started walking, but I could feel someone walking and watching behind me. "Daddy, where are you? I can't find you."

I heard footsteps behind me, and they stopped when I turned around. My pigtails swept against my shoulder. I stopped to listen. Hearing nothing, I started to walk toward the noise I heard before. Walking into the darkness, I began to cry. "Daddy, is that you?" I turned to see a disheveled older man with emerald green eyes holding a rope in his hands.

"Your daddy isn't here, he doesn't know where you are. You're staying here with me. Now I think we need to play our game." I woke myself and Carter, jumping to an upright position and screaming. "No!"

Carter continued his hold on me. "It's okay, I've got you." I felt like I was soaked to the skin and my face was wet with tears. "Bella, I have you. Don't cry, angel, don't cry."

"Carter, I am so scared."

"Daddy," I heard Molly's little voice. I knew she was close. "Daddy."

"I'm in here, Tink, come on."

Molly came in and climbed on the couch between us. Carter put his arms around us both. "My girls," he sighed. "Daddy is here, Tink. I'll take care of you both." He was very loving with Molly and me, though Molly deserved his affection, I did not. I was not worthy of the kind of love he could give and I was unable to be what he deserved. It saddened me greatly because I wanted this. I wanted this badly: someone who could love me, a home, and a family.

The telephone rang and Carter released us from his hold and Molly crawled into my lap, sucking her thumb and patting me lovingly. I kissed the top of her head and ran my fingers through her long dark hair breathing her in. She had the smell of innocence, something that I hadn't had in a very long time.

What exactly happened to me? I didn't remember but bits and pieces.

The one thing I knew for sure was that my innocence ended a long time ago, or at least that was what I was assuming from flashes of pictures that I had yet to put together in my mind. What exactly did happen to me, and why had it been suppressed? How long ago did this happen? Was I a child? Was I an adult? Was it a few weeks ago, months ago, or years ago? I didn't know. Why couldn't I help myself? All I could remember was what was in my dreams, and nothing else. Could I trust what I had in my dreams, were they real? And if they were, how much of it was real?

The only thing I did know was that I had never been with any man consciously. Although Ryan had tried to be intimate with me, I would never allow it. It wasn't that I didn't want him, but at the time, I would see flashes of this man's face and it terrified me. Who was this man? And why was it always a reoccurrence of his face? The only way that I knew for sure that I had been touched by someone was because of a doctor's visit ten months ago. Now the gentleman was not my normal physician and he had asked me several questions. He had implied that I had been with someone before, and I knew from my own accounts that I hadn't.

According to him, I had been ripped and torn at some point and had scar tissue from where there had been several repairs done and it didn't appear to be new. There was also mention of scars at the back of my neck and on my back that I was not aware of. I guess this would explain the idea of a rope being put around my neck during my nightmares. Why did I appear as a child if it didn't happen during childhood? I had a lot of questions but no answers.

CHAPTER 4

"Is she okay? . . . Is she going to stay with you? . . . Well, she can't go back to Cooper." He was obviously agitated, running his hand through his hair.

"Landon, you have to keep her there . . . I don't know . . . It's dangerous . . .

He's told her that line thousands of times, why in the world does she still believe it? . . . She needs to stay with you . . . I know that . . ." He clenched his fist and laid it on the table. "Can't you talk to her? Okay . . . Okay . . . Just put her on . . ." I heard him take a long breath as he sat down. "Beth, you need to listen to me . . . I know. I know . . . you can't go back to him . . . That's too dangerous, you're putting yourself and the baby at risk . . . It doesn't matter, he's told you that before, please, just stay with Landon . . . He's not going to stop until he kills you . . . I'm your brother, I'm trying to protect you . . . For God's sake, listen to me for once. Stay with Landon . . . He loves you, he has from the time you were a junior in high school. Can't you see that? . . . I know you're married to Cooper . . . You don't have to do anything, just stay there where he can protect you . . . Please, just do this for me . . . Okay . . . Stay put . . . I love you too . . . goodbye."

Slowly he placed the receiver back on the cradle and took a deep breath, he raised his head facing the sky as he closed his eyes. Attempting to regain his composure, he took another deep breath, standing he started to walk toward us. "My sister, sometimes she's more than I can handle. I wish she had a good man to take care of her instead of the man she is married to." He was very firm in his choice of words and his tone of voice. "You would think after five years of putting up with his terror she would get out." He sat back down beside us, Molly's little frame was still snuggled against me, sucking her thumb. "She's

68

very content with you. I haven't seen her that content with my sister." He stroked her hair and looked down at her tiny face. "She's gone back to sleep, we better wake her. She hasn't taken a bath or eaten."

"Would you mind if I bathed her and took care of her? I would really like to."

He looked up at me and gave me a smirk. "Sure, if that's what you want.

I'm sure she would love your attention."

"If you could bring me her things, I can get her bathed." I lifted her close to me and stood, her body draped in my arms.

"Okay, I'll be in soon."

Carrying her to the bedroom, I laid her down on her father's bed while I stepped into the bathroom to fill the tub. Soon the bath was run, and I returned to the bedroom picking her up to carry her back to the bathroom.

"Molly, it's time for your bath." I sat her down on my lap in the floor and undressed her. She moaned a sleepy little groan.

"I sleepy." She started rubbing her eyes with her fists.

"I know you're tired, baby, it won't take long. I'll sing to you if you want, or we can read a book when we are done, okay? You have to open your eyes for just a little while. I'm going to sit you in the tub. Here we go." Lifting her, I gently sat her down in the bath, being careful that the water was not too hot for her, and wiped her face tenderly. I bathed her quickly, she being so sleepy I held her up with one hand and washed her with the other.

Lifting her from the bath, I wrapped her into a big oversized fluffy towel and held her next to me, drying her. Her porcelain skin was so perfect.

Grabbing a brush from the sink, I carried her back to the bed and sat down, and quickly finished drying her tiny body, keeping her wrapped. Brushing her hair back out of her face I tied it with a ribbon I had in my purse.

I soon heard Carter's footsteps as he entered the room. He looked at us both so strangely as if it was a familiar sight to him. Molly was in my lap curled against me, wrapped in the towel with her head resting against my arm.

"Hey, do you need help?"

"No, I don't think so."

He sat down on the edge of the bed with his arms crossed over his knees.

"You handle her well. It's like you have been doing this for years." He handed me Molly's gown and panties.

"She deserves to have a woman in her life, a good woman, someone to love her and teach her what it is to be a woman of value." Carter looked up at me sincerely as I cradled Molly in my arms, kissing her cheek and caressing her hair.

"I think I've already found her."

"No, Carter, I don't think you have. There's too much uncertainty in my life. She needs someone stable. I'm not that."

"Bella, can't you see? Molly has trusted you. She wouldn't just let anyone do this. She needs you in her life." He hesitated momentarily. "So do I." His response sent chills down my back. I wanted to respond to him. I wanted him; not wanting to ever leave him. I found great comfort being with him, why did I react so differently with him than with Ryan? I cared for him, I had feelings for him. What had happened to me?

"Carter, you don't know what you're saying." He placed his fingers to my quivering lips.

"I know what I'm saying. I know what I'm feeling, and it's something that I haven't felt for anyone for a very long time. I'm very patient but I want you to know I intend to pursue you. I intend to win your heart, no matter what it takes." I gasped at his response; it sure wasn't what I

70

expected. He knew there were problems, and he still intended to pursue a relationship with me.

"I think the feeling you have is the Nightingale effect, Mr. Blake."

He raised his head and tipped it to the side slightly with a smirk. "What exactly is that, if you don't mind me asking?"

"This has happened many times over," I explained.

"I see, so what you are saying is that it isn't possible to have true feelings?"

"That isn't what I'm saying. What I'm saying is it's possible to be overshadowed by someone that took care of you in a crisis and was there for you."

"Sort of like I'm here for you, isn't it?" I didn't respond verbally to him.

"Don't try to hide it, you have feelings for me, and I know it. You forget it's my business to find the truth in situations. I see it every time you look at me.

Your eyes sparkle and glisten when I look at you."

Okay, so I couldn't hide it. I did like this man very much and might I dare to say, love him. I couldn't drag him into this wreck of a life I had, he's had enough. Moving closer to me, he sat with his leg crossed under him and both hands on either side of my knees. He bent to within inches of my lips, feeling the heat from him. My breath hitched and he stopped, not moving for a few seconds. This was monumental for me. I couldn't move, he had placed a powerful spell over me.

"Bella, you have enchanted me." Leaning in, he kissed me softly and briefly left my lips only to return to kiss me more passionately. My eyes closed, and I took every beat of my heart to mind. He hadn't touched me other than to kiss me, and I felt like we had been lovers all our lives. Opening my eyes, I noticed he was holding me in his gaze. My eyes never left his, and I felt him looking into my soul. His smile had disappeared, and he looked at me soberly. His beautiful dark blue eyes had taken me in. I could die in them. He inched back slightly and looked down at a lovely sleeping Molly still curled in my lap.

"Don't you think we better put Molly to bed?" I shook my head, and he leaned in to collect her from me, taking her gently to his chest.

"Come on, Tink, Daddy will tuck you in," he whispered softly to her. He stood at the foot of the bed with Molly held close and motioned with his head to come with him. I followed close behind him, as he took her to a small bedroom. With one hand, he pushed down the quilt and deposited her on a small canopy bed fit for a princess. He covered her tiny body and kissed her cheek. Stepping back, he stood beside me and wrapped his arm around my waist, pulling me into his side. I looked at her angelic face, and her hair was sprawled against her pillow. She is every bit an angel. "She will always be daddy's baby girl," he whispered in my ear. I had to agree she was a beautiful child and very loving. She was mine for a few minutes, she was my daughter, and she certainly had him wrapped around her little finger.

Turning to me, he reached for me and put both arms around my waist, resting them at the small of my back, forcing me to put my arms around his neck, not that I minded. Who wouldn't want him to put his arms around them?

"Shall we retreat, my angel?" I shook my head yes. He reached the door and turned out the light as we walked out and into the living room. He escorted me to the overstuffed couch in front of the fireplace, motioning for me to have a seat, and I obliged. He walked over to the fireplace and reached to the mantel for the remote and soon had a fire going in the fireplace, not to mention the one he had started in my heart. He walked toward me purposefully and turned the lights off in the room, leaving just the glow of the fire making flickering shadows on his face. This was awesome, who would have thought I would be here with him?

Picking up the remote on the table, soft music started to play in the background. "Finally, a moment alone with you, I've been thinking of this all day." He touched me and I felt my body tremble. I enjoyed his attention but it frightened me.

He looked at me with sympathy. "You don't have to be afraid of me. I would never hurt you. I just want to spend some time with you." He cupped my face and smiled sweetly; his eyes had grown dark. "Trust me." I felt my heart rate quicken, and my breaths had shortened. I was scared to death, but was trying desperately to let him take me away from the nightmare of my subconscious. "I want your heart, all of it. It doesn't matter what has happened before. I'll do whatever it takes to have it." He slowly leaned in to hold me in his arms, taking his time. His arms were soothing and acted as balm to my shattered soul and my broken heart.

"It's okay, we aren't doing anything wrong here," he whispered in my ear.

"Let me hold you and kiss you. It's all I want to do." He pushed my hair away from my neck, and I could feel his breath on me and heard his breathing become ragged. His fingers traced down my shoulders to my back as he pulled me closer to him. "I have anticipated this all day." He started to kiss me softly and slowly from the back of my ear, his fingers slowly pushing the neck of my shirt down to kiss my shoulder. His lips against my bare skin were soft and light.

"You are so beautiful." He could feel my body tighten against his touch, his nose against my neck and in my hair. "Relax, just enjoy being here. We aren't going to do anything that you aren't comfortable with." He stroked my back softly and looked into my eyes, my gaze never leaving his. Tracing my face with the back of his hand, I took in the smoldering look of his eyes and the flickering of the firelight against his skin.

"Carter, I'm frightened. I'm frightened of what I feel for you. I can't remember ever feeling like this, I'm not sure what it means. I just don't want to cause you any more pain." I wanted him, I wanted him close to me, I didn't ever want to let go. I was totally consumed by him.

"I know, I feel the same way. I haven't been with a woman since Andrea died. I have spent all my time either working or taking care of Molly. I need someone in my life, someone to love me and for me to love in return. My intention is for a relationship, this isn't a conquest. I'm ready. I know you have some difficulties, but I am willing to help you. I'm willing to be patient. I want you any way that I can have you. Please, don't run."

I felt my body relax under his loving expression, looking at him like he was my last breath I would ever take. Pushing my hair behind my ears, he cupped my face in his hands. Closing my eyes, I leaned toward him and kissed his sweet, soft lips, taking in every sensation my mind could handle.

Running my fingers into his unruly dark hair, I heard him gasp under my touch. Gently he pulled me toward him as he continued to kiss me tenderly.

I felt the heat rise in me, and my body trembled at the thought of his touch.

I wanted to be totally his, to be lost to him. His breathing was rapid and ragged. I could feel his heart beating franticly as we continued to kiss each other. The strange electrical feel of his hands against me was incomparable to anything I had ever known. Leaning back from him, I knew it was time to stop or we weren't going to.

He stilled, his eyes partially closed and his lips slightly parted. His lips glistened in the light of the fireplace where I had kissed him. "Wow, that was an unexpected pleasure," he murmured. "I liked it." He made an attempt to catch his breath.

I continued to look at him with wonder. He was a fine sight; his hair was askew where I had run my fingers through it. He was completely relaxed, and I was under my own compulsion to touch him. It's evident that he knew what I was feeling. "You are going to be my undoing, Bella." I saw him swallow hard.

"I am sorry, I never meant . . ."

"Don't worry about it, I am just glad you stopped. I don't think I could have."

I sighed heavily. "I am sorry, I don't know what came over me. I'm not like that."

"It's okay, Bella, you're human, just like everyone else." He ran his hands through his hair. "I'm sorry, I should have known better. I put us in a situation I shouldn't have."

"What do you mean?"

"I don't believe in putting myself in a situation that won't allow me to control my emotional state. It's dangerous, it can take you farther than you ever want to go. I guess it sounds a little old-fashioned, but I don't believe in a physical relationship anymore before marriage."

"Why not, I don't understand?"

"Bella, God put a man and woman on earth to enjoy each other, to give each other pleasure, but it wasn't to be outside of marriage." He sat up a little straighter. "I want to live my life his way, not mine. He has done a lot for me, and now he has brought you into my life. I have great respect for you and I don't need to add to the trauma you have in your life."

I felt a little embarrassed that this had happened. I had enough problems dealing with the physical part of a relationship. The fear of being alone with any man in that capacity was frightening for me. I had never been close enough for a physical relationship because of my past.

He picked up my hand and kissed the back of it as if a gentleman from the Old South. "Don't, I know what you're thinking. It isn't your fault. I want this to happen, but only when it's right. It's important to me."

"I don't know what to say to that." I found myself staring down at my hands, feeling very uncomfortable. "I have never felt like this before."

He put his thumb and forefinger under my chin, raising my head to look into my now very confused face. "I know. We're going to be just fine. Don't worry." He grinned at me. "You're a very desirable young lady, any man would be a fool not to fall in love with you." I felt heat radiating from my face. I knew I must be blood red by now.

"I would prefer that you stayed at least tonight, but if you like, I can call Landon to stay with Molly. It's up to you." I looked at him wondering what he's anticipating. He shook his head and grinned. "No, I don't want you to get the wrong idea, I want you to stay because of the trauma you have experienced"—and then pointed to himself—"and I could use a nurse. I can't say I feel the best in the world."

I looked at him with great concern. "What's wrong? What kind of symptoms are you having?"

"Just a little headache and some dizziness, I don't think it's anything serious."

I sat straight up in front of him and put my finger in front of his face. "I want you to follow my finger." I moved it from side to side and up and down.

"Do you have a flashlight?"

"Yes, it's on the counter over there. I can get it."

"No, you sit still, I'll get it." I rose from the couch and walked to the bar and picked up the slim-line flashlight and carried it back to the couch where he sat with his head back against the headrest. Sitting down beside him, I placed my hand on his face. "I need to look at your eyes. I want you to just sit still, I am going to shine a light in them to check the reaction." He sat very still. I placed my hand above his eye and lifted the lid on each eye and checked them for response. "There doesn't seem to be anything wrong."

He reached up and wrapped his arms around my waist and grinned. "All the better to see you with, Bella." He was so playful. I loved his humor, his laugh, and he had the most beautiful dark blue eyes, I thought, I had ever seen.

"You can't blame me for trying. Besides, I wasn't lying. I don't feel a hundred percent, and you, my angel in white, are my cure."

"Flattery will get you everywhere, Mr. Blake."

"It's bedtime. You take my bed, I'll stay here."

"Why don't you come in with me? I can keep a better eye on you, and maybe I won't have those freaky nightmares."

"Bella, I can't. If I come in there, I won't be able to keep my hands off you."

"We are adults. You don't have to worry about me anyway. I have never let anyone get that close to me."

"I really wish you would."

He stood from the couch and looked down at me as if he had found a single glass of water in a desert. How did he do that to me? He extended his hand to me, and we walked to his bedroom. Following him, he kept his head down and my hand close to his body.

Walking into his room with him set me ablaze. The remembrance of his soft lips on mine, I couldn't get it out of my mind. I wanted him to do it again and again. The feel of stubble on his unshaven face, his unruly dark hair running through my fingers was feverous. The smell of his aftershave on his skin was lethal to me.

Reaching over, he flipped the side lamp on and looked down at me with those smoldering dark eyes as he started to sit down on the bed. "Are you sure you want me in here? You're comfortable with this?"

"I want you here with me, I feel safe. I need that."

"Would you like the bathroom first?"

"I can wait if you need in there."

"I'm okay, you go ahead." He began to take off his shirt, revealing his chest in the open button-down. "You can have a clean shirt if you like, there are plenty in my closet."

"I wouldn't mind having that one back, if you don't mind."

"Really?" He smiled at the thought and gave a little chuckle. "You want this one back?"

"Yes, I would."

"Well, I always aim to please. You certainly may have it." He slid it down his well-developed shoulders and handed it to me and pointed the way to the bathroom.

"Thank you, I shan't be long." I looked up at him, batting my eyes.

"Ms. Cameron, you certainly know how to unravel a man."

I walked off to the bathroom feeling pleased with how I had handled myself. I liked being here with him. It felt like home. He knew how to put me at ease; I hadn't felt this good around anyone for a very long time.

I slowly undressed and pulled on his shirt, rolling up the sleeves and smelling the scent he had left behind. Brushing out my hair, I let it fall down across my chest. Hey, lifesaver, my purse was sitting on the vanity beside me.

I got to brush my teeth, certainly making me feel better. One last look in the mirror before I left the room, I took a deep breath. *What am I doing?* I was in a strange apartment with a stranger, a stranger that looked at me and acted like we had been married for years. Who was I kidding? In some ways, I felt the same.

Thinking of all that had transpired from our first meeting was like being under the influence, sending flashes of pictures before me. His beautiful face with long eyelashes and dark blue eyes that looked through me, they melt me.

The ache of not being near him was evident when I tried to go home. His feelings were unmistakable being worn on his sleeve, natural or unnatural, it was yet to be seen. I couldn't say that I was much better. It's addictive just to be in his presence. Okay, the moment of truth began now. I opened the door and walked into the room, finding him on the end of the bed in PJ bottoms and his chest bare. I couldn't help but stare at him. He was glorious, his chest sculpted and firm. I was not sure, to coin his phrase, I might not be able to keep my hands off him.

"Ms. Cameron, aren't you the beauty? I still think it looks better on you."

"I love the smell of it."

"Oh, I see, so what does it smell like?"

"You, very much like you."

"You make it very hard to resist you." Standing, he walked to the bathroom and looked over his shoulder at me then closed the door behind him. I looked around taking the scene in. The room was large with a king-sized four-poster bed decorated in shades of blue, yellow and white. The dresser had one perfume bottle on it and a couple of pieces of jewelry which appeared to be wedding rings. Moving closer, I looked upon them. One of them was a diamond engagement ring on a chain and two wedding bands lying together on a glass tray. It must have been Andrea's rings and his band; I felt an echo of sadness wash over me. How hard this must be for him, he obviously loved this woman. Was I now competing with a ghost?

He walked out and was behind me at the dresser and wrapped his arms around me. "They were Andrea's. When she was at her worst during her illness, she couldn't wear her rings on her finger any longer, so I bought a chain and put them on it. She wore them around her neck. She never

79

took them off once they were on her hand, she said it was bad luck. I couldn't just get rid of them, I kept them for Molly. Maybe when she gets old enough to understand, she will want them." Leaning into me, he kissed me softly behind the ear. "I didn't think I would be saying this to anyone but Molly, but it's time for bed. Tomorrow is church. I would like for you to go with us. I can take you to your apartment to change in the morning before we go."

"I don't think God exists for me, Carter."

"Bella, don't say that. He exists for everyone, it's your choice to go to him.

You have to make that choice, I can't do it for you." He stood and caressed my hair. "Come on, it's time to go to bed."

He walked me toward the bed and I clambered into this large pleasing bed and he covered me with the quilt like he was tucking in Molly. Walking to the other side of the bed, he shut the lights out and crawled in beside me, lying on his back. I could hear him let out a deep, heavy sigh. I rolled over toward him and he wrapped an arm around me and I placed my head on his shoulder, my hand resting against his chest. "Good night, Bella, sweet dreams."

"Good night." I whispered.

I was awakened by the small sweet voice of Molly. "Mommy," I could hear her crying. "Mommy." Untangling myself from Carter, I walked toward her bedroom. As I reached her door, she stopped as soon as I made the first step in her room. Unthinkingly, I switched on the light.

"What's wrong, Tink?" She sat on her bed with her blanket in her hands, crying. Walking over, I sat on the bed beside her, and she immediately grabbed hold of me. I wrapped her up in my arms, trying to soothe her.

"Shhh. It's okay. I'm here, Daddy is here, and no one is going to hurt you.

Did you have a bad dream?" She shook her head

yes and curled into my arms, weeping softly. "Would you like for me to rock you?" She shook her head yes, and I picked her up and carried her to the rocker and gently rocked her back and forth. Her sweet little face lay against my chest. Feeling the warmth of her body, I wrapped her in her blanket, comforting her.

"What was your dream about, Tink?"

"Monsters, they tum out of the closet."

"Ah, Tink, there are no monsters here. Daddy takes care of them. Did you know that?" She shook her head in silence. "Daddy would never let any monsters in here." She curled up tight into a ball and put the blanket up to her face. "Would you like for me to tell you a story?" She shook her head yes.

"Okay. Once upon a time, there was a castle, and in the castle there lived a king and his queen. The queen very much wanted a baby, but for many years, they weren't so blessed. The king was unhappy because he wanted his beautiful queen to be happy. Each night, the king would say a prayer for his beautiful queen to be able to have a child. It was his one desire to keep her happy. So it came to pass that one day the queen came to the king, and she was so happy that the king asked her, 'Why are you so happy, my queen?' She bubbled with delight. 'This time next year, my sweet husband, you and I shall have a child in this kingdom.' They both were very blessed by the arrival of a very beautiful dark-haired princess with big blue eyes, so blue they looked like a crystal sea. The king loved his little princess very much and always strived to give her all the things he thought would make her happy. One day, the king's happiness was dashed by the thought of losing his queen. The queen became very ill, and it was very certain that she would not get well again, not that she didn't want to. It was that her body was so weak she just was unable to get well again. 'How will I raise my little princess alone if her mother should die?' But the king did not give up. He searched the kingdom for doctors to care for his queen, but it was to no advantage. The king would soon be left alone with his princess.

"The king decided that he would raise his little princess with the assistance of his sister, Duchess Beth, and the Duke Landon. They all loved the little princess Molly. She was very well taken care of and loved by all of them. One day there was a new lady among them. Lady Isabella came into the king's life, and she admired him and had a great love for him. She also loved the little princess, and the Lady Isabella wanted very much to be part of their little family, to be able to love the king and his little princess and eventually they would all be a happy family again." I looked down, and my little princess Molly was fast asleep. I continued to rock her when I heard a rustle at the door behind me.

"Is that how the story ends?"

I looked over my shoulder in a start, blushing. "For now it is." I felt a little uncomfortable that Carter had heard the story. "How long have you been here?"

"Long enough to hear the beautiful story you told my daughter." He came and sat down on the floor crossed-legged in front of us. "I enjoyed that little story, and so did she." He pointed at his daughter who was sleeping peacefully in my arms.

"I was trying to make her feel better."

"Was it true?"

What? Then I thought of the story. "Is what true?"

"That you love us and would like to be part of this family?" He shook his head and grinned at the thought. "Okay, maybe love is a little strong for now. Is it true?" I could see the anticipation and questioning seriousness of his expression.

Boy, he *is blunt. How am I going to answer this one?*

"Bella, you don't have to hide your feelings, I

already know the answer. I just want to hear you say it."

Squirming in my seat, I tried to come up with any answer but the obvious, but I couldn't. "I'm trying very hard not to fall for you too quickly, but you are making it exceedingly difficult."

"I was right, you do have feelings for me, more than I thought you did.

Ms. Cameron, you do have a way about you."

"I'm not one to share my feelings, especially early in a relationship.

There's too much of a chance for it to fall through."

"Bella, I intend on making this work. I don't want to push. I just need you to talk to me. I want to know what you're thinking. I want you to know that you can tell me anything. I don't want you to be afraid to talk to me."

"I promise to talk to you more about what's going on with me if you promise to be patient."

"Enough said, I'll certainly do that." He slowly stood in front of me, bending down to take Molly. Pulling her close, he kissed her and placed her back in her bed where he covered her up as she was peacefully and silently dreaming of kings and queens. Turning away from Molly, Carter reached for me and put his arm around my waist. "You're a beautiful woman, Bella. Thank you for the lovely story and the love you have given Molly. It's something that she has needed for a long time." He quickly kissed me and then chuckled. "I stole a kiss, hope you don't mind." I could almost feel my eyes sparkle at him, feeling more like a teenager on her first date, hoping not to get caught by her father.

"I don't mind at all. In fact, I can't think of anything better."

"Shall we return to the bedroom? It's three in the morning, I need my beauty sleep."

"Lead on, Mr. Blake."

I followed behind him just as timid as before.

Taking my hand, he assured me, rubbing my hand. He got into bed and motioned for me to lie down beside him. I slowly climbed in beside him, wrapping his arms around me gently. He lay in bed, spooning next to me.

"Bella, thank you for all that you have done for Molly and me. I appreciate so much that you're willing to care for her as she was your own.

You don't know how much that means to me."

"I enjoy her, I enjoy taking care of her."

"You know what I mean, she's just a little girl. She needs a woman once in a while, and I need you."

"I'm not going anywhere. I like being with you both very much."

"Just take me at my word, Bella. What I say is exactly what I'm thinking.

Life is too short to play around, I learned really quickly."

"Good night Carter. Beauty sleep, remember?"

He nuzzled my hair and kissed me delicately. "Good night, Bella."

Walking in the dark, I could see a single stream of light in the window as I heard feet shuffle behind me. Panic started to fill me. "Daddy, is that you?"

Taking a few steps toward the noise, I smelled liquor and cigarette smoke, it burned my nose as I got closer. The smell of the hard liquor was nauseating to me. "Daddy, where are you? I'm scared, Daddy." I could feel the hot sting of my tears falling down my cheeks. I looked around for him, not being able to see him. I could see old cars all in various stages of being painted.

"Isabella," I heard in a low-pitched whisper.

"Daddy." I heard the footsteps behind me again. I was frightened, and my breaths had become short and erratic. Suddenly a disheveled man stood in front of me. He had a rope in his hands and coming toward me, his emerald green eyes looked at me wickedly.

"Bella, run," I heard a familiar voice but it's soon gone.

I awoke to find myself sitting straight up in the bed, panting as if I had run a marathon. Shaking uncontrollably my clothes were soaking wet. Carter was sitting behind me with his arms wrapped around me, attempting to comfort me. He's rocking me soothingly.

"Shhh, Bella, I'm here. It's okay. It's a bad dream, it's not happening now."

My breaths were short, and I was gasping for air. I was disoriented, looking around the room still back in this brick warehouse trying to find my father until I realized I was with Carter in his home. He's still holding me close and rocking me, the hot tears still running down my cheeks.

What happened then? Who was the man and where was my father? He told me to run.

I turned to face Carter, crying and gasping for each breath, my chest heaving like a child. "Oh god, Carter, what happened to me?"

"I don't know, angel, I don't know." He had hands on both sides of my face, wiping the tears away.

"I'm so scared."

He leaned in to kiss me, and I reciprocated feverously. I just wanted him to take that memory away. He kissed me passionately and pulled me to him tightly. The feel of his body next to me was intoxicating. I wanted him; there was no doubt in that. My body relaxed under his touch, holding my breath anticipating, aching for him, and leaving me breathless. Touching him, I could feel the tightness of his back and the shortened breaths he was taking.

His lips parted and brushed against my shoulder, the warm breath upon me was like an uncontrolled fire on my skin. I was lost to him; there was around, the environment had blended to us. Suddenly I was no longer afraid, my eyes closed, taking in his scent and savoring every moment.

"Bella, stop, baby . . . we can't do this . . ."

"I want you," I whispered urgently. "I want you to love me. I need you to love me."

"Bella, we can't do this, you're not ready for this. As bad as I want to, I'm not ready either."

Trying to calm myself, I took slow, deep breaths. Sitting in front of me, he was running his hands through his hair, trying to calm himself, taking deep, ragged breaths. "Bella, it's not right. Eventually we may get to that point, but we can't. It isn't that I don't want you."

"Just hold me, please." I wanted to have his arms wrapped around me.

Reluctantly he took me into his arms, and I rested my head against his chest. "Carter, I saw him, I saw the man in my dream clearly. He's the same man I've seen awake. The same one I have seen in my apartment, the same one I saw yesterday in the park. I was in a brick building that I think must have been a garage or a warehouse. I was looking for my dad. I could hear his voice, he told me to run. I never saw him. There was another man in the building, and he was following me, he stood in front of me with a rope. I ran with him right on my heels. I wake up before I know who he is or why he is chasing me. He sends terror through me. I can smell the cigarettes that he must have been smoking, and the alcohol that he was drinking."

"It's going to all work out, Bella, you'll see. There is no one going to hurt you as long as I'm here with you. We'll get through this together. I'll do whatever I can to help you, I promise." He sat stroking my hair and rubbing my shoulder for what seemed to be an eternity but was no more than a few minutes. I had become accustomed to the feel of him and the smell of what was definitely him and his cologne. All he had to do was touch me to calm me. This was totally different for me.

"We better get up if we are going to church today."

He patted me and gave me a squeeze. "I'll take you past your apartment to change before we go on if you want to accompany us."

"Carter, I don't really think that it is the place for me."

"You don't have to, but I wish you would. Just go with me once, Bella. If it isn't for you, I won't ask you to go again. I think it will help you."

"Okay, I'll be ready soon. Would you like for me to assist you with
Molly?"

"You can if you want, but you don't have to, I've been doing this for almost three years. Andrea was sick before she had Molly. She was diagnosed while she was carrying her. The doctors advised her to abort Molly and take treatments. She refused, Molly meant more to her than her own life, that's why Andrea and I had difficulties."

"What do you mean?"

"Let's just say at the time, Andrea was what I wanted, when I found she wasn't going to survive, I started drinking heavily. I spent more time in the bar than I did with her." He shook his head and ran his hands through his hair, exasperated. "Andrea needed me, and I wasn't there for her or Molly. I didn't turn my life around until I took Andrea's dying wish to heart. When I was truly broken and went to God, he turned my life around and made me new. I couldn't get back the time I lost with Andrea, but I could with Molly, something that meant more to her than her own life, our daughter. She loved me enough to hold on to a part of me even if it meant losing her own life."

Looking down at his hands, he rubbed his ring finger where his wedding band once existed and swallowed hard.

"I should have been there for her. I could have, I chose not to."

Not knowing how to respond to this, I leaned into

him and rubbed his back affectionately. "I'm sorry, Carter."

"Don't be, it was a long time ago. I've had to deal with this on my own for a long time. It was of my own doing, I'm still healing. It doesn't mean that I don't want a relationship, I do. I miss having a companion, someone to love and someone that will love me back."

CHAPTER 5

"I want to bring a message today that may seem a bit controversial to most. This message was lane on my heart several weeks ago, and I feel someone here needs to hear it, maybe more than one."

I sat close to Carter with Molly sitting in his lap, holding her blanket to her face and her thumb in her mouth, she cuddled up to him. Wrapping his arm around my shoulder, he looked at me and smiled broadly, his eyes glistened. He seemed very pleased to have me here with him; he had introduced me to everyone as his girl.

Beth and Landon set in the pew beside us. She seemed fidgety and uncomfortable, but then again she was close enough to go into labor, of course she would be. Sitting in a very upright posture as you could at about eight and half months pregnant, she rubbed her stomach slowly. I could see Landon was a little concerned.

"Beth, are you okay?" I said in a low voice.

I could see her eyes were a bit squinted. "I'm okay, just some Braxton Hicks. I've had them before." Landon looked at me with a knowing gesture that he thought it's more than that, but I took her at her word and remained still, listening to Pastor Collins with great interest.

"Every one of you here, rather you know it or not, has someone in your life that has been assaulted. Now this can be physical, mental, spiritual, or sexual, all of them causing damage in the wake of their path. It is considered assault in that it is any type of non-consensual contact through force or manipulation, deception or threat. The statistics are staggering, affecting one in four women and one in six men. Up to 14 percent of the victims are assaulted by their spouse, 40 percent or less are reported, so this could be many more.

"The victims in this situation remain in that position

for a large part and are unreported because of shame or embarrassment. This could be your story or the story of someone that you love."

I sat squirming in my seat uncomfortably knowing there was panic in my face. Carter gripped my hand and squeezed his fingers around mine. My breathing became staggering and shallow. I felt sweaty, and my heart began to race. He knew, he knew and he shouldn't. Carter hadn't told him, had he?

"God wants you to know that the suffering will not go on forever, he can and will help you if you want him to. The victims in this auditorium have suffered a loss, a great loss, and grief is okay, but you need to allow for forgiveness."

That's my cue, I couldn't take anymore. I stood to walk out, and I heard Carter whisper, "Bella." I continued to walk out, trying to control my breathing and the panic that had entered me. I found myself at the door hearing footsteps behind me. Feeling his arm wrap around me, I closed my eyes and paused where I stood. He stood with his body against my back, his arms wrapped around my waist. His nose was against my neck, and he kissed me unexpectedly. "Bella, it's okay. If you want to go home, I'll take you. I didn't know that he was going to preach on this subject, I'm sorry." He held me tighter against him. "Give me a few minutes, and I'll get Molly and take you home."

He broke his embrace as I took a couple of deep breaths, feeling like I had just been hit in the stomach. Standing listening to my inner being and struggling desperately, I needed help. *God,* help *me.* I stood next to the door with my feet feeling like they were glued to the floor, but my mind was willing them to run. Hearing feet behind me, I shuddered. Feeling an arm around me, I began to tremor as if I was cold.

"Bella, it's me. Why are you shivering, are you cold?"

I shook my head no, Carter stood beside me with Molly in his arms. Her head lay on her father's shoulder with her thumb in her mouth as she slept peacefully. His face was shrouded in worry and concern. "You're going to have to talk about this sooner or later, facing it is going to make you stronger.

Right now, you're giving the attacker all the power. Take it back, don't let him win."

"I don't want to carry this around, I hope you know that."

"Of course I do. You have to take control, give it over to God, Bella. I can't save you, but I can lead you to him. It has to be your choice and when you are ready. I can't do it for you. I wish I could take the pain away, angel, but I can't."

After a silent ride back to my apartment, he allowed Molly to sleep and assisted me from the car. Taking my hand, he kissed it as a fine gentleman.

He looked up at me through those long lashes of his, and his dark blue eyes shined. "Ms. Cameron, you are at your castle."

"Thank you, Carter. I have enjoyed our time together, I want you to know that."

"You make it sound like I'm leaving and never coming back. You won't get rid of me that easy. Like I said, I intend on courting you, I will be back."

I managed a grin. "I hope that you will, Mr. Blake, I look forward to it."

Carter started to walk me to the door, and I hesitated.

"What?" Carter stood a little off balance that I had stopped.

"I would like to tell Molly goodbye, if it's okay with you."

"Sure, go ahead."

Molly continued to sleep sweetly in her car seat.

Leaning in, I kissed her on the cheek quickly as not to awaken her. "Sweet dreams, precious." Slowly I stepped back from the car and shut the door gently. Turning around, Carter stood in front of me, his hand reaching out for me.

"Come on, I'll walk you to the door."

His expression was unexplainable. I wondered what was going through his mind. Was he thinking about what happened today, about what happened to me? Did he still want to be with me? He walked me to the door and stood looking at me with those beautiful eyes of his. He cupped his hand under my chin and drew me close to him until our noses were almost touching. "I'm going to kiss you," he whispered. His lips brushed mine, and he softly kissed me, then a little more fervently. My knees felt weak at his continual kisses; the thrill of his touch encompassed me. Barely removing his lips from mine, his breathing had quickened.

"I'll call you later. Are you sure you won't come back to the house with me?"

"We both know I can't. Not that I don't want to."

"Call me if you need me, my number is in the book, and so is Landon's, his last name is Mason. One of us will always be able to be reached." He took the key from me and opened the door to let me in. Looking down at me he took a short breath in and run his fingers along my cheek.

"Goodbye Angel."

Oh, I didn't like this. I didn't want him to leave, but I knew he must.

"Bye, I'll talk to you soon, okay?" Saying this was more of a plea than a question.

"I'll call around bedtime. I want your voice to be the last thing I hear tonight." He gave me a wink and walked off to the car. Before he got in, he turned and gave me a wave. How did I get so caught up in him? It hurt to say goodbye and I barely knew him. My heart clinched within me, and I could feel tears pooling. *Stop this,* Bella, he's *coming back,* it *isn't forever. He's coming back. He said he would,* he *even said he would call you tonight.*

Taking a deep breath, I walked into my apartment. The silence was deafening. I never noticed before how eerie it could be. Closing the door behind me, I took a few steps forward and laid my purse on the table. I needed to go on as usual and forget the nightmares and leaving this beautiful man that had entered my life. Being surprised that he hadn't already run, I could still feel the warmth of his arms wrapped around me. Why hadn't anyone else found him and taken him for their own? I was just as glad they hadn't, and then I remembered. "I'm still healing, Bella." His words came back to me. Was he even ready to take the mess that I was on?

The ringing of the phone startled me, and I jumped, feeling as though every nerve ending in me had surged. Anxiously, I reached for the phone.

"Hello."

"Where have you been, I've been trying to call you for days?"

"Oh, Lily, it's you." My voice was shaking.

"Bella, what's wrong with you? You sound disturbed?"

"The phone startled me, I'm fine."

"You were supposed to meet me after work the other night, what happened?"

Grinning partially, I remembered staying with Carter. "I stayed at work."

I cleared my throat. "I had a patient that needed me to stay with them."

"Bella, you take your job way too serious. Why didn't you call me instead of Carolyn?"

"I stayed with a patient that needed me," I repeated with a little more prominence.

"You called and finally left a message and said you would explain, so give it up. What happened?"

"I . . . uh . . . took care of my patient." I took a slow breath and dove in. "I met a wonderful man, Lilly. You would like him." I could hear Lilly squeal on the other end, and then she laughed.

"You didn't? Oh, how exciting. Who is he?"

"Carter Blake."

"No! He's gorgeous and one of the most sought after bachelor I know."

"Yes," I whispered.

"Oh my goodness, Bella, I can't believe it. Are you going to go out with him?"

"I already have." I grinned as if she could see me over the telephone.

"What did you do? Tell me all the details."

"Lily, he is so close to perfect it's scary. We went to the park on a picnic. I spent the day with him and his daughter."

"Wait a minute, daughter? That's a ready-made family, Bella."

"Yeah, I know. You would have to meet him and his daughter."

"You have to tell me all about him, what's he like, how did you get with him? You know, the details."

"Well, I came onto work, and I was assigned to him as soon as I came to the floor. Lilly, I don't know how to explain any of it. I was drawn to him from the time I stepped into his room. It was like I had known him all my life."

"Well, how did you come to stay there with him?"

"I can't say a lot other than he asked me to, and for some reason, I wanted to and did. I got to know him, and he was released from the hospital. He went home sooner than I thought he should, I was concerned. He asked me to go with him." Pausing, I remembered the ride home with his hand lying on mine. "I went with him."

"Isabella, you didn't? The girl that I have to drag

out with me to meet people and you went home with a total stranger?"

"Well, like I said, you would have to meet him. He can be very persuasive."

"For you to do something like that, I can imagine. So what happened?

Fill me in on all the good stuff."

"It's not what you think, believe me. Neither one of us is ready for that kind of relationship. I went home with him, we spent some time together, and we danced in front of his fireplace and talked."

"He sounds like a romantic."

"He is." I felt a little tremor of sadness that he wasn't with me now.

"What happened?"

"There was nothing physical if that's what you mean. He's different, his intention is to, and I quote, to court me."

"But you stayed, didn't you?" The amazement was rising in her voice.

"Yes, but I slept in his room and he slept on the couch, nothing happened.

I don't think that it would have anyway, not with the baggage I carry around."

"Bella, you don't get it. He is an eligible bachelor, and you are a beautiful woman. The problems you have are obstacles, but with the right person, you will be able to work them out."

"I'm surprised that he hasn't run already."

"You told him?"

"Well, what I can remember."

"Does he understand?"

"I think so, he is trying to anyway. He did witness one of my nightmares."

"You're having nightmares again? I thought they had gone."

95

"That's not all, I've seen this man in broad daylight, and he wasn't really there. I've seen images of him in my apartment and at the park with Carter's daughter."

"Bella, you haven't had nightmares for a long time. I have never heard you say that you had seen this man. What do you think triggered it?"

"I think maybe seeing Molly."

"You mean his daughter?"

"She is about three years old and a total doll. I can't imagine how anyone could do something to a child that could cause them that kind of trauma, that's not all, Daddy was in it, and he was telling me to run."

It wasn't long before I completed my call and I was once again in the silence of my home. I never felt the eeriness a noiseless house could bring before. Turning on the stereo I allowed it to fill the air with some familiar sweet tunes that I had enjoyed for years, bringing me relief.

The rest of the day and into the evening had drug on. I didn't think it would ever get to bedtime hoping that the night wasn't going to be much the same. I was hoping for a dreamless sleep, at least if I did I hoped that it would be of him and not the nightmare that followed me daily.

Blinking my eyes, I thought of the past few days and things that had developed from them. The water rushed over me from the shower as if washing all the cares and pain away. If only it were that simple. Closing my eyes, I could see his face, his long lashes shading his dark eyes, his soft lips that were drawn like a bow, and his unruly, soft dark hair. Smiling to myself, I wished he were here, my heart yearned for him. Just for him to put his arms around me would be enough to satisfy me. What had happened to me? Even Ryan who tried so hard to make our relationship work, I never sat back and thought of him like I did Carter. He's etched in my soul.

Reaching out of the shower, I grabbed the heavy towel from the ring and wrapped it around me then wrapped the other around my head. The bath was filled with steam, and I stood in front of the sink mirror and wiped some of the condensation from it. What did he see in me? I was just an ordinary girl. I never thought of myself as being exceptional, my eyes were dark brown with gold rims, and my lashes were dark and long, shadowing them. My heart-shaped face and high cheekbones were a background to my lips that I always felt were to full.

I took my hair from the towel and gently massaged it dry and combed it through. My hair always seemed to be to fine and thin for my liking, it never appeared to be full and lush like I wanted. There were few styles I was able to wear it in because of that. I wore it in layers to give it the appearance of fullness. I always envied women that had thick, lush hair. I dressed and I quickly brushed my teeth. *Hmm,* much *better.* Stepping into the bedroom, I grabbed my well-worn PJs and tied my hair back in a ribbon, knowing the effort was futile.

It's getting late and close to time for bed, my heart sank. He said he would call, why hasn't he? I had waited for him to call since he left me today.

I knew it's against what he believed, but maybe I would have been better off staying with him. At least if I had more nightmares or seen that dreadful person again, I would've had him there to comfort me. No, this was crazy. He barely knew me and me him, why did it matter? I had lived alone for at least three years, why did I need someone now?

The phone rang, and I ran to get it.

"Hello." I gasped from running.

"Hi, angel, you running a race?"

"No," I giggled like a teenager. "I was getting ready for bed, and I heard the phone. I was hoping it was you." I smiled to myself.

"Well, it is. How are you doing, you okay?"

"I would be better if you were here."

97

"I'll come over and stay with you if you want. I can bring Molly with me, she isn't hard to pack up."

His answer surprised me. "You would do that for me?"

"Yeah, if you need me, I will."

"I miss you."

"Glad to hear that, I miss you too. I will do whatever it takes to make you happy, I hope you know that."

"I know you would, I just don't like to ask anyone to do anything for me."

"If I'm going to be your guy, you're going to have to trust me."

"I do trust you. Maybe I trust you way too much."

"All you have to do is say the word, angel, and I'll be there."

Sitting on my bed, I debated on having him come be with me or to go to him. I really didn't want to be here alone. "I thought you wanted to court me."

"I do, I intend fully on courting you."

"That isn't going to be easy if you and I are together in the same place all the time."

He paused. "That's true but I don't want you to be fearful either. You know I would be there."

"I know. I guess I could have Lilly come and stay with me."

"Do you want me to come be with you tonight, are you sure you're okay?"

"I'll be okay. I want to do this your way. It's only right, I shouldn't be afraid of a ghost. That's what it is. I don't know who it is or what it is, but I can't let it rule me."

"I understand." There was some disappointment noted in his response. "I just don't want you to be frightened. You know if you need me, I'm here."

"Yes, I do." I smiled at the phone.

"I would like to take you out on a real date if you

don't mind. You know, the hearts and flowers kind of thing. If I can remember all of that, it's been a while."

"Sure, I would love that."

"Do you have anything planned for tomorrow evening?"

"Yes, a matter a fact, I do."

I could hear his breath catch, and I was grinning. "Oh, okay."

I tried to hide my private joke. "I have a date with an extraordinary man that seems to have old-fashioned values. I think I'm going to enjoy seeing him very much."

"Um, okay," I could hear a little chuckle in his voice. "How about, I pick you up around six. We can go out to supper, I'm not sure what else we may do."

"Sounds good." I was having a hard time controlling my feelings, gushing with excitement. "I look forward to seeing you."

"Ms. Cameron, you have done me a great honor. Not many men have the pleasure of saying they are escorting an angel on a date."

"Carter, you're making me blush."

"So, there isn't anything wrong with that."

"I'll see you tomorrow evening then."

"Good night, Bella. Sweet dreams."

"Good night."

Hanging up the phone, I felt the emptiness once more. What in the world had happened to me? This man, this gorgeous, intelligent man had absolutely turned my world upside down. Turning off the light I climbed into bed. Who was I kidding? I would never sleep tonight. I was too excited; I couldn't wait to see him no matter what or where we'd go. I just wanted to be near him, that's all that was important. Maybe I could get Lily to go with me on a shopping trip tomorrow, maybe a new dress. Yes, that's it, a dress. Very few women wore a dress to go on a date anymore. Why not? It's feminine, and he's looking for the normal. Forget the normal. I was going for being a woman. Where did that come from? I was a fan of my old jeans and tees, well, not this time. I'd call Lily in the morning. Slowly I drifted off thinking of his searing dark blue eyes, luminous smile and unruly dark hair, it's calming and that's what I needed.

I awakened to the sun just peeking through the curtain in my room.

Good, it's morning. Thank goodness no nightmares. I lay and stretched hugging the pillow close to me. I needed to call Lilly to see about a very important shopping trip. Grinning to myself, I wondered, what he's doing now. Was he thinking of me? Was he even awake yet? I bet he was, and I could see Molly wrapped around his neck hugging him tight. Oh, she loved her daddy. Time is wasting, I better get up.

Slowly, I got up and walked into the kitchen, loosening my hair from the ribbon in it, what's left's still up anyway, and turned on the coffeepot in hope of an instant charge. Picking up the phone, it began to ring and I jumped.

Oh, who could that be?

"Hello." There's no answer.

"Hello, is there anyone there?"

There was still no answer and I felt the tingles of anxiety run my spine and the line went dead. All I heard was a dial tone. Hanging up, I dialed Lilly.

"Lilly," my voice sounded a little shaky as I spoke.

"Yeah, it's me, what's wrong? You sound upset."

"No, no, I'm okay. I just got a strange call, it was probably nothing. I was just going to call you to see if you wanted to go shopping with me. I have a date tonight and . . ."

"You have a date? How exciting, is it with Carter?"

I couldn't help myself, and I giggled like a little girl. "Yes, and I can't wait."

"Well then, I guess a shopping trip is in order. When do you want to go?"

"I can be ready in an hour, that sound okay with you?"

"I'll see you about ten o'clock?"

"That sounds great. Thanks, Lilly, I haven't done this for a long time."

"I like the way he makes you giggle. I'll see you soon."

"Be seeing you then." Hanging up the phone I proceeded to get ready to go with Lilly for the day. I could hardly contain my excitement; I was going out with Carter this evening. This had to be perfect.

Before I knew it, it was time for Lily. I pulled my hair back as I heard the doorbell ring. Running to answer it, I opened the door as Lily came busting in. She's all smiles, giddy almost. Before I knew it, she's hugging me and squealing.

"Oh, I can't believe it. You're going on a date, with Carter Blake, for heaven's sake. We have to find the perfect outfit for you. Maybe we'll even stop in and get a manicure, might as well do the whole thing." She bubbled with enthusiasm.

"I want something feminine, something pretty?"

"Yeah, I get the picture, understated but glamorous. We'll find something just right."

"Come on, let's go."

We spent the day at Bateman's, one of the best local stores we had, and Tangles, where we both ended up getting our hair done by Jonah. He's one of the most talked-about stylists in Maine, he didn't disappoint. My hair was done in a magnificent upsweep that looked like I had a ton of hair; little curls hung at the sides of my ears and the nape of my neck. The manicure that we had treated ourselves to made me feel like a pampered princess.

"We must get you a dress, that's next on the list."

I took a long, exaggerated breath trying to collect myself. I could feel butterflies rise in me. Closing my eyes, I continued to take slow, deep breaths.

The attempts to calm myself weren't helping much. I heard a slight giggle from Lilly, which was now stroking my back.

"Oh boy, you got it bad, you're going on a date not before a firing squad."

"Lilly, what if I get involved with him? What if I fall hard for him and he leaves when he finds what being in a relationship with me is like?"

"Too late, dear, you already have fallen for him. Give it time, it's just a date."

I slowly opened my eyes and took control of myself. The anxiety attacks were terrible, especially when you didn't know what brought them on.

Lilly, looking especially pretty, smiled and continued to giggle. "I have never seen you like this, and don't worry. He likes what he saw or he wouldn't have asked you out. Come on, let's get you a pretty dress and some shoes to match, and then maybe we'll get some extras to go with it. Have fun with it, enjoy it, he likes you."

"Okay, let's do this."

Spending most of the afternoon trying on multiple dresses, I settled on a navy blue sheath that fitted my body well but still remained conservative. I liked the feel, and Lilly insisted on it. "He's going to love it, it's perfect. You couldn't have found a dress that fit the occasion any better. You're going to knock him off his feet."

"Do you think so?"

"You look gorgeous."

"You can't hide what's happened to me, Lilly," I said, despondently.

"You are what you are inside. Come on, think of this as a fresh start, and leave the baggage behind. You never know, maybe he's the one."

"Whoa, slow down. I haven't had my first date with him yet, well, not an official one yet anyway."

"Give him a chance, don't hide from him. Let him get to know you, give yourself a chance to get to know him."

Lilly smiled brightly. "Always the optimist, aren't you?"

"Always." She winked.

When I finally got back to the house, I had about two hours before our date. Lilly remained to assist me in getting ready as I felt clumsy, but I managed. I decided on a simple strand of pearls, and pearl earrings adorned my ears. I finished putting on my stockings and my black kitten heels; they made a perfect match to the dress. The doorbell rang as I was trying to buckle the strap of my shoes. Lilly smiled at me. "Oh, that's him, you ready?"

"All but my shoes."

"Do you want me to answer it?"

"No, I'll get it. Do you mind letting me have a few minutes with him? I promise I will introduce you."

"No, go ahead, don't keep him waiting."

I picked up my shoes and carried them to the door. Straitening my dress, I reached for the knob and turned it.

There he was, I drank in the sight of him. He was gorgeous, dressed in dark blue jeans with a white shirt open at the neck, and a navy pinstriped jacket with the sleeves pushed up on his forearms.

"Isabella. Wow, what a knockout."

"You are much too generous, but thank you." I waved him in. "Please come in."

Carter waltzed in with ease and confidence. The only words I could come up with to describe him was earth-shattering, his smile was to die for. "You, ready to go?" Seeming to be unshaken from what he told me, that he hadn't dated since his wife had died. I was, on the other hand, felt like I was in a million pieces before him.

Sitting down in the overstuffed chair next to the door, I attempted to put on my shoes, the straps on them giving me a bit of a challenge. "Yes, as soon as I can get my shoes on, we can go." Seeing me having difficulty, he sauntered over and thence kneeled down in front of me. Grasping my ankle he placed it on his bended knee, slipping my shoe on and fastening the buckle with ease and looked up at me with a boyish grin. Reaching down to his handsome face, I ran the back of my fingers across his cheek.

"There, that wasn't so hard. I have some things planned tonight I think you're going to like. I'm a little out of practice, I haven't done this sort of thing for close to six years," he said as he rose and stood in front of me, offering me his hand. He assisted me to stand. I had finally found a good man, and I was terrified.

"What?"

"You don't seem to be to unnerved by this, I mean you tell me you haven't been out for some time."

He grinned and raised an eyebrow at me. "Are you nervous?"

"You could say that. And you?"

"I've just been shaking in my shoes all day, Ms. Cameron."

We both had to laugh at ourselves. Lily walked in to say her goodbyes to us. "Carter, this is my friend, Lilly Drake. Lily, this is Carter Blake." She extended her hand to him, her eyes never leaving him. Well, I guess it wasn't just me, he was gorgeous. She appeared totally stunned by him; I didn't remember seeing her respond to anyone like that.

"It's nice to meet you, Carter. Bella has told me a lot about you."

"All good I hope," he laughed.

"Well, she has pretty much made you into a knight on a white horse."

"Lily!" I squirmed.

"Well, I'm not sure about that, but I think she is pretty amazing."

Reaching for my hand, he looked down at me with those beautiful dark blue eyes and I melted. "We better go if we're going to make our reservations."

"Yes, we should." I felt very shy and reserved as I looked up at him through my lashes and gave him a grin.

"Oh, one more thing, Lilly, you are staying tonight, aren't you?"

"Yes, if you want me to."

My eyes never left him. "Don't wait up."

He escorted me out of the house, holding out his arm, I locked mine around it. Giving very little attention to anything around me until he had escorted me to my door, I found our ride for the night was a Charger, candy red no less. He flipped the keys in his hand and motioned for me to take a seat. I slid in and he walked around to the driver's side and started the car with a roar. "I thought you might enjoy this. I don't drive it much. I save it for special occasions." He smiled broadly then laughed. "I bought it a couple of hours ago. Insurance totaled my car. Devil of a way to get a new one, but then I wouldn't have met you. We have reservations at the Lighthouse, have you been there before?"

"No, I haven't." I sat, enamored by him. Gazing at him, I was awestruck.

He glanced over at me and smiled. "Good, I picked the right place, you're in for a treat." I knew he felt the stare I had held on him. "What is it, Bella?"

His words finally brought me back to earth, but I never took my eyes from him.

"Nothing, I . . . I . . ." *Oh my, I have lost my voice.*

He chuckled nervously. "Now there is something, what is it?"

I finally released my stare and looked down then returned my admiring gaze at him through my lashes. I had lost my grin; I'd become very serious in my assessment of him. How could I tell him what I thought? What would I say, that I thought he was the most gorgeous man I had ever seen; that he was my comfort, my solace; that he had touched me somewhere inside that no one had ever been able to before?

"Bella, you're making me a little nervous here. What is it?" His jaw was starting to tighten, and I saw he was getting very uncomfortable without an explanation.

"I'm a bit overwhelmed."

"Overwhelmed, why?"

"This is kind of hard to explain."

He was still very uncomfortable, and I could see his face tensing. "Just be honest, Bella, that's all I ask. Good or bad, it doesn't matter."

I took a deep breath as I assessed him. He's scared, so was I. His fear of rejection was the same as mine. He had no reason for it, but I certainly did.

"Carter, I have only been in one serious relationship, and it ended badly.

I just don't want that to happen again. I think you are the most loving and thoughtful man I have ever met in my life. This was a leap of faith for me. I do not disclose my feelings for people often." I could see the tension slowly leave him, and he let out a breath as if he had been holding it. His face remained serious but relaxed. He took a fleeting look at me then back on the road.

"Bella, don't ever be afraid to tell me how you feel or what you're thinking.

If we are going to make this relationship work, we have to be honest with each other. Frankly, the feelings I have for you scare me to death. God is in this, let's see where he takes it. Everything is revealed in his time, not ours.

Just relax, angel, and enjoy the ride."

"How do you know God is in this? I mean, it could

have been chance, you know, luck."

"No, angel, there is no such thing as luck. God places us where he wants us when he wants us to be there. There is no such thing as chance. Bella, I prayed for this, for him to bring someone into my life he wanted, that he would introduce me to the person he wanted and he would let me know. You are what I prayed for, God knows what we need when we don't, and he knows when to place them there. I have faith that God will reveal to you who he is and that you see that you need him in your life. He will in his time and in his own will."

Wow, what *do you say to that?* "I don't know that I understand that. What happened to me, an all-powerful and all-knowing God would have never let that happen."

"Bella, God does not mess with the free will of man. We live in a world of sin, we were born into it as a baby. It's like Molly running and then falling.

I can't keep her from getting hurt, but she knows I will be there to love and take care of her when she does. I know what is going to happen, and I try to protect her. She knows I will be there for her and do all I can. All I can do is to teach her and be there when she is ready to accept me. What happened to you, what you remember, is tragic. It wasn't your fault and it wasn't God's.

He wants to help you if you will let him, he's just waiting for you to accept him. When you are ready, you come to me or my pastor, and we'll talk to you about it. I don't want you to feel you are being pushed. I can't save you, and neither can the pastor. We can lead you to him, but you have to be ready to accept him by faith. He deserves your love and your surrender to him."

I sat and pondered this; so much so that I had forgotten the ride and we were soon parking at the Lighthouse. Carter opened the door and offered his hand to me. Taking it, he pulled me to him, never saying a word but looking at me as he saw into my soul. He looked to me for

107

permission and never said a word. Leaning in, he placed his hand at the small of my back and traced my face with his index finger to my lips, his intention was clear. I closed my eyes, and he kissed me softly then looked at me sincerely, cupping my chin; I felt my breaths shorten.

"I have wanted to do that since I picked you up this evening. Promise me that you will tell me everything. Don't be afraid, you're safe. At all cost, I will take care of you. I want you to be comfortable with me. I will never place you in a position where you will be or can be harmed."

Oh my, he was dead serious. He had no idea how screwed up I was, I didn't even know how screwed up I was myself. I shook my head, and he still looked at me seriously, searching. Finally I managed to speak, "I will always tell you, no secrets." He tipped his head back and closed his eyes, the tension relieved. He refocused on me. Leaning in, he kissed me on the cheek.

"No secrets. Come on, our table is waiting." Placing his hand on the small of my back, he guided me into this small intimate restaurant, lit low. We were met by the hostess and were guided through the hardwood floored room and French doors that led out to a wood deck. The deck lay over the sound laden with small wooden tables covered in white linen tablecloths. The tables were made for two with cane back chairs, and the linen-clad tables were graced with globe-covered candles. The wooden deck was covered in pots of tropical flowers of pink, white, and orange; and the salty smell of the sound rose. The view of the sound with its blues and green was picturesque.

Carter pulled out my chair, allowing me to sit, and assisted the seat back to the table then took his seat across from me. The hostess took her leave, and the waiter arrived in his dark suit with vest and linen shirt. He politely introduced himself then made his suggestions. We're left as Carter looked over the menu. He raised an eyebrow and grinned. His demeanor was relaxed and controlled. "Have what you like, I'm a meat and potatoes man."

"I'll just have whatever you have."

"Okay, Ms. Cameron, whatever you wish. I'm just glad to be here with you." Folding the menu, I gently lay it on the table and smiled brightly at him. "I am glad to be here with you."

"Did you buy that dress especially to go out with me?"

I blushed and bit my lip. "You did," he said in amazement. "You look radiant. Blue is my favorite color, I like the look, very Jackie."

"Jackie?"

"Kennedy, Bella, the first lady and a lady of style and grace."

"Yes, of course. Thank you, sir, I appreciate the compliment."

Our waiter returned, and Carter graciously ordered for us both. He caught me looking around in amazement of the setting we had both found ourselves in. The gulls flying overhead screeched over the sound and I watched them land with grace and ease on the small islands of sand that remained in the water. It's an incredibly romantic place.

"You like this?"

"Yes, it's beautiful. I love the smell of the ocean, and the water is lovely."

"It came very highly recommended by a person I know well and trust."

He watched my expression, and I was a little puzzled. Smirking, he raised his glass of water. "Landon, he used to bring Beth here, well, way back when. Unfortunately, she met Cooper."

"He dated Beth?"

"Yes, a long time ago. He dated her in her junior and senior year of high school. It was pretty hot and heavy, my mother always thought that they would get married."

109

He sat rubbing the rim of the glass. "She met Cooper when Landon was away training at the academy. He was gone for months at a time, and it left her with more time on her own than she needed. She would go out with her friends to parties, she met him at one of them. She was going through a rough spot, a rebellious part of her life, met up with this bad boy that was already on the force. It has never been a good situation. We all work together, it makes for a very sticky situation."

"Did he love her?"

"Landon?" He rubbed the back of his neck, looking a little uncomfortable.

"Yes, he did. He still does. I don't think he will ever give up on it. Cooper isn't good to her, he hits her for pastime, and she won't leave him. She's under the false impression that he loves her and that she loves him. He has never loved her."

"Oh, I see. That's where you're going, wasn't it? You were going after her when you had the accident."

He shook his head in agreement. "She had called me, Cooper was drunk and angry, and it's not a good mix. He drew back to hit her, she ran to the bedroom and locked the door behind her. I could hear him yelling at her in the background that he was going to kill her. She was in a panic. She told me he had his revolver. For her to be in enough panic to call me, it was bad."

He sighed at the thought. "I called Landon as I was leaving and told him the situation, he beat me there. I had also called some of my buddies on the way there so whoever got there first could take him down. On the way there, I swerved to keep from hitting a deer that had crossed in front of me. I don't remember much after that until I was in the hospital and heard your voice. I heard you call my name."

As we finished our meal, he reached over the table to me, and I took his hand eagerly. "I have one more surprise for you, you ready for this?"

"I'm ready to be alone with you," I said, then feeling I was being way to forward for my own comfort, even though that's how I felt.

"My thoughts exactly, Isabella, how did you guess?"

The restaurant lights dimmed further, and music came on behind us, soft and inviting. The deck lit up in tiny white twinkle lights as the larger lamps had disappeared. He stood, never letting go of my hand. "I wasn't expecting this, Ms. Cameron, may I have this dance?" I stepped in closer to him as the music played "Let It Be Me." We swayed back and forth to the sweet melody. My head rested against his chest as he held me next to him, his cheek resting on the top of my head. My hand rested on his chest as he covered it with his hand. Slowly we danced around the deck. He held me close and I listened to rhythm of his breathing. He twirled me around and brought me back into his embrace. He made me a much better dancer than I was. Everything had disappeared to me, except for the two of us. I loved the touch of his hands, and the scent of his cologne was carried on the ocean air. He continued to dance me across the floor and started to sing softly the last verse of the song, having a beautiful intoxicating voice.

All too soon, the music ended and he continued to hold me in his embrace, looking down at me seriously. There was something so exhilarating about it; his eyes shined in the now-glowing sunset. It sent chills through me, and I began to anticipate his next move, his next breath, next word. I could feel my heart beating frantically within my chest, my breath had left me. I couldn't take in the shortest breath as his gaze held me tightly. I could see him swallow, and he seemed to be thinking of what he would do or could not do, I was not sure. The feel of his hands on me had caused my skin to feel extremely sensitive, heated. He raised his hand to my face, keeping me in his embrace and running his finger along my bottom lip, and proceeded to tip my chin. He moved in close to my face and hesitated. "I'm going to kiss you, Bella," he said in a low, hushed voice. Leaning in closer, he kissed me. The very feel of his lips on mine ignited fire in me. I didn't know if I should run or stay. He had awakened something in me that I thought was never there.

Stepping back, he held his gaze on me. I knew he was searching me, attempting to search a reaction from me. My feet were fixed to the spot, but in my mind, I was willing my feet to pick up and run as hard as I could from him. Looking at me warily, he drew his fingertips down my cheek. "Don't run, Bella, I'm scared of what I'm feeling too. I would never hurt you." *How in the world? He knows my thoughts,* what *I am feeling?* He placed his hand in mine and led me to the front of the Lighthouse and paid the check as we left.

CHAPTER 6

Keeping me close, he stepped onto the deck of the restaurant and smiled.

"Surprise, Ms. Cameron." He motioned off to his right. "Your carriage awaits, my queen." I was taken aback and looked on in awe of what he had now in front of me, a white carriage with gold-and-red plush seats drawn by a white horse, majestic in his look and demeanor. Atop the carriage was a gentleman dressed in period clothing of old England.

Carter led me to the carriage and took my hand, steadying me. Sliding over the plush satin cover of the seats, he quickly slid in beside me. The rim of the carriage was covered with white and pink roses with an occasional daisy mixed in.

Raising his arm, he wrapped it around my shoulder. "Knightly enough,

Bella?" I thought back to what Lilly had said before we left, how I talked of him made him sound like my knight on a white horse. I giggled when I realized what he meant. "I guess Lilly was right." He managed a little chuckle.

"Mr. Blake, you certainly are a charmer, a girl could easily get spoiled."

He was having way too much fun with this, and he laughed a little more boldly.

"My aim is to spoil you, Ms. Cameron, is it working?" I was totally flabbergasted by him, but I loved every minute of this, being completely lost to him. No man could be this perfect; no one could know me this well. It's almost as if he had been reading a book on me. The hopeless romantic that I had always been, I knew I was going to fall for him, and fall rapidly and hard. Being here with him was comforting. After all this time, I had found the other piece of me. We rode along the sound, and the parkway cuddled together like we had been in love for years. The orange, pink, and blue colors streaked the sky line with a soft, gentle breeze blowing against us. His arms were warm and inviting me to come closer to him. I lay my head against his chest with my hand placed softly against his leg as he settled in and placed his cheek against my head.

There were few words exchanged, just a peaceful ride, the two of us enjoying time together. His hand traced up and down my arm, leaving me trembling under his touch. He looked down at me with those deep blue gorgeous eyes and smiled, one that was reserved just for me. "Are you cold?" I shook my head, and he removed his jacket and placed it on me as I shrugged it on. I hug it to me, taking in the smell of it, his smell. The cologne he wore mixed with his natural scent was intoxicating.

"Ms. Cameron, I do believe you are smitten."

"You are way too observant, Mr. Blake. I can't hide a thing from you, can I?"

"Not much gets past me. One of the perks of my job I guess. Sometimes it isn't pleasant to know how to capture the thoughts or feelings of someone else. That's the downfall of it. There are times I would rather not have that ability."

It's now that I realized that he was just as vulnerable as I. Maybe it wasn't as terrible for him to know how I felt. Did I know how I felt about him? I thought for a moment and nuzzled my cheek against his chest. "I can't tell you how much this evening has meant to me Bella. You have made it very enjoyable for me, I hope you have enjoyed yourself."

"I have, I can't believe I'm here with you. I can't remember an evening that I have felt, I don't know. Wanted, I guess. I'm very comfortable with you."

"Good, I want you to be. I promise you, we will

never do anything you don't want to do. I would never do anything to hurt you intentionally. I want for us both to be able to share what we are feeling with each other without fear." He looked at me, expressionless. "I haven't let myself feel anything for a very long time. I'm ready to move on. I'm ready to live my life, I need to be loved, and to give that love back to someone that will share their life with me. I don't know what is going to happen with us, but I'm willing to take a chance. My feelings are very real. I can't say that I'm in love with you, it's too early for that, but I know enough that I don't want this to end."

Wow, these were some powerful feelings he was unloading. I looked into his handsome face, trying to take in all that he had just said. I was relieved, but what did I do with this information? Sad thing was, I thought I did love him. Yes, I thought I did. *Careful,* Bella, *you're getting in too deep too fast*, my subconscious told me, but my heart was telling me go for it. *Love this man, he's perfect*, you *know you want to. Just take a deep breath and tell him. What do you have to lose?* I was captivated by him; all that came to mind was what it would be like to belong to him.

"I'm not sure what to say. Carter, I have so many different feelings right now I'm not sure how to sort them out. One of the biggest is fear. There's a lot about me you don't know. I'm scared. I'm scared of how I feel about you, but it's more than that. I'm scared if I walk away, I'll never feel this way ever again. I feel like I can't take my next breath without you. It's so hard to explain, I don't know you. How could this be?"

"Bella, don't try to read too much into what has happened, just let it go. It doesn't matter what has happened in the past, not to me. I'm not looking for perfection, just who is perfect for me. Life is way too short for dealing with things you can't change."

The ride back left the carriage ride lingering in my mind. The touch of his hand on mine brought me back to reality. The tension had continually built from the time we danced and had grown since. Turning, I saw that my glance at him had been met with his; I hadn't realized we had stopped.

Sitting with is arm curled around the steering wheel, his eyes were fixed on me. Sitting in the dim light of the streetlight, I sat and gazed at him. The light reflected off the window on to him, encircling his face. His expression bathed in desire, his eyes smoldering, not allowing me to keep my eyes off him. I could hear the beat of my heart quicken and the pounding of it against my chest. My body began to tremble under his touch and I couldn't move. I didn't want to, aching for him to touch me, to kiss me.

"I thought we would come back home for a while, a chance to get you to myself before I take you home." He shifted slightly in his seat and ran his index finger down my cheek. "I want to be alone with you."

"I thought . . ." My words sounded weak.

"Molly's staying with her uncle Landon for the night."

I felt my breaths becoming shorter, and my heart beat so unruly, hard and rhythmic, I felt it was going to beat from my chest. "Bella, don't, don't think anything in to this. I just want to be alone with you." He found his way over to my side of the car and offered his hand to me. He took my hand and kissed it softly, tucking it through his looped arm, having it rest against him.

I love being close to him, feeling his movement as he strode along beside me.

Opening the door to his home, he walked me in to his living room where he stopped at the door, allowing me to take in the room. The room was dimly lit by the fireplace that popped and crackled, making itself known. The light of the room was reflected from the candles that were flickering on the mantel and the table before us, mirrors was strategically placed under them.

Two glasses sat on the table before us. Listening to his footsteps, I heard him drop the keys on the counter with a clink as they fell. His footsteps clicked on the floor below him as he made his way back to me. Wrapping his arms around me with an innocent hug, his fingers were light and caressed my skin as he help me remove his jacket. Laying it across the bar, he motioned for me to take a seat on the couch. My eyes never leaving his, the gaze he had seemed eternal, capturing me. Backing up to the couch, I felt the coolness of the leather on the backs of my legs as I sat down. Holding to my hand, his eyes were staring into me relentlessly, making me shiver. "Bella, you are so beautiful." Never saying another word he sat down on the couch so that he was facing me with one leg bent under him.

"I have been waiting for this all day. I hope you don't mind that I brought you back here this evening." I smiled back at him shyly.

"Mr. Blake, I hope you know that it's dangerous to leave candles lit in your absence." This brought him away from his seriousness momentarily. "I do, Ms. Cameron, I like to live dangerously." He smirked then continued.

"My sister assisted me. All I had to do was ring her cell. She knew when we left the carriage ride. She set this up, with my approval of course. I do believe she would like to get me out of her business. All kidding aside, she just wants me to be happy. She sees that chance with you, so do I."

I felt my face turned crimson. "I want that too," I said feebly.

He leaned in toward me, reaching to my hair, and I flinched. "Relax," he said in a whisper. He began to remove the comb from my hair then the pins that had held my hair up all night. Slowly and tenderly, he removed each one, searching my face. My dark brown hair fell down onto my shoulders and over my chest. After releasing the last pin, he ran his hands through my hair, shaking it loose, causing it to go tumbling down my back. "I love how your hair sweeps down over your shoulders." Closing my eyes and sighing, I relished the feel of his hands running through my hair. "You like this, Bella?"

"Mmm, very much."

I could feel him move closer. His breath was falling on my shoulder and into the bend of my neck. "Bella, you're safe, relax." He took me closer to him and wrapped himself around me.

I started to relax under his words, bringing my arms around his neck and laying my head against his shoulder. He lightly kissed my cheek and ran his hand down my back. I caught the scent of his cologne, taking me away. We were truly alone. No one else mattered, nothing else mattered. Right here and now, he belonged to me and I to him.

The heat radiated off his body as we were encircled by a woman singing in the background. Singing of what her life would be without the love of her life, not being able to breathe or live without him. The music soon faded, and all that was left was the pop of the fire as it spat and sputtered embers onto the hearth. He broke the embrace enough to keep me from leaning against his shoulder. Tilting my face with his fingers, he leaned closer to me with a little smirk, his eyes danced. "Ms. Cameron, you have me under your spell.

Ever since I heard your voice, you had me." He looked away momentarily for the glasses on the table and offered one to me. The liquid bubbled to the top in traces and the fizz released from the glass like a roman candle. "To a beautiful evening together and many more to come," raising his glass aloft, he clank the glass against my own. Taking a drink, it was crisp, sweet with a bite. "Sparkling cider, always a pleaser, my sister the partier." I had to laugh; he was shocked at his sister's choice. He smiled and took the edge out of the moment. "I have her fooled. I do have champagne somewhere in the fridge along with something else you may like." Standing, he headed toward the kitchen that was still etched in darkness. "The cider is fine, I like it." I stood to walk toward the kitchen. "Can I help you?"

"No, it's ok, I have it." Sliding back into the room with ease and grace, he held a small silver tray and placed it on the table before us. Reclaiming a seat on the couch, he sat on the overstuffed surface of the chocolate brown leather. "Come sit by me, this is a treat. I made them myself." Sitting down, he guided me to sit next to him and to lean back into his arms. "You said you couldn't cook."

"It's pretty hard to screw up strawberries. They taste really good with champagne. I have never tried to eat them with sparkling cider." Taking the strawberry, he lifted it by the stem and dipped it into the cider and took a bite. "Well, it's not bad." He lifted another and dipped the tip into my glass and held it up to my mouth. "Taste." I bit down into it, letting the coolness of the cider wash through my mouth and down my throat. The strawberry was sweet with crystallized sugar, and the sweet and sour bite of the cider, refreshingly crisp. Not bad for a bachelor's idea of romance. "You like it," he whispered.

"Mmm."

"I take that as a yes." I could feel him smile as his face rubbed gently against my own. "I have enjoyed every minute of this evening." He ran his fingertips from my hands slowly up to my shoulders. Sweeping my hair away from my shoulder, he leaned down and kissed me just below my ear and ran his fingers delicately down my arm. The touch of his fingers, the feel of his breath on me sent tingles down me. The effect he had was phenomenal, and he knew exactly what buttons to push.

My body tightened; I was not sure if I was fearful or if it was welcome.

119

My mind was shattered, feeling lost to him. I was enamored by him; I had never felt this way before. It's foreign and frightening to me. Noticing stress from my body, he stopped and left his hand on mine.

"Mr. Blake, are you trying to seduce me?"

He let out a small laugh. "Why, is it working? I told you I'm out of practice."

"You do make a girl weak in the knees."

"I'm glad to hear that I can turn your head."

Turning around to face him, I sat down on his lap. He appeared a little off from my approach, but not enough to knock him off his game. The soft glow from the fireplace reflected on his perfect face, just enough to reflect the light into his eyes and to bounce off his unruly dark hair. I took the drink from his hand and placed it with mine, leaving them on the table behind him. He leaned casually back on the arm of the couch. Leaning into him closing the distance between us, I kissed his soft wet lips still tasting of cider.

This was something I had wanted to do all evening. Yes, it's healing to me.

Realizing now that I had taken the lead and kissed him first, I sat back with my arms around his neck and looked down into his beautiful dark eyes.

His eyes had turned to smoldering pools of blue. "You have my attention, Ms. Cameron. What do you have in mind?"

Saying nothing, I placed my hands onto his chest, my eyes never leaving his. I could feel his hard-toned chest underneath the thin fabric of his shirt that was Carter Blake. Running my hand up and over his chest once again, I leaned into him and kissed his soft wet lips. He never moved and took in all the emotion that was pouring from me, the raw passion that was being delivered through each kiss, each breath, and each touch. My fingers ran through his hair as I savored each small kiss that was returned by him.

Leaning back, I reengaged eye contact with him once more. Still having his complete attention, his gaze never faltered, leaving me to do exactly as I pleased. My fingers ran down the edge of his button-down shirt to the crease where his shirt was open.

Slowly, I unbuttoned each one, pushing it to the side, his chest exposed.

I withdrew my gaze and planted small kisses on him from the base of his throat and across his chest. My breaths had become short and stacked, my heart beating thunderously in my chest. Carter placed his hands on my face and drew me to him and kissed me passionately, taking my breath from me.

The fire rose in me, I knew I had allowed myself to get way too close. His kiss had become hot and hard against my lips, hungry. Gliding his lips along my chin and to the edge of my mouth coming up breathless, he released my face and raised his index finger and stopped. "Wait," he said, breathless. "Give me a minute." He took a couple of deep breaths. "Bella, you really know how to unravel a man. I'm really having a hard time controlling myself." He ran his fingers through his hair, closed his eyes, and took another deep breath. He licked his lips like he had been in the desert and opened his eyes. Suddenly, I felt very exposed, vulnerable. Why did I do that? That wasn't my normal, I had never done anything like this.

"Sorry, I shouldn't have done that. I'm not sure why I did. This isn't me, I have never done anything like that before." Now I felt embarrassed.

"Bella, I don't mind you kissing me or . . . or showing me affection, it just took me a little by surprise. I'm not judging you for your actions, I rather enjoyed it. I just want to make sure we do what's right. There is a time and a place for intimacy, and I don't think either of us is prepared for this." He soon relaxed as I sank into his arms. "It isn't that you aren't desirable, you are. We have to stop before it goes too far."

I shifted under him, finding solace in his arms. I was so confused, why?

This should be a normal thing for two adults. Were we really taking things too fast, too deeply? We barely knew each other, and we had such chemistry, so much fire between us.

"Why? Why is this so hard? I've never had this kind of emotional connection with anyone before." I remained trembling in his arms. My voice was weak, just above a whisper. Carter's breaths remained somewhat ragged and I felt his heart hammering hard under my cheek.

"It isn't any easier for me. I've been waiting a long time for the right woman to come into my life. Emotions and feelings work both ways, they can consume you to the point they burry you or bring life to you. You get too close to the fire before you can control it, you are going to get burned." He sat stroking my hair and kissed it.

"We certainly are not so far gone that we're dead." He chuckled and gave me a little squeeze. I was beginning to wonder if I was even capable of having those kinds of feelings for someone.

"Is it wrong to feel that way? I mean to have that kind of attraction for you or yours for me?" I said to him shyly, not sure why I even asked this question. I began to choke at the thought that I had said it out loud.

"There is nothing wrong with it. Bella, we're human, we were made to have feelings for each other and feelings toward the opposite sex. It's not something that's dirty, it's only made that way by those who do not respect what intimacy is for. Physical relationships were made to give each other pleasure between a man and his wife, something that no one else could share with them. It's reserved for the person you love, it connects you with that person in that it says this is me, I'm yours and yours alone. You should never be ashamed of what you feel for someone. If it's in the right context, it's right and welcomed. It doesn't mean that I don't have feelings for you just because I stopped, and it doesn't mean it's dirty. Don't get that idea, it's damaging and hurtful."

I felt the car stop and roused quickly. "Hey, sleepyhead, are you awake?"

He tapped me on the knee. "I'll come over and get you." Opening the car door, I felt the cool air, and it jarred me awake pretty quickly. "Ms. Cameron, you are home, shall we?" offering his arm to me. I took it and found that I was a lot more off my game than normal. Standing slowly, I took a step and seemed to have two left feet. Feeling my knees start to buckle Carter quickly catches me.

"Just call me Grace."

"Isabella, I do believe you need assistance." Reaching down, he swept me up into his arms effortlessly. His embrace was filled with love and gentleness as he carried me to my door. "Thank you, Mr. Blake, but you didn't have to do that."

"I know I didn't have to, but who is going to pass up getting one more chance to hold onto a pretty girl?"

Standing at my door, I felt a little awkward. He didn't say a word, he just looked down at me with that beautiful smirk of his, and his dark eyes were wide and full of admiration. "I had a wonderful time tonight. It's been a long time since I can remember enjoying someone else's company. I would like to see you again, soon."

"I would love that, Carter, very soon. Thank you for the dinner and the carriage ride, it was one of the most romantic evenings I have ever had."

Feeling a little shy, I looked down and then back into those beautiful blue eyes. "I like spending time with you."

"I'm glad to hear that. I was hoping you would like it."

It became quiet as we stood there in our own little

world for what seemed to be an eternity just looking at each other, anticipating what the other was going to do next. He made the first move and leaned in toward me and cupped my face in his hands. Following his lead, I reached to embrace him and let my hands rest on his muscular back. He watched me cautiously then looked down at my lips and back into my eyes. He brushed his lips against mine. Once more, he leaned in to kiss me, letting his lips brush mine, kissing me gently and lovingly. His lips slightly parted, and he nibbled at my lower lip, running a line of small kisses up my jawline to my neck then to my collarbone, taking my breath from me.

"Wow, you pack a powerful kiss, Ms. Cameron, I'm breathless."

"Just want you to remember me, Mr. Blake."

"There is no chance that I would forget you, ever." Pausing briefly, he looked me up and down then at the ground momentarily and back up at me with his head cocked to the side. "You're an amazing woman, Isabella, I've never met anyone like you." He hesitated. "Well, I better go, do you have your key?" I shook my head and handed them to him; he in turn unlocked the door with the pop of the latch, letting us know that we had entrance. "Good night, Isabella, Do you work tomorrow?"

"No, I have four more days of vacation left."

"I'll be home, or I'll have my cell phone. I'm in the phone book if you need me, or you could always call the department, they know how to get hold of me or Landon if it's an emergency. I'll call you tomorrow. I'm glad Lily has decided to stay with you, I want you safe."

"I hate to see you go."

"I hate to leave, angel, but I have to. I'll call you, call me if you need me."

As he turned to leave, I watched him walk away, feeling the chill of the early fall upon us. The click of his shoes on the sidewalk had a lonesome sound, and I craved to have him wrap his arms around me. Standing at his car reaching for the door, he looked back and gave me a quick wave and was soon gone. Though I was not alone, I felt desperately so.

Locking the door behind me, I walked over and sat down in the chair next to the fireplace of my apartment, hoping to take the chill from me. The wood logs in it were not comparable to that of the fireplace at Carter's, but it did bring back sweet memories of earlier in the evening. His voice echoed in my head, "I'm just glad to be here with you." What comfort that had brought to me. Even though the night had had some intense moments, he seemed to take them in stride. The uncomfortable became comfortable, explaining it was perfectly normal to have intimate feelings as long as they were at the right time and with the right person.

How could he know me as well as he did in such a short time? It was as if we were two lost souls that had been reconnected. Staring into the fire remembering the pop and crack of the fire at his home, the passionate kisses that apparently brought Carter to the edge of loss of control, his voice echoing in my head, "Bella, you really know how to unravel a man." I was still amazed at the effect that I had on him.

My knight in shining armor on the proverbial white horse, a statement made from Lily ended up as reality at the restaurant. The majesty of the carriage and the sheer beauty of the magnificent horse carrying us away for the evening were unexpected but welcome. The romantic restaurant and the dance we shared were etched in my mind, how was I to sleep?

Taking the lap comforter from the back of the chair, I sat there thinking of the way he looked, the heavenly way he smelled, and the touch of his fingers sending delicious, sweet chills down my body as I slowly drifted off.

The room was cold and damp; the chair was hard

and unforgiving.

I couldn't move, fixed to the spot. What's worse was that I couldn't talk, I couldn't scream. I tried but nothing came out. The smell of liquor and cigarettes filled the room. It's so strong that it's toxic, burning my eyes, nose, and throat. Looking around, all I saw was a broken mirror, a four-poster bed in the middle of what appeared to be an old warehouse. I sat, barely taking in a breath and listening intently. The voices of two men were slowly tuned in but remained faceless to me.

"Arnell, you can't keep that girl here forever. You may have taken her, but eventually her family is going to find you, and her," his voice was excited and angry. "How could you do something so stupid? You have a family to think about for God's sake. What were you thinking about?"

"Let it go, Gage, this is my affair," he said darkly.

I could hear their feet shuffle and the smell of cigarette smoke that was thick enough to choke me. Who were these men and why were they here? I started to feel my heart race and my chest sucking in for air. Where was I?

"I'm coming after you, little girl, I should be able to get some good money from you. Most men want them young. Especially those who are untouched, it gives them a little more of a thrill."

He's behind me, I felt his breath, and the smell of cigarettes and cheap liquor reeked. I couldn't see him but I knew he was there. He ran his large rough hands down my arms and brought his hands closer to my chest.

"No! No!" I awakened myself, screaming, and the tears were streaming down my face. I was still in the chair with the comforter over me. The fire was warm, but I was soaked in perspiration. My chest hurt, and I couldn't get my breath as I sat there curled up with my knees to my chest, rocking.

126

I felt hands on my shoulders shaking me. I started screaming.

"Isabella, what in the world is wrong with you? It's me." I was still screaming. I was not able to comprehend that Lily was in the room.

CHAPTER 7

"What happened?" I heard the click of footsteps and the drop of keys on the table. The voice was muted, but it's a male voice. I tried to open my eyes, but I couldn't force them. I didn't know where I was. Who was with me?

There were now two voices, a male and female voice. Their voices became louder as they came closer.

"I don't know what happened, she woke me up screaming. When I finally got to her, she wouldn't let me near her. I found her curled up in the chair in a fetal position."

"Have you called a doctor?"

"Yes, Dr. Bentley. He was her doctor sometime back. He's been here and has given her a sedative."

I felt the weight of the bed shift under me, I was so tired.

"Isabella, it's Carter, can you hear me?" His voice was filled with concern.

Trying again to open my eyes, I was unable to force them open. Making an attempt to raise my hand, I could only raise a finger. "You are going to be fine. No one is here that will hurt you."

"You know?" Lily asked him, shocked by his revelation.

"I know enough."

I could feel him pick up my hand and rub it against his face. His lips brushed against the back of it as he pulled it up to his cheek and clung to it.

I could hear Lily and Carter talking, but most of the time, it was difficult to understand what they were saying.

"I haven't said anything to her. She doesn't know."

"What do you mean she doesn't know? She would have to know?"

"Carter, she doesn't know, she doesn't remember

and no one has ever told her. We have never spoken of it."

Told me what? What didn't I remember? What happened to me, what did he know that no one has told me?

"It's better that she doesn't know for now."

"Just when was anyone going to tell her? That's not fair to her." I could hear the anger in his voice.

"Carter, it was devastating to her for more than one reason. It's a bad memory she doesn't need to remember, it's of no benefit to her."

"What if we had gotten married, don't you think she would have asked questions? Doctors aren't going to lie. You can't leave her in the dark forever.

Is this part of why her other relationships went bad? She wanted more, and they knew about it?"

"Ryan did," Lily answered hesitantly. "He knew about all of it. He was there when, when it happened. He still loved her, but she couldn't get past everything else that had happened. She thought that he didn't know."

"And everyone let her believe he didn't? Do you know how cruel that sounds?"

Continuing to gather what strength I had, I was determined that I was going to say something or at least open my eyes. I slowly fluttered my eyes as Lily continued her conversation with Carter. My mouth was so dry I felt like I'd been on a long trip in the Sahara.

"Carter," I whispered his name. I could see him barely through very sleepy eyes.

"Yes, it's me, angel. I'm right here." He breathed a heavy sigh of relief.

"I'm not leaving you, you're safe here."

"Where am I?"

"You're at home, in your room."

"It's so blurry. I can't focus."

"It's just medicine."

"What happened to me?"

"You were in the living room, Lily found you in the

129

chair by the fireplace.

You scared her pretty badly."

Swallowing, I tried to wet my mouth enough to talk. "Why?"

"Don't you remember anything?" Lily asked, a little confused that I would ask such a question.

Fighting to stay awake and focused enough to enter the conversation, I wanted answers. "I remember coming home and sitting down in the chair and thinking about our date. I got sleepy and covered up in the chair."

"You don't remember anything else?" Carter probed.

I lay quietly, trying to remember as some things started to come back, bringing a cold chill with it.

"I remember the smell of cheap liquor and cigarettes. I couldn't see anyone, but I could hear voices, two male voices."

"Two men?" Carter rubbed his beard, making a scratching sound against his hand.

"Two, I think so."

"What time is it? Where is Molly? She should be with you."

"It's 5:00 a.m., angel, Molly is still with Landon and Beth, she's fine, why don't you go back to sleep now okay?"

"No, Carter, I can't."

"Why not?"

"I want to know."

"You want to know what?"

"I want to know what you were talking about. You both know something that I don't, and I want to know what it is."

"We'll talk later. Right now, I want you to sleep, you need it." Smiling down at me, he pushed my hair away from my face. Closing my eyes, I slipped away.

The room had become cold as the afternoon or early

evening sun was coming through the window making me squint against it. Turning my head, I saw Carter sitting in the chair next to me, leaning forward with his arms on his knees and his hands clasped. His smile was welcome, his dark hair. Oh, I wanted to run my fingers through it.

"Well, sleepyhead, it's about time you woke up. I was beginning to wonder if I were going to see you today."

I continued to look up at him dreamily. Wait a minute, he's changed. He wasn't in the same clothes I saw him in earlier. He's clean shaven where he hadn't been this morning. I looked at myself. I was no longer in my dress, and I was in one of the few nightgowns that I owned. My hair was straight and hanging down at my side; I never wore my hair like this.

"What's the matter, angel?"

"Something's not right."

"What do you mean?"

"You aren't dressed the same, and you're clean shaven. I'm not in my dress.

I'm in one of my nightgowns. I rarely wear one anymore, I wear my pajamas."

"Isabella, everything is fine. You're home, I'm with you."

"I don't understand. I saw you earlier and you were in the clothes we went out in, I was still in my dress."

He made his way over to the side of the bed and sat down beside me. He put his hands on either side of my hips and looked down at me guardedly. I could see he was concerned, he was choosing what to say next.

"Isabella, it . . ."

"Carter, what is going on? Why am I in bed? Where is Molly? You should be with her. What's happened to her?" I could feel the panic raising in me, and I felt sick to my stomach and terribly uneasy. Carter raised his hand to stop me and continued to search for his words.

"Molly is totally fine. She's fine, she's with Beth

and Landon." He hesitated and took a deep breath. Oh, this wasn't good. It's taking too much time.

"Carter, please tell me what's going on, you're scaring me. I know what I saw, you were here with me earlier."

"Yes, that's true. I have been here with you. Bella, what you remember was two days ago."

I gasped and pulled the covers up around me.

"Oh my god, what happened? What happened to me?"

"Bella, you came home and went to sleep in the chair. Lily woke up to you screaming, she couldn't do anything for you, so she called Dr. Bentley.

Then she called me, I have been here with you ever since."

"How did I . . . How did I get changed? Who took care of me?"

"Lily did at night, I have been here during the day to take care of you."

His smile melted me.

"You . . . you took care of me?"

"Well, don't sound so surprised, Bella. I can take care of you."

"No, no, that's not what I meant. Did you . . . ?"

"Change you?" He smirked. "Yeah, with my eyes closed." He laughed.

"You're kidding, aren't you?"

"Yes, Isabella, I'm kidding. I wouldn't do that unless it was an absolute necessary thing to do."

"Carter, I don't remember what happened." Sitting up in the bed I was face-to-face with him.

"You told me that you had a nightmare, you could smell alcohol and cigarettes and there were two men talking."

I closed my eyes, and I started to think of what I could have been dreaming, but I couldn't.

132

Footsteps entered the room as I opened my eyes.

"Carter, I brought Molly by to see . . . Well, Izzy, you're awake."

Then I smelled it, the cigarettes and the alcohol. "Oh, Carter, that's it," wrinkling my nose. "The smell, I remember."

"What do you mean the smell?"

"The cigarettes, the alcohol, I smell them."

Landon walked a little closer. "It must be me. I went with Beth to her home to get some of her things while Cooper was gone. She needed to get some things for her hospital bag. Their whole house smells like it."

Carter directed Landon to move back. "That's what you're talking about?"

"Carter, I was there. I was in a warehouse, garage, or . . . or something that resembled one. I was in a chair, and I couldn't move. They threatened me." Gasping, I remembered. I couldn't say anything else. I remembered Carter and Lily talking too. It's related and I knew it.

"What?"

"Nothing, I remember you and Lily discussing something. Something

Lily said that I didn't remember. I want to know what it is.

Carter looked uneasy and shifted a little where he was sitting. "Bella, I'm not sure I know what you're talking about."

"You and Lily were talking about me, and there was something, something that I didn't remember. I heard it said I was better off not knowing."

Carter looked at me blankly. "Angel, I don't know what you think you heard, I really can't answer that."

I sat thinking and then it came to me. "Dr. Bentley, he told you not to tell me anything. He told you I had to remember it on my own, didn't he?"

"Isabella, I can't tell you because I don't know."

"Carter, you know what I'm talking about. For some reason, you have chosen not to tell me." I felt more like a spoiled child now, sulking. Carter looked down at me, not knowing what to do next.

"Isabella, you're right, I do know something. I just don't want what I know to hurt you. You have blocked it out for so long because it was painful."

"Please, if you think anything of me at all, tell me." He rose from the bed and turned from me, rubbing the back of his neck, obviously frustrated.

"I don't know what to say. I can't hurt you like that."

"We promised each other there would be no secrets between us. You made me promise to tell you anything I remembered or anything I felt. It works both ways, Carter," my voice was raising. He remained turned from me and rubbed his face with his long fingers and sighed.

"Okay, I guess if you are going to find out, it's better coming from me.

Just give me a few minutes, I need to get something." He walked from the room, and Landon followed him.

I could hear muffled voices talking back and forth coming from the living room. On occasion, I could make out a sentence or a few words. I could hear the click of Carter's footsteps pacing back and forth, and I knew he was trying to pull it together.

"Just get it, Lily. I need to tell her."

"You're not helping her like this, Carter, you know that." Lily choked. I could hear the distress in her voice.

"Call Bentley, tell him we may need him. I can't let her think I'm lying to her, she knows, Lily. Landon, stay with Molly, maybe she can come in a few minutes. I know she wants to see Bella, I'm not sure it's the right time."

I heard his footsteps getting closer, and it wasn't long before he was at the threshold, stopping momentarily he entered the room. His beautiful face was full of tension and pain. I'd done this to him, forcing him to do something he didn't want to do.

Carrying a small white box with a Pink ribbon wrapped around it he sat down on the bed in front of me face-to-face. "Isabella, I didn't want to tell you this, it wouldn't have been a good time for you to remember this at any time, but this is it." He placed the box in my lap.

"Before you open it, I want you to know that it doesn't change anything.

I still want to be with you, my feelings haven't changed." Watching his face, I knew that what's in the box was life changing. "This isn't going to be easy for you to see, you sure you want this?"

I shook my head, but I was cautious. I could feel my body react before I touched the box. I remembered this box, I was not sure I wanted to open it.

It's like opening Pandora's box. My hands shook as I picked it up, and I felt sick at my stomach. Feeling a cold rush come over me, I heard a faint cry from long ago. My heart sank as I felt like I had no blood left in my body.

Pulling the ribbon from around the box I laid it aside. I looked to Carter for verification of opening it. I could see the panic in his face, and he swallowed hard. Tears had started to well up in his eyes.

Lifting the lid, tissue paper popped up, and I slowly unwrapped the contents. I found a crocheted blanket that had been handmade, pink with green ribbons running through the edge. I looked at it, puzzled. Beside it was a tiny bracelet with the words Baby Cameron in tiny blue letters. Picking up the blanket, there was a piece of paper under it, a birth certificate: baby girl, mother's name: Isabella, father's name: Unknown. Picking up the blanket I smelled the fresh scent of baby powder still on it.

I began to hear the clatter of instruments and voices and the weak and tiny cry of an infant. "It's a girl," the

135

doctor cried. "Take her now, she's fragile." I could see the nurses around me. "Doctor, we have a problem. I need you now." The anesthetist is standing by me, placing a mask on my face. "No, no, I want to see her." I heard myself say. The room was filled with doctors and nurses running everywhere. I saw her in the nurse's arms, her body limp and her color dark and ashen. Reaching out to the nurse, I wanted her to hand her to me, but she didn't. She placed her in a small incubator and continued to work with her tiny figure. I could hear instruments crash to the floor. "Ms. Cameron, are you okay?"

"Please don't take her away. Please."

I could feel my breath leave me, the room was getting dark where I was, and the voices were getting hard to hear.

"Ryan!" I tried to scream, but I couldn't. "Ryan," my voice was barely over a whisper.

"No, Jenna. Bring her to me please. Jenna, please don't let her die. Jenna!"

"Bella," a soft voice called to me. I knew the voice, and I slowly came back.

"Bella, come on, angel, come back to me. Don't zone out on me, come back." I could feel the touch of his hand shake against my face.

Looking up, my eyes met his magnificent dark blue eyes; tears had tracked down his cheeks. I felt hot silent tears slide down my face, feeling exposed. I wanted to hide, but I didn't know why.

"Jenna?" I choked back a sob. I wanted to cry so hard. I couldn't, I was dumbfounded. Carter, watching my every move, slid in closer to me. "Jenna, they took Jenna away from me." I felt so empty. "She died, Carter, she died.

They wouldn't even let me hold her."

Carter leaned toward me and wrapped his arms around me. I was unable to hold to him. My arms remained held up and clutching her blanket to my chest. He never said a word as he held me, rocking me back and forth in his arms. The harder he held to me, the harder I cried.

"Oh my god, Carter, my Jenna, she's gone." My hair lay against my tear-soaked face. Then I thought, Ryan, I was asking him for help. Did Jenna belong to Ryan? I couldn't remember. She belonged to Ryan, she must have.

I pushed back from Carter harder than I had to and covered my mouth with my hand and tried to collect myself.

"Carter, she belonged to Ryan, didn't she? Jenna, she belonged to him."

Carter started to shake his head. "No, angel, she didn't. That's what you wanted to think. You and Ryan never had a physical relationship. Bella, Jenna belonged to someone else, maybe your attacker. You wanted to keep her because in your mind she belonged to Ryan. He found you beaten in a street where someone left you. You were gone for months, he beat you so badly that you went into labor early. Jenna wasn't strong enough to survive, she was just too little."

"What else do you know that you aren't telling me?"

"Nothing, I didn't know that until Lily told me."

"She knew? She knew all this time and never told me?"

"Yes, Bella, she knew. You have to understand, you nearly died when you delivered her, and there were a lot of things you blocked out. You spent some time in the hospital. It was bad, Bella, and they didn't want you hurt any more than you already were." Carter raised his hand and pushed my hair behind my ear and out of my face. "I didn't want to tell you, I'm going to try to do some digging and see what I can find out. For the mean time, I want you to rest."

He started to slide away from me, and I reached for his arm and grabbed tight to it.

137

"Don't go, please don't leave me."

He stood and wiped his face with one hand from his cheeks down to his jaw. "I'm not going anywhere. Molly is here and she wanted to see you. She's been calling you Mommy for days, and she has begged Landon to see you."

He paused for a moment, and that oak of a man came over to the end of my bed and kissed me softly and dropped to his knees. "Bella, I'm not going anywhere. We need you, don't ever leave us again." I wiped his cheek with the back of my hand and he rose to his feet. "I'll be right back."

He walked from the room as I tried to straighten myself and put the things he handed me off to the side of the bed. It wasn't long before I heard little footsteps bouncing on the floor toward my room. Molly, the little freight train she was, bound in the room with a huge smile on her face, her hair bouncing off her shoulders as she tried to climb on the bed, not quite making it. Carter reached over and gave her a boost, and she crawled her way up into my lap.

Carter took the seat beside the bed, and Molly looked up at me with pure joy.

"I missed you, Mommy." She threw her tiny arms around my neck. Carter sank into the chair and waved his hand, not to correct her.

"Well, Tink, I have missed you too." I continued to hug her tiny body next to me and smelled the innocence on her and stroked her long dark hair.

She released me and sat down in my lap and giggled. Those big eyes of hers shined with glee.

"Molly brought her picture book with her, she wanted you to read to her and look at the pictures." Carter handed me the book.

"Oh, okay. Let's see what you brought for us." I took the book and looked at the front, and it made me smile. "*The True Story of the Three Little Pigs*, my favorite."

I sat at my bedroom window and looked out onto the lawn and the fountain that arose from the pond near the complex. Now what? Carter now knew part of what was going on with me and my history. He was sure to leave, and I wasn't sure if I could handle the abandonment. Then again he deserved someone better, after all he and Molly had been through over the past few years. He didn't need what baggage I had, and I was sure there was more to come.

I sat in the wing-back chair with a lap quilt over me that he had lovingly placed. I had very few days left of my vacation, and he had no more than two left. It would be hard to see him once we both returned to work; maybe it was for the best. Who would want to be with someone like me that had no idea of what had happened to them? My past had been wiped out, and what I now had haunted me.

I looked away from the window and picked up the small blanket that had once belonged to my baby girl. Who was she? Was she really the product of an abusive man that had no face, or was Ryan her father? Carter had told me that she didn't belong to Ryan. If that were so, why didn't I see her as something of a disgusting crime of hate? She was still a baby, and she was innocent. She was not asked to be brought into this world. She was my baby, and she was gone.

Raising the blanket, I clutched it into my face and smelled the sweet smell of lingering baby powder that still remained. How long had it been since I had her? How old was I when I had her? Sitting back, I tried to go back in my mind to when I was still in the delivery room. The room was cold, and voices surrounded me. I was like a spectator standing in the corner watching a movie. I could hear the doctor talking, and the nurse's feet walking across the floor.

I could see Jenna with the nurse as she sped away to

139

the small incubator where Jenna lay limp and ashen. She had let out one fragile cry, and I had begged them to let me hold her. "Please bring her to me. Ryan, please help me." They ran to Jenna, and I looked up to see Ryan standing beside me. I tried to relax to see how much would come to me, but it was difficult as it played out before me.

"Ryan, please help me. Please don't let her die." The anesthetist was standing beside me, placing a mask over my face. I tried to scream through it but I couldn't. Ryan looked down at me then back to the anesthetist. He was panicked. I couldn't move either of my arms, both were strapped to boards in attempt to keep my IVs from being dislodged. I could hear instruments fall to the floor and the doctor shouting at the nurse that stood by my knee. "We have to do this now, or we're going to lose them both, step lively." My head was turned to see her tiny body until I could see her no more.

I sat in the chair trying to make sense out of it as silent tears fell into my lap. I could feel the hot stream run down my face, but it didn't seem to matter. Not only had I lost my daughter, I was probably going to lose Carter and Molly too. I felt numb, empty, and cold inside. I longed for Carter to touch me, but then if he did, it more than likely would feel like a hot poker with the situation I now found myself in.

I heard footsteps enter the room, but I never moved. There was no other sound until they came to a stop by my chair. Carter sat a cup of tea on the table beside me and took the chair from by the bed and drew it closer to me.

"How are you doing, angel?" His hand caressed my hair.

Wiping the tears away with the back of my hand, I took a deep breath. "I could be better."

"You're going to be fine. I know it's hard to understand, but it will get better. Give it some time, you have just opened up an old wound that they should have let

140

you deal with long ago."

I looked away from him, not bearing to look into his face. I felt so insignificant, so used. I was like a broken doll, and I would never be whole again. I looked at my hands as I twirled the quilt in my fingers.

"Isabella, what is it? You can talk to me, I'll listen. No matter what it is, I'll listen."

"Carter, you don't want me. Not after all of this, and there is more to come. This is just the beginning. I can't do that to you."

"I'm not running, Bella, I won't. I found what I want. No matter what comes out or doesn't, you're stuck with me."

"You don't understand, I'm broken, I don't know what's coming next. You and Molly could be left alone again."

"Wouldn't I be left alone again if I left here and never come back?"

"You don't understand."

"I do understand, and I'm not leaving. I told you before, Bella, I want your heart. It doesn't matter to me what happened before me. I'm with you now, that's all that is important to me." Reaching over to the dresser, he gripped my hairbrush. "Do you mind if I brush your hair?"

I shook my head no, he rose gracefully from the chair he was seated in and started to brush my hair in gentle strokes.

"I comb Molly's hair until I think my arm is going to fall off. She always tells me, 'More, Daddy, more.'"

I could feel his fingers run through my hair and then came to rest on my shoulders. The hands that once sent electricity through me now allowed me to feel nothing. I felt nothing but fear and hate for the person who had done this to me. I wanted back what fire I felt for him to return. All I felt was cold and empty. This was no life for anyone, not Carter certainly. To have him live with me, he might as well remain with the memory of his dead wife. I was just as much benefit to him. I would just as soon be dead myself to what else might surface now.

"Bella, it will get better. You knew when and if you found out what had happened to you, it wouldn't be good. I'm here, Lily is here, and you have friends and family that care about you. They aren't going to abandon you."

Sitting very still, the burn of tears continued down my cheeks and into my lap. "Carter, you have no idea of what you have walked into. There will be more that is going to come out, and you hold a prominent job. What's that going to look like on you and Molly?"

"Is that what you have on your mind, what other people will think?" His gaze stayed on my face, and I tried to turn away but I couldn't. "I don't care what anyone thinks. Frankly, it isn't anyone else's business. As for Molly and me, we are fine with whatever comes out. It wasn't your fault, can't you see that? You were a victim. We will eventually find out what all did happen and who was involved, and I promise you, I will see the son of a . . ." He clenched his fist and then took a deep breath calming himself. "I'll put him away Bella, for good. He will never touch another person."

What could I say to him? He was going to stay. No matter what I said, he was going to stay. Kneeling in front of my chair, he looked into my eyes and held my hands in my lap. I knew I must look the worst I had ever looked. I didn't know how he could stand to touch me, to look at me. I wanted to push him away before he could walk away.

"Isabella, it isn't going to be an easy road, we both know that. I want you to know I'm here for you. Please, let me help you, let me be here for you."

He raised one hand to my face, and I leaned into it and the strength he possessed. I wanted his touch, I craved it. I wanted him to want me and to chase away all of this like it had never happened, but I knew better. I closed my eyes and soaked in his warmth and smell. His cologne still lingered on his hand mildly from where he shaved earlier, mixed with soap and his own scent. Dreaming of what my life with him might have been like if this had never come out was interrupted when I felt his soft lips against mine. The power of the emotion behind them once again left me breathless.

When I opened my eyes, he was so close to me his nose was almost touching mine and his face was full of pain and concern. I wanted to take that away from him, but I didn't know how. I was the one that had put it there. He swallowed hard as he looked at me, his jaw was lax as he sat before me.

"Carter, can you do something for me?"

"Of course, Bella, whatever you like."

"Can you"—he looked at me intently—"can you just hold me?"

Standing up, he swept me from the chair, holding me close to him with my head against his chest. His arms wrapped around me like he was carrying a baby. Covering me, he lay next to me with his arms cradling me. My head remained on his chest where I could hear the rhythmic sound of his heart beating beneath his shirt, his breathing was quieting, being a comfort to me.

Only he could bring comfort to me, there was solace here and I wanted to stay and never leave it. My mind conflicted with my feelings. I knew in my mind this could never last, but in my heart, I knew I couldn't take my next breath if he was no longer there. He had become my lifeline, my spirit was attached to him, and I knew if I was severed from him, I would ultimately die.

Lying beside me, he stroked my hair and laid his cheek against my head, assuring me that he was there without saying a word. Sometimes no words need be said, only the presence is needed. I hated how I needed him because I knew inside I could not willingly keep him at my side. Who knew what kind of dark past was about to surface?

"You don't have to worry, I'm here no matter what comes out. You belong to me. I will never leave you," he whispered. How did he always know what I was thinking? He had a direct line to my body and my soul. I should know that by now, yet it still surprised me when he revealed exactly what I had on my mind. He gave me a little squeeze and remained there quietly.

"You always know the right thing to say to make me feel better."

"Well, I try. I just want you to be happy, it's important to me. Everything, no matter how bad it gets, will work out. No matter of worry or fretting about it is going to take it away. It is what it is, and we just need to deal with it. We can't change what has happened, but we can concentrate on what is here, and I'm glad I'm here with you."

I soon closed my eyes and rested against him, taking in his scent and the feel of his sculpted chest against my face. The warmth from his body was comforting, and I soon drifted off.

The smell of cigarette smoke filled the room. Waking, I started to look around. There was nothing but old chairs and what looked like chains. The smell of alcohol and cigarette smoke lingered in the air. It felt damp and cold around me, and the fear rose in me. I tried to move from where I was, but I found that I couldn't. When I did move, I felt the tightness around my neck and I heard a chain shake behind me. My hands were chained to the arms of the chair and so were my ankles. I tried to speak or scream, but no sound escaped me.

Wait, wait. What's around me? If I could see or hear something, I could tell Daddy where I was if I could get away from them. I felt sick at my stomach feeling swollen inside and out. My stomach was large, and I was having a hard time getting my breath. My face hurt, and so did my eyes.

My muscles ached, and I felt a trickle of something running down my face. I soon looked down to my legs or what I could see of them. What was running down my face was blood as I observed it falling to my leg.

"You're going to get caught if you keep this up." The gruff, deep voice echoed in the room. Being unable to see anyone, my hearing was heightened.

Looking around the room, I looked for a chance to escape if I got the opportunity. I wasn't going to stay here any longer than I had to. I was in danger, and so was—yes, that's right—the baby. What about the baby? I had to protect it?

"Don't you worry about it, you're not involved with this."

"I know about it. That makes me an accessory. That girl is eventually going to go into labor, what are you going to do then?"

"I'll deal with it when it comes. I'm sure someone would pay a large amount of money for a baby."

"Arnell, you're already in line for kidnapping, trafficking, and assault if they catch you."

I sat wondering how I was going to get out when I felt a gush, and it soon grew dark.

"Mommy," a tiny voice called. "Mommy, woked up." Feeling a small hand on my cheek, I fluttered my eyes to find Molly looking down at me.

"Mommy, are you in theral?" Sitting on her knees with her blanket in hand, a thumb in her mouth was this precious little girl. Thank goodness for my little lifeline.

"Yes, I'm here, sweetheart." She grinned around her thumb. I looked up to find Carter asleep with his arms still wrapped around me. I put a finger up to my mouth in an attempt to keep Molly quiet. "Daddy's asleep, let's go in the other room, okay," I whispered to her. She shook her head yes. "Is Uncle Landon with you?" She shook her head again. "Okay, why don't you go ahead to Uncle Landon and I'll be in as soon as I tidy up, okay?" She shook her head and got off the bed and ran back toward the living room.

I tried to quietly get out of bed without disturbing him. I knew he was tired. No doubt he had been here day and night. He looked so peaceful I didn't want to disturb him, but as soon as I moved, his eyes opened and he looked at me through foggy eyes.

"What's wrong, you okay?" he said with a raspy voice.

"I'm okay. I was just getting up to see Molly. Go back to sleep, I'm fine."

"Molly? Is she here?" He ran his hand down his face, trying to wake up.

"Molly is fine. Landon brought her, she just found her way into us."

"Okay, let's go see about Tink." Sitting up and trying to shake off the sleep he had been in, he ran his hands through his unruly hair. No matter what, unruly or not, it always looked perfect. I sat on the end of the bed taking him in, and he caught my gaze. He started by straightening his shirt and running his hands through his hair once more then looked at me again.

"Okay, what is it?"

Realizing I've been caught, I grinned and looked away. "Nothing."

"Come on, Bella, I know better than that."

"To be honest, Mr. Blake, I'm admiring you."

He looked away and smirked then looked back. "Like what you see, do you?" His cheeks turned bright red.

"Well, Mr. Blake, do I see a blush?" I couldn't help but giggle at the thought.

"I guess that is just the effect you have on me." Standing up, he reached for me and took me into an

146

embrace. His body against mine was like a drug. One drug that was toxic and addictive. It had become soothing and electrifying at once.

"Isabella, you're addictive and a wonderful shot to my ego."

I wanted so badly to tell him how I felt about him, that he completed me.

He was the closest thing in my life to making me feel whole. It was going to be very hard not to fall in love with him. And yet I thought I already had. I hated it when we were apart and soaked in every touch, hug, or kiss from him like a sponge. We had known each other hardly a week and it was painful to be without him.

I had to think of him and Molly. When everything finally came out, it would more than likely turn my life upside down, and it would destroy him.

Eventually it was going to fall apart, and when it did, I had no desire to see him in pain. I knew he was strong with everything he had to deal with, but I didn't need to add to the pain he had already been through. Then again, maybe he was right, that there wasn't any such thing as chance. Maybe God gave us a choice, and he knows when and where we are going to be and this was what was meant for me, for us, something that was good for me and hopefully would turn out good for him. Wait, did I believe that?

CHAPTER 8

Slipping into a robe, I made my way into the living room with Carter following close behind. On the first step across the threshold, Molly ran to us with glee, wrapping her arms around our legs, connecting us.

Lily, Beth, and Landon looked up from the coffee in front of them with an amazed look on their faces, as if I had come back from the dead. Beth, barely able to move, got up with a push from Landon and was soon standing before us. She was obviously grieved, and I wasn't sure why. Walking gingerly toward me, she put her arms around my neck and kissed me gently on the cheek. Stepping back, one lone tear slid down her face.

"I'm sorry, Bella."

Then I realized she was upset over Jenna. She felt pain for a child she never knew, and I nodded in recognition. From one mother to another, we understood each other.

"It's okay, I'm okay."

She turned to her brother and hugged him and kissed his cheek. It was obvious that she loved her brother and she was also in pain for him because of what had happened to me and to his wife, Andrea. He had so much pain in his life, when would it stop?

"Aunt Bethe." Molly tugged at Beth's leg. "Why is everybody sad?"

Everything just kind of stood still for a moment. Everyone was stunned, not knowing what to say. Landon stepped in and picked Molly up and kissed her cheek.

"Uncle Wandon, why is everyone so sad?" The total innocence and insistence of a child to have answers from their questions had always been amazing to me.

Walking over to the chair in front of the hearth, Landon sat down with Molly on his knee.

"Well, Molly, let me see if I can explain this to you."

Molly looked at him intently and with the wonder of a child. The question as to why the grass was green would have been easier to answer.

Carter looked away and hugged me close to him. I could feel the pain radiate from him as if it had taken him back to the day Andrea had passed away. Beth stood with one hand lying over her stomach and one around Carter.

Landon looked into Molly's little face and attempted to explain. Seeing some strain in his face, I knew it had been difficult for all of them, and trying to explain to a two-year-old the concept of death was not an easy task.

"Molly, do you remember when Daddy told you about Mommy, that Mommy had died and was in heaven with Jesus and the angels?" Molly bobbed her head up and down, and he continued trying to choose his words carefully. "Okay, well, Ms. Bella had a little girl, but she was born too early.

She had a baby in her belly just like Aunt Bethe, but Ms. Bella's little baby was born too early, and she got sick. She was too tiny, and she got sick and God knew that baby Jenna was not going to be able to live here with Ms. Bella, so he took her to be with him. Jenna was even smaller than some of your dollies. You see, God knew that baby Jenna was a special little girl and that she was never going to get well. Now, I don't want you to think that when you get sick that you are going to die, okay?" Molly continued to listen.

"Jenna is in a beautiful place, and she is there with Jesus and his angels. So because Jenna died and went to heaven, Ms. Bella is sad over her little girl, and her friends and Daddy are sad because they don't like that Ms. Bella is sad. You understand?"

"Uncle Wandon, if heaven is good, then why is

149

mommy Bella sad?"

"Because baby Jenna is not here for her to hold and love like your daddy does you."

She thought for a moment, and then a smile came across her face like she had hit the jackpot.

"Uncle Wandon, Mommy is happy now." Landon looked at her a little puzzled, and I could feel Carter take a ragged breath like he knew what she was thinking. Looking at him, he ran his index finger and thumbs from the outside of his eyes to the bridge of his nose. I slowly leaned into him and kissed him tenderly on the cheek.

"What do you mean, why is Mommy happy, Molly?"

"'Cause her gots a little girl to play with now."

She jumped down and ran to me, and I bent down to catch her. Holding her up to my face, she looked at me with those big beautiful eyes, and she put her tiny hands softly on my face. She boldly said, "Me wuv you." Then she said something unexpected and without hesitation, "Me be your little girl, Bella." My heart melted, and I couldn't say a word. I would surely break down if I did. Taking a deep breath, I tried to swallow it down and hugged her to me tightly. Carter wrapped his arms around us both.

"I'm sure Bella would love that, and so would Mommy."

"Wuv you, Bella. Wuv you, Daddy." She then reached and patted her daddy's face and wrapped her arms around his neck. Carter took her to him, lovingly running his fingers through her long hair. "I love you, Tink," he said in a low voice. She finally wiggled her way down and ran off to play with acceptance of what was told her.

Standing slightly slumped beside me, Carter rubbed the back of his neck as if he was in deep thought. Watching his face, I knew he was reliving Andrea's death. The drawn-down look was difficult to see. The man that was normally upbeat and at peace looked distressed and

150

emotionally drained.

Thinking of seeing him with Molly and the love he displayed for her left me wanting that kind of affection. It was unconditional, leaving him vulnerable.

It was my chance to tell him how I felt, but how could I do that in a room full of people? Telling someone you had only known for a second really didn't warrant the L-word either although that was exactly where I was headed.

Taking his hand, I led him away from the group. No one even noticed we had left the room and stepped out on the ivy-covered veranda. There was a chill in the air, but at least for the moment, we were alone. As soon as the door closed behind us and we were out of the sight of our company, I placed my hands on his strong, muscular upper arms and pulled him closer to me.

Instinctively, he lowered his ear to mine.

"You with Molly and the love you show her has to be the sexiest thing I have ever seen," I whispered to him, and I could see a small grin on his face as we walked across the cobblestone veranda overlooking the man-made pond in front of us.

Never taking a look at him, I looked out onto the pond and the wooded area behind it. His hand rested on my hip. I took the opportunity to put my arm around his waist, looping my thumb through his belt loop. My voice felt like it was caught in my throat, trying to utter my thoughts without success, I closed my eyes and tried to control my breathing as it had now risen to an uncomfortable rate. I made an attempt to calm myself, recollecting my inner being.

What's wrong with me? Just say it for heaven's sakes. He said not to hide anything from him. He had already told me he wasn't leaving, and I had to trust him that he was in. Looking down at the stone wall, it was now or never.

151

This is your moment, take *it.*

"A girl could easily be swept off her feet and fall in love with you." Okay, there it was. Not too needy, not clinging, just enough to let him know I was not a lost cause. I felt his eyes on me though he never moved or said a word. My heart began to race, and my body soon had lost the chill of the fall air. Was it a mistake to say anything? Cautiously, I looked up to meet his beautiful blue eyes; and honestly, I could drown in them, my face blank as his.

That vulnerable look he had earlier lingered. Shifting to stand in front of me, he placed his hands on my upper arms and I steadied myself by gripping his forearms.

"Just say it, Bella, that's all I want." Standing there looking at me, searching my face, he waited with expectation of my next words. This was it; this was what I was waiting for.

"If you want my heart, Carter, you may have it. It belongs to you."

His face lit up like a child's at Christmastime.

"Really?" The glow bounced off him.

My somber expression had finely softened. Why should I be afraid? His feelings were evident, and he wore them on his sleeve.

"Really?" He sounded a little stronger from his reaction.

"You have my heart and have it since the first moment I saw you."

Breaking out a little half grin, he caused my heart to sink to my feet. "Just what I wanted to hear. I think maybe, we can work with that."

"Have I told you how happy I am to have you here?"

"Well, in not so many words, but I get the picture." Rubbing my arms with short, gentle strokes, he encased me. "I'm happy to be here, more so now that you have enlightened me."

"You know it isn't going to be easy dealing with whatever happens to come out. It's already muddy."

Sighing, he looked at me attentively. "Bella, we will take this as it comes, that's all either of us can do."

"What other hideous things are going to come out? I don't want to hurt you, I couldn't."

Carter gave a little chuckle. "This is the most I have ever heard you talk.

I've broken down a gate. Look, you don't have a worry in the world with me."

He then began to run his hands up and down my back. "We will deal with it when and if it comes. I'm a big boy, I know what I want, okay?"

"But what if . . ." My words were soon closed off by the softness of his lips on mine, and I melted in his arms. Oh, the affect he had on me. My breath was catching as he held me, my skin had become sensitive and sending tingling rhythms through me. His kiss was powerful, and it consumed me.

"Ms. Cameron"—he attempted to catch his breath—"you never cease to amaze me. Wow!"

"Wow!" I said to him as I stood shaking in my shoes before him. "What did I ever do that good in my life to have you walk into it?"

"I think you have that backward, I'm a lucky man."

Laying my head against his chest, I could hear the steady rhythm of his heart. He rested his cheek against my head and held me up to him so close I wondered if I could even take a breath, but it was comforting and lovingly done.

"I hate to break it to you," he whispered, "but we are going to be missed shortly, and eventually someone is going to come looking for us."

"Just one more minute, I just need one more minute with you."

I couldn't let go of him. I wanted him as close as he

could get, and if this was all we had for now, it was going to be good enough. I was not sure how I would react if I knew it were about to be physical. It intimidated me, yet I desired that closeness that only two people can have. I didn't remember what it felt like to be with my attacker, but I did remember from some nightmares that I was fearful of him or them, whichever it might have been. Would I be able to let my guard down enough when it came to that point? It was too early to vex over that anyway, but it came to mind. What had happened in the past was just that, in the past, and wherever it went from here was going to be with the man I gave my heart to.

"As bad as I hate to, we need to go in."

I knew he was right, but I wanted so badly to just have him to myself.

"Maybe we can sneak a couple of hours later alone." He cupped my face in his hands. "After the rest leave, maybe we could go out for a little while or maybe we can watch a movie together. I like the classics."

Now how did he know? Never mind, it didn't matter. He escorted me back into the house, and Beth was sitting on the couch with Landon crouched down in front of her. Lily was nowhere to be seen. Landon had his hands placed on her knees, talking to her softly, but the closer we got, the more I realized she wasn't just sitting there. Her face was strained, and she was in pain, a great deal of it.

"Breathe, Beth." Landon was trying to keep her calm, and it seemed to be working. She kept her eyes on him and never strayed. Landon looked momentarily at his watch, counting. "Beth, listen to me, we are going to the hospital this time. When did they start?"

Carter broke his hold from me and joined them. "What's happening?"

Landon never looked away. "She's having contractions. I don't know when they started, but judging from the intensity, she's been having them a while."

After Beth caught her breath, she shifted slightly. "I have been having back pain since last night. I didn't think it meant anything. I've had pain before."

"You have had pain since last night? Beth, why didn't you say something, I was right there with you?"

Carter looked around. "Where's Molly?"

"Lily has her, she's okay." Landon took a deep breath, trying to compose himself.

Carter slapped him on the back and walked over to me. "Better get dressed, it looks like we are headed to the hospital."

"Just a minute, let me check her. Why don't you guys go in the other room and let me take care of her."

"Why, do you think there is something wrong?" It was the first time I ever heard panic from him.

"No, but we are girls in case you have forgotten. It won't take long. I promise she'll be fine."

Carter slowly bowed out and took Landon with him.

Beth, taking some slow, deep breaths, waited for the boys to leave; then she leaned closer to me. "They're scared, Bella."

"I know, but I'm not. It's going to be okay, women do this every day. We aren't even sure that you're in labor, that's why I had them leave the room."

"I really don't think I am, I haven't had pain in my belly. It's all in my back."

"You can still be in labor with back pain. Why don't you just lie back on the couch and try to relax, take some slow, deep breaths. I'm just going to cover you a little to keep you from being exposed. I'm going to check your abdomen to see if I can feel a contraction, and I want to see if you're dilated or if I can see the head, okay? But you have to trust me." Beth shook her head, and I started with her abdomen. Her belly didn't appear to have any firmness, but certainly all baby.

I smiled a little, Beth looking at me, questioning.

"What?"

"I can feel his little butt. He's right where he should be. I'm going to go ahead and check to see if you're dilated, I promise I won't hurt you." I continued to check her, and she was attempting to relax. "Has your water broken?"

"No, I don't think so."

"You would know if it did. Do you have other symptoms, do you hurt when you go to the bathroom, anything like that?"

"Sometimes I do, but not always. Why?"

"Because you could have a urinary tract infection, or a kidney stone can cause back pain, it doesn't always have to be labor. You're close enough and it could put you in labor, but you haven't had any more pain since the boys left the room, have you?"

"No, I haven't, I'm just uncomfortable."

"I do think it warrants a trip to the doctor, but I don't think you're in labor yet."

"I think we can let the boys back in." I stood and covered Beth again, and she adjusted her clothing.

"Bella, can I talk to you before the boys come back in?"

"Sure, what about?"

"I have something I need to talk about, and I don't know whom to talk to. I have been keeping something from a lot of people, and I feel someone needs to know in case something would happen to me."

Her look was downcast, and she played with the tassels on the throw that was over her. "I shouldn't draw you into this, you already have enough to deal with, but I need someone, someone that I think would understand my situation."

"Beth, you can tell me anything, and it will never go any farther than right here."

Taking a lingering breath, she started. "You know

I'm sure that Cooper and I have a rough marriage."

"Yes, Carter has mentioned it."

"About ten months ago, I moved out and moved in with a friend of the family briefly. Cooper had beaten me enough that I had ended up in the hospital and I couldn't go home. In that time, I found out that I was pregnant."

"Okay, but I don't see that it's a problem, Beth."

"I'm getting to it, I'm sorry." She hesitated briefly and then continued,

"I went back home after I healed and stayed with Cooper up until the day Carter was brought into the emergency room. When I called Carter, Cooper was drunk and he had chased me up the stairs where I locked myself in our room and called him. Cooper had always had a hot temper, and the alcohol didn't help. He isn't the man he was when I married him. I guess it took the alcohol for him to put two and two together and figured out that the baby didn't belong to him." This had thrown me for a loop, I had no idea. "When he figured it out, he threatened me and he had threatened to find the man the baby belonged to and he would kill us both. I couldn't let him find out who it was, I knew he would do it if he could."

The sharpness had hit me. I knew who it was, but I had to hear it for myself. "Beth, who is it?"

"You mustn't tell anyone unless something would happen to me, you have to promise me that. I don't want this baby to be left with Cooper, it would serve no good purpose."

"Of course, it will never leave me."

"The baby is Landon's."

"Beth, you need to tell him. He has the right to know you're carrying his baby."

"I can't do that. Cooper would know who the baby belonged to then, and I'm sure he would make good on his promise. My life is such a mess, I can't do that to him."

"Beth, the man loves you, don't do this to him."

157

"How do you know that? I mean, Landon has always been so hard to read."

"Oh my goodness, can't you see how he looks at you? He would do anything for you. He was there the night Cooper came after you when Carter couldn't get there. He didn't hesitate today when he thought you were in pain.

You said yourself that he was scared. He was afraid for you because he knows what you have been through with Cooper and with this pregnancy. He loves you, it's all over his face. Look at him, Beth."

"You sound like my brother."

"Well, listen to him. He's pretty smart."

Beth grinned and then she let out a laugh.

"What?"

Beth continued to laugh.

"What is it?"

"I don't know why I didn't see it. You love him, don't you?"

"What do you mean?" Oh, this was uncomfortable for sure. The one man

I admired and had any feelings for in years, his sister was worse than him. I must be terribly translucent.

"He sees an angel, I know him well. I have no doubt that he has fallen for you fast, and he has fallen hard, but I never figured that for you. You glow when you talk about him. You would make him so happy. He has been alone for a long time. I watch you with him, you follow his every move. I saw the pain when Landon was talking about Andrea, and you saw the reaction Carter had. You hated that it still affected him that way."

"Of course it did, Andrea was his wife and he loved her. I feel like I'm living with a ghost of someone that he deeply loved and admired."

"He loved her, Bella, she is Molly's mother. She will always be part of his life, but that is his past. He adores you, he hasn't left you since the night he brought you home from your date. He had Landon bring Molly to him so he could stay with you. He sat in that chair beside the bed for two days waiting for you to wake up. Eventually, you are going to have to admit your feelings for him."

"Beth, that isn't what we were talking about. We were talking about you and Landon. I can't keep a secret like that from Carter. He will find out, and what will he think of me then? We swore there would never be any secrets between us."

"Bella, you're a caregiver, you are expected to keep each patient's privacy.

You have seen me as a patient."

"You're my boyfriend's sister."

"There you go, you are my brother's girlfriend. That's a start, don't you think?"

"I think we better call the boys back into the room before this gets any deeper. Just keep in mind what I said about Landon. He would make a great father."

"Bella, I'm already married. I have a husband that will never change.

What feelings I have for Landon can't be changed, but I can keep my distance. I have to, I have no choice. It's wrong. I have to stay with Cooper."

"Fine, just remember the child you're carrying needs a father that will love them." Standing, I walked to the bedroom door where the rest of the family had congregated away from the turmoil. Opening the door, Landon was the first to jump to his feet.

"You can go in, she's okay. I do think she needs to go to the doctor. It is more than likely false labor or a urinary tract infection more than full-blown labor, but you need to stay with her." Landon let out a sigh of relief and headed to Beth. Molly and Lily sat on the floor playing with her dolls, and Carter's lean body was against the wall with his arms crossed, appearing a little calmer and collected than a few minutes ago. I stood like a child in

159

front of him with my arms behind my back. I knew he could tell I was harboring a secret. A smirk slid across his perfect lips, and I soaked it all in.

"It seems that you do well under pressure. You took control pretty quick in there."

"It has become second nature with patients, be calm, or your patients will overrule you. I just did what I had to."

Gliding over, he walked behind me and wrapped his strong arms around me and pulled me into him. "I love that you care about Beth and what happens to her, that you do indeed love my daughter as much or more than I do if that is possible, and that you trust me enough to give me your heart."

"Mr. Blake, I aim to please."

"You can please me more when the family leaves and Lily leaves for work for us to have some alone time together. I think I would like to celebrate."

"Okay, but only when everyone else is gone. I want to be alone with you, without interruption. Our courting session has been pre-empted by my breakdown of sorts, and I would enjoy spending some time with my new boyfriend."

"Boyfriend? Okay, I like that. I like that very much." His breath was hot on my skin, and he kissed the curve of my neck. I took a sharp breath from the kiss he had given me, and he gave me a gentle squeeze.

"Hey, Carter, I'm going to take Beth into to urgent care and see what they can do to help her." He stopped short when he saw Carter with his arms around me. "I'm sorry, I should have knocked." We both laughed. "No, it's okay," Carter said with a little sneaky grin on his face that he always cleverly pulled out. "Just call us when you find out something. Oh, and don't let her go back home to Cooper. It's hard to tell what he would do to her."

"She isn't going anywhere but to the doctor and

home with me if I have to sit on her."

Carter chuckled. "If you can get anything through that head of hers, you're doing better than I am."

Landon let out a little chuckle of his own and rolled his eyes. "She will listen, I will lock her in her room like a rebellious teen."

"All I can say is good luck in taming her, you're going to need it. You see"—looking over my shoulder with his arms still wrapped around me—"I already have mine trained."

"Ah, I can't believe you, me, trained? Keep dreaming, I let you believe you're in control."

"See what I mean?" He kissed me on the cheek. "She's trained, and she doesn't even know it."

Landon backed off with a grin. "I'll see you later. I'll call you and let you know how Beth is doing. If she has to stay for some reason, I'll stay with her.

I'm not leaving her."

"I know you will take excellent care of her, you always have."

"I'll talk to you later, buddy."

Carter waved him off and he walked away.

"Let's have something to eat, and while we do that, we will decide what we want to do the rest of the evening."

"What about Molly?"

"She usually goes to bed early anyway. We will find her a place."

"She can sleep in Lilly's room since she is going to be gone."

"Sounds good to me," I gushed.

"Okay then, that's what we will do."

We walked into the living room with his arm around my waist. I loved having him here; it's a comfort, anything to be wrapped up in the security of his arms.

"I think I'll make some fresh coffee, and we will discuss supper." Walking over to the coffeepot, he started his process. He had been such a fixture here he knew where everything was. Lily strode into the room, her hair pulled back neatly into a ponytail and uniformed, ready to walk out. Fastening her watch, she stopped and looked up. "Are you going to be okay? Carter is here, and I know he isn't going to let anything happen to you."

"Yes, I'm fine. Go to work, he knows what to do. If I get to out of hand, he will just call the white coats to come get me." I had to laugh at her, you would think I was a child. Carter had been with me almost every day and night and had seen me through the worst I thought I could possibly be.

"Oh, Bella, honestly, only you could make a crack like that. I have to go, I'm late. Later." Just like that, like a storm that had passed quickly and out the door, she took off. The wake of Hurricane Lily had slid in and out quickly.

Carter stood holding a cup of coffee with one arm wrapped around his chest, leaning against the bar. "Boy, she knows how to make an exit, doesn't she?" He stood blowing on the surface of his coffee and taking a sip. "It's not too bad. My coffee is usually more like battery acid. Would you like some?" I nodded my head, and he sat his down on the bar and brought me a cup. It's perfect and made just the way I liked it. He had even added some half and half to it to make it rich. I smiled at him in appreciation.

"How did you know how I took my coffee?"

"Wild guess, anyone as spicy as you needs a little sweetener to even them out."

"You're an animal."

"Only for you, angel," he growled.

"Daddy," Molly's tiny voice broke the conversation and the eternal gaze Carter had on me. "We are in the living room, Tink." Molly appeared with her thumb in her mouth and blanket in hand, walking straight to me, and curled up into my lap, leaning her head against me, her tiny hands against my stomach. Stroking the length of her hair, I wrapped the other arm around her tiny body. Leaning down I took in the smell of her baby soft hair. Carter came over from the bar where he was topping off his coffee and sat down beside us, crossing his ankle over to the opposite knee and relaxing. Molly removed her thumb from her mouth. "Sing to me, Mommy." What could you say to that?

"What would you like me to sing to you, Tink?" This was uncomfortable for sure, singing in the shower was one thing but having an audience was another. I had never sung for anyone before or in front of anyone, but I hated disappointing Molly. Carter sat watching with a grin on his face, waiting to see how I would react, thinking I was sure that I would back out. He was enjoying this.

"*Dumbo*," Molly blurted out.

"*Dumbo*?" I looked over at Carter, questioning what she meant.

I could see a small smirk on his face. "'Baby Mine' from *Dumbo*, it's her favorite."

I looked back at her, but she remained with her head against my chest.

With her blanket in one hand holding it tight in the same hand she used to put her thumb in her mouth, the other she wound her fingers through her hair.

"Oh, I see." I sighed as I tried to remember that picture, and then it came to me. "Okay, I think I remember that one." My voice was a bit shaky as I started I break out into the best rendition I could accomplish for her.

Playing with her hair absentmindedly, I laid my cheek down on the crown of her head, taking in the sweet smell of her youth. The smell of purity always amazed me. She had become my child in a sense that we bonded quickly.

She needed a woman in her life, and I missed my child that I had never met.

Carter watched me intently being immersed totally

to a child's lullaby that I had never sung to anyone before. He had sat his coffee on the table and had turned, with one leg tucked under him, his left arm propped up on the back of the couch, not noticing until I was nearly finished singing to the precious little girl that had quickly fallen asleep.

"Dear God in heaven," I heard the silky voice of the man that I was slowly falling madly in love with. "Your voice is beautiful, Bella, you're gifted."

His gaze was upon me. "Where did you learn how to sing like that?"

"I haven't ever sung for anyone before." My voice was weak and timid, not my normal. It didn't even sound like me. "I just didn't want to disappoint her."

"No disappointment for her or for me. You'll be her best friend for life."

Running his long fingers down my jaw, I gasped at his touch, speaking volumes for him. "You're so good with her. She loves you, you know. I can't say I blame her." Reaching down, he picked Molly up into his arms and held her close to him.

"Daddy," her tiny voice managed one sleepy word, and she was back to sleep.

"Let's put her to bed."

I took the lead, and he followed me into Lily's room where we placed her in the bed and tucked her in with her favorite blanket and one of my old dolls. Leaning down to her and brushing her hair away, Carter gave her a kiss on the forehead. "Sweet dreams, Tink, Daddy loves you."

Tucking the blanket in around her, I kissed her softly. It amazed me and Carter at my reaction as I reverently got down on my knees and smoothed the covers and clasped my hands.

"God, please take care of our baby. She deserves the best you have in store for her. She is a precious life that you have allowed to people to create in love.

164

I'm a poor image for her at best, but I'll try my best to give her what she needs. You have the power to change things, I'm willing." Carter bent down on one knee beside me and whispered a prayer that was inaudible to me. I didn't have to guess, I knew what he was praying for. He had a great love of God and family it's evident in his life, and I knew he prayed for me. With his hand resting on my back, I could feel the sheer and honest affection from him. What did I do to merit him? The road to love for me was going to be a rocky one filled with deep holes and crevices that could burry anyone that followed me. I laid my hand on top of his that rested on Molly's petite one.

In a very short time, I had come to think of them as my family.

When his prayer was through, he turned his hand over and gave mine a squeeze and rose with grace then assisted me from a humbled position before him. He caught me to him as I stood and kissed me warmly then looked down at his little girl peacefully sleeping, her hair sprayed against the pillow in long curls, with an angelic look on her face. I couldn't help but think about what Jenna would have looked like if she were still alive. I had no idea as to how old she would have been or how old I was when this happened. Lily would not discuss it, and I wasn't sure if she had mentioned to Carter.

Carter turned and flipped the switch on the wall and led me from the room with his hand against the small of my back that radiated little shocks warmth that filled me. Every fiber of my being was affected by his one touch.

He didn't have to say a word to me; my body reacted to him without one syllable. Escorting me into the living room, he led me to the couch and motioned for me to sit. The overstuffed couch felt welcome and comforting.

Placing a pillow on one end, he motioned for me to lie down and he covered me with the throw that had been left there.

"Carter, I've been in bed for days, I'm fine. I feel good."

"My intention is to take care of you, and I will. Now, humor me, Ms. Cameron."

"Okay, fine. By the way, what do you have in mind for supper?" I remembered that he told me he wasn't much of a cook.

"I have a few tricks up my sleeve. Just keep me company, and I'll take care of supper." Retreating toward the kitchen, I watched him through the open bar. I could see perfectly from my angle. I was watching him, every move he made was almost musical. I had always felt clumsy and awkward and out of place with anyone I had been with. He had an essence of a God; his movements were sleek and purposeful. Beth was very pointed with her observations; she certainly came to the point. It had me feeling uncomfortable, and Lord knows I had enough to deal with. I was hoping that Carter wasn't expecting more than I might be able to give him. What relationships that I had in the past never worked out, they always ended in disaster. If it didn't affect one, it was the other or both and normally left one or the other shattered, and on occasion both. It wasn't that I wasn't capable of love, I just didn't give it freely. Physically, I was unable to put myself in the position, but it hadn't appeared to be that way with Carter. I wanted him any way I could have him. He was different, he didn't expect that from me where most of the others did. Ryan on the other hand ended up on a collision course with me. I had no doubt that he loved me, but now that I know some of what went on, I could understand why it didn't work out and why I would get to the edge of total surrender to him and hit the brakes.

It wasn't that Ryan hadn't been patient, he had the patience of Job. I had dated him in my junior year of high school, and I liked that bad boy image of his from the

166

moment I had laid eyes on him. If I could track back, maybe I could figure out how long ago it had been that Jenna had died. No, bad idea, I was already saturated with all that had surfaced. I didn't need that kind of turmoil. Regaining my stare and mind on the present, I watched Carter standing at the stove with a towel over his shoulder, testing his creation.

"It smells wonderful."

"I told you, I have a few tricks up my sleeve. I had to learn how to make a few simple dinners for Molly and me so we weren't eating out all the time.

They aren't great, but they are filling."

"You, sir, are a man of many different talents."

"What makes you say that, just curious?" He drew up one brow and gave a smirk.

"You seem to be able to handle just about any situation."

"You mean aside from catching the bad guys?"

"Yes, aside from my being able to catch the bad guys." He was smiling as he continued with his cooking.

"You always seem to amaze me. I've never met anyone like you. You're never shakable, you always know what to do. You're a wonderful brother and friend and even a better father to Molly. Being both mother and father to her must be very difficult. You have been a caregiver to me, a cook and fortress when I've needed all the help I could get. You have been my safety net when I had nowhere to fall."

"Isabella, you make me sound like a saint."

"Maybe I see you that way. Anyone else would have run by now." Playing with the tassels on the blanket that lay over me I looked down, "Especially after everything that you now know and more to come."

"Bella, I'm not afraid. I'm not going anywhere, I have no intention to run.

You think way too little of yourself." Walking over

to the table, he placed a bowl of homemade spaghetti and salad down and quickly fixed a plate for me and a glass of what looked like sparkling cider. Sitting up, he placed the tray in front of me.

"It's sparkling cider. I remembered that you enjoyed it when we had it before." He strode over and picked up his own and joined me on the couch.

Taking a sip of the drink, he appeared to be in thought then left it behind.

"How is it?"

"It's wonderful. You've been holding out on me."

"There must have been something more in that medicine than to help you rest."

I took his little joke and smiled brightly back at him. It was good, and the comfort of homemade food was always settling. It wasn't long before we have finished, and we have settled in for the evening. It's been quite some time since Landon had left with Beth, and we hadn't heard a thing from them.

"What about an old movie? What is your pleasure?"

"I don't know, is there one that you like in particular?"

He thought for a moment. "How about *Casablanca*?"

"I haven't heard of that one before."

"Oh, I think you'll like it. It's an old black-and-white film."

"Sounds good to me."

"You're certainly easy to please."

"I don't care so much what we watch, I just want to be with you."

"Well, aren't you sweet?" Leaning down, he gave me a quick kiss on the forehead as he rose to take away the dishes. "I'll take these and put them in the dishwasher, and we will watch the movie."

"You're spoiling me terribly."

"Are you telling me I'm creating a monster, Ms. Cameron?"

"Take it how you like, Mr. Blake, I'm going to start expecting this."

"We will have to see about getting you back on your feet sooner than later." He was making his way into the kitchen with a handful of plates when the phone rang, and he started to set them down.

"I can get it, go ahead. It's probably Landon with news on Beth." The phone continued to ring once more before I managed to pick it up.

"Hello." There was no answer, only little noise on the other end. "Hello, is anyone there?"

A gruff and gravelly voice answered back, "I see you have a boyfriend."

"Who is this? What do you want?" My voice was beginning to shake, and my hands could barely hold the receiver.

"Well, Isabella, isn't that a fine how-do-you-do, and we knew each other so well, intimately you might say."

"You stay away from me, and don't you ever call me again." Carter's footsteps were getting closer. "Bella, who is it?"

"Oh, he is the protector, isn't he? He won't be there all the time, we will meet up again, and when we do, it will sizzle just like before." My hand shook uncontrollably, I dropped the receiver and it met with a bang against the wall.

I stepped back, and Carter was right on me.

"Bella, what's wrong? Who's on the phone?"

It didn't take long for my feet to make their way into the bathroom where I immediately stripped and got into the shower. I felt dirty and would never get clean. The gravelly voice of the man on the other end I recognized as my attacker. This was never going to stop, I felt sick, violently sick, stomach aching and in excruciating pain. I felt his hands and breath on me. I sank down the wall of shower as the water washed over me and cried hysterically, barely being able to grasp a breath. The water pelted me, and I scrubbed my skin until it was rose in color.

"Bella, honey, where are you?" I soon heard his footsteps outside of the bathroom door. "Bella, are you okay?" I couldn't answer, my chest heaved and gasped for the short bursts of air into my lungs. "Bella, answer me." I couldn't answer, the man's voice kept running through my head and I kept scrubbing.

"Isabella, if you don't answer me, I'm coming in whether you're decent or not." I continued to sit on the floor of the tub against the wall, my knees drawn into my chest. I shook so hard my teeth chattered like I was freezing.

Opening the shower, Carter reached in and turned the water off and lifted a towel along with a robe from the rack. "Isabella." His voice was soft and low. Reaching out to touch me, he made contact with my arm, and I winced as if I were in pain. Tears were rushing down my face uncontrollably.

"I can't get him off me, I can't get clean." He wasted no time in wrapping the towel around me and one around my hair and getting me out of the bath. He lifted me as if I were an infant and sat me on my own bed. Drying me off and placing a robe over me, he pulled me up close to him, and I sobbed into his neck irrepressible, I cried until there was nothing left to cry out.

When I finally settled down enough to take some normal breaths, Carter started to question me. "Bella, who was on the phone?" I shook in his arms.

"It's okay, you're safe, I'm here. You need to tell me what happened."

"He threatened me, he knows you're here, it was a warning." My voice was shaking and barely above a whisper. "He knows you're here, and he said you wouldn't be here all the time. He would get me, and he would do it again.

Oh god, Carter, this nightmare is never going to end."

The telephone rang, and I gasped. Carter answered it this time. "Hello."

There was a brief silence. "Are you taking her home with you? . . . Okay, that's good. No problems then? . . . Well, that's easily fixed with antibiotics . . . Yes, I'm sure she is . . . Keep me posted, will you? I'm staying with Isabella . . .

No . . . I'll tell you about it later, we may have to look into some things . . .

For now . . . Just keep Beth out of trouble for me, and I'll take care of the rest . . . In the morning . . . Good night, Landon, kiss her for me." He hung up the telephone, never taking his grip from me.

"Well, Beth is okay for the time being, it looks as though she has a urinary tract infection and false labor pains. They sent her home on antibiotics, and she will be staying with Landon, so that's a relief."

"Yes. Yes, of course."

"I'm staying with you, no one is going to get to you. Later, I'll make some kind of arrangement for a plainclothes man to be with you when I can't be there. We will find him, Bella. When I do, he's going to wish he never set eyes on me."

CHAPTER 9

Morning found me with a shot. The light from the bedroom window had just enough of a break in the drapes for the sun to hit me in the face. Slowly wakening, I stretched and realized that I was alone. The spot beside me was still warm, but Carter was nowhere in sight. Sitting up in the bed quickly, I looked around the room looking for any sign of him, and then I heard a shuffle from the bathroom and watched to see what or who was coming.

What if it wasn't him, what if it was the man who called last night just waiting for a chance for Carter to be gone? That was crazy, Carter wouldn't leave without someone being here to protect me. Still panic ripped through me. Watching the door intently, I picked up the nearby glass vase that was heavy enough to knock out King Kong if need be. At least it would give me enough opportunity to flee.

I heard footsteps coming closer toward the door, and soon the object of the muted noise leaned against the doorframe with a towel wrapped around his neck. Using one hand, he stood wiping his hair in an attempt to dry it, his movement fluid. Here in the light of my room stood the object of my affection, and he looked smoldering, intentional or not. Standing clothed in his faded jeans, his chest was bare and sculpted, his body in a perfect V.

"Good morning, I hope you didn't intend on coldcocking me with that."

He pointed to the vase in my hand. Startled by his appearance, I swallowed and answered slowly with a shaky voice. "No, I just . . . I woke up and you weren't . . . here."

"I told you, Bella, I'm not leaving until we have some sort of protection around you, even if it means that you live with me."

Now that one would be a hard to explain to his

church family, wouldn't it? "She's staying at my house, but nothing is happening, she's under my protection." Setting the vase down, I sat staring at him in awe. Sitting on the edge of the bed, he laid the towel on the chair and ran his fingers through his damp hair that laced a trail down his chest and back. I was always mesmerized when I looked at him, but never like this.

"What's wrong, Bella?"

"Oh, ah . . . nothing." I looked down from where I was sitting, aware now that he had caught me.

"I know better than that." Standing he gracefully slid into a white oxford shirt leaving it unbuttoned and sat back down on the edge of the bed.

"Just . . . ah . . . I'm not used to waking up with a man in my bathroom."

He smirked.

"Bella, we are grown adults. Nothing happened here that you should be ashamed of. I woke up, you were still asleep, and so I took advantage of a hot shower."

"You're gorgeous." It was out of my mouth before I could stop it. He chuckled a little, and I was mortified.

"Thank you for the compliment, I do believe you have a lot more going for you than I do." Then I remembered last night. Oh, that had to be embarrassing for him, now that I had thought of it, it was for me was. A shiver ran through me and straight to my heart. He had opportunity to take advantage of a vulnerable moment, but he hadn't. He had taken care of me in one of the most intimate ways a man could have taken care of me. He had even taken the time to dress me in my PJs and had combed my hair as I sat numb in front of him. The more I thought of the gesture, the more my feelings grew for him and the person that he was.

"I'm sorry, you know, about last night. I know how you feel about, well, our relationship, and I put you in an awkward situation."

"Let's put it this way, Bella, I saw who you were, not the physical body, the emotional side of you. Let's face it, I'm a man, the physical body is a turn-on. It wasn't the time or the place. I would be lying to you if I said I weren't attracted to you physically."

"I never meant for it to happen the way it did."

"Isabella, you're beating yourself up. Nothing happened, let it go. I told you, I'll take care of you. There is no reason to be embarrassed or ashamed of what happened. Your reaction to the call you received was a normal one."

I lay back onto the bed and stared at his expertly sculpted body. He was to die for with his piercing dark blue eyes and unruly inky, dark hair. He could have any woman he wanted, yet he was with me, a broken woman that no doubt would never be able to be fixed.

"Bella, you're staring."

I immediately felt my face flush crimson. "I'm sorry. You want me to be completely honest with you?"

"Yes, always. I want you to tell me whatever is on your mind, I've told you that before." Carter, looking down at me, took the breath from me; and for a moment, I felt like we had been with each other for years. This was right, he was here, and he was certainly mine for the taking.

"Have I told you just how ridiculously handsome you are?"

"In not so many words, but thanks, I wasn't fishing for a compliment."

Coming in closer, he came within inches of my nose. "You, my dear lady, are the most gorgeous woman I have met in my life." He kissed me on the temple and stood from his position at my side. "Come on, get up. We have a few things to do today. You are going with me to the training center."

Looking at him questionably, I didn't understand the purpose. "Why, you haven't been released to go to work yet."

Standing in front of me buttoning his shirt, he already knew what I was thinking. "Oh, yes, the nurse in you. Well, my angel in white, I'm going for practice only, no rough stuff. I promise I will be careful, plus I have my own private nurse if I need something." I frowned at him, knowing he wasn't totally ready to go back along with the lack of sleep from taking care of me.

"Don't worry, baby, I'm fine. We are going to meet Gus."

"Gus?" I questioned having no idea of what he had in mind.

"Gus is a self-defense instructor, and he is meeting us today at the training center. He is going to instruct you on self-defense. After that, we are going to the firing range. I need to put some time in, and I'm going to show you how to fire a gun." Sitting in the chair beside the bed, he put his shoes on and continued with his details of the day.

"Why do you want me to do that?"

"For one, I want you with me. Two, I haven't been released yet, and three and most importantly, I need to know that you are going to be able to protect yourself if for some reason I can't be there."

"Carter, I don't like guns, they kill people."

"They also save lives, Bella, and this isn't up for argument. You are going with me, and you will learn. You will use my handgun to learn, and then we will purchase one for you later on. I will be with you, I want you to go through a concealed carry class. You need to know how to use it and use it well."

"You're serious about this, aren't you?"

"Deadly." His eyes were stern, and he had lost his playfulness. "I'm very serious when it comes to your safety." After a deafening silence, his look softened. "Bella, I can't take a chance on your life. Even if it would cost me mine, I'm not going to let that happen to you again." Reaching out to me, he cupped my chin in his hand, his eyes focused on me. "You understand I can't go through another loss. I lost Andrea, I'm not going to lose you too." Seeing the pain on his face was more than I could bear. I could only imagine what it must have been like for him. To lose his wife and be left to raise his infant daughter had to be devastating.

"Okay, I'll do it, for you."

A relieved look came upon his face, and he exhaled sharply. "I would do anything for you, Carter." A smile arose from him that would have lit the room.

"Get dressed, I'll meet you in the living room."

"What about our girl?"

"Molly?" Then he caught it. "Our girl is going with us." Turning to leave the room, he looked back. "You never cease to amaze me, Bella." He turned and strode from the room. My body warmed with delight of us acting as a real family. My main concern was to make him happy, and I would do whatever it took. Sliding to the edge of the bed, my body felt stiff and achy. I was hoping a hot shower would relieve some of the pain. Turning on the water to fill the tub, I stopped and looked into the mirror at my reflection. It was distressing, what did he see in me? I felt I was just a plain, ordinary-looking woman. The dark circles under my eyes were a tell-tale sign of sleep deprivation and medicine-induced sleep. Pulling my hair back into a ponytail, I placed my hands on top of the cold vanity. My eyes looked tired and large and apparently swollen from lack of sleep.

Turning to get in the tub, I poured lavender oils into the water. The heat of the water sent the aroma wafting through the air. Lavender was known for its calming affects, I used it often for stress relief, but it was soothing nonetheless. Ridding myself of my outer attire, I slipped slowly into the bath and let the warm water wash over me. I sat there and let some of the things that Carter had told me of his feelings and those that he had spoken of God and what it meant to live for him. He certainly tried to live what he believed.

I loved that he was honest and demanded that in return, but didn't keep me from being fearful. Did God really want me for who I was? Did any of what had happened to me before matter to him? Was he there? Carter tried to explain it to me, but I still had questions about why. Why do I need to get saved? Why did he allow me to be in the situation I was in? Did he still love me after what I felt was my fault? The questions would have to wait. Carter was waiting, and we had a set time. This bathroom ritual was going to be cut short.

After breakfast, we were off to the training center and firing range, and *nervous* was not exactly the best word to describe what I was feeling. The car hummed as we drove through the familiar area of town in which we both lived and into the hustle of the city. People were starting to decorate their homes for Halloween with assorted pumpkins, scarecrows, and black cats along with many other traditional witches and zombies. I wasn't taking much of the sights in only that they were there. Molly was chattering with her father, but I was so far off I didn't pay much attention to what was being said.

The voice from the night before from the unsettling call I knew, and yet it wouldn't come to me. The harder I fought to remember, the further it seemed to be. I was tired of the enigma of trying to tie everything together.

This all had to happen within the last five to six years. I was fifteen years old going on sixteen when I met Ryan. We had met at a mutual friend's home for an after party on a Friday night. Ryan was the center for the Dexter High School Panthers, and every girl in senior high wanted to date him. He had asked me to meet him after the game once and we then started dating. Friday after the game we would stop and get something to eat or go to one of the other players' home for an after-game party. I hadn't seen him for at least a year; he was to return to Knoxville where he was to teach this past fall. When we had called it quits, we tried to live in the same area, and we ran into each other way too often for him to continue with his life, so he had decided to take a job teaching at the university in Knoxville.

"Isabella," Carter's voice awoke me from my thoughts, and I tried not to look shaken. He always seemed to know what I was thinking, and I didn't really want to bring Ryan up today. He wasn't part of my life any longer, and I just wanted to move forward. "You were a million miles away, you okay?"

I turned and addressed him with a smile that wasn't my normal, but maybe it would slow down the questions. I wanted to spend my time with him, not with a memory of what was. "I'm okay, just a bit under the effects of all the medication I have had in me."

"Dr. Bentley said it would take a couple of days to start leaving your system. Tomorrow you should be feeling more like yourself."

"I'm sure I will."

"Well, we're here."

While Carter removed Molly from the car seat, I stood looking at this ominous building. It was old and brick and looked more like a prison you would see in a horror film. The buildings spread out for miles in any direction, and there were smaller buildings surrounding it. The grounds were kept well, and there were several cadets out running in military style down a paved road lined with large oak trees that were shedding their leaves at a steady pace. He gathered up Molly, and we walked to the building. "Bella, it's going to be fine, don't worry. This is something everyone should know how to do."

We walked into the training center, the large open area was more like a gymnasium than a room. We were greeted by a couple of officers I was sure knew Carter well.

It wasn't long before we were met by a gentleman in his early to midforties. His hair was light brown, and his hazel eyes were gentle but commanding. His stride was graceful. It must be the workout they did.

I had seen the same stride and grace in the way that Carter carried himself.

Reaching out his hand, he shook hands with Carter and greeted Molly warmly. He extended his hand to me. "Ms. Cameron, my name is Gus

Holden. I was asked by Carter to teach you some simple self-defense moves.

We will start out with some simple moves and go on to some more advanced ones."

"It's nice to meet you. I have to admit I'm a little anxious about this."

"Don't be. We are in a safe harbor here. It's a nonthreatening atmosphere, no one is here to hurt anyone. It is to help you learn to defend yourself in case of an attack. What you learn in this class could save your life."

"Okay. Just tell me what I have to do."

"The main thing is to keep from getting into a position that makes you a target. Always be aware of your own surroundings. Never ever give up when you are in a situation where you are in danger, that's what gets people killed.

Walk with confidence always. When you find yourself in a situation and you have opportunity call for help if you see it coming first. That means if you are coming home for example and you are getting ready to get out of the car and see someone that you aren't familiar with and you feel uncomfortable, always go with your first instinct. Call Carter for help, call the police department or someone else that can see that you get to safety. If for some reason you are out and being followed, stop at a police station or call 911 for assistance.

If you don't have time to do that or you're in a

situation where you can't get help, these moves will help protect you and allow you to get away. The first one I'm going to teach is how to get out of a choke hold."

Listening to every word, I was still shy about some of the things that he wanted me to do to address the attacker.

"Bella, you're not going to hurt me. I'm protected, so give it all you got. Practice is also good to get out aggression and stress." He continued to encourage me, all I could think was that I was a preserver of life, not to inflict pain and suffering until he came at me from behind, then the nightmare was brought back. His voice rattled through my head, and I could feel his arms around me in a steel vice. I remembered feeling helpless to what I knew was coming. I wasn't going to let him do it again. The first thing I did was throw a punch to the groin and turned and started throwing knees to the abdomen and chest, and my attacker was found on the floor. My breath taken from me, I had short heaving breaths, attempting to regain it. I stood in a fight stance, waiting for my attacker to take to his feet. Seeing the man that had caused me so much pain I wanted him to suffer for what he had done to me.

I refused to be helpless as I was at the time he held me imprisoned, not being able to get out.

"Bella," I heard his voice, and it brought me back to reality. His voice was dumbfounded, and I saw Gus on the floor before me, shaking his head and getting up. Carter turned me to him and looked at me. The fire still flaming from me, I felt my muscles tense and my jaw tightened. "Relax, take a deep breath." Gus made his way to his feet. "You didn't tell me she packed a punch, Blake."

"I didn't know."

Starting to relax, I took some deep breaths. "Bella, look at me and take some slow deep breaths. It's okay, you did what you were supposed to." Gus came around behind him.

"Is she okay?"

"Yes, she's fine. She's been through this before. I wanted her to be able to defend herself if it happened again."

"It would appear she learns fast. See if you can get her to sit down."

"Bella, come with me, and we will sit down on the bench."

Following him aimlessly, he put his arm around my shoulders and took my hand and sat me down on the bench. It was then I realized that Gus was sitting beside me and Carter was on one knee in front of me with a wet cloth, wiping my face. "Bella, what happened? Talk to me, baby." Chills ran down the length of my spine. "He can't hurt you, he isn't here."

"I felt him, he used to come up behind me and put his arms around me like a steel trap. He would tell me what he was going to do to me and what I was going to do for him. He would drug me, I think, I remember the sting of a needle. I don't want to remember anymore." I choked back the fear, refusing to cry. "I just want to forget."

"Blake, she is going to have no problem, but if you want me to, I will continue to teach her for her peace of mind and yours. She's good, and I think she could learn a lot from this class. She could join the academy if she wanted, she would make a good cop."

Carter shook his head. "No, she's a protector, a caregiver, she preserves life, and you know as well as I, sometimes it comes down to taking a life to protect ourselves and others. Bella, you sure you're okay?"

"Yes, I'm fine." But I wasn't, and I knew it. The fear in me had risen to the point that it crippled me. The thought that came to me was that he was arming me with just enough information that I could accidently kill someone in a fit of rage or fear of being put through what had happened before. I knew bits and pieces, and eventually I would remember it all.

One hour later, I found myself behind a gun. The weight of it in my hands was alarming, heavy, the coldness of it. Thinking of Carter, I was going to do this for his sake and not my own. After he had instructed me on how to load it, he laid it down on the shelf in front of us. "Here, I want you to wear these." He handed me a pair of safety glasses and earplugs. Taking them, I put them into place. "I don't want you to be nervous about this, we're here to practice. I want you to get the feel of the gun. Hold it in your dominant hand and steady it with the other. Make sure you have your balance with your weight on both feet. Don't lock your arms, I want you to line your sight with the red dot on the target. Take the safety off and squeeze the trigger. Take your time, you don't have to rush." Carter stood behind me, correcting my stance and guiding me to where my hand placement should be. "Whenever you're ready, Bella." Pulling back on the trigger slowly, I kept my eyes on the target ahead of me. My body shook with adrenalin from earlier today. Taking a deep breath, I tried to relax. The gun fired and gave me a little kick, the sound echoed, and my stomach churned, making me nauseous.

"I want you to aim a little more to the left, and you should be dead-on."

Correcting the position, I fired again. I fired several rounds before Carter let it rest and then assessed the target. The aim was almost dead-on twice, and once through the center, the rest were in the black and some off the black target zone. More than likely, the first few shots that had fired. "Not bad, Bella, for the first time. It's really pretty good. Have you ever fired a gun before?" I thought about the question and remembered my father showing me how to use his 9mm he had at home. I had only fired it once, but he had let me on my own insistence. But when I misfired and shot one of the family pets, it had devastated me and I never wanted to pick up another gun.

"Once, but it was a long time ago." I didn't go into detail on what had occurred, I had just let it go.

"We will come back, and you can practice some more, but for now, I need to put some time in myself. I won't be long, then we will see about getting a firearm for you. We are going to look today only. You have to go through a concealed carry class first." I shook my head to let him know that I had understood and stepped back and met Molly in the glassed-in room behind him. Standing and watching him had become a favorite pastime. The more time I spent with him, the more I wanted to be with him. The more he tried to protect me, the more I had wanted him to; and the more feelings he revealed to me, the more I wanted. I watched as he stood and fired his gun in the smooth grace he had and the tension that it caused in his shoulders.

Even under his shirt, I could see the muscles in back as they flexed at his movement.

I loved him, but I really didn't want to admit it to myself or to him. It came down to could I give him what he deserved. Purity certainly was one thing I couldn't offer obviously. Even though I had not been with anyone of my own choosing, I had still been spoiled, and there was no way to change that. I couldn't go back. Being faithful to him would be no question. I had no desire to ever have more than one man in my life. I was raised believing that once you were with someone you were with them for life that was just the way it was. Could he love me after everything came out, every grotesque detail? I still couldn't fathom why he had stayed with me with what he already knew. I was taught that young ladies were to protect themselves and preserve themselves for their husbands so that they solely belonged to their husband. Virginity was a gift to be unwrapped only by the man she loved. My soul ached and angered because of the way it had been taken from me. It was what had made me different and had set me apart from the others and was a treasured part of me, and my intention was just that, for it to be a gift that was clearly for my husband. I couldn't get over someone else's hands being on me, how could he dismiss it?

Molly sat playing with her coloring book and offered me the box of crayons. "Will you color with me, Momma?" Her sweet little face looked up at me in expectation. Scooting in closer to her, I took the page next to her and started to color with her. I noticed most of what she colored was blue, not one shade of blue, but many shades of blue. "Molly that is very pretty, but why is everything blue?"

"I like blue, and when Mommy come see me, her is in blue lights, her has a white dress. Hers so pretty, hers in a party dress and goes to her feet."

"Have you seen Mommy again?"

"Yes." She did not say much, but then she started to talk about what

Andrea had said to her. "Mommy say make sure to wuv Daddy for her, so me told her me would."

Curious, I asked her some questions although I wasn't sure I believed what she was saying, but I had heard patients talk about seeing their loved ones that had passed on before them. "Why did Mommy tell you that? Is there something wrong with Daddy? Is there something supposed to happen to Daddy or you?"

She pushed her hair away from her face and then she continued with her answer. "Mommy says Daddy might go way, but me not know what her means." Shivers ran down me, and I ran cold. "When, Molly, did she tell you?"

"No, but her scare me, her said her scared for you too. Her not like Daddy not be here for you."

Molly had just finished her story and Carter walked in, and I immediately was on my feet. I ran to him wrapping my arms around his neck, almost knocking him

184

off his feet. "Isabella."

"Carter, you can't go back to work yet."

"Why not, I go back to the doctor in a couple of days? I'm fine, I haven't had any pain, and I haven't had any changes in vision or balance."

Putting my index finger to his lips, I stopped him in midsentence. "Listen to me, something is going to happen, and I have a chance to stop it. Molly was visited by Andrea, she told her to love her daddy as much as she could, that her daddy may not be with her much longer. Carter, I couldn't stand it if something happened to you if I could stop it."

"You don't honestly believe that, do you?"

"Why not, she told her that I was in need of help, that you needed to be there for me and I needed to be there for you. She was right then, wasn't she?"

"Isabella, I can't go just on a child's dream."

"You believed her before, why not now?"

Cupping my face in his hands, he tilted my face toward his. "Baby, I can't live my life on what-ifs. If God decides to take me, I'm not going to be able to stop him. Not that I want to leave my daughter or you, but I have no choice in the matter."

"It's a warning, Carter, can't you see that?"

"It will be okay, I promise you. I have no intention of leaving you."

Releasing his hold, he took me into his embrace, and I rested my cheek on his chest as he stroked my back soothingly. "You have had a rough day, why don't we go pick up some of your clothes? I want you to go home with me. I can look after you better there."

"Carter, that isn't wise," knowing that if I were with him alone, things could definitely get out of hand.

"I know what's going through your mind, Bella, and I will take care of it.

You will have your own room. I will see to it."

185

"But what about?"

"Angel, don't fret so much. It will work out."

As the day passed, I couldn't get what Molly had said from my head, but it didn't seem to disturb Carter in the least. He wouldn't let me know if it did anyway. I had at least one full day off if Dr. Bentley released me today. It wasn't my choice to see him, but under the circumstances, well, to go to work, I had to.

Carter had gone into another part of the house to plan my room, and I sat on the couch before the fireplace that cracked and popped in a display of reds, yellows, and gold. The consoling effect it had given me had made it feel right to be here. Molly lay on the floor in a peaceful slumber. She had played to the point that she had fallen asleep on her belly while she was coloring and was now wrapped in her blanket. In my heart I knew I had to get a grip on my life. The events over the last few days had left so many people in mayhem it had to stop. Having Molly and Carter in my life, I had to let go, I had to find a way to get out of the self-persecution instead of letting it choke me.

"Yes. Yes, she's here." Striding into the room with a self-indulgent grin, Carter walked toward me carrying my cell phone. "Just a second." Handing the cell phone to me, he winked at me. "It's your mom, I do believe she was a little more than shocked to hear a man's voice." Laughing at his expression, I took the cell from him. "I'm sure she is."

"This should be good." He slid in beside me on the couch and scooted in to me as close as he could get, teasing me.

"Hello."

"Isabella, who was the man with the sexy voice?" I couldn't help but smile at her reaction.

"Hello to you too, Mom."

"You're holding out on me, is he as handsome as he

sounds?" She bubbled with enthusiasm, always the matchmaker.

"Yes, Mom, he is." Carter sat with a huge smile on his face. He was getting so much enjoyment from this.

"You must tell me, is the young man single, are you dating?" She shot the questions in rapid-fire at me, and I had to snicker.

"Mom, calm down and I'll tell you. It's no secret. Yes, he is single, yes, we are dating." Carter had started to hold a chuckle in with his fist to his lips.

"Keep going, baby," he coaxed.

"Tell me more," my mother prodded.

"I met him at the hospital." Carter shook his head, allowing me to tell her the rest. "He was one of my patients. He works for the Maine law enforcement as a detective in Portland, and he is my boyfriend." My mother squealed in delight and forced me to hold the cell away from my ear. Carter chuckled as he could hear her on the other end.

"Oh my, oh my goodness, I'll have to tell your father. What's his name?"

"Carter Blake, and he has taken care of me like a baby."

"You deserve to be treated like a baby. Let him baby you. You need someone to be good to you." She contemplated for a moment, and I knew what was coming. "Let's see, Carter Blake," she drew out. "Carter Blake." She was putting it together, I knew it was coming.

"You would like him, Mom. You and Daddy will have to meet him sometime."

"Oh yes, of course. He's Grayson Blake's son, isn't he? Oh, Bella, you hit the jackpot. He is one of the top notable bachelors, and he is pursuing you."

"Yes, Mom, he's mine and I intend on keeping him."

"Oh, honey, I'm so happy for you. You will invite

Daddy and me to the wedding, won't you?" I gasped at the idea, and Carter, following my expression, didn't help matters.

"Mom, we barely have had our first date. I think that is a little soon."

"I know, I know, but a mother can dream."

"Believe me, if that happens, you will be the first to know."

"Oh, before I go, I talked to Lily, and she said that you had been ill."

I wasn't going to go into detail, she would just worry and she was too far away to be here and she would be. "I'm fine, just a little anxiety, but I'm doing much better now."

"I can understand why you would be. Carter took care of you?"

"Yes, he did." My mother's questions started to make me squirm in my seat. Tapping me on the leg, Carter got up and walked away.

"He likes you very much, I can tell. He seems like a very good man."

"He is, Mom. I'm a lucky girl," I gushed.

"Well, I better go, honey. I need to check on your father, call me when you can. I love you."

"Love you, Mom." Turning off my cell, I placed it on the table beside me with a clank as it hit the tabletop. My mother, always the dear heart, knew how to sustain a marriage. She and Daddy had been married for years and still looked at each other like they were on their honeymoon. I was sure they had their disagreements, but I never heard them raise their voices to each other.

My grandparents were like that too. Always the loving couple, holding hands even in their sixties. My grandmother always ran the house and saw that my grandfather had supper on the table when he came home, and my mother was no different. Call it old-fashioned, but I wanted that kind of relationship. I wanted the type of love they had for each other and to love one another, to take care of the other one.

"Mom excited, is she?" Carter's voice broke through my thoughts, and I turned to find him standing behind the couch, looking down at me with that drop-dead look of his.

"You could say that."

"Hey, you couldn't get a better catch than me." He laughed out loud.

"You heard that?"

"Yes, I did."

"I wouldn't laugh if I were you. She has us married already."

He smiled widely at that. "I knew I liked her."

"How long did you talk to her, you certainly charmed her?"

"Long enough. Come, I have a surprise for you." Standing, he took my hand and led me into where his study had been. He had totally transformed the room. The hardwood floors had large rugs with blue, yellow, and white Victorian roses on them and a gold border. The bed was covered in white linen and a down comforter that had a cornflower blue border and a light blue lace coverlet at the bottom, setting off the white walls. Mustard, cornflowers, and daises graced the white-and-gold-trimmed Victorian tables. White sheers fell from the ceiling and tied together at the posts of the bed with yellow ribbons over a white four poster Victorian bed. In the corner next to the bay window and at the edge of the fireplace was a chaise lounge in cornflower blue strewn with white and yellow pillows and yellow and cashmere lap throws. The mantle was a glow of white and blue candles in various heights and styles. Walking to the window, I looked out onto the ocean, and the waves rolled in with a roar. I loved the ocean, the sight of it, the smell of it, and the most recent the memory of it.

I looked around in amazement of what he had done, and then I saw the wall at the side of the bed, scriptwriting stenciled in blue. It was one of the most heartwarming things he had ever done for me. The inscription read,

"The most valuable possession a man can gain on the earth is a woman's heart."

"You did this?"

"I had some help. It's been in the works for a couple of days. Do you like it?"

"Like it? I love it. It's beautiful." I looked around the room in admiration; there were pictures of Carter and Molly together and separate ones of each of them. Lying on the bench beside the chase was a stack of frames that matched the others, empty. Pointing to the empty ones and gliding over to pick them up, he offered the gold-colored frame to me. "These are for you to fill with pictures of us together, there are others for your parents and friends in the bureau. I want you to treat this like your own home. Anything you want or need, I'll get it for you."

Standing in the center of the room, I attempted to take it all in. The flowers were fresh, beautiful, and full of fragrance. The room itself was a sanctuary, but the sentiment behind it meant more. How could I have found such a man?

"I can't believe you did all of this for me."

"Isabella, I would die for you."

Walking up behind me and running his hands down my arms, he embraced me, holding me against his firm, sculpted body. The power from him radiated through me.

"You better get ready, you have an appointment to keep."

CHAPTER 10

A week had passed and Dr. Bentley had released me to return to work against his better judgment. Carter had returned to work the day before; the only time we had together were evenings at home. I had spoken to Dr. Bentley about my concerns on many things along with the intuition of Molly, and of course he seemed to feel that what Molly had told me held no relevance. It came to mind on occasion, but I tried to push it back. Maybe he was right. I took most things way too serious.

It would soon be lunchtime, and Carter met me most days as I left the floor. I enjoyed every minute I could get with him. Molly had been engrossed by him the past couple of days and barely let him out of her sight. Kids and animals have a sixth sense of things coming, and it put me on edge. Stepping off the elevator, he was standing before me, leaning against the wall with his arms crossed, his legs crossed at the ankle casually. He was dressed in his dark blue suit jacket and pants and a crisp white shirt that almost glowed against him. His tie, the shade of his eyes set against his dark hair, made him look dangerous, way too attractive to be left alone. Walking toward him I noticed the other women looking him up and down and turning away when they noticed I was watching, but he didn't seem to mind. Coming closer, he extended his hand to me, catching mine, and drew me in and kissed me quickly.

"How's my angel in white?"

"I'm fine." My face flushed, and I felt a little intimidated in his presence.

He looked gorgeous, but his dress led me to believe he was not just at work today. "Where you headed dressed so dashing?"

"Business, nothing too important, just thought I

would have lunch with my best girl."

"Oh, okay. Will you be home when I get off tonight?" my voice was almost pleading.

"I should be, but if not, Landon and Beth will be there with Molly when you get there."

"With both of us at work, I don't know what we would do if Beth went into labor. Molly has no one to go to."

"She has Mrs. Freeman next door, they will manage. If something were to happen, you can reach me on my cell. I promise I will be close by."

We made our way to the cafeteria and picked through the assorted meals, finally settling on one. We sat at the table closer to the corner of the room, it seemed less congested there and was much quieter, I couldn't eat and I hadn't been able to sleep, my stomach had been tied in knots for days.

"Bella, is there something you want to talk about?"

"What?" Carter's words threw me.

"You're obviously distracted, and you haven't been eating much lately.

What's wrong, angel?"

"Oh, nothing. Just a bit tired, I haven't been sleeping all that well. Getting back to work seems to have helped some."

"But?" Looking over his steepled fingers at me, I knew he already had the answer.

"Nothing, just trying to find a routine, I'm fine, really." Leaning forward, his look was piercing to the point it burned me. "You know I can tell when something is upsetting you. I will find out."

"Don't worry about me. You have business to attend to, and I'm keeping you from it."

"I hit a nerve I see."

I hung my head before him, knowing that I had been defeated. I couldn't get anything by him. Looking up, he raised his brow. "Okay. It's me, isn't it?

Look, Bella, I'm fine. Nothing is going to happen. I promise you, I'm coming home all in one piece. Please, don't worry."

Leaning my cheek against my fist, I tried to secure myself. I hurt, literally ached. What would I do? "You're right, it's crazy. I shouldn't be thinking about anything like that. You will be home, and I will see you tonight."

Reaching across the table, he took my hand from my face and covered both of my hands in his. "Can you at least smile for me? I'm going to be gone a few hours, and I'll be back. You act like we are an old married couple." He smirked.

I gave him a halfhearted smile, and he accepted it. I felt the warmth of his touch that I so often craved and etched it in my memory. "I'll be coming back home tonight to see my girls.

"Okay."

"I promise you I'll be back. I know the last few weeks have been a tumultuous ride for you, but I'm here and I'm not going anywhere. I don't want to leave you like this."

I didn't want to stand in his way, I was stronger than this. I had to find my position and take it.

"It's okay. I know you have business to attend to. I'll take care of Molly, and we'll have a nice dinner when you get home."

He looked at me, astonished that I had taken the rein. I could do this. I had a job that demanded my ability to stand on my own, why couldn't I do the same in my personal life?

"Sounds good to me, I'll be looking forward to it." His megawatt smile went from ear to ear.

I dreaded having to leave him, but it was inevitable. "I guess I had better go back, they will be sending a search party for me."

Standing, he took me to his side with his hand, leading me at the small of my back. The gesture was intimate, and I loved that he wanted to be there.

He led me to the bank of elevators where we would be parting, and I sunk inside. Using the Call button, he leaned his forearm against the wall, and his look at me was unreadable. I turned to say goodbye and enclosed my body, putting his tall frame in front of me; and leaning in, he kissed me deftly, leaving me speechless. Stepping back but never leaving the enclosure around me, he studied my face and grinned. "I'll see you tonight," he whispered. The elevator doors opened, and I unwillingly stepped in, watching him until the doors would no longer allow it.

The day moved on in a steady pace. The next time I had looked at the clock, it was four in the afternoon. Thankful I had been busy enough it hadn't allowed me much time to dwell on if Carter was safe, he would be coming home.

The marble floor was unforgiving as I walked out of trauma 3. I gathered my wits and headed for the desk. The simple photographs and paintings were the only color that the hall had to offer giving the appearance of sanitation and coldness. It nearly sucked the life out of me. I had never really noticed before how desolate it was, and it only added to my disheartened mood.

Carol sat at her normal post, clicking away at the computer, busying herself placing orders. Peering up from her work, she gave me a cheery smile.

"Hey, girl, how's it going?"

"Not bad." I lied.

"How's tall, dark, and sexy . . . ," she said in a low voice.

"He's good."

"Oh my goodness, Bella, just good?" Laughing, she lifted my mood. "He certainly is a powerful force to reckon with."

194

"He's wonderful, Carolyn. Honestly, I don't know what I would have done without him, he's been very good to me."

"See?" she bragged. "I knew he would be good for you. He's got the whole package. He's smart, wealthy, he's a good man, and he has good taste."

Blushing from her response, she decided to have some fun with me. "Oh, look at that. You've got it bad."

"Okay, okay, you win. He has me. I never thought I would meet someone I would never stop thinking about. He treats me like a lady, I've never had that. He makes me feel special."

"You do have it bad."

Marilyn walked in behind me, her coolness felt as soon as she walked in the room. "Well, still hanging out with the million-dollar mogul boyfriend?

Bet I could show him a better time than you ever could." She stood toying with me, knowing that Carter was a hot subject with me.

"Marilyn, I'm sure with your reputation, you would have no problem finding a man. Being an easy mark should make it exceptionally effortless.

"Your goody-goody act must be stifling to a man with that kind of sex appeal. Rest assured, dear, I will get my chance."

She turned on her heel and walked away with a sneer on her face. Thank goodness, I didn't have the strength to deal with her.

Carol cleared her throat. "That woman would steal candy from a baby and stand back and eat in front of them."

"Don't worry about it, Carol. A man might get her, but they would bring her back in the daylight."

I walked on to the break room, and my cell rang, startling me. "Bella, it's Beth." She had alarm in her voice. "I need help," her voice was shaking by this point.

"Beth, what's wrong?"

"I can't get Landon on the phone, I need him. I think I'm in labor this time."

Her voice was fading, and I couldn't understand why. "Beth, I can barely hear you. Is Molly still with you?" She squeaked out a yes. "Beth, hand Molly the cell if she is there." I could hear her moving her hand around from the crackle of it against her.

"Mommy," Molly's little voice came on the cell.

"It's me, baby. What's going on with Auntie Beth?"

"She lying on the floor. Uncle Cooper was here."

Chills ran through me. "Molly, did Uncle Cooper hit her?"

"Not know, her told me go in my room and lock the door. Wots of noise, Mommy, me was scared."

"Okay, is he gone?"

"Me think so."

"Can you get Mrs. Freeman?"

"Tant get her, Auntie tried."

"Baby, you need to get Mommy's blanket off the couch and cover Aunt

Beth and then put some pillows under her feet. Do you know how to call Uncle Landon?"

"Yes, it's the 3 on Auntie Beth's phone."

"Okay, you call Uncle Landon. Stay right there with Aunt Beth, and I'm on my way. Can you do that for me?"

"Yes, I stay right here."

"Listen, if Uncle Cooper comes back, go back to your room and lock the door. Don't let him in, okay? You call 911 if he comes back. Can you remember that?"

"Yes," she said with a little cry caught.

"It's okay, baby. I'm coming home."

I tried to contact Mrs. Freeman, but I was unable to contact her with the number Carter provided.

"Carol, I have to go. Will you call the supervisor so I can talk to them?"

Collecting my things, I made my way back to the desk and contacted a squad to be dispatched then talked to the house supervisor and told her of the situation and I was on my way. It was time to call Carter. Dialing him in urgency, I could hardly get the numbers in the cell. The cell rang, and I felt my heart in my throat, not knowing what I was going to find when I got there.

"Hello."

"Thank God, what a relief."

"Bella, I'm on my way home. I should be there in about fifteen minutes."

"Carter, you need to get home, I'm on my way there." I was trying to control the terror in my voice.

"Why, what's wrong?"

"I'm not sure what happened, but Cooper has been there and Beth is in labor. She called me because she was unable to get Landon, Molly is with her.

I called an ambulance, they should be there about the time we arrive."

"Is he still there?"

"Molly said she didn't think so, but I told her if he came back to go to her room and lock the door."

"Bella, listen to me. If you get there before I do, I don't want you to go into that house. Do you understand?"

"Carter, we need to get to Beth and Molly. Beth, heaven forbid, could be in danger. Her life may depend on me getting into that house. I can't stand by and just let her lie there."

"Isabella, my daughter is in there. If he is in there and gets spooked, he will use her. Now listen to me, don't do it."

"Carter, please let me do this."

"Isabella, if you think anything of me at all, don't go in there." The cell went dead and I lay it on the console, knowing I was now on my own. I would try to contact Landon, maybe he could get there before either of us.

Hoping that Molly had hit the speed dial on Beth's cell, I tried to contact him through the police department. They effortlessly connected me to him.

"Hello." His voice was controlled and smooth.

"Landon, thank God, it's you."

"Yeah, it's me, are you missing my best bud?"

"Landon, we have problems."

"Well, what is it, my angel of mercy?"

"Landon, it's Beth, I think she is in labor."

"In labor, why didn't she call me?"

"She tried to, you must have been out of range."

"I'm on my way, I should be there in ten to fifteen minutes."

"Landon, wait, Cooper has been there."

"Cooper? How did he know where she was?"

"I don't know, but we need to get to her. Molly is scared, she said it was loud. She went into her room and hid. I'm on my way home."

The anguish in Landon's voice was clear. "I knew I shouldn't have left her. She insisted she was okay."

"Landon, you can't blame yourself for this. The important thing is to get to her."

"I'll be there soon. Bella, if you get there before I do, don't let her die."

The cell died, and I lied it back down. I happened to think that Dad's 9mm was in the glove box. He always wanted me to carry it, as Carter, he too insisted on it. I never had it loaded; I kept the clip separate in case I was stopped by a patrol. I had it near if I needed it; I wasn't going to let Beth lie there.

Soon I was rolling into the driveway, watching for any sign that he was still there. There was no vehicles close or any movement anywhere. The door was ajar, and there was no sign of Molly outside or at the door. Pulling the gun from the glove box loading it, I unclipped the safety. Molly and Beth were my concern, and I was going to protect them at any cost. The boys had not yet made it, it was now or never. I opened the car door, leaving it open. I walked to the front door. Reaching for the knob, I cautiously walked into the room where it was eerily silent. Each step was pushed by adrenalin, and I was ready to fire on him if I had to make the choice.

I walked closely to the wall and stopped for a moment to listen. There was no sound, not even a shuffle. The only sound was the beating of my own heart, and it beat like thunder. I could hear my pulse in my ears as I walked farther in. The cold stillness ate at me, feeling like someone was watching each step my breath caught.

Looking into the living room, I could see the top of Molly's head, and she jumped when she saw me and ran to me. I returned the safety on the gun and placed it in my scrub jacket as I bent to pick Molly up and hold her in my arms. I patted her back and praised her for being there with Beth. I kissed her cheeks and wiped away the remnants of her tears that still remained and then sent her to watch for her father. It would give her something to do while I assessed the situation with Beth.

I got down on my knees and assessed her. Her color was pale, and her skin was cool. Checking her pulse, it was barely palpable. She was in shock, and I was getting nervous. Palpating her abdomen, I attempted to feel for fetal movement in which I found none. Looking down at the blanket on her and the floor, I didn't have to remove the blanket to know that she was bleeding. It was evident with the pool of water and blood that surrounded her. Touching her face, I tried to get a response from her. "Beth, it's Bella. Come on, talk to me." I pleaded with her. If something happened to her, Landon wouldn't be the only one affected, it would ravage Carter.

I couldn't let her die, but I felt helpless. I was limited to what I could do where I was.

Looking over my shoulder, I saw Carter coming in

the door followed by Landon at breakneck speed. Coming to a halt at the sight of Beth's unmoving frame, he looked at me in desperation. "Bella, how is she?" He was visibly shaken by the appearance of his sister, he was notably vulnerable.

"She's alive. We need to get her some help quickly."

Landon broke through the door and fell to his knees, picking her up and laying her head in his lap, followed into the living room by the ambulance crew. They worked with her franticly. While they work with her, the earlier conversation with her came to mind. I needed to tell Carter about the conversation between us. Landon and Carter had the right to know what had happened and Beth's wishes.

Attempting to lead him away from his sister, I took him by the arm and tried to pull him back. "Carter, let's step back so they can get to her."

He stepped back away from her reluctantly. Looking back, I placed my hand along his cheek and aimed his face to me. "I need to talk to you, it's important."

He shifted nervously and looked at me, waiting for the revelation I was about disclose to him. "What is it?"

"Carter, this is difficult for me to tell you. I hope that you know I would never intentionally keep anything from you without a good reason."

"What are you trying to tell me?" His face had become full of anxiety and distress; I hated to see him like this.

"It's Beth. There is something that she told me that you need to know.

She made me promise not to tell anyone unless something happened to her.

Beth was keeping a secret, she was protecting someone. The baby she is carrying is not Cooper's."

"What? What are you telling me?"

Taking a breath and a brief pause, I tried to come up

with the best words to tell him what was needed to be said.

"Bella, you need to tell me what it is you're holding back, I don't understand."

"She was protecting someone she loved. She thought by keeping it quiet, she was protecting them. Cooper had threatened to kill the man the baby belonged to, so to protect them, she let Cooper believe the baby belonged to him. The night you went to her and had the accident, Cooper had been to a bar and had a few and figured out that he wasn't the father."

"You're talking in circles, come out with it."

"Carter, Cooper isn't the father of her baby, Landon is."

"What do you mean Landon is. She was never with Landon. Cooper wouldn't let her out of his sight."

"The time she was admitted to the hospital for assault, Landon took her home with him. She was with him a few weeks. He is the father of this baby, she knew and she had me promise not to tell anyone."

"I don't understand. She always came to me when she was in trouble."

"Not this time. You were to close to the subject. She was afraid for him and for you. She loves both of you, she couldn't take the risk of one or both of you being killed by a man that had threatened the very ones she was the closest to."

He ran his fingers through his hair in frustration. "That can't be."

"It can, and it is."

Looking back at me, his expression had turned icy. "How could you keep something like that from me? You promised me you would never keep anything from me? I thought we understood each other."

"Carter, it was not just between two people, it was between a nurse and a patient. She asked me not to tell, and I didn't."

"She is my sister. She could die and she is carrying a child that may die because I didn't know. Landon may lose his child and the woman he has been in love with for years. He had the right to know Beth is carrying his child."

"I'm sorry. There's not much else I can say."

"Sorry isn't going to cut it, Isabella. I thought we were better than this."

He moved away from me. "I have to talk to Landon. He needs to know what's going on." He walked away from me, and my heart shattered. Molly ran to me, and I picked her up, holding her close. I stood stalk still, watching them as the crew loaded Beth for transport. As the crew walked away, Carter guided Landon to sit down. I know the conversation had turned to what I have told him. Landon looked at the messages on his cell, and the distress had harnessed him. He took the cell and threw it against the wall where it broke into pieces and skipped across the floor. Carter stood and sent him toward the car. Looking over at me, his mood was still angered. "You coming," He motioned to me, and I carried Molly and approached him cautiously. As we walked toward the door, I deposited the gun on the table and followed them to the SUV Landon arrived in. Carter took his place behind the wheel. With Landon a wreck, he was in no shape for driving. I slid over the back seat with Molly and secured her in a car seat that Landon had had placed for her, little did he know his own child might use it if it were to survive.

Sitting in the waiting room holding Molly who was now sleeping soundly in my lap, I watched and wondered now what Carter and Landon thought of me. The cold, icy feeling I felt from him could not be coincidence. Not that it mattered, I could understand if Carter hated me for keeping that secret, but I felt I needed to keep my word to Beth. She had told me in confidence, and I felt a sense of duty. From my type of work, you do not disclose anything a patient has told in confidence, it is part of the record that only was shared between the nurse, patient, and physician. At some point, Carter might understand it, but for now, all we could do was to wait, wait for what was to come. Landon sat in the chair, bent over with his hands cupping his face, his arms supported on his knees. Carter stood in the corner of the room with a stale cup of coffee in his hand, staring out into the night from the large pane glass window that was now showing the dusk. The couch was open, so I deposited Molly there where she curled up and continued in a sweet dream.

Cautiously, I approached Landon and sat down in the hard metal chair beside him. I wasn't sure what I was going to say or do. I felt as helpless as he, and I felt somehow that my presence wasn't any good for either of them. I laid my hand on his shoulder, and he started talking, it's all he needed.

"Isabella, what am I going to do? All I ever wanted to do was love her and to protect her." He rubbed his face and as he straightened in the chair. "I never wanted anything more than to love her. She walked away from me and I still loved her, she married another man and I still loved her." He ran his hands through his ruffled hair tensely. "Why didn't she tell me? I would have gotten her out of there. I would have done whatever it took." He choked back a sob, and my throat tightened.

"She loves you, Landon. She did what she did to protect you." He turned in his seat to look at me. "Cooper threatened her that he would kill the man that the baby belonged to. She knew he would do it. She wasn't afraid for herself, she feared more for you and the baby she carried than herself. I knew, Landon, she told me. I'm sorry, I should have told you. She asked me not to say anything because she feared for you, and she feared if Carter found out, he would go after Cooper. She was concerned for his safety." I wrung my hands trying to control my feelings. "She asked me to keep it from the both of you, as a professional, I'm bound. As a friend, I should have told you. I asked her to release me from it, and she denied me. She did ask that you were told if something happened because she did not want that little baby to end up in the hands of Cooper. She wanted you to fight for him."

"Bella, I don't blame you. I should have figured this out way before now.

I don't want you to think that this happened often, it didn't, it was one time.

We were together, and I wanted to have her there to protect her. My feelings for her left me vulnerable, and the trauma and fear she was living with left us both in a situation we should have never been in. I respect her marriage to Cooper. Even though he is about the most worthless human being there could be on God's earth, she chose him."

"I don't know what to say, I know from the little time that I have known her that she is still in love with you."

"That's my girl and my baby boy in there, they are fighting for their lives, I feel so helpless."

I couldn't believe what was being brought to my mind. God had no use for me, why was I being told to pray? *Tell him to pray,* and *I will hear him.*

"Landon." I took his hand. "Pray for them. Pray that they will be brought back to you. Pray for their protection and for God's hand."

He cleared his throat, and I sat quietly with him as he prayed silently.

My eyes closed, I offered no prayer, I felt I had angered God long ago and he would never hear the cries of a wretched person of the gross sin that I had been a part of. My heart ached for him and the injustice of feeling the child that he might never get to see or to hold while he was a living being. It would be a miracle of God for them to

204

survive what Cooper had done. I could feel the icy coldness of pain that consumed me. My life was one of no meaning or concept. I had people in my life in whom I loved and cherished with every breath of my being, but I felt unworthy of being loved by them.

As a young girl, you dream of the young man that will fall in love with you. The knight on the white horse that will take you off to his castle. You plan your wedding down to the shoes you will wear. I could remember standing in front of my mother's standing mirror with her shoes on and a white well-oversized dress and a sheet for a veil, dreaming of my wedding, carrying a hand full of daisies that had been picked from the yard. That dream of that perfect day had been long gone, and I was irrational to think that Carter could ever consider me to be that kind of perfection I felt a wife to be.

The perfect bride was untouched, pure, and innocent. That part of me had been gone for a long time. I couldn't be honest with him because I didn't know what was true and what wasn't. It wasn't that I wouldn't love to have him as a husband somewhere down the road, it just didn't seem realistic.

How could he love me? I was used and broken, still that girl dreaming of the impossible.

I felt warmth gather around me, and I looked from where I sat. Carter was on one knee in front of me, and he laid a hand on my knee. His head bowed and his body shook. The heat resonated from him, and I could tell he was in pain, the physical and mental pain of the uncontrollable, yet he was calm. I clasped my hand over his and sat quietly as these two men of God prayed. I made an attempt, but I felt it went no higher than the ceiling.

The minutes turned in to hours before we heard anything. I stood at the window and looked out onto the dark night with my arms wrapped about my waist, pleading with God for a miracle. The doors finally opened as a

205

physician clad in green scrubs made his way toward us. Landon immediately stood, and Carter stood stiff at his expression. I walked over to them and placed my hand upon his shoulder, hoping for the best, but waiting for the worst.

"Hello, I'm Dr. Fields." He offered his hand to each of us and then motioned to the chairs behind us. The fellows took their seats, and I stood behind Carter with both hands on his shoulders. "I wanted to let you know that Beth has made it through a rough time. She is stable for now, she lost a lot of blood, but we are in process of replacing it. We did deliver her, it involved a caesarean section. The baby was in distress, and it was imperative to get to it as quickly as possible. The placenta had pulled away from the uterine wall and was causing most of the bleeding, she also had a small tear in the uterine wall that we repaired. My main concern is that she took a pretty good fall. Does anyone know about that?"

Carter spoke first. "No, we weren't aware of a fall. Her husband had been there, and he has a tendency for violence. We found her after the fact. We aren't sure what happened."

"She is still unconscious, the blood replacement and volume of fluid we have given her should help her, but she hasn't regained consciousness yet. I don't look for that to happen for a while. She's still under some pain medication, and has gone through a pretty traumatic event."

Landon stepped in. "What about the baby, is he all right?"

"The baby is doing fine, bouncing baby boy, as healthy as anyone I have seen. Good set of lungs on him." Landon breathed a sigh of relief, and the tension left from Carter's shoulders.

"When can we see them?" Landon had asked, anticipation in his voice.

The doctor grinned broadly. "You can see the baby

through the nursery window now. Beth, give her an hour or two while they recover her, and you may see her as well."

"Dr. Fields, would it be possible for Landon to hold the baby?" I asked, knowing that he would need something to hold to.

"We don't normally allow anyone other than the parents to hold the babies."

"I'm the father," Landon replied without hesitation.

"I see no problem then, why don't you follow me back and I will see what we can do."

Carter picked up Molly and held her close to him to where her face lay in the crook of his neck. He reached back for me and clasped my hand; I stopped him for a moment.

"You want me to go?"

"Yes, I want you there."

The doors opened and we headed toward the nursery and the doctor escorted Landon inside. Looking through the glass, there was a baby boy in the warming bed being tended to by an older nurse. He wailed, and his hands and feet moved in excitement, his lips trembled as he cried. It wasn't long before Landon stood beside the warmer clad in a yellow hospital gown. The nurse smiled and lifted the baby from the warmer and placed him in Landon's waiting arms. He walked him over to the window and showed him off to us, and he rocked and swayed the little fellow, and he stilled in his arms, sucking his tiny fist. Landon kissed his tiny face, and the tears flowed down his cheeks in relief and the love of his new son.

"All is right with the world when a baby comes into it," Carter murmured, seeing tears come down his cheeks.

"You softy," I teased.

"There is nothing like the birth of a child to show the power and the love of God, Isabella." He stroked his daughter's hair and rocked her gently in his arms. "She is one of the most precious things in my life. I know how he feels right now. The next best thing to happen is Beth."

"He loves her, you know. He told me, I have no doubt he does."

"He never stopped loving her, he has always been there. He was crushed when she married Cooper. I don't know if I could have loved someone like that. He had a few dates after he and Beth separated, but he couldn't offer them what they needed, he still loved my sister."

I was a bit uncomfortable. He kissed me on the cheek as we stood there watching Landon admire his baby boy. "I'm confused."

"What on earth about?" He chuckled.

"I thought you hated me."

"Bella, just because I get angry doesn't mean my feelings have changed."

He turned to face me, "Yes, I was angry, I'm over it. I learned a long time ago to never let the sun go down on your wrath. You never go to bed on your anger, it serves no purpose, and you never know if the person you are angry with will be there tomorrow. We have no guarantee of our next breath."

He had forgiven me, what liberation that had given. Standing on tiptoes, I kissed him, not hesitating and bold in my delivery. In a pause, he stood there with his eyes slowly opening and looking down at me. His brilliant blue eyes shined at me. "You do unravel me, Ms. Cameron. A man could fall madly in love with you."

"I challenge you, Mr. Blake, to do just that." I taunted him.

"When will you ever cease to amaze me, Bella?"

"I hope I always mystify you."

Landon stepped out of the nursery and stood in front of us, the proud papa cuddling his son. "Isn't he something? His tiny little fingers and toes, they are all there." He smiled in appreciation of the life he held in his arms.

"Isabella, thank you."

"Thank me, for what?"

"For taking care of Beth and being her friend and for this little man of mine, I never had anything overwhelm me like this."

"Landon, I didn't do anything. Molly stayed with her, and she did what I told her."

"You told me the truth. It's going to be rough, but maybe Beth and I can work things out. We will have to do something. Our little boy is going to have a home, one with both of us."

"And we know that God causes all things to work together for those who love him. Now the Bible doesn't say it's for Jay over here or Susie over there or some things depending on who or what does it. The Bible says all, inclusive. It might be a good thing, but then the bad in our lives also is part of God's plan. He doesn't make it happen, but he's there when it does, and it can be used for his glory if you will let it. Those who are called according to his purpose, everyone that will allow him is used by him. It doesn't matter if you're rich or poor, old or young, healthy or ill, heavy or thin. That's just it, God looks on the human heart, and he doesn't look at the physical. He uses us if we are willing vessels.

"If God is with us then who then shall be against us? God's power goes beyond any mortal understanding." I couldn't grasp it, but I knew it's there.

"He gave his own son, sparing his own child that was perfect, and delivered him. He loved you yesterday when you thought all hope was gone, and he loves you today just as you are."

I was squirming in my seat. I had agreed to attend service with Carter.

Uncomfortable was an understatement as the pastor delivered his sermon. I felt hot and weak, and my anxiety rose. God was speaking to me and I knew it, he had before when I was here. I felt sick at my stomach at the things I had been involved in. The things that had never been proven, but from what I remembered was not pleasant. It was not by choice what had happened, but it happened just the same.

"No one can separate you from the love of God, the Bible plainly states it. No one or anything can separate us. Not only can we not be separated, we can't be taken from his hand once we are his. He can take any circumstance and use it for his glory, and he can pull you out of whatever situation you are in. God doesn't ask you to clean this up or to do this or that, he wants you and he will take you just as you are, if you will trust him."

When altar call came, I stood with the rest, Molly standing in the pew between her father and me, snuggling against her blanket. Carter left the pew and walked the aisle and dropped to his knees along with some others.

Landon remained, standing stuck still in place, his eyes closed in silent prayer.

My feet were firmly planted to the floor, my breath catching and the room suddenly becoming very warm. I felt myself sinking, and there was no way to stop it. The last I remember was arms wrapped around me. Landon was there, I know he more than likely had eased me down, the arms I felt were not human. The arms brought peace that I did not understand. Instantly, my heart lightened and I felt pure relief. A small voice was telling me, "You are my child, and I will lead you. Come to me, trust in me, and do not lean on your own understanding."

I found myself looking up at Carter in a haze, propped against his knee.

Landon, Molly, and Pastor Collins were all gathered around me as my eyes began to focus. Carter's face was pale and questioning, his beautiful, soft blue eyes pleading for a response.

"What happened? I walked the altar and you were

210

fine. I heard the others gasp, and I looked back, Landon had caught you."

"I don't know, I felt hot and a little dizzy. I'm sure it's nothing."

"Do you think you can sit up?"

I made an attempt. "I think so if you don't mind supporting me?" He assisted me up and placed himself directly behind me. I leaned against him, trying to take in a deep breath. Molly sat on her feet in the pew beside me, blanket in hand and thumb in her mouth. I smiled at her, and she soon snuggled into my arm.

"It's okay, Tink, I'm okay. Did I scare you?" Molly shook her head yes.

"I'm sorry." I kissed the crown of her head and smoothed her hair away from her face.

"You gave us a scare, are you sure you're okay?" Pastor Conley looked on in great concern and with reason. When I finally grabbed hold of my senses, everyone had left except us.

"Yes . . . Yes, I'm . . . fine," I stammered. "I'm sorry, it must be lack of sleep. I haven't slept well for a while, it must have just gotten the better of me."

"Are you ready to go home now?" Carter wrapped his arms around me and pulled me closer to him. The strength in him gave me great comfort and the feeling of security.

"Yes, I think so." Standing, I was a little shaky. I felt like I was in a rowboat on the high seas. Carter slid his arm around my waist and pulled me close guiding me. Landon had taken Molly's hand and had already led her to the door. Once at the door, I stumbled slightly but quickly recovered my equilibrium.

"Isabella?" Grabbing me tight to him, Carter's hold almost sucked the life from me. "Something is wrong."

"I'm fine, really." Trying more to assure myself as well as him, I straightened.

"We're going to see a doctor, Bella."

"No, I want to go by and see Beth."

"You're not able to do that."

"Yes, I am. I want to see if she has awakened."

"Isabella, please."

"I want to see Beth, Carter." He let out a groan and looked at me with a slight grin.

"You're a stubborn woman."

"Yes, it's one of my better qualities. It keeps me on my toes with you."

Nearing Beth's room, Carter bent down and picked Molly up and proceeded into the room. I took a seat at the opposite end of the bed, leaving the seat nearest her for Landon. Walking up to the head of the bed, he put Molly down and leaned over and kissed her softly on the forehead. Beth lay silent, never offering a response. "Hey, Neff, it's me, wake up." Did he just call her Neff? Beth never stirred, and he stepped back and watched her soberly. In full control, he stood and watched as Landon entered the room with his new son, all smiles, looking down on his tiny face and kissing the precious bundle he held. Sitting down in the rocker next to the bed, he held the baby in one arm and picked Beth's hand up in his as he took it and kissed it.

"Hey, Mommy, wake up and see this baby boy of yours." Hoping for a response that never came, he rocked the baby back and forth and hummed a sweet melody to him. Once the baby had fallen asleep, he moved Beth's arm and placed the baby in the crook of her arm and placed Beth's arm over him and supporting them both with his.

"Mommy, here's your boy." He sat close to her and supported his son as the tiny infant rubbed his head against her arm. "Beth, honey, our boy is here.

He's safe and happy. I gave him his name, the one you picked out. Gavin Carter Mason is here, and he wants to see his mommy."

My heart broke for him for it seemed Beth would

never wake up.

I blinked back the tears that burned in my eyes as he rubbed her arm and supported them.

"She wanted him named after me?" Carter stood, stunned.

"Don't be so amazed, you are her brother. Gavin is my middle name, and she wanted yours as his middle name. Cooper had no idea why she wanted to name him Gavin. I didn't know why then, it's obvious now. She told me one evening that is what she wanted."

Carter revealed a boyish grin. It was good to see the loving side of him, it made him human. Molly clamored on the bed at her side, dragging her well-worn blanket with her. She patted Beth's hand, barely touching it.

"Auntie Beth, woked up," she protested. "'Kay, I pray for you." She squeezed her eyes tight and clasped her hands together so tight that they became ghostly white.

"Pease, God, help Auntie Beth to wake. Amen." Her sweet, gentle innocence made a new pool of tears float in as one tear dropped and traced down my face to my lap. "I wuv you, Auntie Beth."

The room was still, all that could be heard was the small sounds of Gavin as he moved his head and sucked his fingers for comfort. Landon picked up his son and held his tiny body lovingly. He started to feed little Gavin, and Beth's eyes fluttered.

"Beth?" Landon leaned closer to her, still attempting to feed Gavin.

"Wake up, honey," he coaxed. "We're all here." Beth's eyes fluttered again as she slowly tried to open her eyes and focus.

"I'm waiting, Neff," Carter added. "Wake up, sissy." Beth's struggle was completed; she opened her eyes and took in a deep breath then searched the room.

"Welcome back, baby girl." Landon let out a sigh, relieved that she had woken. He took in a deep breath and blew it out slowly.

"Landon?" She looked around the room. "Carter," Beth managed, sounding panicked.

"I'm here sis, we all are." Carter's face seemed to release all the tension and anxiety of the last hours. He started to look and act more like himself.

"The baby, what happened to the baby?" Her voice trembled as he she spoke the words that seemed to be coming from her heart that I thought might break her before Landon had opportunity to speak.

"I've got him," Landon stated proudly as he rocked and fed his son. He turned to show Beth the tiny infant he cradled in his arms. Beth turned her head, following Landon's voice.

"My boys," she trembled, and tears flowed quickly down her face.

Landon sat down on the edge of the bed where Beth could see him better without interrupting Gavin's dinner. "Look, Mommy, look what a handsome boy we have." Beth gasped and choked back more tears.

"You know?"

"I know. Why didn't you tell me? I would have taken care of you. I would have never left you." Beth never said a word, but I knew the answer and he would know soon, all of it. Landon never pursued it any longer, he just looked down at her adoringly and his son. What a beautiful picture, I had never seen Landon in this light.

"He's beautiful, Beth, thank you."

"Oh," Beth cooed. "He looks so much like you. Will you forgive me for not telling you? I wanted to, but Cooper threatened to kill us both. I couldn't let him, Landon, I couldn't let him know. I'm afraid for you and the baby, I don't care about me, I got myself into this. I should have never married him. I was still in love with you, and he knew it."

Landon choked on the words that she had just

214

spoken. His face went pale, and he watched her attentively. He was anticipating what she would say next, I could see it. "Do you still love me, Beth?"

She could no longer deny her feelings; it was written all over her face that she was still very much in love with him. Carter looked down at the floor and then slanted his head back at his sister. "Tell him the truth, Beth. You have told me before, if it's true, you need to settle it." Beth looked over at her brother. "Life is too short, we almost lost you both. Don't wait."

"I don't know what to say," her voice trembled. "Cooper will never let me go, he hates me, but he doesn't want anyone else to have me either."

"Beth, do you still love me? It's a simple yes or no question." Getting up and circling the bed, he handed me Gavin. "Do you mind holding him for me?" Not saying a word, I reached for Gavin and held him close to me and rocked him gently. He snuggled into my arms as if he belonged there. I could smell the sweet smell of him that always reminded me of purity, a child that is brand-new and untouched by the world. He made some sweet noises as he put his fist to his mouth and sighed. Landon made his way back to Beth, and he knelt on one knee by her bed. Taking her hand in his, he looked into her face, and sincerity flooded him. He brought her hand to his lips and kissed it tenderly. "Beth, I asked you this before, and if you don't give me a straight answer, I will never ask it again."

"Landon, I do love you." Landon placed a finger to her lips.

"Just listen to me for a minute." He hesitated but only for a second.

"Elizabeth Jo Blake, I love you. Do you hear me? I. Love. You. None of what has happened in the past matters. I forgave you a long time ago for leaving me and marrying Cooper. I forgave you for not telling me about the baby. I need to know right here and now, will you marry me?"

Beth, now fully dumbfounded at his proposal, cried like her heart was broke. "You don't have to worry about Cooper, you press charges, I have enough to put him away for the rest of his life."

With that, Beth shook her head yes.

"Landon, yes, I will marry you." Sliding in closer to her, he hugged and kissed her gingerly. Landon leaned back, and his face and Beth's both tracked tears.

"I will never let go this time," Landon exclaimed. "We are going home as a family, you, Gavin, and I."

"Gavin," she sighed. "You remembered."

CHAPTER 11

Past Halloween and now past Thanksgiving, our unit had grown into a family of sorts. Molly had her third birthday just days after the birth of Gavin. Landon was enjoying his new family. They weren't married yet, but with not being able to find Cooper, they would be able to annul the marriage on abandonment if nothing else. Gavin was growing in leaps and bounds; he had inherited his mother's raven black hair along with his father's hazel eyes.

Beth had moved in with Landon on a permanent basis and had filed charges of assault and battery, but the court was going after two counts of attempted murder. Divorce papers had been filed with no one to sign them, Beth had signed without reluctance. Cooper had left presumably the day he left her on the floor fighting for her life.

Carter, Molly, and I had become a family of our own. Carter still insisted on courting me as he put it, even though we lived in the same home. Nothing out of reason happened, not that it couldn't, it was something he strongly believed, and it was never pushed. The longer we were together, the stronger my feelings grew. My heart soared each time I saw him. I continued my work as before, and Marilyn took a jab at me each time she had the chance. I also spent time at the training center with Gus and at the firing range taking self-defense and practicing with firearms. Carter had no idea. I didn't want him to know because I knew how he thought. If he knew, he would think I was insecure and needed him to be with me more. He had a job that he did well, and I did not need to get in his way.

The self-defense classes, no matter how long I had done them, still left me sore and depleted. It was something that was never reflected when Carter was home. Oftentimes when Molly was watching TV, I went straight to the bath and soaked in the aroma of lavender. For the most part, the nightmares had stopped, but there was always a lingering one here or there.

Christmas was upon us, it was my favorite time of the year. I always went all out with decorating, gifts, and entertaining. Christmas took me back to being a little girl lying on the floor under the tree looking at the lights. I would fall asleep there, many times admiring the twinkle of them. My intention was to have a family Christmas here this year, decorating it to the point that it would look like a Norman Rockwell painting. Carter had been gone on a business trip and had left Landon in charge of all of us. Need I say, he had his hands full basically living in an estrogen ocean with the exception of Gavin who was too young to care or attempted to do anything to manage female's emotions. He spent the last two days with us picking out a tree. I took great pains picking out the perfect one. The living room was just right for a seven-foot-tall tree.

While Landon unloaded the tree, I called Lilly and spoke with her. I hadn't seen her much since I had moved out, and I felt it was time to catch up and invite her for Christmas. She seemed very excited when she answered the telephone. She began telling me that she had met this wonderful man and that he was just right for her.

"Lily, when did you meet this guy?"

"I met him not long after you met Carter. Come to find out he works with Carter. His name is Jay Clayton, and he is an absolute dream. I call him J.C., Oh, Bella, you'll love him."

"I'm sure he is wonderful."

"I was going to call you later because I had something to tell you, it is serious."

"Okay, since you have me now, what is it?" I was expecting anything but what came out of her mouth next.

"Bella, I'm getting married, and I want you and Carter there, and bring Beth and Landon too. I want you to stand up with me."

"Lily, aren't you rushing things a bit?"

"We aren't getting any younger, Bella, and besides I found him, finally, after all this time. This is what I want. Please, just be happy for me."

"Of course I am."

"Have you and Carter talked about getting married?"

"No . . . not yet. I'm not sure that I'm ready for that, but if he asked, I'm sure I wouldn't turn it down either. I come with a lot of baggage, I really don't know if he or I are ready for what we might have to deal with." There was a brief lull in the conversation. "I called, Lilly, because I would like for you to have Christmas with us. You can bring Jay with you, I'm sure there won't be a problem. I miss having you to talk to."

"I would love to come. I'll see you soon, call me again when you get a chance, okay?" With that, she hung up. I could hear a male voice in the background calling for her. Sliding the cell phone in my pocket I sat down with a box of ornaments beside Beth.

"You really get into this, don't you?" Beth started going through the ornaments; she picked them up and gazed at them, admiring them.

"Christmas has always been my favorite time of the year. People do not seem as stingy or shutoff. Most of them are more charitable and loving, it makes me feel like a little kid."

"You are a true romantic, Bella." She smiled, so that she glowed.

"This is the happiest I have ever seen you, Landon is good for you."

"I never realized how much I missed him or loved him. He doubts on me constantly, and Gavin is going to be very spoiled. He carries him constantly."

"He loves you, Beth, he has for a long time."

"He had never told me until we were in the hospital, after I had Gavin. I knew he did, but he would never say it. I knew he meant it when he told me and then asked me to marry him. After all I have put him through and the years we spent apart, he still loved me. I was never sure."

"He loves you, Beth. I have seen it since day one."

The cell phone rang. Looking down, I saw it's him. It's Carter, and I picked up quickly.

"Hello."

"Bella, didn't take you long to answer. You missing me?"

"Yes, I was hoping it was you. When are you coming home?" My voice shook with excitement and my heart quickened, I couldn't wait to see him.

"I should be home in about an hour or so." I could hear his smile over the phone.

"Good, I have a surprise for you."

"Oh, well, maybe I should come home a little faster."

"Don't do anything that will get you hurt, I want you home in one piece."

He chuckled. "You don't have to worry, I'll behave myself."

"One thing before you go, I want to have a family Christmas here this year, if it is okay with you of course."

"You know I'm not going to deny you, although I can't see my parents coming."

Hesitating, I marveled at what he was saying. "Your parents, I didn't think . . . Never mind what I thought."

"Did you think they didn't exist?"

"No, you just have never spoken of them."

"We will. I'm getting into some heavy traffic, I better go. I'll see you soon."

"See you soon." I squealed with delight. "He's

coming home."

"Isabella, really, you're worse than some teenager."

"I've got so much to do before he gets here. He will be here in about an hour."

Landon walked into the room with the stand for the tree, observing the excitement.

"What's going on?"

"Carter's coming home," Beth said in an exaggerated response then giggling at me.

"Come on, guys, I haven't seen him in two days."

"Could it be the love bug has bitten you, Ms. Bella?" Landon joked then started setting up the beautiful pine we all had brought home.

"I do believe it's bitten someone else, Mr. Mason. Have you looked at yourself lately?"

Landon stepped away from the tree, which was now standing straight as an arrow. "I would love to tease you endlessly, but some lady I know demanded that this tree be set up in a hurry."

I smiled at him, knowing it was me he was talking about. "Now I wonder who that could be." We all let out a hearty laugh. Molly heard the commotion and joined us.

"Tan I put the orgaments on, Mommy?"

"Orgaments?"

Molly was very matter-of-fact, shaking her head, exaggerating. "You know, orgaments, the things on the tree, orgaments."

I couldn't help but laugh, it was so cute. "You mean ornaments, and yes, you may help us." She jumped up and down and started clapping her hands.

Her little face beamed with excitement.

If only Carter could see this. The assurance was that he would be here soon, and it wouldn't be soon enough. The evening drew on, and it was getting late. He was at least forty-five minutes late. I began to pace the floor with the others not really noticing. Beth was busy with feeding

221

Gavin, and Landon was entertaining Molly. I guess the Grinch was entertaining enough for her at the time. Supper would wait, but not for much longer. The table was set, the candles were lit, all that was missing was Carter. Looking out the window, I saw snow starting to fall and there was at least two new inches of snow on what had already been on the ground.

Turning, I went back to the kitchen and checked on supper when I heard the latch on the door. I ran to the door, but he had opened it and was standing inside, shaking off his coat. "Hello, angel, sorry I'm late." I grabbed him and hugged him, not saying a word, fear had consumed me. He laid his coat across the chair at the door and hugged me tight.

"Glad you missed me." He kissed the top of my head. "I'm late because I stopped to pick up a surprise for you." I could hear chatter following, the sound of familiar voices. Letting loose of Carter enough to look around him, I saw them walk in, shocked at who I saw.

"Momma, Daddy?"

"There's my baby girl." My father dropped his things at the door and pulled me into him, and I cried uncontrollably. It had been almost a year since I had seen either of them.

"I think you better give Mom a turn." He stepped back, and Mom stood in front of me with a beautiful smile and her arms open wide.

"How's my little girl?"

"Momma, I'm fine. I'm so glad to see you and Daddy. I was so worried.

Carter was supposed to be home almost an hour ago."

Carter looked over at me and smiled. "Am I forgiven?" His eyes twinkled and shined.

"Of course you are." I stood on tiptoes and kissed his cheek.

"Come in, Momma, Daddy. I want you to meet the rest of the family."

They followed me in to the living room. Molly ran to Carter when she discovered her father was home. I introduced them to Landon, Beth, and Molly and told them of little Gavin. "Of course you have met Carter."

"Yes, your Carter is a fine young man," my mother boasted. "He picked us up at the airport. Our flight was delayed that's why we were late."

Carter's face turned red from the compliment. "Your mother is a charmer, she just might take me away from you." He grinned widely. I couldn't be upset with him; he had brought me a wonderful gift even if he had been late. Being late on a snowy night like tonight was bad enough, but I hadn't seen him for a couple of days and I had missed him more than I could have imagined. I was just glad to see him home.

My eyes set on him. "Dinner is on the stove, everyone, help yourself."

Carter had gotten my meaning as everyone else filed into the dining room and kitchen, leaving us there alone. He remained in front of me, and I loved that he knew what I wanted, a few minutes alone with him. He slid his arms around my waist and looked down at me. "Ms. Cameron, you are beaming.

What happened to you while I was away, and what have you done to the house?"

"I'm so glad you're home." Stepping a little closer and I tightened my grip around his waist as he rested his arms at the small of my back. Looking up at him, he had that normal adorable boyish response of his.

"I decided we needed some Christmas, so Landon helped me get a tree, it's mostly decorated. I left one very important piece for you to do. Beth helped with garland while Gavin was down for his nap, and Molly did the orgaments on the tree." I grinned as I remember her.

223

"Orgaments?" Carter raised a brow that caused a crease to form on his forehead.

Laughing at his response and Molly's choice of words, I explained.

"Orgaments, you know, the things Molly says goes on the tree."

"Well, I haven't heard that one before, she comes up with some good ones." He kissed my forehead and gave me a squeeze.

"I can't believe you're here, I'm glad you're home."

"So am I. I missed you, but I think we better join the rest before they think we abandoned them."

Spending the evening with my parents was a treat, I loved that Carter had done this. He had this planned before he left. He would take care of the business end, then he would pick up my parents on the way home, but he hadn't planned on the weather delaying the flight.

With the confined room, Landon had taken Gavin and Beth home.

My parents took my room so I set up in Molly's room with her. One short story and she was off to sleep. She was never difficult to be put to bed; some simple lullaby or a story was enough. Carter had come in before story time and kissed his daughter sweetly, and she had giggled with glee. I watched her face, she was almost as happy to see him as I had been.

I covered her up and placed her blanket beside her. The night before her father had come home, she had cried for him, and it had nearly broken my heart. Molly lay now in her bed sleeping in complete peace.

Walking away, I stood in front of the gold-framed mirror above her antique dresser. Mom had brought me a delicate white gown that was adorned with lace, ribbons, and pin tucks fitting the innocence of an untouched bride. She meant well and it was beautiful, but it only served as a reminder of what I could no longer offer. I ran my finger

224

over the rim of the lace that came just short of the peak of my chest. Feminine and delicate in its appearance, making me feel like a woman, but the feeling also brought the thought that I could never be brought back to innocence. Picking up the robe, I pulled it on over my shoulders and then pulled my hair from the collar, allowing it to cascade over my shoulders. I looked at my reflection deeply as I dragged the brush through my hair and then set it down on the surface of the dresser. Turning, I walked toward the kitchen, finding Carter sitting on the couch, unaware of my entrance to the room.

"Pop, it's only a couple of days . . . The place isn't going to fall in if you aren't there . . . Yes, I know . . . I know . . . I want you to meet her. You'll love her, Pop . . . No . . . No . . . She is good with Molly and Molly loves her . . .

Yes, I know . . . Yes. I do . . . Will you at least think about it, I would like to have both families here for Christmas . . . Okay, give me a call . . . Let me know and I'll pick you up . . . Miss you too, Pop. Tell Mom I love her."

I walked toward him, and he turned around. "Hey, I thought you would be asleep by now."

"I couldn't forget about you." I couldn't believe what was coming out of my mouth. It was true, I wanted to be with him every second. He patted the seat beside him, "Come sit by me." He didn't have to ask me twice. Sitting down by him still shook every nerve in me. I had been closing in on three months since I met him and the sight of him still made me weak in the knees.

"You look gorgeous, Bella. I don't think in the few months we have known each other I have seen you this happy."

"I found someone that understands me, someone who is able to look over my past and still want me for who I am." Carter shifted in his seat.

225

"Did you ever doubt what I feel for you?" His face became serious. "Bella, I know what I want. I always have."

Tipping my head so I could look directly into his face, I could see he was earnest in what he was saying. I never doubted his feelings for a second.

"I don't want you to get the wrong idea, I believe you, I just don't understand." I looked down at my hands as I fumbled with the buttons on my robe." Carter cleared his throat and tipped the glass in his hand for a drink.

The ice in the glass clinked on the side. He was giving me opportunity to elaborate, in which I didn't.

"What don't you understand, Bella?"

Shrugging, I never lifted my face to his. "I just don't . . . feel like I'm worthy of your affection. I feel like damaged goods. I certainly don't feel like I'm someone that is wife material for you. My innocence, it's gone, Carter."

The glass shook the ice as it landed on the table. He tilted my face toward him so that he was looking into my eyes, to my very soul.

"Isabella, I don't ever want to hear that again. Being pure, it's wonderful, but what happened to you was not of your choosing. It was brutal and cruel, it should have never happened. I know it carries guilt, but you have to let go of it. The guilt belongs to the man, men or otherwise that did this to you. As far as I am concerned, it's gone, it's over, a chapter in your life that is over, it's done. To me, you're innocent. I've never touched you. You are my life, a survivor, and I'm proud to say you're mine." He ran his long fingers down the side of my face, and it sent chills through me. "I love you, you have to believe that."

His words took me by surprise, I had no idea. My hand fanned across my chest, feeling that I might faint. Getting a grip on myself, tears welled in my eyes and a smile slowly filled my face. Relief had flooded me, and I was between laughing and crying.

"What?" He searched me and studied my face and my actions.

"I can't believe what you just said to me. I'm not sure I heard you right."

"You want to hear it again?" He smiled and chuckled when he realized what I had meant. "Isabella, I love you. I'll say it as often as I have to so that you will come to believe it. You know what?"

"What?" I beamed at him.

"I'll do one better. I have one of your Christmas presents in my pocket, one of which was a point of my trip. I have one other that I went for, but you will have to wait for that one."

"We weren't going to exchange presents until Christmas Eve."

"I know, but I'm like a little kid in a candy store."

"If you're going to give me a gift, can I give you one?"

He thought a moment, and then he answered, "Yes, I guess that's fair."

Jumping to my feet, I headed to the tree and pulled up a small gold box. I knew it was perfect for him. Grandfather told me it had been in his family a very long time. It had been passed down from a father to a son-in-law for as long as he could remember, but since there were no daughters, he had given it to me to pass on to someone that was special to me. He had told me, "I want you to give it to your young man. The man you intend on marrying.

When you have a son and he takes a wife, it is to go to him. It is a ring of protection and good fortune. It is meant to protect the leader of the family and the family he leads. The ring is very old, and it is said to have protective qualities in it. It has been blessed and has been dipped in the River Jordan.

Please have him wear it on his left ring finger, remember what I say."

I bounced back to the couch in front of him filled with excitement. Like a child, I trembled with excitement and anticipation. "Open mine first." After handing him the gift with both hands, he took it in his. "It's something my grandfather gave me, he wanted someone special to me to have it."

"It must be something for you to be this excited." Sliding in closer to him, I hooked my arm through his. When he opened the box, the look on his face was priceless. "Bella, honey, where did you say you got this?"

"My grandfather, he wore it. His father-in-law had given it to him. He wore it, and many other men in the family had worn it. It was said that it held protective properties and has been dipped in the River Jordan. He told me that the person that wore it was to wear it on their left ring finger. I'm sure it's an old wives' tale, but it is a personal piece, I wanted you to have it."

"My ring finger?"

I shook my head, smiling at him, waiting to see what his next reaction was going to be.

"Isabella, I think your grandpa wanted you to have this. It was meant for your husband."

"I know," I whispered. "It was meant for protection of a relationship and the leader of the home. I want you to have it. If you don't want to wear it, it's okay, but I would like for you to keep it." I wasn't sure now what his reaction was going to be.

"Bella, I don't know what to say." He was obviously touched by the gift and took it from the box and examined it. The ring was two-tone and had a gold cross in the center of a silver field, otherwise very plain but attractive.

"Do you like it?"

"I love it. You sure you want me to have this?"

"Yes, I couldn't be surer of anything."

He smiled broadly. "You never cease to amaze me,

Isabella." He handed me the ring. "I will wear it, but for now, I want you to put it on my right ring finger." I looked at him, a little puzzled. "When the time comes, you can put the ring on the finger where it belongs." I took his hand and slid it on his finger, and it fitted perfectly.

"My gift isn't that flashy, at least this one isn't." He pulled four tickets from his pocket and handed them to me.

"They're tickets for *Cinderella*. We're going to the theater?"

"Yes, if you want to go, I can exchange them if you want to see something else."

"No, I love it. It's one of my favorites, thank you." I leaned in to kiss his cheek. I took in the smell of his cologne mixed with his own scent and the feel of his skin against my lips. He definitely left me intoxicated. My body shook inside with excitement, feeling more like a child at Christmas, but then again more like a woman totally in love. I didn't want to admit it to myself, but I had fallen for him, hard. There was no recovery from this if he walked away. I was his; and there was no doubt, little by little, he had won my heart and the feelings grew deeper and larger every day.

"There are four tickets here."

"I thought your parents might want to go, Molly can stay with Landon and Beth. She couldn't sit that long anyway. I thought we might meet

Landon, Beth, and the kids later for a late dinner so we could all be together.

I do have other gifts for you, this one just happened to be early."

"You sure this is okay with Landon and Beth, they do have their hands full."

"I have already talked to Landon and to Beth, and they are fine with it. I want you to wear your prettiest dress and go do all the little things women do before a date. Take Lily, Beth, and your mom with you, it's on me."

"Lily is going with us too?"

"Lily and J.C., they already have their tickets, and possibly my parents."

"You know about J.C.?"

"Yes, I know. Lily is all he can talk about."

"Did you know they are getting married?"

"He told me that he was going to ask her. I couldn't say much, we both know you have stolen my heart. I can't tell him that he isn't ready, maybe he is. I hope Lily is ready to be a detective's wife."

"I think she is. She is a lot stronger than I am. I wonder every time you walk out that door if you will be coming home."

"It's a chance we all live with, even you."

"Me?"

"Bella, you never know what is going to walk into that door. Anyone could come in there with a gun. a needle stick that had been used on someone with a life-threatening disease, your job is just as dangerous."

"We both know your job isn't the safest in the world. I never know when or if you are going to come through that door. I can't help it. I don't know what I would do if something happened to you."

Carter ran his fingers down the side of my face, his touch soft as a feather.

"You aren't going to get a chance to find out."

Moving in closer to him I lay my head against his chest. The beat of his heart was soothing. His arms wrapped around me gave me comfort from the panic that had filled me earlier. He was home, and I was wrapped in his arms where I fitted perfect. My promised hand lay softly against his chest, and I could smell his cologne that had become so familiar to me. I was his and his alone. I had come to believe that. My mind drifted as his cheek lay against the crown of my head. *God, if you can hear me,* thank *you. He's more than my heart could have ever dreamed of. I don't know that you even care about what I think after all the sin that has been in my life. I know he is one of the best things that have ever come into my life. Please protect him and bring him back to me, back home where he belongs. I couldn't bear it if something happened to him.*

The living room was lit barely from the breaking dawn. I found myself on the couch alone covered with a quilt. I looked around slowly. Not seeing Carter, I picked the quilt up and laid it across the top of the couch. Walking back to his bedroom, I looked around. He was nowhere to be seen. Walking to the bathroom where the door was barely open, I looked in. The light was out, and there was no sign he had been there or that his bed had been slept in.

Walking to Molly's room, I glanced in so as not to wake her, to only find that he was not there. I felt a chill run down my back, one of unease and regret that I hadn't told him how I felt about him. I loved him, there, I admitted to myself. Finally after all this time, I did indeed love him. I walked slowly through the house to find a note on the coffee table that was carefully placed where I would find it.

Bella,
I had to leave. I got called out about 3:00 a.m., but I should be back before everyone is awake. There has been a death at the old warehouse, not sure what has happened. Landon is with me, so if Beth needs something, she will be calling you. We will talk soon, something I wanted to discuss last night but didn't get the chance.
I love you. I'll see my girls soon.
Carter

I held the note clutched in my hand against my chest. What if he didn't come back, what if last night had been it? No, no, I couldn't think like that, it would eventually drive me crazy. This was part of his job, and he

231

knew how to protect himself. I had to depend on it. Right now, it was all I had.

I sat on the edge of the couch recounting when we had met. He was dependent on me for a short time, but he was sure and confident of what God could do; and if he didn't restore his sight, he would have handled it.

He was just as sure that he had met me because of God's grace. We needed each other, and God saw to it that we met. Looking down on his bruised cheek and the cuts, he had peace, a peace that I didn't understand, that's what had intrigued me. Remembering picking the glass from his hair and staring into his face, wondering what had happened, why this gentle soul had been brought to me and the feeling of needing to keep him alive not for just him, for me.

Never forgetting the first touch, the first kiss that had sent electricity through me, not understanding what I felt. I still had trouble with understanding that, what I felt and how I felt for him was a normal thing and was not dirty or dreadful. He was the right man for me, he loved me for who I was in spite of what had happened before him, no matter what else might come out, it didn't matter.

"Bella . . . honey."

Looking around, he stood beside me and made a slow descent to the couch. I wondered why he looked puzzled. Then I realized, I had been crying and had gripped the blanket and the note to my chest. My legs were drawn into me, and my face was wet from tears. I was shocked to see him. I hadn't heard him walk in. I was so taken by my thoughts I hadn't heard him.

"Bella, you okay?" He laid his hand against my face and I dropped the note and it floated to the floor. Throwing my arms around his neck I kissed him without hesitation. He wrapped his arms around me slowly, not understanding what had happened. I wanted him, now, and it didn't matter there was a whole house full of people. It didn't matter my

232

parents were two doors down from where I sat. By this point, he understood I wasn't passing on this. I initiated on something I knew I would finish if he wasn't strong enough to stop it. I understood his reasoning, but the thought that was brought to mind was that we had no guarantee of tomorrow. It was important to me to let him know I was his and that I loved him. Yes, it was wrong in God's eyes. I knew that. I also knew it was important to him, but it was the only way I felt I could be close to him. This was my way of connecting with him, something that I could share with him. I wanted to wipe out every negative experience I had with my aggressor, this animal that had caused me such great pain and replace it with the loving touch and intimacy that Carter's touch promised.

I could barely take a breath; feeling his heart beat thunderously under my hands. His breathing increasing and a hiss released from him when I ran small subtle kisses from his jaw into the crook of his neck. My hands ran through his unruly, thick dark hair; the feel of it through my fingers reminded me of silk, soft and light against my hands. Standing up from the couch, I never turned from him. I watched his face for any disagreement and met none. He looked at me with great affection and love. Taking him by the hand, I walked backward toward his room. His eyes locked with mine, and he followed me. After the last step into his room, he shut the door behind him.

He gazed down at me, his face at ease but his breath catching. His blue eyes searched me as if he was asking questions, and I was giving no answer.

He stood stock-still and looked at me in bewilderment. The tears were gone, and I was totally into seducing him. I had turned into a woman he didn't know. Reaching for him, I pushed his jacket off his shoulders, and it fell to the floor. Continually I looked into his face, losing myself in his beautiful deep blue eyes. His hands were placed on my waist, but he was not pushing away. My eyes

233

continued staying fixed on his as I slowly started to unbutton his navy blue button down, one button at a time, tracing my finger down his chest as I went. Making it finally to his waist, I pulled his shirt and then unbuttoned the cuffs so they fell free. Running my hands against his chest, I felt the soft prickle of chest hair against my hand. I traced his chest down to the rim of his jeans and let my hands run up his back and over his shoulders to remove his shirt. I stood and admired him; my hands against his well-developed body. Workouts had made him firm and sculpted. Leaning in, I kissed him delicately, the first time my eyes had left his face since he stood before me. Carter's hand tilted my face once more to his. He was so close to me the heat radiated off him onto my body, now sure of my intent. "Bella, if we do this, we can't take it back. I don't think I'm strong enough to stop it this time."

"I don't want you to stop." My voice trembled as did my body under his touch. "I want this. I want to feel close to you, I need it, It's all I want. I want you to take all the pain away, all the bad memories of what that hideous man did to me and to know I have you, that you love me."

"I do love you. I want more than anything to be with you."

"I want you, Carter. I want you more than I can ever imagine wanting anyone in my life."

I began kissing his chest once more, tracing my fingers down his arms, and Carter's response hit me. His eyes closed briefly, then he breathed deep and let it out slowly. Opening his eyes he looked at me like he could see through to my soul. Stepping back just enough for him to see a full view of me, I removed my robe, revealing only the gown that I had thought hours ago had shown me as a bride, untouched and innocent. I had no intention on stopping, I wanted this. All I wanted was his love, the feel of his hands on me. He stepped closer, and I never made a move to walk away. I took in some deep breaths and closed my eyes as he approached me. Picking me up like a baby, he deposited me gently on his bed and removed the comforter from under me. His touch was so feather light I could barely feel it. Lying there with him looking down at me, I still wondered what he was going to do.

Bending toward me, he kissed me passionately, with more fire than I thought possible. Kissing my cheek and down my neck, he pushed my gown over to the side to trail kisses to my shoulder.

Looking down on me once more I could tell he was troubled by what was happening, but it had gotten the best of him. He deftly and slowly started to unbutton my gown and started to push it back. "Isabella, dear God, you're beautiful." His hands shook as he started to touch me then he drew them back into a fist at his sides. Rising from the bed he stood and replaced his shirt and drew in a sharp breath. I couldn't help but feel rejected and hurt.

"Why did you stop?" I started to choke back tears. He didn't want me after all. It was this man, this animal of a man that had stopped something yet again that I wanted and hurt someone that I loved. This was too good to be true, I knew it. Carter sat on the edge of the bed with his shirt on, but it remained unbuttoned.

"Bella, you are my lady, I need to protect you, and unfortunately, that also means from me. I want our first experience to mean something. If I do this now, I'm no better than the man that abused you."

"I see, you don't want me either." I sat up on the bed and slowly buttoned my gown once more.

"No, Bella, that's not it at all. I want you more than you could imagine, but I made you a promise. When it's right, God will make it beautiful for us both. You are untouched by me, it has made you an innocent in my book no matter what that monster did to you. I love you, as bad as I want this . . ." He rubbed the back of his neck in frustration.

"Carter, I want this, I want you to be a part of me. You, just being here, consumes me, every breath, every feeling every time my heart beats. I can't sleep unless I'm next to you. I can't function, and simple tasks are difficult.

I'm in deep here, and I don't know what to do next."

"Let it be, Bella, it will happen." He placed his hands on my shoulders, forcing me to look at him. "I love you. I've already told you that. It came on just like it should have. It wasn't rushed, and it can't be. My love for you isn't going away just because we aren't acting on it."

"I knew this was too good to be true. You don't want me because of him, nobody does." My heart broke as I realized at the thought he didn't want me, not the way I wanted him.

"Isabella, listen to what I'm saying to you. It is simple as this. I am in love with a beautiful woman. That woman deserves to have a loving husband on a wedding night that she has dreamed of all her life. I know you better than you think. You want the white gown with the flowers on the perfect day in a church surrounded by family. You want a honeymoon somewhere romantic with a man that loves you and will love and take care of you for the rest of their life. Am I right?" All I could do was look at him. "I can bet you right now that you stood and looked in the mirror when you were little and dreamed of that day, dressed up in one of your mother's dresses with too big a heels and a veil made out of a sheet or towel thinking about the man you would marry. I get it, I get it, Bella. Don't ever think for one second that I am not enamored of you."

His words tore me like a knife. He did know, he did understand, and I was lost. It didn't take the desire away from me. "What could have happened here, Bella, would not have taken the pain away he put you through, no one can. God is the only one that could help me when Andrea was going through her struggle, and he is the only one that

236

can help you. I'm here, I'm not going anywhere." His arms then reached for me and I sunk into him.

"You don't understand." I sniffed back tears that threatened to choke me.

The only thing I knew was I loved him, and I lived in fear now of losing him.

He sat holding me tight against his chest, and he kissed the top of my head. In a voice that was obviously distressed, he voiced his feelings. "I understand more than you know, Bella." My soul shattered before him, and the feeling of loss was totally evident to me. I was in the same room with his arms around me, but I couldn't have felt more alone if I had been secluded somewhere on a deserted island.

Carter rocked me in his arms and pushed the tears from my face as I leaned into him. "We'll get through this, Isabella. Please, don't give up."

CHAPTER 12

The day had turned cold and damp. With the chill and snow, it seemed colder than usual. Not wanting to but doing, I went on with my day as nothing had happened between Carter and me. It was a struggle. I wasn't sure how I felt about our earlier encounter. I was ashamed of how I felt about him and how I had acted on it. I knew that I loved him and lived in fear of what he must feel about me. Nothing felt like it made sense anymore. I was hurt and felt rejected, but in respect to Carter, I knew he was right. I could never remember being the one that initiated anything of an intimate nature.

The family had eaten, and I had retreated to my room for a time trying to regain my composure. I sat on the chaise lounge in front of the bay window hoping to understand. Sitting with the quilt lain over me, I watched the waves crash as they hit the beach. The water looked dicey, cold, and fierce even in the winter as it rushed in to meet the shore. My parents were sitting at the breakfast table with Carter and Molly, enjoying their company. I'm sure my mother was already in tune to something being on edge. I wasn't good at hiding my feelings, and I didn't expect it to be better now.

Looking over on the table beside me there was a carefully placed Bible on it. More than likely he had sat it there, hoping that I would one day pick it up. At this point, I felt anything was better than what I was feeling. Picking it up, it fell open to 2 Timothy 1:7: "For God hath not given us the spirit of fear; but of power, and of love and of sound mind." The scripture hit me like a ton of bricks. God never wanted us to live in fear and not be consumed with ourselves. We have the power to overcome and help others; he gives a peace we will never understand. This was what Carter was talking about, having peace that went beyond our understanding, the peace that I saw in him. In my heart, I could hear a voice speaking within me. "Come to me, daughter, and I will make you whole." The thought of God speaking to me scared me to death. If he could speak to me, he knew everything that had ever gone on in my life, and I was doomed for sure. I lay it back down on the table beside me. My heart longed for more, but I couldn't. Fear was my greatest enemy. I wanted to try and leave the fear behind, just let it all go, but it hung around my neck like a noose, sucking the life out of me. I picked it up again and held it to me, trying to take comfort from it and opening it once more, fighting the fear that consumed me. The Bible seemed to have a mind of its own, falling open to 1 Peter 5:7. "Casting all your care upon him; for he careth for you." My mind started to settle. God cares about me, he cared about how I felt and he could take care of it. The verse found me on my knees beside the chaise. I attempted anything I could so that God would hear me. "God, I don't know what to do anymore, I'm troubled and fearful, and you are all I have left. I don't know what it is I have to do, but I know you have the answer. I'm scared. I don't know what is going to come out from my past. I don't want to lose what you have given me. Carter is the best thing that has ever happened to me, and I don't want to lose him because of my insecurities.

I want to show him how I feel, but I don't know how. I want what he has, God, the peace of knowing who you are and what I'm to do to serve you.

God, help me not to live in constant fear. Thank you for hearing me." Wiping my face and turning to stand, I found Carter standing there, looking a little hurt but more concerned.

"I didn't mean to interrupt."

"Ah, no, you weren't interrupting me." Feeling a little naked from what he had witnessed, I wasn't sure how long he had been there.

"Your mom is starting to ask questions as to why you disappeared. I kind of knew, but I made some excuse so you had some time to yourself."

He stepped toward me, knowing that I was past being vulnerable, and took my hands in his. "If you want to talk, I'm here. If you would rather talk to someone else, I can arrange that. I know I'm not going to be the easiest to talk to right now." He looked down at my hands and rubbed his thumbs over them. "I want you to be happy, Bella. I don't want you to be fearful of what you feel. This is partly my fault, I'm sorry. I should have not let it go that far."

"It's okay, I understand." I did understand, but I never made a step to get closer to him. My feelings for him ran raw and cut me like a knife. I loved the comfort of his touch, but for now, it hurt. It hurt me that I couldn't be any closer. My feelings for him were far from being restrained.

"Isabella, don't you think I know you better by now?" He looked at me in a way I had never seen before. "I know what you're feeling."

"Then why did you stop me?" I snapped at him. It was something I thought I would never do. "Why? I wanted to be with you. I needed to feel you next to me. It makes every bad feeling and fear leave. I have times where I feel like my next breath will never come. You rejected me, Carter, hurt and vulnerability is only half of what I'm feeling. You could have left me last night and I would have never been able to touch you again, never be able to see you, to feel your arms around me. Every minute of the day you aren't with me, I'm incomplete. I have allowed you to unlock me, everything that I am, and I can't stop it. I can't stop what I feel about you." The pain and the anger had surfaced with every breath. "The monster that raped me and left me shattered in pieces, he took everything from me. My innocence, my youth, and my future and left me with nothing. I didn't even know I could feel anything for anyone until I met you."

240

Carter approached me, gingerly reaching for me. "Can I hold you?" He held his arms open for me. "You don't have to if you don't want to." Standing there watching him, knowing what I had said, I couldn't understand where all the anger had come from. I would have never raised my voice to him before or to tread on the subjects I hit. I took some deep breaths, never moving.

He stepped closer and slowly wrapped his arms around me, and I shuddered.

I made no attempt for a moment to reciprocate his gesture. "Angel, I can't promise you nothing will ever happen to me. It's not my decision, but I will tell you this, my choice is to be here with you. I'm never going to leave you."

Carter kissed me on the forehead, and my eyes closed and I was unable to resist putting my arms around him. It was crazy for me not to respond, we both knew that my feelings for him weren't nonexistent.

The door behind us rattled. We continued to stay as we were. Who cared if someone walked in? I wasn't trying to hide my feelings, and Carter never budged. His cheek brushed against mine, and he whispered softly, "Take it one step at a time. I'm here, I'm never leaving."

I could hear the footsteps leave as I stood still. This was where I belonged, I fitted perfectly with him. "I want to talk to you if you don't mind." I shook my head yes, and he guided me down to the chaise and sat beside me. Sitting with his forearms on his legs and his hands clasped, he seemed to think intently and then ran his hand through his unruly dark hair. "Isabella, I heard your prayer and I'm glad you are starting to think in that context. I've wanted to talk to you about God and what it means to be saved and what it means for us as a couple. God has a plan for all of us, and he has a way that he wants us to live, and even though we may want to do it different, his way is perfect. It's always right, even if we don't understand it."

Carter shifted a little and turned toward me. "God has put me in a place, I believe, to talk to you about what he wants. Bella, he loves you, no matter what has happened. Once you accept him, all things that you have done, seen, thought, heard that was not of God is gone. He forgets them, and you are a new person. We are created for him and for his pleasure to carry out a mission. You see, God has a purpose to everything, his purpose for us is to ask forgiveness and to serve him." He sat for a moment and thought and ran his hand across his unshaven face. "I'm not very good at this. Okay, we were all born into sin. Babies are born with a sin nature. None of us are without sin, but when God sent his son, he sent him to a dying world. He knew that man would fall, and he made a way for them to come to him, and that way was through the death of his own son, a perfect sacrifice. The only bridge between us and God is through the blood of Jesus, his son. Jesus died on a cross for the salvation of all, everyone that would accept him as their savior, and all we have to do is to ask and to believe in him. We are saved and preserved for him. No one or anything can take us from him. When we die, we are going to end up in one of two places. Sin separates us from him, and those who do not accept him, hell is their home for eternity. Our soul lives on even after our mortal body is gone. Because all people are sinners, even I, we all deserve hell. God can't look upon sin, he allowed his son to die on a cross, he was buried in a borrowed grave, and as God had told before, he rose on the third day and returned to heaven. If we repent for our sins, he forgives us and we have the gift of eternal life. God has the power to take the fear and the pain away, Bella. He has the power, let him."

"I don't know, Carter, I can't live a perfect life."

"That's just it, angel, you don't have to. You live your life for him, we aren't perfected until we are in heaven, but he does expect us to live for him. I can't do it for you, you have to be ready and accept him yourself." He looked at me warmly, looking straight through me as if I were a pane of glass. "More than anything, I want to see you come to God, but I want the assurance, Bella, that when something does happen to me, I want to see you coming toward me, I want to walk the streets of heaven with you."

I didn't think I could have been more touched by him. As much as my heart longed for him, it now wanted everything he did. I wanted to be here with him, but even more, I never wanted to be separated from him even in death. "You think about it, Bella. When you're ready, God will me meet you where you are. I promise you that."

The days went on before Christmas, and it was the day that Carter had planned on us to see *Cinderella*. Lily, Beth, Mom, and I were preparing for our outing at the spa. Tangles, I was sure, would be busy with this crew. The spa was always a welcome sight. I rarely went for the whole treatment, but this was a gift from Carter. Tonight would be wonderful, I could feel it. My mother always made things fun, and this was going to be no exception. We were all going to the spa for some pampering. Jonah would be taking care of our hair, and it was unsure as to who would and what other services Carter 1 had taken care of. We all reached the door laughing and enjoying our day when Jonah and Carter met us at the door of the spa.

I was surprised to see Carter there. He stood at the entrance with Jonah with a boyish grin. Jonah stepped toward us eagerly. "Welcome, ladies, welcome. Won't you come in and enjoy yourself?" I looked back at my mother, and she placed a hand on my shoulder and nodded with an approving grin. I took a half a step and was met by my handsome date for tonight.

"What are you doing here?" I smiled at him, thinking how handsome he was. He took my hand and looped it through his arm. "I'm here to escort my angel to her room of dreams." I could actually feel my eyes sparkle at him as he watched me. "Not that I feel you need a makeover, just something to add to this evening." He walked me to a back room where we were alone. The room was filled with the sound of a rushing ocean and seagulls. The aroma lifted through the room of peppermint, and the lights were dimmed to a relaxing level. In the middle of the room was a massage table with towels, sheets, and robe ready for use.

"This is wonderful . . . but isn't it a little pricey?"

He turned me to face him and framed my face with his hands, his eyes reflecting me. "I want you to enjoy yourself. I don't want you to ever forget this. This is our night, and I have a lot planned for you, so I'm going to have a little pampering myself, not something that happens often, and I will see you this evening." He started to turn away then he rejoined me. Placing a finger to his lips and then letting it fall, he took a step toward me. "Just one more thing, don't worry about what you will wear, I have it covered." Leaning in with a sneaky grin, he kissed me quickly and walked to the door. He was met by a very pretty tall, slender blonde. "Bella, this is Monica. She will be taking care of you today, and Jonah will take care of the rest. I love you, see you tonight." With that, he winked and walked out the door.

"Ms. Cameron, I will serve you today." Monica stepped forward and shook my hand; her grip was soft and delicate. "Mr. Blake has left specific instructions for us, so we must get started." Handing me a robe and showing me to the dressing room, she led with her hand toward the door. "Please take your time, undress only to the point that you feel comfortable." Her smile was warm and was ready to take care of any need I might have. Stepping into the dressing room, I found it luxurious. I was not there long before my mother entered from the opposite end of the room.

"Isabella, isn't this wonderful?" She met me,

carrying her own robe and preparing to change. "Your Carter is a wonderful man."

"Yes, Momma, he is." After changing, I had sat down on the chair in front of a well-lit mirror. She could hear the questioning in my voice.

"What is it, honey? I know something is bothering you, and it has been since the morning after we got here. Daddy has even noticed. It takes a lot for him to notice anything."

"I love him, Momma."

She sighed then she giggled softly at the statement. "I know that. You can see it, it's as plain as it can be."

"That's not it, Momma. I haven't told you everything."

She sat down in the chair beside me, laying her robe across her lap. "Then what is it, honey? You should be happy."

"I am, but, Momma, things are starting to come back to me. Things that I didn't think would make a difference, but they do." I twirled the sash on my robe and wound it around my fingers.

"Does Carter know about any of this?"

"Yes, he does."

"Then what is there to worry about, Bella? Carter loves you. He wouldn't do this for just anyone. Look on this as a blessing."

"Momma, I remember Jenna. I remember partially the attack, and I don't know what else he did to me or how many. I have scars on me that have never been explained, and my feelings the fears of what I'm feeling seem to be getting in the way."

"Isabella, only you have the control to stop this. Carter is a good and understanding man, let him make the decision of what he thinks he needs to do. You can't be afraid all your life to share your feelings because of fear.

Something that might be, may never come. If he

loves you, he will understand all of it."

"Momma, what did happen to me?"

She looked a little haunted and not really willing to talk about it. She patted my hand and leaned in to me. "Honey, let it go. You know about Jenna, that's enough. I hope you never remember." That infuriated me.

"Momma, how could you say that?"

"I almost lost you, honey, twice, because of it, leave it alone. I know that you want answers, but maybe you're better off not knowing everything. Just take comfort in knowing that Daddy and I love you and Carter apparently loves you." She kissed my forehead and started to go on the other side of the screen to change. "Try to enjoy now and forget the past, we can't change it anyway."

She walked away, and I managed to walk back into the massage room where I was met by Monica. She stood at the table clad in a black-and-white shirt with a black apron over it with the Tangles logo on it. "Ms. Cameron, please come, relax, and let me take care of you." She aided me to the table and instructed me to lie on my stomach and assisted me with the sheet and my robe. "I want you to be comfortable. If at any time something hurts or is uncomfortable, please tell me." She spoke softly, and her hands were firm but gentle. "Mr. Blake has arranged for a massage and hot stone treatment. I think you will enjoy it. Close your eyes, take some deep breaths, and listen to the music. We will continue." Her touch was healing, soothing, and I soon forgot what my conversation had been with my mother. Enjoying music and the aroma in the air, I dreamt of Carter and what tonight would be like.

He had wanted me to dress in my prettiest dress; I could see the two of us sitting in the theater, loving every minute of being together. We had both looked forward to this. Between his job and mine, it left us little time to spend together. My parents were here and had planned on staying through Christmas. Carter's parents on the other hand, well,

I wasn't sure of what to expect. Grayson and Iris Blake hadn't been talked about much. What would they think of me? Well, never mind that, I would just concentrate on Carter and what he wanted. There was nothing I wanted more than to make him happy. What a wonderful boyfriend I had. He was good to me even if I didn't always see eye to eye with him. I didn't always understand, but I was getting there. The thought of just hearing him laugh made me smile. I liked the idea that he took care of me, and I trusted him completely, which was not something I could say about most people I knew.

"Okay, Ms. Cameron, we're finished here. If you like, you can go into the changing room and dress, have some refreshments, and they will call you for your manicure."

"Manicure?"

"Yes," She giggled slightly, but she was professional. "Mr. Blake has you well taken care of dear. You are down for a full day of pampering, enjoy."

She wasn't kidding. Before going home that evening prior to our night out, I had been fluffed and puffed to the max. He had treated us all to a massage, manicure, pedicure, facials, makeup, and styling. I felt like I was ready for the red carpet by the time we were finished. After returning home, I went into the bedroom to change and found him sitting on the chaise.

Music was playing in the background, barely audible as a fire flickered in the fireplace. He was a picture sitting there very comfortable and well dressed in black dress pants and jacket with a crimson red button-down unbuttoned at the neck. His sleeves peeked out from under his jacket enough to disclose silver cufflinks trimmed in gold. His dark hair was tousled and gelled perfectly in place. He watched me as I entered the room, and that boyish grin that I loved so much soon appeared, and without hesitation, I blushed and grinned back at him.

"Ms. Cameron, I wondered when you would be home."

"I had a day in town that some handsome gentleman arranged for me.

He pampered me like a princess, and I just couldn't disappoint."

He rose slowly from the chaise, giving me plenty of time to admire him.

"Ms. Cameron, you could never disappoint." He sauntered toward me and slid his arm around my waist. He glided me around the room to the music, laying his cheek next to mine. "Ms. Cameron, you are beautiful." When the music stopped, he continued to hold me next to him, his cheek next to mine.

I felt his breath against me, making me shudder in tiny ripples down my back.

"Tonight is going to be wonderful." He kissed me on the cheek before taking a step back, his voice soft and charming. "I have your dress for tonight, it's hanging in the bath and waiting for you. There are also some shoes and some other girly things I thought you might enjoy." He grinned sheepishly at me.

I smiled at him, wondering what he had in mind and what he had done.

"Mr. Blake, what have you done?"

"Just a present for my angel, you deserve the best." He stood smiling at me then stepped back and put his hands in his pockets. "Well, how long are you going to make me wait?"

Kissing him quickly, I stepped into the bathroom and shut the door behind me. I surveyed the room to find everything a woman could want to wear on a date. He had bought everything down to the shoes. He even went as far as to buy silk stockings and some other very feminine effects unheard of for a man to purchase. On the counter, a black beaded evening purse, beside it on a hook in a

248

garment bag, a crimson strapped dress. I dressed quickly in the very feminine dress, leaving it partially unzipped, being unable to reach it well enough to continue. I placed the dark red kitten-heeled shoes on my feet that were jeweled delicately across the foot with small rhinestones. In a box tucked into my purse was a set of ruby earrings surrounded with diamonds.

I put them into place and looked at them carefully. The woman before me in the mirror, who I hardly recognized, was well polished and gleaming. My hair, adorned with rhinestone combs pulled off to one side, draped over my nearly bare shoulder.

"Isabella, are you about ready?"

Carter's words tore me away from my view. "Coming." I picked up the beaded purse and walked into the bedroom. Carter stood in front of the fireplace with his hands in his pockets, looking at me. The look on his face was indescribable. He stood still and watched every step I took toward him.

I could understand, in some respect, the dress was form-fitting but modest, clinging to me where it should, hitting just above my knee. It was more on the idea of old Hollywood-style elegance. Stepping in front of him and turning around, I looked over my shoulder. "Could you"—I suddenly felt shy in his presence—"zip me, please?" I could feel the heat radiate off his body as he took a step closer to me. His touch was gentle as he zipped my dress.

Turning to face him, he still looked at me in wonder.

"Carter, are you okay?"

Not sure what to think at this minute, he just stood there and looked at me, stunned. His stance of confidence had changed to more of vulnerability, his eyes never left me and his jaw was tense. "Dear God in heaven, Isabella, you look like an angel." He let out a sharp breath and was guarding himself with great restraint.

I stood in front of him, shy and nervous, which was not my normal from recent. Something about him had changed. His whole demeanor had changed, this confident man had suddenly had become very defenseless.

"Isabella, I . . ."

I stepped closer to him, knowing we were both treading on thin ice. I whispered against his cheek, "I thought the same thing when I saw you sitting there." I brushed his face with the tips of my fingers delicately. He continued to look at me with admiration and great restraint. Clearing his throat, he picked up his keys from the table.

"We should go." He took me by the elbow and showed the way with his unoccupied hand. We were soon joined by my parents, Lily, and J.C. Once I gathered my jacket and did one quick look in the mirror, the room loomed with excitement. Above the chatter, the doorbell rang. Walking to the door, I was met by a gentleman dressed well in a suit and tie with a fine linen blue shirt. His salt-and-pepper hair was swept to the side and well styled; he carried himself with great assurance and was joined by a beautiful brunette woman who was marvelously dressed in an ice evening gown that flattered her hourglass figure perfectly.

"You must be Isabella." The gentleman extended his hand, and a partial smile along with an equally brilliant smile on the face of his wife. "I'm Grayson Blake, and this is my wife, Iris."

Stunned at their appearance, I stood still and soon come to the realization these people were Carter's parents. "I'm sorry, come in." Carter made his way through the living room to me.

"Hey, angel, you ready to go?" When he got to me, he stood in bewilderment. It was as much a shock to him as it was to me. "Pop, why didn't you tell me you were coming?" Then he stepped toward his father and was greeted with a slap on the back and a quick hug. His mother smiled wide and took him in and hugged him like she would never let go. "Mom, it's so good to see you." A tear stood in his eyes as he admired his mother.

Iris framed her son's face with her hands and smiled at him. "My baby boy." She sniffed back tears.

"Mom, Pop, I want you to meet Isabella. Bella, this is my father and mother, Grayson and Iris Blake.

His mother looked at me approvingly. "Isabella, so nice to meet you, dear, Carter has told us so much about you." In the back of my mind, I was hoping that he hadn't told them about the darkest part of my past. Iris stepped forward and embraced me. "I hear you have captured my baby boy's heart."

My face heated, I knew I was blushing.

Grayson took my hand and kissed the back of it as Carter had in the past.

"He failed to mention how beautiful you are."

"Thank you. It's very nice to meet both of you."

"I'm sorry, son, that we came on short notice, but I wasn't sure if I could get away at all."

"It's okay, Pop, but I wish you would have called. I could have picked you up."

"What! And miss the surprise, not in your life." Grayson's eyes shined at him.

"Mom, Pop, why don't you come in. We have a few minutes, and I can introduce you to everyone." They followed Carter in, and I finally took a deep breath, my chest was tight and I felt like I was smothering. I had no idea they were coming. I stepped out onto the concrete porch that circled under a short awning and took in a couple of breaths feeling the cool air on my face. I wasn't there long before I was joined by my mother.

"Isabella, my goodness, what are you doing out here?"

"I'm okay, Momma, I just got a little warm and I needed some fresh air to soothe me."

251

"Are you still having panic attacks?"

"Once in a while, it's nothing really. I've learned to live with them."

My mother stepped in close to me and gave me a sideways hug, her arm draped across my shoulders. "You have nothing to worry about, you know.

I've never seen anyone more in love with someone as I have seen the love that comes from him for you. He pursues you like you are his next breath."

"I love him too, Momma." I smiled to myself. "He loves me for who I am, not what I can give him, and I admire him for it."

"Bella . . . Bella."

I looked over at my mother and smiled. "That's him." I gushed like a schoolgirl and turned and tried to walk the maze back to him. "I'm coming."

It wasn't long before I found myself in plush red seats surrounded by my parents, his parents, and Lily and J.C. But no one kept my attention as Carter did. He had held my hand through the entire play. Watching Cinderella as she swept the dance floor with her prince and sang to him ten minutes ago, all I could think of was waltzing the floor with my now-acclaimed prince.

My life, so unlike a fairytale, had become one through the love of one man.

I smiled through tears as I watched them dance across the floor with their newly proclaimed love. Feeling a bit sentimental and foolish at the thought of crying over a child's story, I rubbed my eyes with my fingertips when Iris offered me a lace handkerchief. "I never go anywhere without one, dear." She smiled kindly and was very gracious.

"I can't believe I'm crying over a fairytale."

"Don't worry, dear, I have seen this at least ten times, I always cry here.

I used to bring Carter to see it when he was a little

252

boy. It was always his favorite." She smiled freely at me. "Seems he has found his princess he has searched for all his life. Look at him beam." Subtlety, she pointed at his direction. He was self-absorbed, watching every step, but he had a smile that would light the room.

"I certainly hope so, Mrs. Blake."

"Please call me Iris," she whispered.

As the play started to end the last act, Carter leaned toward me and whispered. "Come with me."

"Where are we going? It's not over yet."

"You'll see, come with me." He stood and walked me to the back of the theater and then around to the end of the stage and to the back where we could watch from the edge of the curtain.

The show closed, and the cast took their bow. The master of ceremonies took the stage in front of the cast and crew and spoke of different charities and thanked the cast for their hard work. Then he introduced Carter. "I'll see you in a few." He walked onto the stage confidently and took front and center. He shook hands with the MC and was given attention immediately.

"Hello, everyone, for those of you who do not know me, I'm Carter

Blake. I work for the Portland police department and have worked through the theater for a charity that is close to my heart and has been for many years.

I have Andrea's place, it's a home for abuse victims, a home provided for women and their children who are victims of abuse. The money raised here tonight will go to Andrea's place and to a women's project called Where the Heart Is. I started Where the Heart Is as an organization for women who are diagnosed with cancer. My wife, Andrea, died almost three years ago from terminal cancer. I watched her struggle with many things, but one that made the biggest impact on her was the inability to share simple things with her daughter and me.

Where the Heart Is, hosts charity events to provide women and children that have been affected with this terrible disease. Like Cinderella, realizing her dream to marry her prince and looking to brighter days, Where the Heart Is allows those that have been affected and their family to have a dream and to leave their disease behind them even if it is for a short time. This is in hope that it will allow them the strength, self-esteem, and the confidence that the fight takes from them. As you go home tonight, ask yourself this, what would I do to provide my loved one, one more wish, one more dream that would make their life feel normal? Everyone should have a happy ending, but it doesn't always work out that way. This is in hope that we all have happy tomorrows. Thanks, everyone. Merry Christmas to all of you, may the God of heaven bring us all peace this Christmas season."

Before Carter left center stage, he was joined by the master of ceremonies.

Looking at Carter, he whispered something to him then turned to face the audience. "Mr. Blake has asked that you remain for one more scene of Cinderella, I will announce the end of the festivities at the close. Merry Christmas, everyone, and may your dreams come true." He stepped back and nodded at him. "Mr. Blake." He stepped back off stage. I stood watching in bewilderment of what he had in mind. He started to walk toward me and then directed me to come to him. Reluctantly, I slowly walked to him.

Walking on stage, he led me onto the center of the stage. The music began to play ten minutes ago, and the characters from the production had now joined us and were dancing around us. "I wasn't sure you were going to come to me."

He chuckled softly. Being completely stunned, I couldn't utter a single word.

"May I have this dance, Ms. Cameron?" He bowed

and took my hand and swept me across the stage. The song was right; there was no ceiling or floor, he literally swept me off my feet. "You are my queen, Ms. Cameron, and you have stolen my heart." I suddenly had a sense of déjà vu as he danced me around the stage. The moment had felt so memorable, but I couldn't pull it completely out.

The music stopped, and he bowed before me, and in grand royal style.

I offered a curtsy. A burst of applause filled the audience, and the curtain dropped. The cast left the stage, and I was left standing in front of the man I had truly given my heart. "You dance divinely, Mr. Blake."

He gave one of his boyish grins and took my hand and slipped it through the crook of his arm.

"The ball is just beginning for you, Isabella. Just remember you still belong to me at midnight."

Carter led me off the stage, and we met up with the rest of our party.

Paired off in couples talking to each other, I didn't seem to find it strange that the parents were the ones that were paired off, mother with mother and father with father. Lily and J.C. were into each other and had really no recollection of anyone else. I clung to Carter and leaned into him like I could not take another step. He had become part of me, I wasn't sure where I ended and he began. The closer to him I was, the better I liked it and the more secure I was. Most men I guess would have found it stifling, he on the other hand seemed to enjoy the idea and leaned his cheek against my head and kissed my hair, taking me by the waist and pulling me in as close as he could and still walk.

The cold air kissed my cheeks as we walked in Shenanigans, well known for being one of the best restaurants in the area and for their four-star treatment. The dark cherry floors, and wood frame chairs were elegant. Each table, covered in red and white linens, was adorned with hurricane lamps, the flatware of gold set the tables off. The chandeliers were drop crystals that danced across the floors and lit in a low, even fashion, creating drama and sophistication. A small orchestra played in the corner away from the dining area, and a clear framed dance floor glowed below them. Soft ferns and poinsettias filled the rooms and along the orchestra set off by tiny twinkle lights. The hostess had shown us to our table; Carter stood by me and assisted me and made his seat beside me. I watched him dreamily as if no one else existed; no one was in the room but the two of us. I watched him as he spoke and marveled at the way he laughed. His beautiful smile and the way his eyes—oh, those brilliant blue eyes was enough for me to lose myself in and never return.

Before I realized, he had turned to me and spoke, "Bella . . ." He chuckled slightly. "Hey . . . Isabella."

"Yes, I'm sorry. Just, ah, daydreaming."

Grayson laughed. "I do believe your young lady is enchanted."

"Not any more than I am with her, Pop."

I felt my face flush; I might have been as red faced as my dress. Landon, Beth, and Molly walked in behind us, and Molly found her way between us and soon climbed up on my lap. "Hi, Mommy." She beamed and threw her chubby little arms around my neck and hugged me tightly. "I miss you."

Carter's parents and mine both looked shocked, and then it came to me that they had heard Molly call me Mommy. I hugged her and kissed the top of her head. "I missed you too, Tink." Carter looked at us, and he grinned and shook his head slightly.

"Hey, what happened to Daddy here? I want a Tinker Bell special." She jumped down and hugged her father twice as hard and kissed him so hard you could hear it smack. "Wow. That was some kiss, Tink." She giggled in her little girl way and then jumped down to the floor.

The orchestra started to play in the background softly, and Molly motioned for her dad to lean down to listen to what she was saying. He smiled at her then laughed. "Of course, honey, come on."

Looking at me, he chuckled. "It seems I have a dance waiting with a young lady, I won't be long." He stood and walked to the dance floor with

Molly. They started playing "A Dream Is a Wish Your Heart Makes." Picking Molly up into his arms, he swayed back and forth with her as she laughed and giggled at him. What a sweet and gentle picture of them. Molly's delicate pink dress floated against him, showing her white ruffled anklets and black patent leather shoes. Her long dark hair bounced on her shoulders with a single pink ribbon dancing against her back. The love he had for his little girl was unmistakable.

"He has always loved to dance." Grayson spoke in a low baritone voice.

"He has done well raising his daughter, much better than I had expected alone, but then again he has surprised me many times."

I smiled and continued to watch him dance with Molly. "He loves his baby girl more than I could ever imagine anyone could."

"I know a young lady that he also loves very much. I never thought he would ever fall in love again. When he lost Andrea, he was lost for a long time. It appears that he has finally healed from that loss. Thanks to you, Isabella."

"He has loved me and helped me through some pretty difficult times, above and beyond what I could have ever asked."

Grayson stood and offered his hand to me. "Shall we join them? I would love to see you dance together again."

I accepted his offer and he walked me to the dance floor and he slowly danced me over to his son. Grayson was exceptionally light on his feet as he was spinning and waltzing me across the floor. "Isabella, I can see the joy in Carter's face every time he looks at you. Be good to him, he will never fail you." His advice shook me to the core. Why was everyone baring their soul to me, and what proverb could I come back with other than "I love your son, he's everything to me but you would think differently of me if you only knew." I could feel a cold chill run down my spine. What was going on? Was I so dense that it was staring me in the face and I couldn't see it?

The music was complete and Grayson stepped to Carter and smiled genuinely at him. "May I have the next dance with my granddaughter?"

"What do say, Molly, want to give Poppy a whirl?" Molly wiggled and then reached for him, taking her, spinning her across the room before the music started. Molly giggled and laughed. "Poppy, dance with me like Daddy."

Carter watched them as they glided across the floor and took two short steps toward me and offered his hand. "Bella, will you dance with me?"

I didn't offer a word, letting him lead me. "Have I told you that you look stunning tonight? You positively glow."

"Thank you, and yes, in not so many words, you have. I do so enjoy hearing it. You, my fine gentleman, are very handsome. The prince has nothing on you."

"Glad to hear it, thought I might lose you to the prince tonight."

"The only prince in my life is standing right here in front of me. I wouldn't have it any other way."

The music began to play a slow ballad, and Carter took my hand. Kissing the back of it, he pulled me into his embrace. Laying my head against his chest, I could hear the soft beating of his heart. My promised hand lay against his chest, and he covered it with his own and wrapped his arm around my waist. His cheek rested against mine even though he did have to bend to allow it to do so. I started to recognize the song playing, and it was true, he had become my voice when I was unable to speak. I now was the person I had become because he had loved me. Because you love me, it played and shut out everything and everyone around us. He had my full attention, he consumed me.

The soft whisper from him left me no doubt of how he felt. He had said it many times before, somehow it was different in the sweetness, my heart accepted it. His touch had changed as if I had become a preserver of his life, his hands trembled against me. His voice cracked slightly as he made his pronouncement of the three words that escaped him, "I love you."

CHAPTER 13

My foot had slipped into Cinderella's glass slipper. The night had been magical from beginning to end. Carefully taking Molly's dress and shoes off and slipping her gown over her head, I tenderly covered her. Her long hair sprayed along her pillow, and her lashes fanned against her cheeks. How precious she had become to me in such a short time. Sitting on the edge of the bed, I softly caressed her tiny face when a voice pulled me from my thoughts.

"She is a lovely little girl, isn't she?" Iris had followed me into the room and took her seat in the nearby rocker.

"Yes, she is, inside and out." I never took my eyes off her. "I'm very fond of her. She readily accepted me, a stranger she didn't know, and allowed me to share her father with her."

"Carter was a hard one to get to bed. He would make every excuse from monsters in the closet to wanting a drink of water. I would sit and read to him for hours sometimes. He loved *Where the Wild Things Are*, I don't know how many copies I bought of it. To think now he has a little girl he is raising."

"He's a very good daddy to her." I smiled as I remember him going down the slide with her at the park, carrying her off to bed and tucking her in, hugging her close and kissing her until she giggled.

"I want you to know, and I know I speak for Grayson, we are so happy to see him smile again. To know he has someone that he loves as much as he does you, well, I know he is happy, and I can see that you love him very much."

"Yes." It was all I could manage. I hadn't told him, I wanted to. I was not sure why there was fear in telling him that. He was forthright with his feelings and he knew

260

mine, but I had never stated them.

"Well, Mr. Blake and I will take our leave for tonight. It was very nice to meet you, Isabella. Thank you for being so good to Carter. No matter how old he gets, he is still my little boy." She stood to take her leave, and I kissed Molly on the forehead lightly. Turning the light out, I followed close behind her. Carter and his father were standing in the middle of the room with my father, laughing and talking about some inaudible subject, and it was apparent they were enjoying themselves. He stood comfortably with one hand in his pocket, gesturing with the other. My father and Grayson were laughing together freely until they saw us in the room.

Carter removed his hand from his pocket and looked over his shoulder, and I was soon greeted with that all-too-familiar smile of his, and the older men watched him intently. His father slapped him on the back and continued to watch us walk across the floor to the men in our life. He reached his hand out to me and kissed the back of it.

Grayson assisted his wife into her coat and slipped it over her shoulder and kissed her on the cheek. "Grayson, what has gotten into you?" His face brightened as he looked at her. "Love, darling." He glided his arm around her waist, and she laughed. "Shall we, my dear?" He stepped forward, guiding his wife to the door. "Son, we will talk soon."

"Sure, Pop." Carter waved him off as they made their way out the door.

"Well, I better see to your mother." My father winked at Carter and kissed me on the cheek before he exited the room. We were soon left alone, and he gathered me up to him like I were a delicate flower. His eyes burned into me, and I could feel my body tingle under his gaze, I loved it. My heart quickened as he looked down at me, my breath left me as I looked into those piercing blue eyes.

261

"Bella, I had a wonderful time tonight with you. I look forward to many more just like it." Walking me over to the couch, he sat beside me, the only light now on in the room was that cast from the Christmas tree and the warm flicker from the fireplace.

"I wanted you to remember this night, I hope it exceeded your expectations."

"Any time with you is wonderful for me, I would think you would know that by now."

"My parents love you. You certainly made an impression on my father."

"He seems to be a very good man." Carter smiled broadly and looked down at his hands. He seemed to be a bit disarmed.

"Are you okay?"

I had never seen him like this, he was actually nervous.

"Yes," he chuckled. "I'm fine, just trying to get what I want to say right."

"It's me, remember? I'm the one that has a problem expressing thoughts and feelings." He took a deep breath. "You're struggling with this, aren't you?" I was getting a little concerned. "What is it? Is it me, have I done something?"

"No, it's nothing like that." He took a deep breath and slowly released it.

"Isabella, I knew from the moment I met you that you were a special person.

God has blessed me with so many things, and he certainly blessed my life when he brought you into it." Constantly he was changing direction in where he was looking. He looked at me then at the floor and then back at me. It's as if he was having difficulty concentrating. I wanted to say so much to him, of the way the night had went and that I loved the way he had planned the day and had treated me as a princess. In such, I began to ramble at the unease.

"I was beginning to worry a little. Everyone seemed to know something I didn't. Your mom talked about you when you were a little boy and how she used to take you to see Cinderella and that you liked the book *Where the Wild Things Are*. She talked about how no matter how old you got, you were still her little boy. Grayson talked to me about how much he thought I had done for you being in your life, and honestly. I was afraid of meeting them." Carter placed a finger against my lips.

"Isabella, if you don't let me do this, I am never going to get it said." He collected himself, and I sucked in a breath, not sure what was going on. "It was easier to talk to your father." He reflected a boyish grin, letting me know all was well then stood momentarily. Before I got my head wrapped around what was going on, he was on one knee in front of me. His eyes shined in the light of the fire. "I wanted this night to be special, something you would never forget. I took time to plan everything to the minute. The highlight of my evening so far has to be the dance we shared at the theater. Isabella, you are a beautiful woman, smart, loving. You have become my happy ending, and I want to be that for you." It had finally set on me what was happening, and I was in total shock. Tears were welling in my eyes, and my fingers had met my lips in awe. He slipped his hand into his pocket and pulled out a small red velvet box, holding it in one hand and holding my hand with the other.

"I hope you are ready for this, I know I am." His voice fully serious. "Isabella, you have fulfilled me, completed me. I have walked a lonely road for a very long time, that is, until I met you." He opened the box to reveal a beautiful diamond solitaire that was way more than what I deserved, surrounded with rubies, custom-made with my birthstone. "Isabella, will you do me the honor of becoming my wife?"

Through tears, mine and his, I managed to answer. "Yes . . . yes," I whispered.

"You said yes?" He grinned.

I shook my head and giggled through tears. "Yes."

Taking the ring from the box, he slipped it on my finger. "Cinderella just found her prince." I threw my arms around his neck, and he pulled me from the couch onto his waiting knee.

"Wow, Isabella, I didn't think I would ever be this happy again." He kissed me quickly and picked me up and swung me around in his arms as I laughed and giggled like a schoolgirl. He sat me down slowly. His eyes met mine, and I had no intent on looking away, his grin had left. His hands left my waist and lay softly against my face, framing it. "You have made me a very happy man. I wasn't at all sure what you would say."

I smiled at him sweetly, trying to lighten the mood just a bit. Raising a finger to him, I traced his jaw from his ear to his chin and then ran it against his lip. "I'm deeply, totally, madly in love with you. Nothing could drive me away from you." His expression had shown relief from my declaration of love for him. "You know me so well, how could I say no?" In that instant, I was his and I belonged to no other. I had been released or so I felt from the past, I was his and his only. Loving him was never going to be difficult, not that there would never be any problems. I knew better than that, but for now it was wonderful. My hands dropped and rested at his waist, relaxed under his intent gaze.

He drew me closer to him, the atmosphere around us soon charged, the mood was dangerous. The electricity between us was passionate, and he kissed me like he would never see me again. I felt reckless; Carter had never acted so passionate. He wrapped me up in both arms so tight that my hands could not move from his waist. His kiss became hard, passionate, and wanting, leaving us both breathless.

The emotions between us heightened every sense and nerve I had. The touch of his hands on my body, the smell of his cologne, and the heat from his body all added to an intoxicating affect. His cheek rested against mine, and I could feel the short, chopped breaths that came from the passion he possessed. "I love you, Isabella." He left me totally thunderstruck that my own need and want of him had taken every word, every thought from me. My body tingled with anticipation. His hands now rested at the small of my back and the nape of my neck, and I slowly ran my hands up and down his muscular back to his waist. In an attempt of great restraint from him, I could feel his body tense under my touch.

"Carter, it's okay, relax. Nothing will happen unless you want it to. I'm fine, I can stop if I have to."

His body trembled beneath my touch, I had not let it go unnoticed that my own body had become responsive to his with the same intense trembling and breathlessness it had given me. In that moment, I had an unexplained terror. The fear began to rise with fury, and it had taken me by complete surprise. Why, why now? I had never been fearful of him or being with him.

It lay in the back of my mind, and I tried to push it aside, back to the dark recesses of my mind that had hid all other unpleasantness. His hands moved slowly to my shoulders and down my arms and back again to the small of my back. Carter sucked in a short breath, and I could feel the coolness from it.

"Isabella, I . . ." Never looking at me, his voice has become weak. The normal confident, steady-as-a-rock man had become weak. His voice cracked and broke as he tried to make his intention clear. "I don't think I can stop," his voice shook. "I want you," he whispered softly. "I want you so badly."

Running short, untamed kisses from my ear to my neck, he definitely had my attention. With everything in me, I wanted this, I wanted this to happen.

Stepping back just enough to look into my eyes, he watched me and then kissed me longingly, passionately taking his time and tracing his fingers down my arm, and started to kiss my neck to my shoulders. My thoughts were clouded for his intense fervor. My eyes closed momentarily, and I soaked all this in knowing if I didn't stop this and now, this would happen. His words ran through my mind as tears started to trace my cheeks. *I know what I want, Isabella,* you *certainly can unravel a man. If you let me do this,* I'm *no better than the man that raped you.* My heart sank because of the want and need for him, I had to stop this. He trusted me to be strong when he couldn't. I had always heard from the time was a child that God never heard a sinner until they repented. I didn't take a chance now, I had no strength in stopping this.

I loved him and the passion burned in me. *God,* please *help me,* help *us.* It's wrong and I knew it, but my feelings were getting out of hand and he trusted me. He trusted me to do the right thing. Honestly, I didn't want to do what was right. *Please help me.* In that moment, a small voice stilled my heart and I heard it clearly. "Daughter, be still and know that I am God."

"Carter." He stilled and then took a step back. When he realized what was happening, he took two more steps back and then turned away and ran his long fingers through his unruly dark hair. "I'm sorry, Bella." He turned toward me, looking ashamed.

"Don't be, I wanted it too."

Carter remained about three steps away and placed his hands in his pockets. "I didn't mean for it to get out of hand. Sometimes, I just can't help myself when I'm around you."

"Carter, it's okay." I walked to him, closing the gap between us.

"If it wasn't for the sheer reason that I want to do

this right, we would go tonight. We would go and find Pastor Conley or someone that would do this ceremony, and we could have been together tonight." He stepped back, tension in his jaw, and rubbed the back of his neck, standing with his other hand resting on his waist.

I had to laugh. I couldn't stop myself and I laughed to the point that tears ran down my cheeks and I had to sit down before I fell down. He looked at me, perplexed. "What's so funny?" He almost seemed angry.

When I finally caught my breath, I slowly spoke and made an attempt to sooth his hurt feelings.

"Come, sit with me." He still tried not to approach me. I placed my hand on the couch next to me. "Please? I promise I won't bite." He strode toward me, and I drank in every move he made and the beautiful pout he had on his beautiful face. He sat down beside me with his forearms resting on his legs and his head resting partially in his hands. He took in a sharp breath and blew it out slowly.

"I wanted this night to be perfect." He barely spoke above a whisper.

I had finally become slightly angry with the situation but controlled.

"Carter, look at me." A brief moment passed and I tried not to panic. "Look at me for heaven's sake." I could feel my face tense, and I loved the idea of being his fiancée, but I wanted to be his. I wanted to be married to him. If that was what it took to have him wholly, then I was ready. He raised his head and then turned toward me and watched me intently. "You gave me a wonderful compliment. One that I never thought I would get. To get it from you is the most wonderful gift you could give me." He looked at me like he was totally at a loss. He had no idea what I meant, I could see it. I placed my hand on his shoulder, hoping that he would relax and it would return to the wonderful atmosphere of before. "You have shown me something I didn't think I would see. You let me see your feelings. You let me know that you had a desire for me, I never in my wildest dreams thought I would ever see that from a man. I have had so much pain and torture in my life when it has come to a physical relationship." Lifting my hand to his hair, I pushed it back and ran my fingers through it. "You have no idea how that felt to me. All I remember of a physical relationship is pain. When you . . . when you looked at me and touched me just now, I could feel it, I could feel the love you have for me. Do you have any idea how much that means to me that you would allow yourself to feel that for me even for just a few moments?"

He reflected for an instant and I knew he understood and he shook his head. "I never thought I would be sitting here in my living room having this discussion with you." He shifted on the couch, finally seeing control return to the confident, strong man I knew. "Isabella, I love you, plain and simple. You have no idea of how desirable you are to me. I try very hard not to let that be reflected because it would be so easy to act on. It isn't easy to control when you want someone that badly."

"Don't you think I know that? I've wanted this for months. Every day I'm with you, it grows a little stronger. I want to be with you so bad sometimes that my heart literally aches. If it came down to marrying you tonight, I would do it." I snapped my fingers quickly, never hesitating. "Just like that, I would go, right now. I wouldn't have to think about it. Wherever you are, that is exactly where I want to be."

He seemingly relaxed and his smile returned as a repressed grin. "That's exactly why I love you. You love me no matter what."

My fingers continued to run through his thick, unruly dark hair. "I would marry you now if you were game."

"Don't tempt me, angel."

"I would do anything for you, Amore."

"Amore." He flashed that lovely boyish grin at me and chuckled. He shifted on the couch so that he faced me. "Where did that come from?"

"Amore, love, it means my love."

"Amore."

"You are my amore."

"Oh, okay." He rubbed his face, following his jaw down to his chin. "I like it." He chuckled.

I gushed so that I felt a glow rise from me. "I'm so happy. I don't know what do with this feeling. I've never felt this good."

"You deserve to be that happy every day, and if I have my choice, it will be that way."

"Just curious, did you buy my wedding band?" He smiled but he wasn't sure I could tell if he wanted to answer. His smile had already answered my question.

"Yes, I have. Where are you going with this?" He smirked, and he knew, he just wanted me to say it.

"Well, since you . . . have . . . already picked my wedding band and you have it and you have yours on the opposite hand."

"Ms. Cameron, are you suggesting what I think you're suggesting?"

"Yes, I am suggesting just that."

"I would love to but . . ."

"Oh, here we go, but?"

"Come on, Isabella, my parents would be upset and your father wouldn't be happy and your mother would kill me. You are her only daughter and her only child."

"We could get married and no one would have to know until we married in a church."

"If Pastor Conley would perform the ceremony, it would be a lie. He would never keep that kind of a secret."

"I want to do this, is there any way we can?"

He kissed me on the forehead. "No, as much as I would like to say yes, we can't."

I felt a bit letdown. I knew it would happen but a few days, a few months, it seemed a bit extreme to me.

"We will do this soon, just not now. I want you to have what you have wanted all your life and it will keep me out of the doghouse with my future mother-in-law."

"Oh, mother-in-law. When are we going to tell our parents?"

"They all knew I was going to ask you, that's why they were here. They just didn't know you would say yes."

"My mother even knew? She never batted an eye. She can't keep a secret."

"They knew about a week ago."

"I wondered why you acted so strange. You had this planned for a long time."

He grinned. "I bought your ring a month ago, had a devil of a time keeping it hidden."

"You set the day up at the spa, the play. Did you know you were going to dance with me at the theater?"

"I planned it with Rowland before they started production. He knew we were coming, and the company was in on it."

"I can't believe it. How did you keep it quiet?"

"It wasn't easy, but then again, I was petrified. I wasn't sure you would say yes."

Waking to find Molly had already left the room, I turned to look at the clock. I sat up and rubbed my eyes to look once more. *Oh man, really?*

Ten a.m. I never slept this late. Why hadn't anyone awakened me? Mom, Carter, even Molly. I looked around the room and then out the window. It was daylight out for sure. There wasn't a sound in the house. Sitting there, I pulled the quilt against me and stretched for a moment and started to get up when he walked through the door.

"Good morning, angel, sleep well?" He came into the room, gracefully carrying a tray of some simple breakfast pieces and dressed in a white tee and ripped jeans. Mercy, how could someone look that good? How was I going to deal with that? He placed the tray over my lap and gave me one of those crooked smirks of his that melted me. "I've been watching you sleep for two hours, you must have been extra tired."

"I slept, but not that I can say I slept solid. I had some handsome man walking around in my sleep that I just simply couldn't keep my hands off of."

"Oh, then that explains it."

"What?"

"Well, I had this unbelievably tempting woman running around last night in my dreams, chasing me. I was ready to let her catch me, but she decided to get married on Valentine's Day and left to get her dress."

"Did you say Valentine's Day?"

"Yes. I believe so."

"Couldn't have been me. I got married last night to a wonderful man."

"Now that was a dream, I should have joined you." He sat on the edge of the bed and watched me.

"Where is everyone? I didn't hear anyone."

"They went Christmas shopping. Only two more days until Christmas you know."

"You don't have to go in today, do you?"

"No. I fully intend on spending it with you."

"Good, that was my thoughts, Mr. Blake."

"When you finish your breakfast, we'll go do a couple of things."

"Things, like what?"

"Well, we do have to meet our daughter at the mall around noon. She wants to go see Santa Closet." He laughed as he said it. "She has a way with words."

"Does Santa have her list yet?"

"Oh yes, but there are always last-minute choices you know."

"Are you going to talk to Kris Kringle too, Mr.

271

Blake?"

"No." He took my hand and raised it to his lips, kissing it softly. "I have what I want for Christmas. What about you, any last-minute wishes?"

"Well, maybe just one." I smiled at him shyly.

"One you want to share?"

"It wouldn't come true if I shared it."

"Okay, make sure it comes in the right size."

"I am sure that at the right time, it will be just perfect."

As we sat there, I finished what I was eating and listened to him chatter away about meeting Molly and what all she had mentioned she wanted Santa to bring.

"I see you are finished. Why don't you get dressed and meet me in the living room. We will head to the mall first. I'm not sure what we may do after that." He sat the tray down on the chest and offered his hand to me, and I graciously accepted it. "We need to meet with both sets of parents to let them know you said yes." He leaned his forehead into mine. "I can't let Mom and Pop leave yet." Then he leaned back and looked at me like he hadn't seen me in years.

"You're serious about Valentine's Day?"

"You bet I am. You need to get with your mother to pick a dress. I will see to a planner, and we will need to meet with Pastor Conley."

"That's going to be quick." My head was already spinning from what he was proposing to do in such a short amount of time. "Do you think we can put it together in about two months?"

"I have connections, don't worry. The main thing is that you and your mother pick your dress." I had to smile, thinking in just a little more than a couple of months I would be totally his. "What are you thinking?" He grinned sheepishly and pulled me into him.

"I'll never tell," I teased him. "Do you think your

mom would like to go?

To help pick out a dress, I mean?"

"I'm sure she would be honored. My mom is hard to win over, and you did it so easy."

"I wondered about that. I had a fear of meeting them, I wasn't sure what they would think of me."

"Come on, Isabella, as long as you make me happy, they are overjoyed.

Besides, what's not to like?"

"They don't know me, Carter. What if they knew about me, about what has happened to me? They wouldn't think much of their future daughter-in-law."

"They aren't that shallow, Bella. They just want me to be happy. Believe me, they have nothing to worry about, and neither do you."

"We better get started. Santa and Molly are waiting on us." Leaning in, I made an attempt at kissing him quickly, and he had decided a chaste kiss was not enough. Taking me quickly to him, his kiss was passionate and lingering, taking my breath from me. Taking a breath and slowly opening my eyes, I took him in. "Ah, Mr. Blake, if you really want to leave this room, I suggest you do not kiss me like that."

Carter continued to hold me into him as close and tight as he could possibly do so without taking my breath totally away. "You are intoxicating, Bella." Never letting go, he barely moved his head back far enough for me to see his face. His eyes were stern and blazing into me, his jaw had tightened, and all I could think of at this moment was forget waiting. I didn't care, we were adults and it's our choice. A shock of electricity was sent through me as my mind exploded at the thought of him just touching me. No more than what he was doing was killing me, my will to stop him had never been that strong. "Soon . . . very soon." Kissing my cheek and down to my shoulder, he spoke low, "My present will be you." He breathed. "You. Will. Be.

All. Mine.

And believe me, I'm going to enjoy unwrapping it." He sent chills down me, I had never heard him talk like that, ever.

Looking up at him warily, I bit my lip and assessed him. "I don't think I have ever heard you talk like that." It scared me, but I wouldn't admit it why did it scare me. He had never done anything to hurt me.

"Bella, I'm a man. You torture me just being in the same room, sometimes knowing that I can't have you . . . yet."

Patting him on the chest, I looked into those marvelous blue eyes. "If we are going to meet your daughter, I must get dressed. And you, sir, are not helping." Throwing his head back, he collected himself and had regained full control.

He let out a little chuckle as he looked down at me, using it more as a release, and stopped briefly to think as I had. We were alone, totally and utterly alone. There was no one in the house and no intent on anyone coming home soon. "I know you well enough to know what you have in your mind right this minute. I can't say it hasn't crossed my mind." He furrowed his brow and then gave that little smirk of his. He was so sexy. God help me, he was. He could take every thought I had and just look at me and turn me to jelly. "We are alone, and all we can do now is to get ready and leave for the mall to meet your parents and Molly. Not that it wouldn't be a wonderful way to spend an afternoon, I love my daughter. I can think of something I would love to do more than that."

I couldn't believe this. As bold as I had been and now he was the one taking the lead. I couldn't believe how much that scared me now. I wanted to run, and my feet were planted solid to the floor. This absolutely could not be happening. I must be dreaming, it wasn't real, my throat had become tight.

I was starting to break out into a cold sweat, and my heart was racing like I had run a marathon. I was breathless, I felt totally out of control, feeling as though I was going to faint. My body was shaking, and I couldn't seem to stop it.

"Isabella, you okay?"

Thank God he had me in his arms because I was starting to see black.

"Carter." The darkness was getting closer, my vision had narrowed.

"Isabella." He started to pat my face. "Isabella."

I could feel my legs buckle, and he lifted me.

I opened my eyes, finding myself on the bed and Carter sitting there wiping my face with a cool cloth.

"Isabella, wake up, angel. Come on, honey."

Looking around, I was in Molly's room in her bed, and I feel so nauseated. Carter looked down at me, concerned.

"Isabella, come on, angel."

I looked at him, and he was still in his pajama bottoms and a tee. His hair was wet like he had just gotten out of the shower, the smell of his cologne rose.

"Can you sit up for me?"

My head felt like it weighed a ton, and I was cold and sweaty. My hair felt damp against my face. What was going on? Carter assisted me to sit up and leaned in behind me. Wrapping his arm around me, he reached with the other for what looked like Motrin or Tylenol.

"Here, take this for me." I was so weak that I couldn't manage to take them from him. "Open," he demanded. I opened my mouth, and he places them there and helped me to take a drink. The water had ice in it, but it tasted warm. He placed the glass back on the table and had me lean back into him as he washed my face with the cool cloth.

Swallowing, my mouth felt dry even after a drink.

"Why do I feel like this?"

Gently he held me to him. "You have the flu, I think. Last night after you went to bed, Molly came and got me. She said you were hot, your temperature was 103. I wasn't able to get you awake enough to take something, so I used cool washcloths."

"Where's Momma? Does she know?"

"Yes, she knows. I didn't want her in here, I don't want them all getting sick."

"We have to meet them." I tried to sit up.

"Meet who?"

"We have to meet my parents and Molly at the mall."

"Bella, what are you talking about? We aren't going anywhere."

"We have to, Molly is going to see Santa and I need to get my dress."

"Isabella, what are you talking about?"

"You said we had to meet them at the mall. Molly wanted to talk to
Santa, and I needed to pick out a wedding dress."

"Angel, you aren't going anywhere. Molly goes tomorrow to see Santa, and while I would love for you to pick out a dress, you aren't able. I don't remember saying anything about taking Molly to see Santa."

It occurred to me that I must have been dreaming. Oh no, did I dream that Carter and I got engaged too?

I choked a little about the thought, and I knew I had to ask or make an attempt to look at my hand. I couldn't raise my hand, it felt like lead. "Carter, are we engaged?" Hoping he was going to say yes, but at this point, I wasn't sure.

I could feel him smile, kissing my cheek. "Yes, Bella, we're engaged, you didn't dream it."

My body relaxed as I took a deep breath. Carter was here, and I didn't care about anything else. He would take care of me. The door opened, and I turned my head to see Molly standing there with her blanket and thumb as usual. Carter turned to see her standing in the door.

"Stay there, Tink."

"Mommy okay?"

"She's okay. I just don't want you to get sick."

Her little face looked worried, and her hand raised her blanket to her face and had her thumb instantly to her mouth. She was stressing, I could see it.

"It's okay, Tink, Mommy is fine. Daddy will take good care of me, okay?"

That's all it took, the thumb came from her mouth and she smiled.

"Did you tell her, Carter?"

"Not yet, we will."

She remained at the door and watched.

"Is Poppy and Nanna with you?"

"Yes."

"Tell Nanna or Poppy to turn cartoons on for you. Daddy will be out after I take care of Mommy."

She got ready to walk away, and Carter told her to shut the door.

He took his arm from around me and propped the pillows for me so that I was sitting semi upright. He sat on the edge of the bed and looked down at me. "You scared me last night. I have taken care of Molly before when she has been sick, but I can't remember taking care of anyone with a temperature that high. I think you might have had a febrile seizure last night. You shook, like you were cold, and I couldn't get you awake. You were so tired. I changed your clothes and bed last night. Your clothes and sheets were soaked."

Somehow it didn't bother me that he did. Any other time, it would have embarrassed me to death. I guess I was too sick to care. Carter seemed a little embarrassed, his face was slightly red.

"You okay? About having to do that?"

"Isabella, I would do anything for you. It had to be done, and if we are going to get married, I will be taking care of you then."

There was something bothering him, I could see it. "What is it?"

He looked away momentarily. "I didn't want to say anything because I know it bothers you."

"What bothers me?"

"What happened to you Bella, the scars, what did that monster do to you?"

I tried to raise my hand again, and it wouldn't go and he could see that.

He lowered himself next to me.

He kissed me gently on the forehead. "Don't worry about it. It just hurts to see what someone did to you."

"It's okay. Don't worry about it anymore. I have you, and I have Molly," I said in a very soft voice. "It's all I need."

I knew it had been bad when I slept all one day and didn't realize it. I sat up in the bed, and it had dawned on what I think was Christmas Eve. I woke to see Carter asleep in the rocker across from me. I did feel better, but I was still weak. I had to be able to get up and make this day special for my family and little Molly. I sat on the edge of the bed and pushed my hair away from my face and looked at the man sitting in the chair. A very tired, Carter sat in the rocker, his arms crossed in front of him and his head against the back rest.

Scooting out to the edge of the bed, I place my feet on the floor. Sitting there waiting for my body to collect its bearing, I looked down at my hand to see the dazzling ring he gave me. I hadn't even been able to enjoy it, where I had been so sick I couldn't even look at it.

Stirring, I looked across the room to see Carter open his eyes and look at me. He rose from the chair without a word and offered his hand. "You need to get up?"

"Yes, I feel gross, I feel so dirty. I need to brush my teeth and take a bath."

I took his hand, and he helped me up. "Come on, I'll help you." I gasped, and he grinned slightly.

"What? Oh, come on, Isabella, it isn't like I haven't seen you."

"What do you mean by that?"

He looked at me, a little shocked. "I've taken care of you for the last two days. How do you think your clothes got changed and your bed."

"What day is this?"

"It's Christmas morning. We need to get you going, Molly will be up soon."

He escorted me to the bath and sat me down in the wicker chair that sat there. Turning on the water, he checked it like he was bathing Molly. He ran his hand through it and poured some bath salts into the water. The aroma of lavender mixed with the heat made a soothing smell.

Standing in front of me, he held out his hand and helped me up from the chair.

"I can do this," I told him sweetly.

"Isabella, I'm not leaving. I'm going to help you get in the water. If you want to bathe yourself, it's fine, but I'll see that you get in and out okay."

Oh, sometimes he could be so hard to deal with. I bit my lip and stared into those brilliant eyes that were insistent on his will. I could see I was not going to win this fight.

"Fine," I said harshly. "Close your eyes or turn around, something."

He smirked and had the nerve to laugh. "Isabella, who do you think has taken care of you for the last couple of days?"

"Please, close your eyes."

279

"Bella, this is ridiculous. I have done everything for you, seen everything."

I was suddenly appalled and moved backward. "What do you mean you've seen everything?"

He tilted his head and gave a boyish grin and kissed me on the cheek.

"Believe me, your birthday suit is in fine shape."

"Oh my god, you didn't?"

"I did, and if I have to, I will do it again."

"How could you?" I couldn't believe I was upset over this, but I was.

"Isabella," he said sternly and pointed to the tub. "Get in, now." His voice had become clipped.

I watched him as I started to raise my arms over my head to take off my gown and I was unable. I made several attempts, and I just couldn't seem to.

He hid a smirk with his fist. "I told you, I knew you would need help."

I let my arms drop to my side in frustration.

"Sit down on the chair for a minute," he said to me softly. I obliged him and sat down in the wicker chair across from the tub. He stooped down onto one knee and placed his cupped hand under my chin. "Isabella, I did nothing to you. I took care of you, modestly, but I took care of you. I would do it again if I had to. That's what love is, taking care of each other. You would have done the same for me."

Sitting there stiffly, he stood and took a brush from the vanity and brushed my hair and pulled it back into a ponytail. "Okay, stand up and I'll help you get into the tub." He looked at me, requesting permission. "Do you trust me?"

I did trust him. It didn't mean I was comfortable with it. I nodded, and he stood in front of me. Taking the hem of my gown, he lifted it over my head and wrapped me in a towel. "Can you, ah, get your panties?"

280

Again I tried but couldn't hold to the towel and remove them too.

Reaching under the towel, he pulled them down gently. "This is mortifying."

I could feel my face turn crimson, this was way too intimate for me. He was right, I wasn't ready. One, it was daylight, I was much more comfortable in the dark. At least I was shrouded in the dim light, there was no hiding, no hiding of my expression or my feelings like this.

"Isabella, there is nothing to be ashamed of."

He took my hand as I held the towel with the other, and he helped me step into the bath. Turning his head from me, he held the other hand out.

"Give me the towel and I'll steady you." I hesitated momentarily. "Isabella, I promise, I won't do anything to hurt you, I won't look." I unwrapped and handed it to him, and he slowly assisted me down in to the water.

CHAPTER 14

The embarrassment was consuming me. Carter broke the silence after I had been sitting in the tub for at least five minutes, soaking in the warmth.

"Bella, I don't want you to think that I took advantage you, it wasn't about what I could see or touch." Staying turned away from me, he ran his fingers through his unruly, dark hair. "It was not my intention, I felt like it was my responsibility to care for you. I understand what you're feeling, I felt that way when you were caring for me. The only person that ever touched me . . ." He hesitated and took a deep breath, and the sense of disquiet was felt by me. He was revealing a little more about himself. I had found that I didn't know as much about him as I thought. "Andrea was the only one, and it took a long time to feel comfortable with her. There's a lot you don't know about me, I wasn't easy to live with back then."

The splash of the water never moved him as I rinsed off. I was weaker than I had originally thought, and asking for his help was not something I wanted to do. I had never felt comfortable with even looking at my own body in the light of day. To say it was unnerving to me was putting it mild.

It wasn't that I was heavy, or disproportioned, I just was never comfortable in my own skin and hadn't been for a very long time, not to mention the scars that were left behind.

"What do you mean? I have never seen you as being difficult."

"You wouldn't, I've changed a lot since before Andrea passed away. When something has been ripped from you, it changes you, sometimes for the better, sometimes not. I can see some of me in you. I was fearful . . . not very masculine to admit such things. When I tell you

I understand what you are feeling, it isn't that I have never lived it."

This was incredible, he's baring his soul to me. I wasn't sure how I felt, my skin tingled from just the idea he was here and telling me some very intimate thoughts.

"It will eventually get easier."

"I can't even look at my own body." My voice became soft and weak. "I don't feel comfortable in a room alone with a man, and it has to be almost dark."

Carter rubbed the back of his neck. "You shouldn't be ashamed, Isabella, there is nothing wrong with the human body. It's beautiful, God made us the way we are. Of course we are to be modest, but in the situation of being partners, being brought together as husband and wife, we are to take pleasure in them. It is a gift of God for a husband and his wife to be able to share each other's body. I know we aren't married, but I love you. I would never do anything to cross that line. The first time we can actually feel free to enjoy each other will not be like me taking care of you in a time you needed it."

He continued to sit with his back to me. The silence lingered, and I wasn't sure what to say to that. It wasn't that there was never a thought, but each time something had sparked a fire between us, I had been under the protection of dim light. It was bright as day in here, and I felt totally exposed, vulnerable. I didn't like the idea that he could turn around anytime and see me as I was.

"Isabella, say something, I'm out on a limb here."

"I don't know what to say. Of all the people in my life, I trust you the most. It's hard, and I don't know why. I grew up . . . I don't know how to say this."

"Just take your time and say it. Take a deep breath, and let it go slowly.

Think about what it is you want to say."

My body clenched. I wanted to tell him how I felt. I felt silly honestly after everything that I knew and had went through. "I'm not comfortable with my body. I was raised, I guess, to think of any type of sexual contact or physical contact as being, you know, dirty unless it was in marriage, and I still don't know what I would think of it then. It was not something that I ever embraced. I never really looked at myself as being beautiful. I always tried to hide what assets I had because I didn't want to bring attention to myself.

I have always been fearful that I wouldn't be good enough. I would never be able to please someone in that way. It didn't help that one of my friends found herself pregnant at the age of thirteen. My mother forbid me to see her anymore and then beat it in my head, so much that I was afraid to let a young man hold my hand or kiss me. I'm sure most of them, which were very few, thought I was a freak. After all that I have been through, you would think it wouldn't matter."

Carter stayed still and I could see him shake as he ran his hand across his face. Being unable to see his expression, I wondered what he was thinking. "I can understand that." He never said another word. I sat there for a moment longer and he broke the silence. "Are you about ready to get out?"

I sucked in a breath and tried to relax. I needed my hair washed, and he was the only one there to help. It was foolish I knew to not allow him to help me. "Can you help me wash my hair?" My voice shook as I asked.

"You sure you want me to do that? The only way I can do it is in the tub or shower. I don't think there is enough room at the sink."

"Yes, I want you to help me, if you don't mind."

"Bella, I will do whatever you need done."

I took the washcloth and covered my chest, the bubbles in the tub covered the rest. "I'm okay if you want to help." He turned to find me covered and seemed to be relieved. Pulling off his black button down, he laid it across the chair and got on his knees beside the tub.

"Can you bend your head back so I don't get water in your eyes?"

Bending my head back, I remained covered with the washcloth and resting on my elbows so that my head was leaned back, still supported. He took his hands and filled them with water and wetted my hair completely then filled them with baby shampoo. Its rich aroma made me feel pampered.

I had soon forgotten the stress and the fact that I was fully unclothed before him. He massaged my hair until it was full of lather, and I slowly started to feel at ease with him. Not thinking of anything other than the feel of his hands in my hair, he rinsed all the soap away as I relaxed under his hypnotic spell. He pushed the excess water out and wiped my face with the end of a towel, treating me more like a child. "We're done," he exclaimed, waking me from a wonderful solitude.

Standing, he held a towel in front of me, holding it out to wrap me in it.

He turned his head and assisted me from the water. Once my feet were on the floor, he wrapped me in a thick white towel and led me over to the chair where I sat down. He took another towel and dried my hair then brushed the tangles away and blew it dry, running his long fingers through it. This was something I could get used to after all, I was enjoying his attention. It was warm, loving, and intimate. He began to run the brush through my hair and pulled it back once again in a hair tie. Leading with his hand out to me as a gentleman, I took it quickly. Looking into his dark blue eyes, I watched him as he looked into my face. Never once did he waver, and he took a sharp breath in. "Come," he demanded of me in a soft, even tone.

He led me into Molly's room and sat me on the edge of the bed.

Suddenly, I felt very weak and tired. He turned and walked to the closet and dresser where I had a temporary stash of clothes. I lay down on Molly's bed and closed my eyes, the coolness of her bed was inviting. All I could do was try to take in what energy I could while he roamed around the room.

It wasn't long before he had gathered up what he had in mind. He was definitely complete. "Bella, can you sit for a few minutes, I'll try to help you get dressed." At this point, I didn't much care anymore. I sat on the edge of the bed and did as he had instructed me to the best I could. By the time he had finished with me, I was dressed in a pair of older jeans, my favorites, and a red Henley shirt with a white tee underneath. He looked incredible to me, wearing ripped worn jeans, a navy blue tee, and a red V-neck sweater. He smoothed my hair where he had helped me pull my shirts on. I had to admit when he finished with me, I didn't look bad.

He smiled at me and his accomplishment. "You're beautiful even when you don't feel well." Taking my hand, he slid my arm through his and made an attempt to walk me to the living room. I didn't make it far, and started to feel dizzy. Seeing my reaction, he swept me up close to him and very gently deposited me on the couch, which was already made into a welcoming bed of sorts. It wasn't long before Molly come wandering out of her room, rubbing her eyes and carrying her blanket. Her eyes were rimmed red from rubbing.

She came over and sat beside me, her little body cuddling up to me as close as she could get. Not seeming to be interested in her gifts, it worried me. She wasn't fevered, her cheeks weren't flushed, yet she acted like none of what was under the tree made any difference to her. Carter leaned in and put his hand across her forehead, checking her to see if she too were ill. He shook his head in disbelief. "What's wrong, Molly? Don't you want to see what Santa brought?"

"Dot what I wanted, Daddy." Carter cocked his

head to the side and looked at me, not knowing what she meant, but I did.

Patting her on the back and kissing the top of her head, I assured her that I was fine.

"Mommy's fine, Tink. Why don't you go wake up Granpa and Mim, tell them we are waiting on them, okay?" She wiggled her way down and went to wake them.

Shaking his head, he watched in amazement. "She really loves you."

"And I love her and her father very much."

"I was worried about you. At one point I thought of bundling you up and taking you to the hospital, but then I thought maybe I was being a little premature with it."

I cupped his cheek in my hand, I truly looked at him in a different light.

He did love me, how could he not after taking care of me the way he did. It couldn't have been easy for him after he took care of Andrea so long ago.

"I'm okay, I'll start getting better now. I can't imagine how hard it must have been for you to take care of me."

"I did it because I love you, there is no other reason and it wasn't difficult.

I wanted to."

His lips curled up in a soft grin, and as ill as I have been, I still couldn't imagine him changing me and the bed. He had done the kinds of things that I normally did on a daily basis for myself and others. It was nothing for me to care for someone because that was all I had ever known.

"I just meant you weren't used to taking care of a grown person when they were ill, it isn't easy."

Scooting next to me, he wrapped his arm around my shoulder and kissed my forehead tenderly. "Bella, you are my life, when will you ever get that in your head?"

I smiled at him and kissed him on the cheek. "You are a beautiful man, Mr. Blake."

287

"I wasn't always so good you know." His smile diminished, and his lips descended into a thin line. "I try to do better now, but I can't change the past.

Molly's first Christmas, thank goodness, she will never remember. She was too little, in a lot of ways I'm glad she never will. Andrea died shortly after Christmas, I had just been in church a short while and had tried to make up the time I had lost with her. I spent my time here with Andrea and Molly on her last Christmas. Andrea barely knew what was going on with all the pain medication they were giving her. I wanted to make what I knew was her last Christmas beautiful. The hospice nurse had been there all night, and there would be a nurse aide coming in within an hour to assist her with getting a bath and dressed. I didn't wait for that, I did it myself. As many years as we had been married, I had never done anything for my wife when she had been ill or much of anything for that matter. She had been sick for almost a year, and I had never done anything for her myself. I barely took care of myself, and between my mother and hers, they took care of Molly. I bathed her, dressed her and combed her hair, and changed her bed and let her sleep after that. While she slept, I decorated our bedroom with Christmas lights and a small tabletop tree so she would have a Christmas. That was the only year I didn't have a large tree in the living room. She couldn't have been moved in there anyway. Christmas was always her favorite time of the year. When she found out she was pregnant with Molly, she started planning for her first Christmas. It didn't matter that Molly was not going to be old enough to remember, it was the thought that it was her first. I spent the day in our bedroom with Andrea in my arms with the lights twinkling around us. It was one of the best, and one of the worst Christmases I've ever had. New Year's Day she died in my arms. I held her to me when she took her last breath.

I can only hope that what I did after I started in

288

church wiped out all the drinking and anger she saw before that."

"I'm sure she knew you loved her. I don't know how I would react to something that devastating as a loss of a husband. It must have been very difficult for you to lose her?"

"Yes, it was, but it was a long time ago. It took time, but I recovered.

God allows things in our life so our faith will grow. We aren't always going to understand it, but he knows why and we should never question." He quickly took a deep breath and ran his fingers through his hair. It was hard on him, I could see it, the death of his wife, then being reminded of it with me being ill, even if it was a temporary thing. My thoughts were interrupted as the doorbell rang.

"I'll be right back." Carter stood to get the door, and I watched him saunter across the floor. My gaze on him was interrupted by the sound of feet padding against the floor. Molly was running to me followed by my parents.

She threw her arms around my neck and hugged me tight and wiggled down to the floor.

"Well, young lady, it appears you're feeling better." Looking up, I saw Grayson and Iris coming in behind me. My mom and dad came in and sat down as Grayson and Iris deposited their coats, picking up Molly, kissing her.

Molly was back to her lovely carefree self as she laughed and giggled. She grabbed Grayson's face with both hands and kissed his cheek abruptly. "Wuv you, Poppy."

"I love you too, sweetheart." He sat her down, and she ran and sat down in front of the tree. We were soon joined by J.C., Lily, Landon, Beth, and Gavin. Our family was together, it's truly now Christmas. The gifts were opened, and Molly milled through all of her gifts and was playing with a dollhouse that was made like a tree. She said it's a fairy house and the fairy lived and stayed in a forest. She had yet to name the fairy that lived there, but she definitely had the imagination.

Carter stood before the tree and raised a glass to toast the family.

"I have one more gift, and it's for all of us. It is especially something I think that my little girl is going to want to hear." He picked Molly up in his arms and started to make his announcement.

"My sweet Isabella, glad you're feeling better. This wouldn't be a special day without you." He gave me that boyish smirk of his, letting me know what he was about to announce. "My lovely daughter asked Santa to bring her a very unselfish gift, one that I had not intended on. A month ago, I asked her what she wanted Santa to bring and it broke my heart. She told me that she wanted to ask Santa to bring her one thing, one thing. Now, it isn't what you would think, not the typical doll or bike or any toy you could think of."

He looked at his daughter with love. "Molly, tell them what you asked Santa to bring you for Christmas." Molly smiled and patted his cheek. "I want a mommy for my daddy for Christmas." Carter kissed his daughter and hugged her. "I wasn't sure how that was going to work out, but I found her." Molly clapped her hands. "I asked Isabella a couple of nights ago to do me the honor of being my wife. Since then, she has been ill and hasn't felt much like company. I'm glad she has recovered enough to be by my side today. I love you, angel. I have been a bachelor for far too long, so with that said, Isabella said yes. So, Ms. Molly, you will be getting your mommy for Christmas after all."

Molly's little mouth was drawn into an O. Her face glowed with excitement. "Santa broughted me what me wanted." Everyone burst out laughing. Carter assisted her back to the floor, and she leaped onto the couch beside me, crawling in next to me.

"I wuv you, Mommy," she squealed.

"I love you, Tink."

It had finally hit home. I would soon have a husband and a daughter.

This sweet little innocent baby would be mine. I loved them both so much, how could I be so blessed? As bad as I had felt, my body seemed to heal quickly, my heart lurched. With Molly on my lap, I looked up at him in admiration.

"I love you."

He moved with grace to me and sat beside me on the couch as the room rose in an uproar of cheers as he leaned in to kiss me. He whispered in my ear softly, "I love you, angel."

Grayson was obviously overjoyed at his son's announcement as was my mother. "So when's the wedding, son? We will help as much as we can. Your mother and I would be glad to help host."

"I don't know yet, Dad, we'll have to let Isabella get a breath."

My mother sat down in the chair beside me and took my hand in hers, tears stood in her eyes as she smiled brightly. "He's the one, Isabella, I have no doubt. I've never seen a man look at any woman like he looks at you. Don't worry, we will put this together, and you will have exactly what you want."

It entered my mind of what I wanted and it's simple. I was not sure that they would go for it, but it's what I want, it's more important to me. The way Carter looked the night of the play, the passion he had for charities. The ones closest to him should have the money they were all planning on spending on this wedding. The families dispersed through the house talking among each other and playing with Molly. Landon had congratulated his brother-in-law on his engagement and had given his blessing. This meant a lot to him I was sure. "Andrea would be pleased that you weren't alone and that you were in love again," he had told him. Kissing me on the cheek, he welcomed me into the family, telling me that he was happy for both of us. As they all went into their own little world, it left us to ours. Molly went to play under the tree with her many gifts, and Carter and I sat quietly on the couch together. With as many people in the room, you would still think we were alone. Turning, he looked at me as if there was no one there but us. His beautiful smile and dark blue eyes enthralled me. No matter where we were or what we were doing, the reaction to him was the same. Troubling at times and comforting at others were the feelings I allowed myself to feel. There had been so much turmoil in my life, and now it seemed to have departed, I was truly grateful.

"Do you think we could have a small ceremony with simple things?"

"Like what?"

"I kind of want something simple, big enough for flowers and a simple dress, but I want the money they all are planning on this wedding to go to something else, if that's okay with you of course."

"Isabella, I want you to have what you have always dreamed of, but I will do whatever you want. Where exactly are you going with this?"

"I want the money to go to the charities you sponsor. We will be just as married and just as happy with a smaller wedding, besides I would rather it was just our friends and parents."

"Angel, you don't have to do that. We can afford whatever you want and still give to the charities if you want, believe me, we can do this."

"I know my mother is going to want to spend an outlandish amount on this wedding."

"It's fine, I'm going to do this."

"Carter, you can't do that. My mother is rational, but she has a very good idea of what she wants."

"I want you to have what you want, I can afford it.

Take my word for it, I can afford this."

He smiled politely at me and ran his index finger along my jaw. "I can do this and I want to, don't deny me or yourself of this wedding. I want you to have the best whatever it cost."

"But . . ."

He placed a finger to my lips to still me. "No buts, Bella, I want to do this, and I can afford it. You pick out the perfect dress, the one of your dreams and whatever else you want, I will take care of it."

I could see I wasn't going to win this fight either. He was so hard to say no to. "Okay, when are we going to do this?"

"Whenever you like and we can do this anywhere you like. It doesn't matter, but we will hire a planner to help do some of the legwork so you can just relax and enjoy the ride."

"Mr. Blake, do you have any idea how much I love you?"

"Oh, maybe." He watched me with those endearing eyes of his, piercing and direct. I could only imagine what he was thinking, I know what I was thinking about and it wasn't any way near innocent. Seeing that I had been sick for almost four days, I didn't think I would make it to first base anyway. I could hear my subconscious say, "*You're sick,* not *dead.*"

As the day went on, I started to get really tired, and Carter with his keen senses knew when I had had enough. Stooping down to pick me up, I winced.

I was so sore, but I knew that it would soon go away. "You okay? I didn't hurt you, did I?"

"No, I'm just a little sore." He held me close to him, and I rested my head on his chest.

My father spoke quickly when he saw Carter with me in his arms. "Glad to see someone has some control of her." He laughed, "Glad to see someone loves her as much as I do. Thank you, son, take good care of my little girl."

"I will, sir, thank you for allowing me to have the right to one day soon to have her as my wife."

I blushed in his arms and remained leaning against his chest. "Say goodnight, Isabella, you need to rest." I wasn't going to argue, I was tired and starting to feel very weak.

I waved at everyone. "Good night, Isabella." I giggled.

"Night, Mommy."

"Tink, you want to help tuck Mommy in?" Molly's little eyes lit up, and she followed her father as he took me into his room.

"Carter, this isn't Molly's room."

"No, it isn't. It's a much bigger bed, and I can watch you closer."

"What are our parents going to think?"

"Nothing, I'm taking care of you, that's all this is."

He had Molly pull the comforter and sheet down, and then he deposited me on the bed. "Okay, Molly, why don't you go to your room and bring

Daddy Mommy's nightgown. Can you do that for me?" She quickly shook her head and left and shut the door behind her. He looked down at me quietly but sternly. "Do you need to go to the bathroom?"

"I can do that." I made an attempt to get up.

"Come on, I'll get you there."

"Carter, I'm capable of getting up on my own."

He put his hands up in defense and let me make the attempt. I got to my feet and made two steps and found myself leaning to the side and grabbing on to the four-poster bed. "I guess not."

"Why do you always want to do things the hard way, Isabella?"

"Because, Mr. Blake, I'm a very stubborn woman."

"I can see that!" Reaching down, he swept me up.

"Next time, just let me help you." Carrying me, he assisted me to the bathroom, at least close enough where I didn't have to take any steps. Stepping out, he allowed me a bit of privacy. "I'll be at the door, when you're finished, give me a yell."

As many people as I had taken care of, I had never been on the receiving end of being taken care of, not like this. Of course I have always heard that doctors and nurses are always the worst patients. It had been a beautiful day for us despite my illness. I'd spent it with my family and now my future husband. What a wonderful word, *husband*. To think a few short months ago, I had no offer of even a boyfriend, let alone a future offer of a husband. I truly was blessed with this man. Smart, funny, and devastatingly handsome, this gentleman had literally swept me off my feet in an instant. No longer than we had been together, I couldn't remember ever being without him, nor did I want to think about ever being alone again.

"I'm ready."

Walking in the room, I watched him saunter toward me with confidence as he swept me up into his arms. "You are a beautiful man, Carter Blake." He turned red. Oh my goodness, I'd caught him off guard. I actually had caused him to blush.

"Thank you, Ms. Cameron, glad you approve."

Carrying me effortlessly, he deposited me onto the bed once more and changed me into my gown. He's very discreet about his task and soon was covering me with the comforter. Sitting down on the bed, he dimmed the light just enough that it was no longer bright in the room. Before covering me, he released my hair from its tie. Sitting with his leg crossed over his knee, he sat and gazed down at me.

"What?"

He smiled back, "Nothing, just looking at you. You have the prettiest eyes, your lashes are long and wispy, high cheekbones, beautiful dark hair that lies in long waves.

You're a beauty, Ms. Cameron, and I can't seem to take my eyes off you."

"I think you're a little bias, Mr. Blake."

That boyish smirk appeared again. "Perhaps you're right. I still think you're gorgeous." Bending down, he kissed me lovingly. His hand lay upon my cheek as he continued to kiss me softly. "We're going to have to get married soon. I don't think I'm going to be able to keep my hands off you much longer." He wasn't joking this time, he was dead-on serious about what he was saying. At least I wasn't the only one experiencing these feelings, and it had brought ease to me.

"Close your eyes now and sleep, angel, I'll be in soon." I did as I was told, closing my eyes, and listened as he walked out of the room, shutting the door gently behind him. Not feeling so ill anymore but very tired, I lay quietly in the dark thinking of him. I knew that he was right in having me go to bed, but I wanted to be around him even if that meant sitting and watching him.

The thoughts of his unruly dark hair, dark blue eyes, that would pierce the coldest heart, and his touch on my skin kept me from falling asleep.

Thinking of earlier today, how he took care of me whether I wanted it or not, I began to think of it as an intimate and loving gesture instead of an intrusion. It's what he wanted to do, he loved me, and there was nothing sexual intended. What more could he do to prove to me that was all he was after? I lay there trying to remember what happened to me and when. It's a mistake to try to do this, I know it is. Why turn a relatively good day into a bad one? Maybe my mother was right, leave it alone. Carter loved me, and that's all that mattered. He would protect me and this family. Whoever did this was more than likely long gone by now.

The door squeaked, and the light from the living room washed in. The figure in the door was dark against the light, making it difficult to see who was at the entrance. "Isabella, it's Momma, are you awake?"

"Yes, Momma, I'm awake. Come in and sit down with me." She walked into the darkened room and sat on the edge of the bed and clasped my hand in hers.

"You feeling better? I was worried about you."

"Yes, I'm doing much better. I'm tired, but I think the sick stomach is gone."

The bed shifted as my mother scooted farther onto the bed. "Your young man seems to love and care for you very much. He's done everything for you while you were ill."

"You have no idea what he's done."

"Now what is that supposed to mean, Isabella?" My mother's voice was stern.

"He didn't only take care of me, Momma, he bathed me and changed my bed."

"And what's wrong with that, Isabella?"

"I don't know, it just seemed way too personal for him to be doing."

My mother laughed out loud. "Isabella, believe me, when someone is as ill as you were, it is in no way a sexual attraction. He loves you, he wanted to do this for you and felt you deserved to be taken care of by him. After all, you are getting married."

"I know. Oh, I don't know how I feel about it."

"You are going to have to let the past go if you are going to make this work." She pushed my hair back away from my face and caressed my cheek.

"When you were a little girl, I could kiss your fears and cares away. I can't do that anymore, honey, it's way beyond what a kiss from your mother can do."

My throat had become dry because now I realized as much as I wanted to be with him, it scared me to death. The physical relationship, what was that really going to be like? What was going to haunt me when he finally touched

297

me for the first time? Would I be reminded or would it be a healing for me?

I would prefer the latter if it were a choice. "Mom, what was it like . . . you know, with Daddy the first time you were together?"

There was no answer right away. I think I shocked her. "You don't have to answer if you don't want. I'm not sure what is bothering me, I'm scared, Mom."

"No, it's okay. I just didn't think you would even have a question. It a . . . well, Daddy and I were very much in love. It's not something you can really prepare for. You have to remember that the physical aspect of a relationship is tied to the emotional one. It's an expression of what your emotions and feelings for that person are. It's meant to be loving, beautiful, and above all, a very intimate and private thing."

"I know, I just want to know when it comes to it, I'll be ready to handle what comes with it."

"Don't fret, honey. You love him, don't you?"

"Yes, I've never had a doubt about that."

"He loves you, I can see it every time he looks at you. Relax, when the time comes, he will take care of you and you won't care about what has happened before. That's really what you're nervous about, isn't it?" Shaking my head yes, I should have known she could read my mind. "Carter is a loving, long-suffering, and understanding man, don't sell him short."

"Thanks, Momma."

"Anytime you need to talk, I'm here. I wouldn't worry, he's a very good man." Bending down, she kissed my cheek. "Daddy and I will be here for a while, he decided to stay a couple of days longer since you were ill. We want to spend some time with you and get to know Carter and his family.

We are going out with the Blake's tomorrow evening to get to know your future in-laws. You need to

298

rest, Daddy and I will be around. Go to sleep, I'll see you tomorrow." She covered me like I was a child and walked out of the room, leaving the door barely cracked. I slowly drifted off into a comfortable world of dark blue piercing eyes, unruly dark hair, and the scent on a pillow of the man that loved me.

I awoke with a start to see a figure moving about in the room surrounded by a dim light that brought me straight up in the bed. My breaths were rapid, short, and hard to take in. The shadow started walking toward me in a dimly lit room that had only what moonlight that cascaded through the window. A shiver ran my spine, and I made an attempt to scream being unable to.

The figure sat down, and the weight shifted the bed. Reaching for the light, the figure shed light upon the room with a flip of the switch.

"Bella, you okay?"

Letting go of a deep breath that had now escaped me, I realized it's

Carter. Thank God it's him. Was I dreaming before? What startled me? I was gasping in short breaths for air, and it didn't come quickly. Carter placed his hands on my shoulders and looked directly into my face. "Bella, look at me. Take a deep breath, relax." My breaths remained in short, chopped breaths. "Bella, look at me." He cupped my face in his hands and had me looking directly into his face. "Follow me, follow my breaths." I found myself mirroring him and my breaths started to slow down and I could take a deep breath again. I relaxed and collapsed into his arms, the weight of my body leaned against his chest. He gently rubbed my hair and kissed it. "It's okay, I'm here. I won't let anything happen to you. I promise I'll look after you."

He cocooned my body against his.

My thoughts had left me, my mind and body totally empty. He rocked back and forth in small movements like he's rocking a child. His arms were comforting, my eyes still wide and fearful. I relaxed against him, and flashes of people returned to my mind. Like pieces of a puzzle that doesn't fit together, it's stressful and troublesome to me. It felt like it could fall in on me and snuff out every breath. Closing my eyes, I prayed it would go away.

Flashes of men I didn't remember and a young man that was handsome, young, and timid. I knew him, but how did I know him? I couldn't get over the fact that I felt that he could help me that he wanted to help me, but he was bullied beyond belief. I could see him in great detail. He looked like he was a teenager, maybe fourteen or fifteen, with copper to auburn hair, wavy like a surfer ruffled by the wind, and hazel eyes. He looked at me with pity.

He finally called out my name. "Bella, I'm sorry," he pleaded.

I could feel my body clench like someone had drawn back to hit me, and I ducked my head farther into Carter's chest and grabbed my head with both hands. Every part of my body felt like it was ravaged in pain. My breathing picked up again like I had ran a marathon, feeling my body break out in a drenching sweat.

"Isabella," Carter attempted to pull me from my reverie. "Isabella, it's okay. I've got you."

"No, no, no." I shook my head as I saw his hands coming toward me. His face was plain, and I could see this young man. I knew him, who was he? I could hear my own voice calling his name. "Lee, don't do it. Don't let him do this." The man's voice behind him seemed to threaten him, I could only hear pieces of what he was saying. "Just do it boy, be a man for once! You're such a pansy. How could you be my son?" I could see the fear and determination in his face of what this man was asking him to do. He looked remorseful before he ever took a step toward me.

I screamed out loud and hit Carter in the chest as I saw this young man coming after me. Carter grabbed my wrist and shook me. I was still screaming, and the tears washed down over my face. He pinned me to the bed with his body holding my hands raising them above my head. "Isabella, honey, it's me Carter. You're okay, no one is here but me. Open your eyes, look at me." I managed to open my eyes and look into his face. My screams retreated and returned as sobs. He released me as he saw I had realized he was there. He drew me back into his arms and sat holding me tight against him, stroking my hair. My mother and father had made their way to the door and asked to enter.

Carter invited them as he continued to sit and hold to me tightly, rocking me back and forth. "Is she okay, we heard her scream." It's my father's voice, my sobs almost as loud as his voice. "She's okay, just a bad dream. She's done this before. Dr. Bentley says they're night terrors. It's how her body deals with the trauma of what she has been through. Believe it or not, this one was not as bad as some of the others."

"Is there anything we can do to help?"

"No, not really, just time to adjust. Can you bring me her medicine? It's on the counter and a glass of water?"

My mother stood by him, stroking my hair gently, her eyes consoling.

Carter laid his hand against my face and caressed it gently. "Shhh . . . Bella, I'm, here. I'm sorry, I should have been here with you, maybe you wouldn't have done this." My father returned to the room with my medication and water. I was assisted to sit up enough to take my medication. "Take this, honey," my father coaxed. "It's going to help you feel better." He treated me like he did when I was a child and hated medicine, bringing in a spoonful of jelly with it to help it go down. Taking a drink of water, it went down easily and I leaned back against Carter, once again taking comfort in his arms.

"We're going back to bed, I think you have things well in hand." Carter looked up, nodding at him. "Do you mind looking in on Molly? Just make sure she's still asleep."

"Our pleasure, just take care of our little girl."

"I intend to, sir."

Daddy smiled fondly at him, "Call me Dad, Carter, you're practically family." He nodded in assurance, and my parents left the room. My breathing was almost normal once more, and I could feel the medication taking over.

He eased me back down onto the bed and covered me. My eyes barely open, I watched him as he took his T-shirt off and walked surely toward the bed and crawled in next to me. He turned off the light and pulled me next to him, picking me up to where my head rested on his chest and his arm was wrapped around me, making me feel secure listening to his heart beat in a steady rhythm.

"It's going to be okay. I've got you, angel." His long fingers ran through my hair, and I sank into his touch, curling up almost into a fetal position.

As long as he was here, I was safe. The security of his arms, his reassurance of safety and tranquility was all I needed. The terror of what I saw was still ringing through me. Lee—who was he?—the face and the voice I remembered being so familiar. So eerie that I felt this young man had a close connection. I didn't know if I wanted to know. I could still hear his voice haunting me. "I didn't want to do it, Bella," was all I could hear. The closer I got, the more I wished I never had the first memory.

I lay next to Carter trying to do nothing more than to concentrate on the motion of his chest as it fell and rose with each breath and the sweet beating of his heart against my hand. The appreciation and the respect that I had for him was more than I thought I would ever have for anyone. He had always been there for me, he deserved so much more than what I had been able to give him. The dark of the room was consuming, but it's still and calm. The threat of my earlier terror had lifted and he was there.

My body relaxed in his hold, and I took a deep clarifying breath. Running my hand down his chest barely touching him, I sighed. It occurred to me the most important thing I had never told him. In a soft, fearless tone, I could hardly believe the words that escaped me. "I love you."

Running his hand down my back gently, he kissed my hair. His voice was hushed. "I know you do, Bella, I love you too. I'll always be here for you.

Sleep, angel." I was so tired. A weight had been lifted from me as I slowly drifted off to sleep.

CHAPTER 15

Waking early, I found myself wrapped in his arms. Looking at him, I saw he was serene. This was what it would be like to wake up every morning next to him. His hair was ruffled, and his eyes were closed with his lashes fanned against his cheek. He softly breathed as I watched him sleep. I didn't want to wake him; I could watch him sleep easy enough. He had been so good to me, he deserved some extra sleep, and I knew if I stirred, it would wake him.

In the still of the early-morning dawn, I admired him. It was so hard for me to believe that this beautiful man had chosen me. Out of all the women he could possibly have in the world, he had chosen me. With my faults and all, this precious man was in love with me. I no longer had any doubt.

His cheeks were flushed from the warmth of the quilt he'd lain against, and his lips were slightly parted in an undisturbed slumber. The bow of his lips was inviting, but I dared not kiss him. Still, it would be nice just to touch him. Someday, I would be able to love him freely with no thought of guilt or shame. As it was I felt like we were treading on thin ice. I knew the idea was to have me where he could take care of me if I were to get ill through the night, yet the temptation was there. I'd wait, that's what he wanted, and maybe, maybe that's what I wanted. What could be more special than to wait on something that filled you with joy and love? Every minute, every second, that's what he did for me, being totally captivated by him.

He began to stir as I lay next to him. He took in a deep breath and sighed as he opened his sleepy eyes. He gazed over at me as I watched him. In total delight, I watched his beautiful grin unfold. "Good morning, angel," he murmured. I smiled at him, feeling it from ear to ear, rising up on my elbow to look at him closer.

"Good morning, Mr. Blake." I had to touch him, running my fingers gently down his cheek.

"How long have you been awake?"

"Just long enough to get to admire you."

"Getting bold, aren't you, Ms. Cameron? You like the view from there?"

His boyish smirk was delightful.

"Well, since you asked, yes, the view is fine, Mr. Blake. I intend on enjoying this view a very long time."

Chuckling, he pulled me down to him almost nose to nose. "You may fancy your view, but I happen to like you close-up."

"Why? Are you getting a little near-sighted in your old age?"

"Ms. Cameron, you have no idea of the benefits of having you this close.

The one thing I enjoy most of all is to look into that lovely face and know I can kiss it anytime I like."

"So what's stopping you?"

Smiling, I know he's holding back. Sighing, he kissed me chastely. "A little piece of paper that says you belong to me."

"That, Mr. Blake, can be arranged easy enough, don't you think?"

"It's easily fixed, but we would take the fun out of it for our parents to have a wedding, and I would never dream of denying you a wedding of your dreams."

"I wouldn't care about a large, elaborate wedding just so I have you. It's all that matters to me."

"You have me already, I'm not leaving."

"You know what I mean. I wouldn't have to worry about what other people thought or and we wouldn't have to wait any longer to be together."

"We aren't doing anything wrong, so what others think of me doesn't matter. On the other hand, I don't like the idea that it bothers you." He rolled over on to his side, taking me with him, allowing him to look down on me. I thought of what it would be like to be with him, the physical aspect frightened me. I was looking at him, but it's like I was looking through him and he had caught it. "Bella, what is it?"

"Hmm."

"Isabella, hey, you here?" his voice was full of concern.

He had brought me back. "Oh, it's nothing."

Looking down at me he knew there was more to it. "Isabella, if we are going to get married, you have to trust me enough to talk to me. I know you well enough to know there is something amiss. Now are you going to tell me?"

I hated to admit it, and it did sound strange. "I'm scared."

"Everyone gets scared, Bella, marriage is a big step. In the best of circumstances, it can be very trying. I have no doubt about what I am doing here, and I know it's no mistake. If you have doubts, you need to tell me."

"Oh, no, it's not that I have any doubt about marrying you, there's nothing I want more."

"Good, you had me a little nervous. Tell me what it is, Bella, it can't be that bad."

"I'm afraid you'll laugh."

"Isabella, if it's serious and it's really causing you distress, I promise I won't laugh."

I closed my eyes so I didn't have to look at him as I confessed my fear and I said it so fast I wasn't sure if I had even made a whole sentence. "I'm afraid of what may happen on our wedding night." I cringed and slowly opened my eyes, and he was looking down at me solemnly. His look was far from being laughable.

"You don't have to be, we'll take it slow. Whatever it takes to make you comfortable, that's what I will do. Don't worry. I have a feeling it is going to be a first for both of us. I'm not nervous, and you shouldn't be either. You are going to be with me, someone that loves you completely without any reservation, without a doubt without any thought of what was but what will be. I love you, all of you."

"What could a girl say to that?" I grinned at him, watching his beautiful face. "You're unmatched, Mr. Blake, how could I live in fear for a second?"

His look softened, and he traced my cheek. "Thank you, but I'm far from perfect. I promise you this, no one will ever hurt you ever again."

"You are truly a find." I breathed. "How did I ever get so lucky?"

"Now there is where you have it wrong. I'm the one that is lucky. You love me for who I am, Bella, and that's hard to find." My smile did not go without notice. "You're so beautiful, I thank God every day that he brought you into my life." Leaning down to me, he promptly kissed my cheek.

"I do love you." I had said this without hesitation, without a thought, without fear.

"I do believe you have turned a corner, Ms. Cameron, you haven't only told me once but twice now that you love me. I'm glad to hear it. I was beginning to wonder if I would ever hear those words from you, but I'll tell you this, I would have waited a lifetime for them."

Thank goodness most of the flu had passed. I was still tired and weak, but I was feeling better. By New Year's Eve, I was starting to feel more like myself.

Carter and I were to go to a party that his fellow officers had put together, nothing too over the top, but certainly more than I was used to. It promised to be a nice evening out, but Carter had told me before we had decided we were going that more than likely if we did go, we would come back home before 1:00 a.m. Since I was still recovering, it was the best he thought, but maybe I could talk him into staying a while longer and enjoying himself.

Standing before the mirror in my bathroom, I put the finishing touches on my hair, and then stared at the thin line of my face. Before dressing in the newly bought dress I looked down my frame clad only in my very feminine lace bra and panties. I was thin to start with, but I swore I could see my ribs protruding. My recent illness had taken a toll on me. Maybe it was just me, maybe it was my imagination. There was no doubt that I had lost some weight from my illness, but not that drastic. I concentrated on trying to get every touch perfect before I slipped into an expensive long evening gown.

It wasn't something I was used to. This was not my cup of tea, even the restaurant that Carter and I had went to before Christmas was too high-end for me. Taking the dress from its garment bag, I slipped into a floor-length, strapless jade satin column sheath that fitted my form perfectly. I paired the dress with silver strap pumps embellished with rhinestones and emerald and diamond drop earrings. My hair had been fixed into a French roll with small tendrils of my hair hanging in short curls at my ear and neck. The aim was to knock them dead, but not flashy, after all I was going to this event as Carter Blake's fiancée. What a wonderful thought, it would be the first time he would have me out anywhere together as his now wife-to-be. I was looking for simple elegance, and it appeared that I had found it. Even in the thin state I was in and some paleness left from my recent illness, I felt I did Mr. Blake justice. I was anxious although I really didn't know why. I wasn't trying to impress anyone, and I wanted Carter, my future husband, to be happy. Husband, what a wonderful thought, I would soon be planning for our wedding. It wouldn't be long before I was pouring through bridal magazines for ideas.

I turned to leave the bath then I reached for one last thing, a splash of Décolleté. It was a romantic fragrance that reminded me of being able to walk the streets of Paris. It was my signature fragrance, and I wore it often.

Walking into the living area, I reached the threshold where I was met by stares of those present. Carter's parents had agreed to watch Molly and Little Gavin. Carter had turned to see me when everyone had stopped talking as I entered the room. He walked across the floor elegantly and was soon standing in front of me. Taking me by the hand, he raised it and kissed it softly. "Ms.

Cameron, what a beautiful sight you are." I felt my cheeks flush, and the heat rose in the room quickly. He stood gracefully before me in his dinner jacket and finely tailored pants. His shirt perfectly matched in a crisp Jade against his black jacket and tie.

"Mr. Blake, you look devilishly handsome." My eyes sparkled with delight as I admired this man. He never ceased to amaze me, he always blew me away. His unruly dark hair was swept to the side like he had run his fingers through it. It's always in place as if it was numbered. Carter's cologne raised the mix of his natural scent together, and it was an exhilarating combination.

"Thank you, Ms. Cameron, you look lovely. I can say I am a little worried about taking you out tonight." My smile dropped somewhat, and he watched me then grinned that boyish smirk of his that came so easy.

"Why on earth would you be worried? I'm better now, weak maybe, but

I'm better."

"No, Isabella, that's not the reason. Some handsome brute of a guy may sweep you off your feet, and I wouldn't stand a chance. You are absolutely enchanting."

"Well, I don't think you have a thing to worry about, I happen to think you are the best-looking man I have ever seen. Besides, I'm not in love with any of them, I think that gives you an advantage."

"You have a point there, Ms. Cameron. I hope they

all turn green with envy." He held out his arm and my wrap. "Shall we go?" As we started to leave, I heard this little voice behind me and a little tug at my dress.

"Mommy," Molly had come, dragging her blanket behind her.

"Hi, baby." I held her up against my leg where she had grabbed me.

"Me no feel too good."

Carter bent to pick her up and brushed her hair away from her face.

"What's wrong, Tink?"

She curled up against his chest and put her thumb in her mouth.

Reaching over to her, I felt her head. She reached, wanting me to take her. I took her into my arms and carried her over to the couch and sat her down on my lap. I looked at her like I was inspecting a fine piece of art. "Me no feel good, Mommy." Her voice was almost a cry by now. Her face was flushed and hot.

"Does your tummy hurt?" Shaking her head yes, she leaned up against me. The heat from her little body felt like a cook stove. Carter sat down beside me watching her attentively.

"Tink, does anything else hurt you?" She shook her head yes, "Show

Daddy where it hurts." She started to map out all the pain, first pointing to her stomach then her head and throat. I had Carter to get the flashlight, and proceeded to look into her throat, trying not to gag her. I lay her down on the couch and raised her pajama top slightly. "Let Mommy look at your chest, baby." Looking down at her, I discovered she did have a fine rash. I was not sure if it was from her clothes or if it truly was a rash.

Picking her back up and sitting her in my lap, she leaned back against me. Carter was now fixed on us both. "What is it, Bella, is she okay?"

"She could possibly have strep throat. I see some white patches that could be blisters in her throat, and she appears to have a rash, she definitely has a fever. We need to get her temperature down first, children's Motrin works best on kids. We can try that first, later we can try some Tylenol." Carter got up and headed for the kitchen. "Do you itch, baby?" She shook her head no, but she never moved from where she was resting. Carter promptly returned with some Motrin and had Molly take the complete dose. She appeared to have a problem with swallowing, little delayed because of pain. "The medicine will help the hurting, baby." Cradling her in my arms, I felt the heat as it rose from her body. "I'm so sorry, baby, I hate to see you sick."

Carter sat, watching her warily. "Maybe we shouldn't go, I hate to leave her." Grayson stepped up and looked at him with concern. "Son, she is okay.

Mom and I can take care of her. If we need to take her to urgent care, we can call. Take Isabella out and enjoy yourself, I know how to get you if I need to."

Carter sighed. "Pop, I hate to leave her like this, I have never left her when she was sick."

"Don't deny Mom and me the opportunity to take care of her, we see her so little." Grayson lifted her from my lap and held her to him. Molly soon was burying her head in his neck. "We'll see she's taken care of, we took care of you, and you turned out well." Carter half-heartedly smiled at his father.

"Go on, have a good time." Carter stood and offered his hand to me, and I quickly took my place beside him.

"Pop, make sure and call me if anything changes." Grayson watched him and smiled. "Son, she's okay, don't worry." Grayson leaned his head against Molly's and spoke to her softly. "Poppy can take care of you, okay?" Molly clung to him and shook her head. "We're going to be fine."

Carter had said little since we left, and I knew he

was worried, so was I, little ones run a fever quickly and they left sometimes quickly as they came.

The nurse in me just felt, something was wrong, and I couldn't put my finger on it.

My intuition was getting the better of me; my mind had run over at least ten different things from simple to serious. I felt anxious and very unsettled, just the thought of leaving her. Not that Grayson and Iris couldn't take care of her they were very capable. Listen to me, I acted like I was her mother, and she was never mine.

"Maybe we should go back and take Molly to urgent care." My voice seemed heavy and not belonging to me. Carter kept his eyes on the road and thought for a moment then he glanced over at me nervously. "Bella, we have to give my parents a chance to take care of her. If something happens differently, they will call." Picking up my hand, he placed it to his lips and kissed it gently. "I appreciate the concern, I'm worried too. I'm sure they will know what to do, we can call and check on her later." He settled in his seat and continued to hold my hand and laid it against his thigh. Any other time, it might have sent a charge through me, but now my thoughts were with Molly. Carter took a deep breath; and his face that once looked strained had softened. "I'm looking forward to showing you off, Ms. Cameron. Most of the people I work with didn't know I was dating, let alone getting married. I think Landon and J.C. are the only ones who know."

It wasn't long before we pulled to the front of an old majestic white building surrounded by evergreens and shrubs. We had literally stepped into a piece of the country. The inn was aptly called the White Barn Inn. The snow on the evergreens and shrubs made it look inviting, and it was tastefully decorated for the holiday in white lights and red berry wreaths. It wasn't at all what I had expected, but it was charming nonetheless. Carter parked in front of the inn and was soon on my side of the car and assisted me. "Be careful, it's slick." He pulled me into his embrace to where we were nose to nose.

"I wouldn't want you to bump that cute nose of yours, Ms. Cameron." He grinned and kissed me chastely and turned to escort me in.

Ah, being playful, that's what we needed tonight. Molly would be fine, Grayson and Iris were with her and it's a chance for Carter and me to celebrate our engagement. I was sure there would be a formal engagement party if our parents had anything to do with it. We no sooner hit the door, and all eyes had turned to us. I stiffened from the attention, and as Carter removed my wrap, he leaned in next to my ear where only I could hear him.

"Relax, angel, you're beautiful. I'm the luckiest man here to have you on my arm." He kissed me behind the ear. That of course drew more attention to us.

Placing his hand at the small of my back, I was instantly comforted by him and put on a smile. I had nothing to worry about. I was here with a sinfully handsome man that also happened to be in love with me. How could I have a better evening ahead of me?

The entertainment area was large, and it was a thing of beauty with high rafters and lofts. The wooden tables and bar were highly polished. The tables, which were small and quaint, each decorated with a single candle display to enhance the mood. Landon met us with Beth on his arm; she was glowing in her gold strap gown. Her raven hair in large waves hung at her shoulders, and she was adorned with a single string of pearls. I didn't think I had seen her so well put together or happy. Landon slapped Carter on the back as he reached him, and we were drawn into the crowd.

"I broke the ice for you, brother, they know Beth and I are getting married. No one has any idea that you were even dating, this should make for an interesting evening. You are going to announce it tonight, I mean, the parents already know."

Pulling me in closer to him, he looked down at me and grinned. "Only if it's okay with Bella, otherwise I'm ready to tell the world." I couldn't help my face splitting smile.

"I think that would be a wonderful idea. I also think that getting married sooner than later is okay too."

"Whoa, Carter, you might end up at the altar before I do." Landon laughed, and Carter laughed at him.

"Who's to say we aren't already married?" Carter smirked.

Landon looked at him slyly. "One, you wouldn't do that. Two, your mother would kill you, and three, your mother-in-law would be standing in line after her. It wouldn't be likely you would make it to your honeymoon."

Carter broke into that boyish grin of his that always melted me. "Point well made, I'll try to remember that." He looked down at me and flashed that megawatt smile and leaned toward my ear. "I just might have to take you up on that, Ms. Cameron. The way you look tonight, I don't know if I can keep my hands off you."

His words sent a satisfying shiver down my spine. He had to be kidding, as many times as I had asked him to do that very thing. He had finally confronted me with it, and I was a little nervous that he might pitch it to me.

"Why don't we hit the dance floor and show them how it's done, Ms. Cameron?"

"I'll follow you wherever you go, Mr. Blake, lead the way." With that, he looped my arm through his and led me to the dance floor. I was never a very accomplished dancer, but he was so light on his feet. He danced so well it was hard for me not to follow. He made me appear much more graceful than I was as he glided across the floor. When the first dance ended, the next began as a ballroom dance, and it was completely out of my realm. I had never danced one time in that manner. The music was lovely, and Carter led me back onto the floor. Before the first step was made, I leaned in, "I've never done this type of dance before."

"Just follow me, it's light, graceful, and intimate. It isn't any different from the waltz we've done before. Leave everyone else behind, and let me have you." The music began, and he took me in his arms so close that there was barely room for us to move. Our bodies touched, and we moved as one.

I was tense and the tension was making it difficult for him to move. "Take a deep breath, Isabella, we're alone. Relax, dance with me like we're lovers."

It threw me off balance a little, but then that's all it took. I was caught up in him, and we moved around the floor like we were on air. Watching his eyes instead of my feet, I moved flawlessly, concentrating on him, seeing into his very soul. I could feel and see the want and the need in him, love shown out from him. I adored him, and I could feel that adoration spark into a fire that burned white-hot in me. This was not lust, it wasn't unacceptable to me any longer, and I was not ashamed of my feelings. I wasn't sure what to do with this; I had never felt this way before. His eyes never left me as the music continued to play. He never said a word, there wasn't need for any. When the music stopped, I never let go of our embrace and continued to look into his eyes. Not until the crowd went into thunderous applause did we look away.

We were the only couple left on the floor; everyone had cleared it at some point during the music and we were alone.

My breath had come in short chains. He left me breathless at every turn.

Landon escorted Beth to the floor and smiled in amusement. "Where did you learn to dance like that? I don't remember you ever dancing with Andrea at any function. That was amazing."

Carter looked unsettled. "There's a lot you don't know about me, and that's one of them." He had become guarded, like . . . like this was a secret or something. "Will you excuse us for a moment?" He took me by the hand and walked us off the floor. There was tension in his face and his arms, he's upset over something. We exited the room to the hallway where he took a seat in the lounge. He rested into the U-shaped chair and sat with his arms resting across his knees. Taking the seat beside him, I sat quietly waiting for an explanation to his behavior. I cleared my throat, and soon I was asking the question I knew he didn't want to answer.

"What happened back there?"

"Nothing, I need to call home and ask about Molly." He swallowed hard, and the tension was so thick you could cut it with a knife. "We both know that isn't the reason you cut Landon off like that." He remained silent.

"Remember you're the one who said we needed to communicate if this was going to work. Talk to me," I demanded.

"Isabella, leave it go, it doesn't matter."

"It does matter or you wouldn't be acting this way. We were having a perfect evening together, and whatever this is, has upset you. As your future wife, I want to be there when you're upset and try to help if I can."

"Some things are better left alone, Bella."

Letting the subject die, I stood and paced, and he pulled his cell from his pocket and began to dial. "Pop . . . When? . . . Is she okay?" His voice was on edge, being able to hear the panic. "We can come home . . . What do you mean, it's no worse than when we came . . . ? Oh . . . Have they said when it will reopen? . . ." Carter blew out a breath harshly. "Okay, we can try early tomorrow morning. Are you sure she's okay? . . . I know you will . . . Yes . . .

I'll let Beth and Landon know what's going on . . .
Bye Pop."

Carter placed his cell back into his pocket and ran his fingers through his unruly dark hair. He was frustrated and his lips formed a thin line.

"What is it? What's happened?"

"Molly got worse after we left, and they took her to urgent care. They think she has strep throat, the culture come back positive."

"Okay, at least we know what we are dealing with."

"Well, they aren't sure, so they kept her."

"Why?"

"Molly started complaining of her neck hurting. They kept her because they thought it could be meningitis. Pop went home long enough to get a few things and to call us, but I beat him to it."

"Oh, Carter, I'm so sorry. We need to leave now."

"Can't."

"Can't. What do you mean we can't?"

"Road conditions are so bad they closed the main roads down."

"But you're an officer, you qualify as emergency personnel."

"Isabella, I want to be with my little girl, but not at the expense of hurting someone else. We're going to stay here till morning. We better book a couple of rooms before the others find out."

"Two rooms." My heart sank.

"One for us and one for Landon and Beth. It isn't like we haven't stayed together for months."

"I thought . . ."

"You thought what?"

"I thought you were going to separate us because you were upset with me."

"I'm not upset with you. Just give me a little time, I'll tell you all about me soon."

317

After booking the two rooms, Carter and I made our way back into the party, and the festivities were in full swing. Landon and Beth were sitting at one of the linen-clad tables, swooning over each other. What a picture of two people truly in love. The candlelight bounced off their already-glowing faces.

Carter pulled out the chair and assisted me and then pulled out the chair for himself. He leaned into Landon where he could actually hear what he had to say.

"We're not going home tonight," he announced. "Roads are closed due to the weather, emergency personnel only. We can try first thing in the morning.

We need to get to North Dale, Molly has been admitted. They aren't sure, but they think she could have meningitis."

Landon's face went pale. "That's really serious, isn't there any way we can get there?"

Carter gestured, waving his hand. I was unable to hear what was being said. The band had started to play once more, and it was difficult to hear the person next to you clearly. They were engrossed in their conversation, but the meaning was apparent, we were staying here. J.C. and Lily headed toward us, and Lily was laughing and looking at J.C. like he was God. Before Lily got comfortable, I gestured to Carter that we were walking out for a moment, and he shook his head in acknowledgement. Lily was talking to me, but I couldn't understand a thing she was saying. When we finally made it to the hall, I could now talk to her privately and be able to hear what she was saying.

"I can't believe it," she gushed. "We set the date, it will be the first week in May. Oh, Bella, I can't wait."

Taking her and sitting her down in the chair, I explained about Molly and the closed roads and advised her to book a room. "What about Molly? Is she going to be okay?"

"I hope so, Lily. I can't think about that now. If I did, it would drive me crazy."

"I guess I better take care of a room for J.C. and me before we go back."

"I need to get back to Carter. I think he is going to announce our engagement, and I want to be there when he does."

"Oh, I forgot to tell you that Pastor Conley is here, he's the chaplain for the police department. He's actually going to do weddings at the stroke of midnight if anyone wants to get married. I thought about it."

"You didn't?"

"Yes, I did. Why don't we all do it? We would never forget an anniversary," she said jokingly.

"Carter would never go for that, besides, our parents would kill us."

"Just a thought, Bella." She grinned and walked away.

Not that I wouldn't be up to getting married, but I knew without asking he would never do it. Getting married right now was not really the priority, it's Molly. What's going on with her right now? My baby girl was in a hospital, and I was here, not being able to get to her. I wondered if she was scared. Of course she was, she's just a little girl.

Walking into the room, I saw Pastor Conley at the podium. He had delivered a speech, and everyone had stood to applaud. Carter was standing at the table, motioning me to come and stand with him. His smile was broad, and his blue eyes danced in the dimmed light.

"Pastor Conley is getting ready to speak about the New Year." He placed me in front of him and wrapped his arms around my waist, holding me close to him. The excitement built in me as he held me, he's mine and I loved every minute of being with him.

"As you know, we all have made plans for the New

Year. God moves in so many ways, and we are looking forward to a happy, healthy, and abundant New Year. We start fresh, every year offering us all a new beginning, a fresh start in our life to leave behind the old and embrace the new. There are a few that are celebrating tonight a new beginning or ones to come in the New Year, and I wish you all the best. Just remember to keep God in the center of your lives no matter what happens. All things, good and bad, bring us closer together and closer to God. He's a loving and merciful God and only wants the best for all of us.

"On that note of well-wishing, if anyone has something to celebrate, I would like for you to join me here. Just ask those that are in front of you to allow you to come through. I'm sure they won't mind. I have been surprised by a few, and I'm sure you will find it worth celebrating."

Landon and Beth, among some others, were making their way to the stage. Looking down at me in admiration, Carter gave me a little kiss on the cheek. "Well, Ms. Cameron, are you ready for this? It's going to be interesting to see the reaction."

"Mr. Blake, I wouldn't miss it."

He looped my arm through his and escorted me to the stage behind the others. Landon and Beth were in front of us talking, unaware we were behind them. As we got closer, I could feel eyes following us. It's clear that we were being watched.

Carter leaned down to my ear. "Can you feel the heat, angel? There are a lot of eyes on us."

"Yes." It was making me so uncomfortable. I didn't know why I was very happy to be on his arm and to be called his.

After at least twenty announcements of people becoming engaged, grandparents, or some great achievement that had made in some of their children's lives, Landon and Beth took the stage. Landon beamed at his wife-to-be as Pastor Conley introduced them. "Well, Landon, what have you to announce this year?"

Landon looked over at Beth and then back to the engrossed crowd. "Beth and I are getting married in March, and we aren't only celebrating that, we are celebrating the birth of our new son, Gavin. We are looking forward to a wonderful and happy New Year."

"Well, congratulations to you both. That's wonderful."

Everyone clapped in honor of his announcement, and he escorted Beth off the stage. J.C. escorted Lily and announced their engagement and that they were to be married but the date was unsure. They had hoped for a May wedding, and it was in the works. J.C. was looking down at Lily like he was totally in awe of her. His rugged good looks had made him extraordinarily handsome. He looked to be the stern and strong-spirited type, but in her sight, he was like putty in her hands. Lily shined under him, and she clearly worshiped this man. As the applause died down, Carter took me by the hand and escorted me to the stage. My palms were getting sweaty, and I was well aware that now, indeed, all eyes were now on us. It's clearly a surprise for his fellow officers to see him on this stage. The room became painfully quiet, and my heart quickened. His friends and co-workers were in shock. This man that seemingly had not had a date or a relationship with a woman for so long had not only come to this party with a young woman but had also escorted her to the stage to make an announcement.

"Carter, what an unexpected surprise." Pastor Conley looked past Carter to me and assessed me. "What have you to celebrate this New Year?" It was obvious that Pastor Conley had no clue as to what his announcement was going to be.

"Up until about four months ago, I would not have

been up here. I have to say that God has certainly smiled upon me more than once in the last few months. I survived a car accident that should have killed me. Other than my life being spared, something else came from that." Turning to me, he took his fingers and run it down my cheek to my chin, getting my attention. "If that would not have happened, I wouldn't be standing here today with the love of my life. She's won my heart, so"—he sighed—"Pastor Conley, it looks like your services is going to be needed more than once in my family. I asked Isabella to marry me."

The room remained silent, so much so that if an ant had walked across the floor, it could have been heard. "What did she say?" Landon shouted from the back of the room, and Carter laughed and turned to the group. "She said yes." The group clapped and began to chant, "Kiss her, kiss her."

"Shall we, Ms. Cameron?" Taking one step toward me very deliberately, he kissed me and proceeded to dip me elegantly. The group went into an uproar. He looked down at me, his smile cunning. He was happy, and I was stunned so that I kissed him again and the crowd became louder.

"Carter, I do believe you have plenty to celebrate. The celebration of your marriage will be soon I hope, and I will be more than glad to celebrate with you." He shook Carter's hand and kissed me chastely on the cheek, and I was escorted off by my handsome fiancé.

"Do remember at the stroke of midnight, I'm here, and I will be performing ceremonies if anyone chooses to make their commitment tonight. Write your names down on the list, if everyone here that has made announcement of commitment decides to do this, I'm going to be busy for a very long time."

In the hours that passed, Carter had called his father three times. There didn't seem to be any change in Molly's condition. The spinal tap she had did not seem to indicate

322

meningitis, but she was still very ill. Poor baby, I hated to think that she was there without us and that she had to undergo a procedure such as that. She must be so scared, if she was able to be scared. Carter tried to reassure me, but I could tell he was still very concerned for his daughter.

I stood looking out the window from the hall watching the snow gently fall as it kept mounding on the grounds. It floated down so quietly and peacefully, but it left me with such a feeling of dread and uneasiness that I wrapped my arms across my shoulders to prevent myself from shuddering.

We were going to stay the night here? Why did that unnerve me? It wasn't like we hadn't stayed in the same home for months or that we hadn't stayed in the same room at night at times. I guess it was different when I was suffering from influenza and some kind of nightmarish fight I had during the night looking only for solace. We were both perfectly healthy; my feelings for him had grown just over the past couple of weeks. It didn't help me either to know that he had those same feelings that he had been fighting. I guess it was crazy for me to even think of anything in particular happening between us other than what was needed, sleep.

I felt his arms wrap around me as I stood there, his breath felt on my neck as his head bent to my ear. "Penny for your thoughts, Ms. Cameron."

If only he knew what I was thinking, he wouldn't be standing so close to me.

Shrugging it off, I relished in his embrace, and I felt myself warm just from his presence.

"Just Molly and you, watching the snow fall, hoping it would stop so that we could go home to her. Never thought I would want to leave from being in a place such as this to be able to have time alone with you where you were totally mine."

Kissing me on the cheek, he squeezed me gently to

him. "Molly is going to be fine. I understand you want to be with her, so do I. We can't, so we are going to have to make the best of it and just keep in contact with Pop. She knows we would be with her if we could. God is going to take care of her, I have to believe that."

"How can you be so sure of things, that little girl could get very sick maybe die, and you say God is going to take care of her?"

"Faith, Isabella, and yes, she could die. It isn't that I haven't thought of that. No matter what happens to us, it isn't a mystery to God. He knows every step we are going to take, every breath we need, every good or bad thing that is going to happen, but he is there for us. So if Molly gets well, it's in his will, and if it isn't, I have the assurance that my little girl will be in a much better place than I and I'll see her again. It doesn't mean that I wouldn't grieve or that I wouldn't miss her because I would. God never puts more on us than we can stand."

"I wish I could believe in the God you seem to stake so many things on."

"You can, Bella. It isn't as hard as you think. God knows your heart, he knows what you need, and if you can't pray, he prays to the Father for you when you don't have a voice. Open your heart to him, angel, he'll come in if you invite him. He just waits for us to ask, and he wants to dwell within us and have a relationship with us. He's the best friend you could ever imagine having. When we go to him for salvation, we ask and believe it with childlike faith, knowing that he hears us. We ask for his forgiveness from sin, and he cleanses us fully, never seeing it again. Just like Molly has accepted you and has adopted you as her mother, he adopts us into his family. We belong to him, and nothing can take us from him ever again. As long as sin stands in the way, there is a great divide between God and us. Jesus made a bridge from us to God to make it possible for us to come to God and renounce our sins and become part of his

324

family. It's up to us to accept the simple truth and grab on to it. No one can live a perfect life, I know I couldn't and I couldn't begin to try.

"Just don't wait too long. He calls so many times, and then it falls on deaf ears. We too never know when our next breath will be our last. We live for him and try to live a life that is honorable to him and to serve him. It doesn't mean there will be no fun or strife in your life, it's the opposite really. We can enjoy our life, and he gives us a life that is free and abundant no matter what we face.

"Losing Andrea taught me a lot. It was a hard lesson to learn, I was just starting a new Christian life, something that she had tried to talk to me about for years, and I didn't want to listen. I can see now how many good times and blessings I missed out on because of it."

CHAPTER 16

The crowd gathered in the reception hall as Pastor Conley was about to toast to the New Year. Standing in the crowd next to my promised love and soon-to-be sister- and brother-in-law along with my best friend and her husband-to-be, I still felt a sense of dread. Something was wrong or maybe I was just out of sorts, I wasn't sure. Something didn't fit, something didn't feel right. Everyone was happy and ready to celebrate the New Year, looking around for someone to share their midnight kiss, and some were so celebrated it was hard to tell where they would be by the end of the evening.

Looking through the room and trying to remain calm, I could feel a presence that wasn't there before. I was suddenly fearful. Fearful of something that seemed to be haunting me. Was it me, Landon, Beth, J.C., Lily, Carter?

It couldn't be Carter. Who would be there that would want to do any harm to any of us. All the same, I kept my purse next to me, tucked inside was my Glock 19 loaded and ready for use. I rarely went anywhere without it since I had been training at the academy. Other than Carter, Gus had taught me how to use it and helped me with target practice. Carter had no idea I had been going at least twice a week for months practicing in firearms and self-defense.

If he had, he would have thought I lived in fear and I was determined to stand on my own. One of the few nights Carter wasn't wearing his gun. I guess he thought with it being a closed celebration with fellow officers, he wouldn't need one.

"Everyone ready? Fellows, find your gals, we're going to start counting down," Pastor Conley announced. "It's been a wonderful year, and we look to a brighter one. Start the clock, J.C., it's time." And from then on, all eyes were focused on J.C. "Ten, nine, eight, seven, six, five"—

Carter looked down at me nervously like he knows something was wrong—"four, three, two, one. Happy New Year!" Carter embraced me and kissed me like he was desperately in need of saying something that was unable to be said with mere words. Clasping my face in his hands, he looked into my face, and I saw a beam of light from behind him, one that totally surrounded him. "What is it?" My heart thundered in fear, what had I witnessed? Something was going to happen, and now I knew. Whatever was to happen, I knew it was going involve him.

"Bella, what's wrong?" Leaning into him and holding on to him for dear life, my breaths became sharp and hard to take in. The pain of knowing something was wrong, something was going to happen and I could feel it.

I didn't know when or why, but it's him, and I was not going to let him go without a full outfight. "Isabella, come on," he coaxed, stroking my back.

"If anyone is ready to make their commitment tonight to each other,

I'll be set up shortly," Pastor Conley announced. I continued to stand there holding on to him and loving him the only way I could, hoping that he understood.

"Hey, Carter." J.C. came over to where we stood, not sure rather to continue from the sound of his voice. Carter was slightly knocked off balance letting me know he had slapped him on the back in a friendly gesture. "J.C.," he addressed.

"Would you and Isabella stand up for Lily and me? We would like to get married tonight, if you would do it for us. It would mean a lot to Lily for Isabella to be there and for you to stand up with me."

Moving away slightly but never letting go, I turned to see them both there in front of us waiting for an answer. Carter looked at me and then to J.C. "It would be our pleasure, we would love to."

"That's great." J.C. clasped Lily's hand. "You have

no idea how much this means to us. Can you meet us at the podium in about ten minutes?"

Carter smiled that shy grin of his. "Sure, it'll be practice for our own wedding." J.C. quickly took Lily off to the side, and they talked before heading up to the podium to talk to Pastor Conley. "Isabella, you okay?" I shook my head yes, knowing it wasn't true, I wasn't all right. He knew, it amazed me how well he could read me. "I want to see you in your perfect dress on your perfect day real soon, Ms. Cameron. I want to be down at the end of the aisle watching my angel walk to me"—he pointed as if he saw me walking toward him in a distance—"with your white dress, your veil floating softly against your face with your flower girl and bridesmaid with your father escorting you in. The only person I'm going to see is you that day. It's one I'm looking forward to seeing. Until then, we can stand up with J.C. and Lily and share this special day with them. We get to practice at least twice before our own, we should be really good at it by then." He chuckled.

Taking my hand, he led me to the podium where Pastor Conley, J.C., and Lily were waiting. He came prepared with music and flowers for the bride and bridesmaid. "I'm so glad you could be here with us, Bella," Lily gushed.

"And J.C. is so happy that Carter was willing to do this for us. He thinks of Carter like a brother. I'm so happy. I'll stand up for you when you marry Carter if you like. I wouldn't miss it for the world."

"I would love it if you did. You know I couldn't get married without you, you're my best friend."

"Lily, Pastor Conley is waiting for us," J.C. announced to his bride. Lily took his hand and gave her a bouquet of flowers. Pastor Conley handed me a lovely bouquet of red sweetheart roses, the fragrance filled the small area in which we stood, transporting me to my future wedding. I dreamt briefly and looked over to see Carter smiling at me from the other side of J.C. We were at arm's length. When the prayer was offered for the bride and groom, he reached behind J.C. to take my hand and rubbed my knuckles with his thumb tenderly. Looking over at him with my head bowed, I could see his head bowed and his eyes closed. His cheeks were slightly red, and his lips were parted slightly, offering a silent prayer. I would marry him now if he would do it, I didn't want to lose a moment with him.

The ceremony was short, and I barely paid any attention to it. The only word I heard was *amen.* Pastor Conley spoke a few scriptures in which I did not hear and spoke to the bride and groom directly. Meanwhile, I was in my own world looking into my own future, picturing Carter reciting his vows and committing to me. When I finally came back to know what was going on, he was announcing them as husband and wife. Carter's hand still held mine as J.C. kissed his new wife. I had to say I didn't think at this point he was exactly watching them either. He looked at me with his beautiful boyish grin and mouthed "I love you." My face turned crimson, and I smiled at him shyly.

The room applauded for the new couple, and J.C. picked up Lily and let out an uprising scream. The room burst into laughter. "We did it, she's mine," he declared and she giggled as he carried her away. Pastor Conley laughed with the others. "Well. There goes a happy couple."

Carter stepped closer to me as they left the room, and I could hear his boyish laugh as they left. Pastor Conley made a few steps closer to us and smiled. "You ready to do this tonight?" He looked at Carter for his answer.

Carter looked at me and back to Pastor Conley. "I don't think so tonight. I really want to give her the wedding she wants, one where her family can be there."

Pastor Conley nodded. "I understand. I know you

will be very happy together. Come see me before you make arrangements, there's some things we need to talk about." Pastor Conley walked back to his place to wait and see if anyone else was going to commit tonight, and we made our way back to Landon and Beth. Landon stood and took Beth by the hand. Beth smiled, but she looked tired.

Carter greeted Landon with a grin of a Cheshire cat. "Going to get hitched? I know the pastor well, maybe we can cut you a deal." Landon shook his head and laughed at the suggestion.

"No, not tonight. Besides, I don't think Beth is feeling much like a honeymoon. I thought for sure you and Bella were going to. I've never seen such a perfect couple. You stole the show from Lily and J.C., but don't tell them that."

"Come on, Landon, you know me better than that. I would like to live a little longer. If we went home married, our parents would kill us. All joking aside, I promised Bella a nice wedding with all the glitz she can stand, big enough deserving of a princess. I want her to have what she has dreamed of."

"You're such a cop out. You know you would marry her now if she asked."

Carter looked over his shoulder and smiled at me. "Be careful, she's watching you."

"If that's what she wanted, I would do anything for her."

"I knew you were too soft."

Carter laughed heartily. "I wouldn't talk, you aren't much better. I've seen you get pretty mushy, never thought you would turn to clay."

Beth leaned into Landon, signaling to him that she was indeed very tired.

"You better quit while you're ahead, my sister has been pretty good at making fellows putty in her hands, even me."

330

Landon took Beth by the arm and then snaked his arm around her. "It's past Sleeping Beauty's bedtime. Think I'll take her to the room and get some rest. We'll meet you at North Dale when we can get out on the road."

"We'll see you then." Carter watched as Landon escorted Beth from the room and down the hall.

Turning, he looked at me and pulled me close into him, and I held to him like he was going to get away. "Ms. Cameron, would you like to take another spin on the floor, or would you rather I walked you home?"

"A spin on the floor sounds really good, but you know I turn back into the little cinder girl at midnight. The little girl that sits and cleans among the cinders waiting for her prince to slip the glass slipper on her foot and carry her away is still waiting."

"I think he is going to find you really soon. I can carry you away you know." Reaching down, he swept me off my feet and into his arms as if I were weightless. Giggling as he picked me up, I put my arms around his neck and kissed him on the cheek. The room started clapping, and Carter turned with me in hand to see why everyone was clapping. He's shocked when he found they were watching us. "Make an honest woman of her, Blake," one of them yelled. My face flushed, and I leaned into him. Carter just shook his head and smiled, "Soon, not tonight." He then walked off with me in his arms, his head lying against mine. "Cinderella, let's get you home." He carried me all the way to the room holding me as close to him as possible. He allowed me to slide down his body as we stopped outside our room for the night. Starting to step in he picked me back up. Shocked at his response, I looked into his very serious face.

"You didn't have to carry me back to the room you know. I could have walked."

Never missing a beat, he looked at me with some unknown emotion. I'd never seen him look like this, ever.

331

"Practice, Ms. Cameron, practice for the day I will be carrying you over the threshold on our wedding night, I look forward to it." Kicking the door shut behind him, it slammed with a harsh bang. "Just because we are stuck here in this beautiful place on a beautiful snowy night doesn't mean it can't be romantic. I brought a couple of things with me for you which I think you will like very much. I sent a young lady that we all know and love with your mother to a fine boutique. They picked a couple of things out and did me a favor. Just don't go in the bedroom yet.

Everything for all purposes is in the bath for now. Don't keep me waiting, Ms. Cameron, I'm not one to be kept waiting long." Oh my, what did he have in mind? He had my mother in on this? He had this planned all this time, whatever it was. Allowing me to slide down his body once more, he looked at me like he could see into my heart, read every thought. Right now, it would be a pretty hard read. "Go, go." He sent me on my way.

"The bath is to the right, Ms. Cameron. You'll find a garment bag on the door and the appropriate jewelry on the counter. I'll see you in fifteen minutes, don't be late. By the way, there will be a young lady in to escort you, she'll know where to find me." Taking a few steps and looking back, he could see the thunderstruck look on me. He looked smoldering, his stance had changed and so had his mood. He loved me, but there was something that didn't fit. He's hiding something from me. "Don't worry so, Ms. Cameron, you'll understand soon, I promise you." He grinned and then watched me slowly head to the bath. Entering the room, finding it very unique for a farm themed, the bath was an open big room with a tub on the side wall, and a fireplace divided the bedroom from the bathroom. The fire was lit and was the only light for the moment in the room. Candles were strewn around the room and on the mantel, and there was a scent of fresh flowers. Looking on the door, I found a garment bag as he promised. At the vanity on the counter was a cinched jewel bag along with what appeared to be a hat box. That seemed odd to me, why would he go to this trouble? As I walked on into the room, I found a lamp and turned it on. Walking over to the door, I found the garment bag and started to look at the contents when I saw a shoebox at my feet. Picking it up, I looked in to find a pair of kitten heel pumps. They weren't any ordinary pump, these shoes were beautiful. One look at them and I knew where he was going. These were Cinderella's glass slippers. Sitting down chair, I tried them on and had to smile. They fitted perfectly. Now being overly curious of what I would find in the garment bag, my heart raced in anticipation of what I would find.

My hands shaking with excitement, I unzipped the bag to find a white ball gown. Looking at it closer as I removed it from its hiding place, I found it was a wedding dress. My breath was suddenly taken from me. I took it and held it to me, looking into the mirror above the vanity. That's what he's had planned. I couldn't believe this, and my mother was in on this. That's even harder to believe. Didn't she want to be here? Well, I couldn't question, I had to get dressed, he's waiting for me. Before I was fully dressed, I heard the door open and heard the footsteps getting closer. "I'm in the bathroom." Trying to find my way into the corset part of the dress, I turned to see a woman walk into the room.

"Isabella, you look radiant." She smiled, wiping back tears.

"Momma?"

"You didn't think I would let you do this without me, did you?"

"When did you get here?"

"We came this evening just after you left with Carter. We couldn't miss this, honey."

"What about Grayson and Iris?"

"They wanted to be here, but with Molly ill, they couldn't."

"I don't want to get married without Carter having his family here."

"That's all been taken care of. We are going to do this in a church later, but for now, this is what he wanted to do for you. Don't spoil it for him."

"Oh, I don't know, Momma. He shouldn't do this without them."

"He wants to do this, he had it planned down to the detail. He loves you, honey. Come on, let's get you dressed. Daddy's waiting on us."

She helped me to step into this beautiful satin beaded wedding dress. It fitted my every curve and sat just off the shoulder. In the jewel bag, there was a fine triple-strand pearl choker. Leaning my neck to the side, my mother placed around my neck. I admired it in the mirror. I turned to leave, and my mother stopped me. "Sit down, Isabella, you missed something." She pointed for me to sit on the stool in front of the vanity. Sitting, I looked into the mirror, and I had been transformed totally. My hair remained up but in a sophisticated bun, and small curls were left at my cheek. Looking into the mirror, I could see my mother approach me. A veil, of course, with a tiara attached no less. He remembered everything. I had suddenly become very emotional. Tears just sit behind my eyes, and I tried to hold them back. "You wouldn't want to forget your crown, dear. I always knew you were a princess, just look at you, you're breathtaking." She squeezed my shoulders and looked at me in the mirror. "Time to go. Get your gloves and put them on, and I'll get your flowers."

My flowers were made up of pink peonies, daisies, and white roses with a long pink ribbon attached to them. I had to hand it to him, he paid attention to detail and it wasn't over yet. It occurred to me that was the smell of fresh flowers I had encountered as I came into the room. When I made it to the seating area of the room, I found my father sitting waiting by the door, looking very dapper in his black tux and white dress shirt. "Time to go, daughter. You look lovely, pretty as Mother."

"Daddy."

"It's true, never thought I would see this day come, pretty as a picture."

Leaning in, he kissed me on the forehead. "We better go, your young man is impatiently waiting for you."

As we walked out of the room, it hit me in a few short moments that

I would no longer be Isabella Cameron. I was no longer just someone's daughter, I would be his wife. Oh my, how was that going to work?

Daddy walked me to the hall that Carter and I came from earlier from the New Year's party and stopped at the opening just before walking into the reception hall. Momma kissed me on the cheek and made her way to her seat.

"Oh, Daddy, who's standing up for us, where is Landon and Lily? They were supposed to be here for this."

"Don't worry. It's fine their here." He attempted to soothe me. "Lily will meet us, and Landon is trying to hold the groom together." I giggled nervously at the remark. No sooner had he said that, Lily came bounding in.

"Oops, sorry I'm a little behind. I didn't expect this, and I had already changed."

"It's okay, Lily, I didn't know. Carter set this up, I had no idea."

The music began to play. A beautiful piece of music playing I recognized as the "Butterfly Waltz." "I'll see you up front," Lily announced and then walked away in her pink tea-length dress holding pink roses. I couldn't wait to see him. I knew with the details he had made, he must look amazing.

Taking my arm, my dad looked down at me. "You ready to do this, princess?" After shaking my head yes with a broad smile, he rewarded me with a smile of his own. "Let's go meet him." Pulling my veil down over my face he took my arm he walked me around the corner. The room was lit with candles and Christmas lights. How did he manage this in a short amount of time? It had been less than a half hour ago that the place was full of people celebrating New Year's Eve. Now as I managed to look around, I saw my parents, Landon, J.C., Lily, and Beth. At the podium stood Pastor Conley and my handsome husband-to-be surrounded with ferns, pink peonies, daises, and white roses. Once my eyes were on him, everyone else vanished.

My heart raced and my hands shook. This was it, I was going to marry this wonderful man, and he was only steps from me. His beautiful blue eyes danced as he watched me walk to him, his unruly dark hair perfectly in place, and that boyish grin that made my heart sink to my feet was in full force.

Standing there waiting for me in a perfectly tailored navy suit, he was dressed like royalty. A gold banner down his chest made him look regal and military.

The prince of my Cinderella was here, how could it be anymore fairytale than this?

Stepping down from the podium, he met me and my father three steps from Pastor Conley. My father placed my hand into Carter's as he gave me away. "Take good care of her, son, she's my baby girl."

Carter received my hand and assured my father he would with a nod. He stepped in front of me and raised my veil. "You want to do this? This is your chance to say, it's okay if you aren't ready. We can always do this later if you aren't sure." His face questioned as he watched my response. He's nervous only at the answer I might give; otherwise, he's steady as a rock.

"I haven't been more ready for anything. Question

is, are you ready for this? You've been a bachelor for a long time." The tension from his face had left and he smiled. "Isabella, I have been ready since the day I met you."

"If you're ready, we'll start." Pastor Conley looked down on us.

"Yes, we're ready," Carter answered.

"I think we will get to the heart of this if it's okay with you?"

"Yes sir, that's fine."

"Carter, Isabella, do you come freely, of your own will, to give yourselves in marriage to each other? If so, say 'I do.'"

Looking at each other, Carter spoke first, "I do."

"I do," came from me without hesitation. All nervousness for the moment had vanished when I looked into his beautiful eyes.

"We are here today to celebrate the union of Carter Elijah Blake and

Isabella Jade Cameron. God speaks of marriage as a sacred contract. In this contract, you are to give yourself 100 percent to the other. You are no longer separate, you become as one. One, there is no longer two, one unit, never to be torn apart. This unit is to be there for one another to function, for without the support of the other, the relationship suffers. God meant for marriage to be for a lifetime and holds it in high regard. Today, before God, your family and friends, you enter into a holy covenant, one that is binding before God. It is a lovely thing to see young love, but more beautiful is that of old love, one that has grown and is in the favor of God. We wish this for you both.

"Carter, Isabella, will you love each other, honor each other, and accept children from this union freely. If so, please say 'I do.'"

Carter's eyes never left mine. "I do."

337

We never discussed children. My thoughts left easily. "I do." Hesitating, Carter was watching me intently. He got it, it's apparent. We may never be able to have children together because of my past. Does that even matter to him?

"There is no greater gift than love. God speaks of love of being gentle and forgiving. First Corinthians 13 reads,

"Though I speak with the tongues of men and of angels, and have not charity, I am become as sounding brass, or a tinkling cymbal.

And though I have the gift of prophecy, and understand all mysteries, and all knowledge; and though I have all faith, so that I could remove mountains, and have not charity, I am nothing.

And though I bestow all my goods to feed the poor, and though I give my body to be burned, and have not charity, it profiteth me nothing.

Charity suffereth long, and is kind; charity envieth not; charity vaunteth not itself, is not puffed up, doth not behave itself unseemly, seeketh not her own, is not easily provoked, thinketh no evil; rejoiceth not in iniquity, but rejoiceth in the truth; beareth all things, believeth all things, hopeth all things, endureth all things.

Charity never faileth: but whether there be prophecies, they shall fail; whether there be tongues, they shall cease; whether there be knowledge, it shall vanish away. For we know in part, and we prophesy in part. But when that which is perfect is come, then that which is in part shall be done away. When I was a child, I spake as a child, I understood as a child, I thought as a child: but when I became a man, I put away childish things. For now we see through a glass, darkly, but then face to face: now I know in part; but then shall I know even as also I am known. And now abideth faith, hope, charity, these three; but the greatest of these is charity."

He continued, "Marriage is not to be entered into unadvisedly or lightly, but reverently, discreetly, advisedly, soberly, and in the fear of God. Please join hands."

Reaching for my hands he takes one and I give my flowers over to Lily.

My heart sings and echoes an unfamiliar feeling. I truly didn't ever think there was such a thing as a true love. Of course I had watched my parents for years but I thought of it as something strange and wonderful. It wasn't something I ever expected for myself.

"Do you, Carter, take this woman to be your lawfully wedded wife? To

have and to hold from this day forward, in sickness and in health, for better or for worse, for richer or poorer, keeping yourself unto her as long as you live? If so, say 'I do.'" His face was solemn, and I could feel the love radiate from him. How could I be so lucky to have his love? After everything he had been through and what he did know about me and things that he didn't?

He still loved me, holding out hope that I would one day come to his God.

I could tell I was closer to God than I once was. Maybe it was as simple as Carter had explained. "I do." He smiled.

"Isabella, do you take this man to be your lawfully wedded husband? To have and to hold from this day forward, in sickness and in health, for better or for worse, for richer or poorer, keeping yourself unto him as long as you live? If so, say 'I do.'"

I could feel the tears starting to run down my cheeks, and I smiled sweetly at him. "I do."

His face softened as he heard my answer. His boyish grin that I loved had returned, thank goodness.

"Do you have a symbol of this commitment?"

Carter handed him my ring, and he placed it on the open Bible. "The wedding ring is made of precious metal and is made more precious by the wearing of them. They are a circle, a symbol that has no beginning or end.

The ring is a symbol of the love you share, an outward reflection symbolizing the love and commitment between you that will never cease, and a visible sign of the vows in which you have made to each other."

"Carter, place the ring on Isabella's left hand and repeat after me, 'This ring is a token of my love.'"

Carter recited after Pastor Conley, "This ring is a token of my love."

Pastor Conley and Carter took turns reciting the ring ceremony. "And a symbol of faithfulness, as I place it on your finger, I commit my heart and soul to you. I ask you to wear this ring as a constant reminder of my vow to you, to love you all the days of my life."

"Isabella, do you have a symbol of your commitment?" Carter removed the ring I gave him for Christmas and handed it to me, and I turned it over to Pastor Conley. He took the ring and placed it over the Bible. "Blessed is the one that gives this ring and the one who wears it. Isabella, take the ring and place it on Carter's left hand and repeat after me." I listened intently and recited each word. Carter now as well had a tear tracing down his cheek.

"This ring is a token of my love and a symbol of faithfulness, as I place it on your finger. I commit my heart and soul to you. I ask you to wear this ring as a constant reminder of my vow to you, to love you all the days of my life."

"Is there anyone present who may know a just cause why this couple may not be legally wed? Let them speak now or forever after hold their peace."

Pastor Conley paused for a moment, giving the guest time to answer in which none did. "By the authority vested in me by the State of Maine, I now pronounce you husband and wife. Carter, you may kiss your bride."

His eyes never left me and hadn't the whole ceremony. I had forgotten we weren't alone. "With pleasure," he smiled and kissed me tenderly but slightly chastened. *Oh my goodness, he's mine. He's really mine.*

"Ladies and gentlemen, may I present to you Mr. and Mrs. Carter Blake."

It wasn't long before everyone was congratulating us on our marriage. My mother was crying, and my father was making an attempt at consoling her.

Landon was shaking Carter's hand and then pulled him in for a little slap on the back followed by J.C., Lily was hugging me for dear life. We won't be able to forget each other's anniversary seeing it was on the same day of the same year. Who would have thought? Beth was on the other side of Lily, waiting for her turn between Carter and me. Carter was talking with Landon, J.C., and Pastor Conley as I finally made my way back to him. Lily followed along with Beth, I thought, in an attempt to get them to go back to their rooms. It was rather late, and our ceremony lasted longer than what was intended.

I had to admit it was beautiful, but as beautiful as it was, it was my wedding night and I wanted to have him to myself, plus it meant an early morning to see about Molly if we could get to her. Our poor baby girl, she must be asleep by now. Taking him by the hand, I got his attention. "I can tell I'm married, she's already coming after me." He smirked.

"Don't you think we should check on Molly?"

"Already have." He smiled, and I saw relief in his face. "She's fine, I talked with Pop before the ceremony. Her fever has broken or at least under control.

They think it's no more than strep throat and they should discharge her tomorrow morning, maybe before we get there."

I sighed with relief; a weight had been lifted from me. "Oh, thank God, I was scared."

341

"Me too, but she is fine and we can enjoy our wedding night, Mrs.

Blake." He slipped his arms around my waist as I put my arms around his neck. "That has a wonderful sound to it, doesn't it? You don't have any regrets of getting married like this, do you?"

"No, I think it's the most wonderful thing you could have done. I'm thrilled, but how in the world did you put it together so quickly? It wasn't a half hour we left and we come back and the room has changed and everyone is gone."

"I have some really good friends that wanted to see me happy. They moved the party to the conference room and the rest help decorate."

"It must have taken an army to do this."

"Well, a small one." He cocked his head to the side. "I can think of less pleasing things they have done faster." Bending down, he kissed me on the forehead. "We have a cake to cut, but I suggest we cut it, take our toast, and get out of here."

"I'm all for that."

"Well, Mrs. Blake, you are an impatient one?"

"I just want to be alone with my husband."

"You will soon. Right now, our guests are waiting on us. J.C. is just itching to give the toast."

"J.C., he's giving the toast?"

"I thought it an appropriate gesture, I see him like a little brother."

"How wonderful, I'm glad you asked him."

"Shall we, Mrs. Blake?"

He escorted me across the floor to the main table where there was a small two-tier white cake elegantly topped with a crystal coach. The bottom of the cake was surrounded with Christmas lights and pink roses. We cut the cake, and he smiled at me sweetly. "Be nice," he warned, grinning.

I delicately gave him a bite of our wedding cake, and he in turn fed me my piece. The flavor was wonderful, red velvet with a sweet cream cheese frosting. The toast was given by J.C. Standing tall, he raised his glass.

"To the happy couple, may your days be filled with laughter, joy, and peace, may God smile down on you and grant you many happy years together.

I'm honored to be able to toast this man I consider like a brother to me and his lovely wife. Knowing Carter, there will never be a dull moment. Cheers."

Carter carried me back to the room and smoothly unlocked the door and crossed the threshold easily, although I didn't know how, his hands were full of me and a ton of wedding dress. Kicking the door behind him, he walked across the floor as I admired him. This was it, he's all mine. Reaching for the French doors to the bedroom, he opened them and carried me over to the bed and set me on the edge. The room was lit solely with candles and the fireplace, the warmth of the room didn't keep chills from running down my spine.

Dropping to one knee, he rummaged through the bottom of my skirt and took my foot against his thigh and took off my shoe. "Mrs. Blake, it seems the prince found your glass slipper and returned it to you." He looked at me with that boyish grin and then lifted my other foot and removed my other shoe. "It could take a little while to get you out of this. Running his hand up my leg to my thigh, he felt me shiver. "It's okay, relax, you're with me. I'm not going to hurt you."

Continuing, he reached the top of my stocking. "Mrs. Blake, I approve, very nice." Taking the top, he slowly rolled them down, allowing his thumb to sweep against my bare skin. He did the same with the other and gazed up at me with a reassuring look. I took some slow, deep breaths, trying to control my fear. I felt it rising along with my passion for him.

"Isabella, you okay?" He remained looking up at me, watching my every reaction, but I couldn't say a word. I didn't know what's keeping me from speaking. "Angel, talk to me," he coaxed. I couldn't manage a syllable for him.

He remained kneeling before me and looked at me with compassion. "It's going to be okay, Isabella, I know you're nervous. So am I, more than I would like to admit. Let it go, angel, there isn't anyone here but us." Standing slowly, he held a hand out to me and I took it reluctantly.

Come on, Isabella, flip *the switch,* this *is your husband. You're allowed to be vulnerable in front of him,* you're *allowed to feel.* Without a word, I reached for the sash over his chest and removed it, laying it on a close-by chair. His beautiful eyes flickered against the fire light, and I saw the man I had fallen in love with.

Making one step toward him, I ran my fingers along the lapels of his jacket up to his shoulders and slowly removed it, allowing it to fall to the floor. Drawing my hands flat against the coolness of his white linen shirt, I started to unbutton it, starting at the collar tracing his chest down as I did, allowing his shirt to fall open. He held up his wrist, asking me silently to unfasten the cuff links, and I handed them to him. Taking them from me, he fisted them and put them both in his pocket. Looking down at me, his unruly dark hair fell over his forehead and I admired my husband in the dim candle-lit room. Reaching up standing on my tiptoes, I traced his shirt up his chest and pushed it over his shoulders, baring it.

I made an attempt not to stare, and my breath caught as I watched him.

Placing his hands on my shoulder, he leaned in and kissed me tenderly. His lips were soft, and his hair swept against my face. I was trying desperately to rid myself of the uneasy feeling that was so urgently trying to consume me.

344

Whispering in my ear, he asked me to turn around, and I did slowly.

Stepping toward me, I felt the heat from his body, but he hadn't touched me. I felt his breath on me against my shoulder and his lips were next to my ear. He ran his fingers against my exposed skin at the top of my dress, and I trembled under his touch. "Isabella, take some deep breaths, let me love you the way a man should, it's okay." He kissed me behind the ear and then at my neck, and I could feel the strange hands of my attacker on me. Carter was there in parts of this, only the rest was filled with the man that beat and raped me. The cold chill of that time was filling me. He started to unzip my dress, and I felt it slowly fall away as it pooled at my feet. My heart was beating so hard that I thought it was eventually going to stop.

He picked me up. I was left only in my bra and panties as he swiftly pushed the comforter over and laid me down onto the bed. Standing looking down at me, I captured again a glimpse of him. "Isabella, let it go, let go, trust me." My heart lurched as he drew closer to me. Finding myself once more with this beautiful man, I realized this time he's mine. I wanted this when we couldn't, when it wasn't seen fit in the eyes of God. Now I had it, and it scared me to death. Lying stiffly, I looked into his dark blue eyes, and I heard the words eerily ring in my ears, "Flip the switch." Timid at the thought of touching him, I could hear these words repeated at me. "Flip the switch, Bella." It's haunting knowing at some point I had heard these words spoken to me.

He was tracing my cheek down and across my lower lip with his gentle touch, and my eyes were set on him, and everything left my thoughts but him. The moment he touched my bare skin, a visible chill ran down my body.

He's very in tune to me. "We don't have to do this tonight, I want you to be ready." His face was full of distress and empathy for me.

345

I couldn't seem to move. I had wanted this man for months, and now that he was mine, I couldn't do a thing. My memory kept bringing back a voice saying, "Flip the switch." I was scared, taking short, chopping breaths, I tried to control my fear. *He's going to find out what kind of evil,* dirty *person you are*, my subconscious told me in a whisper. I tried to push it away, wanting this night with him for so long, wanting to be with him. I was terrified, every inch he came closer, I felt the man that abused me. I could smell his breath, the cheap liquor, and cigarettes.

I could see his glaring green eyes upon me as he gazed down at me. I could hear his rough and ragged voice over that of my husband's that made an attempt to calm me. "You're just a total waste. No one will ever want you again after I have finished with you. Used, and by many," he taunted. "There will be no man alive that will want you."

"Isabella, what's going through your head? Don't tell me that you're okay because I can see you aren't." From his stance above me, he retreated to lying on his side and looking over at me. Pulling the quilt over me tightly, I looked down and away from him. The shame was overwhelming, the guilt it had instilled in me. Curling into a ball beside him, the child in me didn't know what to do with these feelings. There was more than one man in the room with us, and one was definitely not welcome here. The dark shadows of my past were covering this room quickly, and I suddenly felt uneasy about being in here with him.

"Isabella, look at me." I couldn't look him in the face, the pain and hurt that had devoured me wouldn't allow me to look at him or touch him. I was paralyzed, but I felt like I wanted to run but being wielded in place, not being able to take a breath without something grabbing hold of me without warning. I stayed in the fetal position protecting myself. "Isabella," he warned me ahead of time, "I'm going to touch you. I won't hurt you. If it hurts, scares you or makes you feel uneasy, tell me and I'll stop."

Reaching over to me, he placed his hand on my now-covered arm and I shuddered trying to allow the touch as he attempted to soothe me, stroking my arm gently up and down in a rhythmic motion. After what seemed to be hours, my mood shifted and I started to calm down. My rapidly beating heart had returned to normal along with my overactive breathing pattern that made me feel like I would pass out.

After seeing the calm, Carter got up and walked to the bathroom and reappeared with a white satin sheath nightdress. "I got this for you," he confessed as he showed it to me. "You deserve to be dressed like a princess all the time. I can help you if you like, or I can leave and let you dress." His voice was a bit shaken, but he stood solid. I still couldn't communicate with him, I didn't understand. I still had the guilt but not from what it came from before, this time it was the feeling of unfulfilled dreams and feelings that it had left in its wake.

Carter left the nightdress on the bed beside me and walked off into the living area, rubbing the back of his neck. After I could clearly see he had left the room, I claimed the nightdress and held it up to me while still being covered with the quilt. I slid it down over me and walked to the bathroom where I looked at the girl in the mirror. All I saw was a young girl with a shattered reflection, one of grief and desolation. Suddenly uneasy about seeing my own reflection, I walked over to the wall and slid down, curling up into a corner holding tightly to my knees and rocking. Hearing footsteps heading toward me, I tucked my head to my knees and my arms clenched tight around me, never looking up. *It's him*, my mind kept running it over and over. A hand rested on my shoulder, and I jerked away and whimpered as I saw the man that started this whole mess. *Why now, why now?*

"Angel, it's me. I'm going to pick you up and put

347

you to bed. It's okay, Isabella, we'll work it out. We're both tired, and we have to get up early to go home, you need sleep." Reaching down, he picked me up and held me close to his chest. His familiar scent had brought me back, my husband had me.

"It's going to take some time, but you'll learn to trust me, I'm willing to wait."

Feeling numb as the tears slid down and burned my cheeks, he put me back into what should have been a marriage bed and covered me with the comforter like putting a child to bed. My heart broke at the thought that I was unable to love this man the way he should be. Crawling in behind me, he deliberately hesitated before he placed his arm around me and pulled me into him. Lying there spooning, he pushed my hair away from my ear and laid his arm around me. "Go to sleep, angel, I love you."

CHAPTER 17

The coldness settled in the room, and the familiar smell of cigarette smoke and cheap liquor came to light. I was in a room with a door shut listening to two men argue. I knew if my breathing was too loud, they would hear me. I wasn't able to hear most of what was being said, but shifting closer to the door, things were clearer. "I recommend that you don't get caught," the one said in anger, "because if you go down, I go with you, and I like my life!"

I could hear the heavy footsteps as they approached the door, echoing on the hardwood floor. Hiding behind the door and wrapping my arms around me, I looked down to see why I was so cold. I had nothing on but a bra and panty set. Looking over into a full-length mirror that was built of old wood and a broken glass, the image was that of a gaunt figure of a young girl that was me. My hair was down on my shoulders and uncombed, but it wasn't all I noticed. My face and arms and the insides of my legs were heavily bruised in different stages of healing. Over in the corner of the small room was a king-sized canopy bed that also looked old and worn with nicks and cuts in the posts. There were cuffs and chains on the wall and at the top of the bed.

Looking into the mirror, I noticed a collar, a collar of what looked like iron or steal connected to heavy chain keeping me from moving beyond the door and marks that had been left on my wrists from what appeared to be from the same.

I hurt everywhere especially when I sat down. Sitting down on the floor gingerly, I tried to become small and hide. What clothing I had lay on the floor in pieces and was no longer wearable. I was stuck here; I couldn't even make an attempt of going out of the windows. The windows were covered with bars. Even if I managed to get out of the chains, I wouldn't be able to get out of the room by window or leave unnoticed. "I'll be back, I want to check on our prize." His footsteps grew louder as he came to the door, and I trembled. *No, he can't do that to me again, I won't let him. I have to get out of here.* All matter of things ran through my mind from trying to hit him over the head with something to just trying to find some kind of escape route, any kind, even if it meant him killing me.

The door squeaked as it opened on its rusty hinges, revealing my captor, the man I hated. "Well, there she is." He picked me up off the floor by the upper arms much more tightly than needed and threw me onto the bed. The smell of cheap liquor was rancid, making my stomach turn. I knew what he was here for, and I was numb. It had happened so many times before I knew what to expect. The closer he got, the clearer this very wicked man and those green eyes became.

"Been waiting for your company, sis, you ready for round 2?" He traced his finger down my throat to my breast. Turning my face from him, he soon grabbed me by the chin and pulled it back to where I was looking at this man face-to-face. "Look, you better get used to this because you are going to be here for a very long time." Leaning into me, he pressed himself into me, leaving me pinned to the hard mattress as I tried to move away. I couldn't, he's much too strong for me. Laughing with a most disturbing laugh, his smile was evil. "You're going to give a lot of pleasure and make me an extreme amount of money. You'll sell well. Men like the young ones, especially those that like to fight. They'll pay for you to do a lot of very rude things to them, and for them, you'll do it if you want to eat. But right now, it's my turn."

He planted himself firmly on me, holding me to the point that I couldn't move. His green eyes blazed at me, he's took everything from me, including my innocence. I could see myself here like I was watching a movie, standing in the corner watching all of it. My heart pounded furiously, and my breath caught in my throat, feeling like I was drowning. I couldn't move, and the hot tears ran down my face. "No! No! Get off me." I gasped, trying to take a breath. "It hurts, get off me. No! No! . . . Help me! Somebody help me!"

Sitting straight up in bed, I took a deep, exaggerated breath, panting like someone had held me underwater. Carter ran from the bathroom and placed himself beside me. He's cautious about touching me until he saw I needed it.

The sweat was pouring off me, my clothes and sheets were wet and my hair was drenched.

Taking me into his arms, he rocked me gently as I tried to regain a normal breathing pattern. I cried mournfully not being able to put my arms around him, they remained in the air at my side. "Oh my god, oh my god, they sold me," I blurted out before I could stop myself. I didn't want Carter to know that. I didn't want to know that.

Carter enveloped me tightly and lovingly rocked me; this was never in my thoughts. After what seemed like hours in which I was sure were only minutes, I put my arms around him and held to him tightly and sobbed. My husband, what a wonderful person he decided to marry, a total screwed-up mess. What else was I eventually going to remember? My heart sank knowing he deserved so much better. I loved him, but that's not going to be enough.

He needed someone that was totally his and had nothing lurking in their past that kept popping up.

"Shh, I'm here, Bella. It was just a bad dream. It's okay, we're together and you're fine, it's not happening." Carter stroked my hair, gently running his long deft fingers through it. When I came back finally to here and now, I found myself sitting in his lap with the sheet wrapped around me. My head leaned against his chest with his arms around me, giving me comfort. This was not what I had intended my honeymoon to be like. Living in fear was not something I wanted to spend the rest of my life with.

I wasn't sure now where this was going to take us. Was it true? It certainly seemed to be. I guess he could be right, it could have been just that, a bad dream. It was real enough for me; the haunting eyes of the man that was in my nightmare with me were all too familiar. I had seen them over and over staring at me. Why wasn't it coming to me who he was? It's the same man that called me months earlier. I was sure of it.

Without moving an inch, Carter continued to stroke my hair, his gentleness was healing to me. I had craved this kind of affection, this was what I needed. I needed him. He was what I'd been looking for. I was right in some respect in his touch taking away the pain, but it also seemed to have opened up a whole new wound. I didn't know if I wanted to deal with it.

"Bella, you okay?" His voice trembled in response.

Taking the back of my hand, I wiped the remaining tears away from my face. "Yes, I think so." Sliding off his lap, I attempted to stand and take control of myself with the sheet still wrapped around me. Watching me his brow was furrowed and his face became ashen. He sat helplessly as he studied me.

"Question is, are you okay?" My heart skipped a beat each moment that went by without a reply.

"I'm fine. I don't like it when I feel like you're threatened." His voice was soft, he ran his hand through his unruly hair and sighed. "I understand what's going on, it doesn't mean I have to like it."

Standing before me, he rested his hands on my arms as he took a cautious step closer. "Bella, don't worry about this, it could be nothing, and if there is something to it, we'll deal with it."

"What if it isn't, what if it's true? I was broken before, this is worse. I can't expect you to accept that."

Crossing my arms in front of me, I held to my arms tightly, and my body trembled at the thought, how many others had touched me uninvited. Looking away, I bit my lip, remembering parts of a nightmare I would much rather forget. This was going to haunt me, I could feel it. My eyes closed. I couldn't look at my own husband. "Bella," placing his hands on my face, he cupped it gently, raising it so that he could look into my eyes. "Bella, look at me, please." Opening my eyes had become a challenge.

What was I going to see in his face, regret, disappointment, or worse, shame?

"My feelings will never change, I told you that. No matter what comes out, it doesn't matter. It wasn't your fault. You weren't consensual in this, it wasn't your idea. If it were, you could have let this go and it wouldn't matter now. It was a crime. A crime against you, you didn't ask for it."

The rage had built in me, and I didn't know what to do with it. If I could remember who he was, I'd put him away. His ghostly appearance in my mind had troubled my days and my nights for so long and knowing that he's still out there, I could feel him.

Clearing his throat, he removed his hands from me and dropped them to rest on the waist of his jeans. "Why don't you, um, go ahead and get dressed and I'll see about getting us some breakfast. We need to get started soon. I talked to Pop, Molly has been asking for us." Running his hand through his hair, I knew that he was frustrated or troubled, but I didn't ask.

"Okay." I looked away and down and headed for the bathroom. Looking over my shoulder as I went, I saw him walk away, grabbing a black T-shirt from the chair as he left the room. Closing the door behind me, I tried to make myself presentable. The dark circles under my eyes had left their mark.

I look tired and anxious. The princess of last night

had turned into something that looked shattered and wrecked. Feeling lost and empty, I picked the brush up and briskly brushed my hair. Clenching my teeth, I hurled the brush at the mirror, watching it bounce off and into the floor into pieces. The anger welled in me as I thought of what my wedding night should have been and how it ended. It wouldn't last, not like this. He would eventually leave me because of this unknown assailant that ravaged me.

I wanted to be normal, just a hint of it. I had tried so hard to make my life normal, and something had stood in the way. "I'm making you a promise, Isabella, if I find this man, I will kill him," I promised the woman that stood looking back at me. Collecting my clothes my mother had been so generous to pack, I put on a pair of faded jeans, white shirt, and royal blue sweater.

Classic and comfortable with my gray boots. I swept my hair over into a side pony and left the bath looking for Carter. I walked on into the living area, but he was nowhere to be found. Taking a key from the table, I walked down the hall looking for him, passing some of who were at the party the night before, but no one that I knew.

Stepping over to the desk, I picked up a paper and grabbed some coffee when I heard the voice of my husband talking to another man. Standing still for a moment, I heard some of what was being said.

"I would have talked to you before you married, you know it's going to be difficult. Any marriage has its difficulties, if you need me for anything I'll be glad to talk to you and Isabella."

"I know, Isabella has had a difficult time with some things from her past and she's struggling," Carter's voice was no longer as strong as I remembered.

It's full of hurt, and I didn't know. Maybe sympathy.

"Carter, you know this all too well. Give her time, you haven't known each other long. She needs the time to get to know you as a man as well as her husband."

"It isn't that simple. There are a lot of things buried that she doesn't know, and there has been a lot of things come out that aren't pleasant. Not that it bothers me, but it does her. I love her, nothing is going to change no matter what happens."

"I have no doubt you love her. Just remember this, God has always been there for you, he'll be there for Isabella. He doesn't want to see his children suffer, but he will allow it if it's what it takes to bring them to him. You learned that, it wasn't easy for you, but you learned."

They continued their conversation, and I tried to put a smile on as I made my way to my husband as I followed his voice down the hall. Walking closer, I caught his eyes, and Pastor Conley turned with a smile as Carter watched me warily.

"Good morning, Isabella," Pastor Conley greeted me with a smile.

"Good morning, Pastor, sleep well?"

"Yes, I did, thank you."

Looking over to my husband, I grinned at him shyly. "There you are. I picked up a paper from the front desk, thought you might enjoy the paper with breakfast." Walking over to him, I slid my arm through his as he held to a box with what appeared to be breakfast sandwiches and scones.

"Good, thanks." He grinned and kissed me on the temple.

"We'll see you soon, Pastor. Thanks." Carter nodded.

"Anytime."

Carter walked off with me arm in arm as we found the door to our room.

Opening the door, I walked in and placed the coffee

and the paper on the table. Sitting down, I watched as he was setting down the box of food he had brought with him. "I didn't know what you would like, so I brought a couple of things. You can go ahead and pick out what you want. I'm not that hungry."

"You need to eat something. No telling how long we will be at the hospital today." I knew why he wasn't hungry, and it's killing me. I could see it in his face, I was the reason. He was trying so hard to be patient with me.

This wasn't going to be easy for either of us. I should have seen this coming way before we ever talked about getting married. This man, the man I was madly in love with, had the patience of a saint. No man would put up with all the baggage I'd come into this marriage with.

I followed his every movement as he sat reading the sports report. The muscles in his jaws were tense, and there was a barrier built between us. "Are you angry?"

He folded the paper and laid it down and picked up the cup of coffee.

Staring over it, I was met with a conflicted smile. His body now relaxed, and his attention was now on me without wavering. "No, why would I be angry?"

"Well, last night and then this morning. It's pretty revealing, you may or may not have a wife that you may never get any pleasure out of. Then you may have a wife that has had many sexual partners, willing or not, it doesn't matter. I'm used goods."

Reaching from across the small wood table, he pushed a small piece of hair behind my ear. "I'm not worried, and you shouldn't be either. It will come in time, and we can work through it, I'm not going anywhere. As far as being used, you were used by a man you had no affection for. It was not in your will to be with him or however many more there may or may not have been. And you're wrong, I find pleasure in you every day you're with me. The intimacy can wait if it has to, I know what you're going through." His fingers stroke my arm, and his expression had gone from a smile to a very serious one.

"How do you know, how can you know?"

"Someday I'll tell you. There's a lot you need to know about me. I have things in my own past I'm not proud of, Isabella, and if people were honest, none of them have lived a perfect life. For now, I want you to work on one thing."

"What's that?"

"Learn to trust me, learn to trust that I'm here for you and that I love you enough to stay, that I would never hurt you. That's the most important thing, building trust."

Never saying another word, he went back to his paper. I returned to eating a few bites and drinking the coffee. I didn't exactly have an appetite either. Soon we would be back to reality, back to jobs, family, and children. I had some appointments to keep this week, maybe I should add Dr. Bentley into the mix with everything else. It sure couldn't hurt, and for now, Carter didn't need to know. I had an appointment with my OB-GYN this week too, that should be fun. I'd rather be hit by a bus, I hated it. Then I returned to work this week, which should also be an interesting. One day I was single, the next I was married. There would be a few that would try to wreak havoc I was sure, but there would be others that would be happy for me.

Picking up the last of the breakfast and packing it, Carter grabbed his coat and the bags and took them to the car. I made one last trip around the room, making sure nothing was left behind. Finding the pieces of the brush still scattered on the floor. Picking them up, I disposed of them in the trash and shut out the light.

Carter's footsteps were heavy as he found his way to the door and turned the key. I felt a chill run down me as the door opened, but no one was there when I walked into the sitting room. Picking up my purse, I opened it slowly.

I'd protect myself if I had to. If it were Carter, he

would be in the room now, instead the room appeared empty. Looking around cautiously, I saw no sign of anyone.

"Isabella, you ready to go?" Carter stopped short at the door. Standing there, I held the gun clutched in my hand. He made a few steps to me and looked at me, stunned. "What is that?" He pointed to the gun that was still in my hand, aimed down to the floor.

Realizing I was still holding it, I placed it back into my purse. "It's a gun."

"I can see that, what are you doing carrying it here, and when did you get it? That isn't the one you learned on."

"No, it isn't. Someone came in the room before you got here."

"What do you mean someone was here before?"

"How long have you been here?"

"Just as I asked you if you were ready to leave."

My hands clenched the table in front of me. "Someone came into the room before you came back from the car. I was in the bathroom checking to see if we had everything. I heard who I thought was you at the door and came out to meet you. When I got here, there was no one in here, and the door was open."

"Maybe it just opened."

"No, there were footsteps, I heard them. Someone was here, and they left."

"Isabella, no one could get into this room without a key, it must have been housekeeping. Maybe they thought we were gone already."

Shifting, I picked up my coat and put it on. "You still haven't answered my question. Where did you get the gun, and when did you start carrying it?"

Reluctantly, I answered him, "I've had it since November. I started carrying it when you went away on a business trip."

"And what else haven't you told me?" He looked at me questioning, and I knew he wasn't going to quit until he knew all of it.

"I continued my self-defense classes with Gus. I've been going for months, not just to the academy but to the firing range. I . . . ah . . . wanted to make sure Molly and I were protected. You can't be there all the time, and I didn't want to worry you. I'm not afraid, I know how to use it and I will if I have to."

"Bella, if you were worried, why didn't you say something?"

"You have enough to worry about without taking care of a weak female.

Well, I took the initiative. I'm no longer weak, I can take care of myself if I have to."

"Just be careful, make sure you're willing to use it."

His face became tight, and I could see the concerned glance he had on me. "We need to go."

Picking up my purse, I pulled the strap on my shoulder and walked casually over to him and put my arms around his neck. Kissing him gently, I needed to break away some of the ice that this situation had created. "You amaze me at every turn." He put his arms around my waist. "You do have a conceal carry for that, don't you?"

Grinning broadly at him, I kissed him again. "Yes, Mr. Blake, I do. Don't worry, I went through all the appropriate steps. Gus filled me in on all the legalities, I know what I'm doing."

His strained appearance had left, and the boyish smirk had returned. "A pistol-packin' momma."

He laughed out loud, throwing his head back as he did. "You fascinate me, Mrs. Blake. I just might need protecting from you."

My boots clicked on the white tile floor of the pediatric wing as Carter and I walked to Molly's room. The stillness of the hall was deafening, knowing there should be the sounds of children. All of those here were too ill to be up and playing and squealing with childish delight. Walking into Molly's room, Carter put his arm around me. If he hadn't, I was sure I would have fallen on the floor.

In the bed lay Molly, very still, and she looked so small. The bed engulfed her, it was so large against her tiny frame. Being a nurse, you would think I would get used to seeing this type of thing. You do become hard to some things, but when it's one of your own, it's disturbing. Seeing the IVs in her and the paleness of her skin shocked me. She looked so fragile. My heart broke for her because I knew if she were feeling better, she would have been up and greeting us without question. Instead, her eyes were closed with no reaction to us at all being in the room. At 9:00 a.m., it was unusual for her to still be asleep.

Stepping away from Carter, I walked to her bed and lay down beside her, trying not to wake her. Carter soon followed me and sat on the opposite side of the bed and picked up her tiny hand, she never flinched.

Grayson placed a hand on his son's shoulder, attempting to soothe him.

The pain had returned to his face seeing his daughter this way. "She's okay, son, the doctor has been in to see her and says its nothing more than strep throat and she's a little dehydrated. She wasn't drinking much because of the sore throat. He started her on antibiotics IV last night and says he will more than likely send her home on antibiotics by mouth."

"Has she had a fever this morning?"

"No, the fever broke last night around eleven. When she found out you and Isabella were getting married, she was a little disappointed she wasn't there, but I told her there would be a wedding that she could be in on. She was happy she was going to have a mommy and a daddy from now on."

"That's my girl, so sweet and precious. Has she

been asleep long?"

"Yes, she's been asleep for a while. She made me promise you would wake her when you came home."

"Pop, I hate to wake her, she looks so peaceful."

"Do it, she'll go back to sleep if needs to."

Lying there next to her, I stroked her dark hair and smiled at my now little girl and watched my husband. Looking over at me, he gave me a little smirk. Running his finger down his daughter's face, he gently tried to wake her. "Tink, it's Daddy, we're home." Molly stirred briefly and kept her eyes closed. "Tink, wake up, baby. It's Daddy and I brought Mommy with me."

Raising her hand, she rubbed her eyes and tried to open them. Sleepily she opened her eyes and looked at her father.

"Daddy," she whispered softly and rubbed her eyes again. Carter sighed heavily and released the stress he had been carrying. The stress he had carried with him this morning was washed away as he watched his daughter slowly waken.

"It's me, Tink. You feeling better?"

"Uh-huh. Missed you, Daddy."

"Missed you too, Tink."

"Wherl's Mommy?"

Carter grinned and chuckled at her knowing I was there beside her curled up. He pointed toward me. "Behind you, sissy. Mommy is right behind you."

Turning her head, she saw me.

Looking at me, she's waiting to see if there was something different about me. "You my mommy for real now?"

"Yes, baby, I'm your mommy. Daddy and I were married last night, and

I'm your mommy now. Is that okay?"

Molly smiled sweetly and put her tiny arms around me. "I wuv you,

Mommy."

"I love you too, Tink."

As the weeks went on, Molly got better and I returned to work. It was closing in on Valentine's Day, and spending it with my husband was the sweetest thought I had. Walking onto the unit, I was met by the wonderful Marilyn Strike. This had been a long time coming, and I was prepared for it.

As usual, her purpose was that of a lion after prey. I had come to expect this from her, knowing that she was never going to let go of my meeting Carter.

"Well, I guess you got the prize after all." She smiled evilly at me, waiting for my response.

"Well, if it is not the diva of North Dale Regional Medical Center. So what do I owe the pleasure of meeting up with you today, Marilyn?"

"Oh no, you just do not get it, the pleasure is all mine. You see, just because you married him doesn't mean I can't still go after him. Believe me, I can do it. Don't think that word doesn't get around, Isabella, I know everything."

I had to say I was a little shaken, but then again, what could she know that I did not. I was the one that lived it. There was no way she could have anything on me. The only one that knew anything that happened other than I did would be Lily and Ryan. I doubt very much my own parents knew the story.

"And just what do you think you know?"

"I know enough to know that at one point in your life, you were used by at least one man, if not many. I can destroy you. And I wouldn't have any problem sitting back watching you, as a matter fact, I would get pleasure from it. You see, I dated Ryan Bentley after you did, and I know a lot of your little secrets, maybe some that you don't know yourself. My intent is to go after Carter Blake, and I'll destroy anybody who gets in my way. So just keep that in

362

mind."

Marilyn walked off, and I finally took a sigh of relief that she's gone.

What a piece of work she was. That was one person. I didn't want any dealings with whatsoever. It always amazed me as to how men fell all over their selves for her. Looks was about all she had going for her. She had no compassion and certainly was not capable of loving someone. With everything that I knew I had been through, at least I had the capacity to love.

"Code blue trauma 3. Code blue trauma 3. Code blue trauma 3." Hearing the distress of a dire emergency, I followed the rest to trauma 3. As I went down the hall I heard the cry of a young woman screaming out for someone named Jack. Looking as I passed a nurse was with her trying to calm her, I continued to the next room where I found a young man approximately eighteen years old. His face had deep cuts and was very swollen. Dr. Reed was there leading the team in an attempt to save this young man's life. "Dear God, I don't think there's a fix to this, but we have to try. Let's give a round of drugs. Start with Epi 1 milligram, and we'll go from there." The team was in full action, but the young man was still flat line after a pulse check according to the monitor. "He's still asystole. Keep going, we have to give this kid a shot. Anyone know if his parents are here?"

"Parents have been called, no one has arrived yet," one of the others had said. "Let's give 1 milligram of Atropine. Someone try to get some labs on this kid. I want to know what all I'm dealing with here." Dr. Reed was well in control of the situation, but it looked bleak. The respiratory team had intubated him and had a ventilator standing by. "Let's check the pulse." He gazed at the monitor as he felt for the femoral pulse. "No pulse, resume CPR.

Go ahead and give him another milligram of Epi."

The efforts were looking pretty futile. The monitor beeped with each compression that was made, and the sound of the respiratory therapist breathing for him was rhythmic.

"How long has it been?" Dr. Reed looked up from him for a moment and watched the monitor.

"Around thirty minutes," I announced after looking at the code sheet.

"Let's try another round of drugs. I don't want to give up too soon. This kid's got a closed head injury I'm sure of it."

The team continued until Dr. Reed called for another pulse check.

Looking at the screen, there was nothing but one occasional blip that wasn't strong enough to sustain life. One beat and the rest was flat line. "Okay." Dr.

Reed shook his head. "Let's call it, time of death: 1823. Sorry, Jack, I tried."

Removing his gloves, I watched him leave the room as the team disassembled.

As I left, the room I ran into Dr. Reed.

"Isabella, glad to see you back. I haven't been here much myself lately.

You got married I hear, congratulations."

"Thank you. Ah, that young man in there, what happened?"

"He and some of his friends were traveling at a high speed and hit a concrete culvert. All of them have died except one, and I'm not sure about that one."

"What was the young man's name?"

"His name was Jack Westbrook. He played football for the Panthers, looks like the team lost their captain. He was a fine player, I watched him all season. The kid could have been good enough for pro ball."

"And the others, did you know them?"

"Only from the games. The only survivor I know through her parents.

Bailey Highland was dead at the scene. She was a cheerleader for the

Panthers. She disappeared about a month ago, along with the only survivor from this accident. Curtis Faraday was the quarterback for the team. He would have graduated this year and had a full ride at Ohio State majoring in electronics."

"And the survivor?"

"Paige Gates. She also disappeared about a month ago. I don't know the story behind it, but from what I gather, the boys found them, at least that's what I can get out of Paige. Jack was her boyfriend. It isn't going to be easy to tell her that her boyfriend died trying to find her. It's going to be harder telling these parents that their children have died."

"Yes, I can see that." My heart was now in my throat. What an awful thing for any parent to go through. Then I thought of Jenna. She was so small, how could God have taken her? She was an innocent in whatever happened to me. It wasn't her fault that I ended up with this man. It didn't matter, there wasn't anything I could do to bring any of them back.

"I need to go in and see Paige, do you want to come along? Maybe you can help her. She isn't going to handle this well, she could use a woman's touch." Nodding, I went along.

When we entered the room, the young blonde was sobbing. IVs were attached along with a heart monitor that reflected the rhythm of her heart.

She was petite in stature and looked overwhelmingly fragile. Dr. Reed greeted her by taking her hand. "Paige, it's Dr. Reed. Has your parents made it here yet?"

She sniffed back a sob. "No, I don't think so. I have not seen anyone yet."

The silence in the room was almost deafening as Dr.

Reed looked down at Paige. Grasping the doctor's hand, she looked at him in quiet reserve. "Jack.

Is he okay? Can I see him? Can he come to me?"

Dr. Reed's brow furrowed out of concern for her. "Paige, I took care of Jack. I am sorry there was not much I could do for him. I wish I could have saved him, but I couldn't."

"No! He can't be dead. You can't let him die. He saved my life. You have to do something, you can't just let him die."

"Paige, there was nothing else I could do. I tried everything. He was just so badly hurt, there was no saving him."

"Jack and Curtis saved us. They got us away from that terrible man. He took us."

"What do you mean? What man? Who took you?"

"Bailey and I were out after a football game and this man. He . . . He told us he was having trouble with his daughter and wanted us to help him.

He said she was having an asthma attack and needed one of us to call and get her some help. When Bailey turned to phone for help, he and another man pushed us in the van. We were there for I do not know how long, he did terrible things to us. He . . ." Paige cried uncontrollably. She was crying so hard that she was unable to catch her breath between sentences.

Dr. Reed clasped her face and looked at her sternly. "What did he do to you?" Her sobs continued, making her unable to speak. "What did he do to you?" I could see the anger rise in Dr. Reed's face as he looked down at her.

He already knew what this man had done, he just wanted her to say it. He needed it for the record, and so that he could do what he needed to nail this guy. "Tell me and I will put this guy off the street."

Paige continued to sob uncontrollably, making it difficult for anyone to understand what she was saying.

Talking through her tears, I understood part of what she was saying, it sounded all too familiar to me. It could have been my story she was telling over again. Walking over to the other side of the bed, I took her hand and caressed her face. "Would you rather tell me in private?"

She nodded. "Do you mind, Dr. Reed? Just give us a few moments alone." Dr.

Reed agreed and walked out the door.

"He's gone now, you can tell me. I promise you, I have heard it all before, you don't have to be afraid. No one is going to hurt you here."

She started to calm down, but the tears continued. "The man, he took us to this big warehouse and put us in a large room by ourselves. There were others there we didn't see, but we could hear them. He eventually put Bailey and me in separate rooms. He put me in a room and ordered me to remove all of my clothes, leaving only my bra and panties." Paige began to heave, she was so upset and crying.

"It's okay, he can't hurt you now, we're here to help you." Her breathing started to slow down, and she continued with her horrific story. Her story was so near to my own that I could remember that I knew it must be the same man, even describing him to what I did remember.

"Paige, I know it isn't going to be easy, but you need to talk to a police officer and give him a statement. We also need to do some test, a rape kit.

This man assaulted you, and we need to get him off the street." Paige began to cry inconsolably as I talked to her. "Paige, you mustn't think this is your fault. Understand me? This man did something unthinkable to you."

"My parents, they don't know. Do they have to know?"

"Yes, they do. You're underage, and they have to give consent for the test."

"Oh no, my mom, she's never going to understand."

367

"Yes, she will. It isn't going to be easy for any of you. I'll leave some information with the social worker, and we'll set up some counseling for you.

Dr. Reed needs to know what's going on. Be honest with him, he's your best friend right now. He isn't going to scold you, he's upset because someone did this to you. I'll talk to him. He'll talk to your parents, and he will be doing your test. You won't be alone, I promise."

"How can you say these things, how do you know everything will be all right?" Paige's anger had risen, and it's time to be honest.

"Because I've been there, Paige, I've lived it. I think the same man that had you and Bailey also had me. I have blocked a lot of it out, but I do remember what you have told me tonight from events in my own past.

Believe me, I know what you're feeling."

"What about Curtis and Bailey, are they alive?"

"No, they aren't. Bailey died at the scene. Curtis died en route to the hospital. You're the only one that has survived. Your friends gave you a gift.

Live your life well in spite of this. Don't let what they have done for you be in vain." I clasped her hand, and she nodded her head in agreement.

After meeting with Dr. Reed about Paige, he went to talk to her parents who were patiently waiting for him in the consultation room. Her parents were just glad she was alive, but it was going to be a long and difficult road for them. It wasn't exactly easy to share what had happened to me with a stranger, but she needed something to cling to, something to bring her hope.

If it meant sacrificing some of myself, then so be it. It was time to do some healing. I needed it, not just for me but for the benefit of my family. My marriage would eventually suffer if I didn't do something.

It was nearing seven in the evening and I hadn't had a break. Heading for the elevators, I pushed the button for

368

the bottom floor mindlessly. My mind drifted somewhat, and flashes of puzzle hit me that didn't fit. It was something I remembered, but it wasn't making any sense. When the doors opened, I walked toward the cafeteria. Looking down the hall, I saw my husband holding on to Marilyn.

Walking on, I made my way into the cafeteria as I heard him calling for me. Ignoring him, I continued on.

"Isabella, didn't you hear me calling you?" He ran up to me, slowing once he made it to my side.

I continued on and sat down at a table away from everyone with my coffee. It was about all I could handle at this point. The events of the evening had drained me, and to find my husband holding Marilyn Strike was the limit.

Following me over to the table, he sat down and stared at me, bewildered at my mood. I continued to look over my cup of coffee and ignored his presence. If he wanted her, he could have her. After all, he wasn't having a satisfying relationship with me. I couldn't blame him for that, a wife that couldn't satisfy him was more than any man could handle.

"Isabella, are you going to continue to ignore me? I came here to see you and to have supper with you before going home." He was reaching to take my hand, but I drew it back from him.

"Are we going to play this all night? I don't know what you're mad about, but I haven't done anything."

"You haven't done anything? What was that display out there?"

"What in heaven's name are you talking about?"

"You and Marilyn Strike, what were you doing with your arms around her?"

"That's what you're mad about, that's what you're upset about?" He chuckled, and it made me furious.

"I don't find it funny, Blake."

"I'm sorry I do. Isabella, how could you think I

369

would want anything from a woman like that? She's spoiled, vicious, and self-centered without an ounce of compassion in her body."

"Then what were you doing holding her?"

"I wasn't, I ran into her. It was either catch her or let her fall. Why are you so upset? You know I love you. I would never do such a thing. My heart belongs to you and no one else."

My heart melted as I sat there across from him. "I'm sorry. It's been a bad night here, and Marilyn has made her threats of coming after you. She told me it didn't matter that you and I were married, she always got what she wanted."

"You don't have a thing to worry about. I have no interest in anyone but you. When your break is over, I want you to finish your shift and come home, if not sooner. I need to be with my wife for a while. It's been a long day, and I just need someone to cuddle up to." He smirked and took my hand and kissed it softly.

"I do love you, Mr. Blake."

"And I you, don't worry about Marilyn. I can handle myself around her."

CHAPTER 18

The drive home seemed longer than usual, giving me opportunity to think about the events of the day and the past. Maybe I shouldn't have let it creep in so often, but it happened. Being alone for so long, now suddenly I had a family. It made me wonder what was in store. Whatever happened next, we could survive it. At least that's what I kept telling myself. Unfortunately for the both of us, we hadn't tried any further to consummate our marriage. I felt incredibly guilty about the situation even though Carter kept telling me he understood and it would come.

Soon I saw the familiarity of our home and I was glad to see it. The thrill of seeing my husband after the day from below had given me a renewal that it might be salvageable. I had felt these feelings for him before. I hadn't exactly been willing to act on them. It occurred to me that I was keeping myself from the one person that had vowed to love me until the day I died. Could I trust him? He had been willing to trust me from the beginning, why should I be different? He had been there for me from finding out about Jenna to finding that I had been sexually abused and physically beaten. I was damaged, and he still loved me and had all this time. He deserved nothing less than my complete surrender to him.

Then I thought of someone else that deserved my completeness of surrender. God. He had asked nothing more from me than just to commit to him, giving my life to him. Carter understood this. Why had it taken me so long to understand? Shutting down the car, I sat there in the garage and completely allowed myself to thank God for who he was. My heart opened to him and it felt like a dam burst.

"God, I'm so sorry I've left you out of my life. I'm sorry for the sins I've committed against you, for denying you for all these years. I know that I'm not worthy of your love, but I know that you are worthy of mine. I ask you for your forgiveness. I don't understand all of this, but I know that I need you.

I believe that you gave your son for me, that he lived and died, and I'm ready.

I'm ready to accept you. Lord, please come into my heart and be the God of my life. I owe everything that I am and what I have survived because of you.

You've been so good to me, you've given me a new life with my husband and daughter, but nothing could be better than to be your child. Help me to be the person that you want me to be. Thank you for hearing me and that you're always there for me. In your precious name, amen."

My tears fell unbidden down my cheeks as I sat there quietly. The weight that had been on me for years had lifted. Not that it had fixed everything, it hasn't, but it had defined who I was for so long that now I could see who I was now that the past had been lifted. I was God's daughter, and I was Carter's wife. Carter knew what he was talking about, there was no earth-shattering moment necessary, just peace and assurance. I was okay, and it didn't matter what happened before, it's all gone.

Collecting my things, I rubbed the back of my hand against my face and pushed the few strands that had managed to come free from my ponytail. It's time to see my husband. I had a new light of him and what he was about.

Walking into the hallway I laid my coat on the nearby chair along with my purse and keys. Looking around, I couldn't see him. "Carter . . . I'm home." Turning, I saw him walking from the bedroom, running his fingers through his wet hair. Fresh out of the shower, he walked into the room in a navy blue button-down untucked and faded jeans. How had I missed this?

I had always admired him, but I had never looked at him this way. Love consumed me as I watched him walk in the room.

"Hey, angel, just get home?" His movements toward me were purposeful, and he looked drop-dead gorgeous. Bending down, he kissed me gently. The feeling of his lips on mine felt like he was kissing me for the first time.

Chuckling, he cupped my face in his hands. "What's wrong, angel, you act like I haven't ever kissed you before?"

My breath caught, and a smile came quickly. "It's just what I needed."

Wrapping my arms around his neck, I stood on tiptoes and kissed him again.

"It's been a very eventful day, and it promises to get much better."

"Oh, well, glad to hear that. So what has made today so much better than any other day?" He slid his arms around my waist and pulled me close to him cautiously.

"Amore, you don't have to treat me like glass. I'm okay, I'm better than okay. I'm never looking back again."

"Something really good has happened to you, what is it?"

"Come over and sit down with me for a few minutes, and I'll tell you."

Following me over, he sat down and put his arm over the back of the couch. Sitting down beside him, I angled myself so that I could see his expression. "I did have something very good happen today. One that I'm sure you will be happy to hear."

"Okay, I'm all ears." He relaxed sitting back against the couch.

"On my way home tonight, I thought about some things. I can't go into a lot of detail, but it had to do with one of my patients and my past. Then I remembered some things that you had talked to me about. That God loved me and that I could have the peace and relationship with him

373

that you have."

Carter's face went pale, and I could see he was anticipating what was coming next. "I sat in the car and thought about you and Molly, thinking that there was no way I could be the wife or mother I needed to be without God.

I couldn't begin to heal or leave any of this behind without him. I have been so conflicted about my feelings and what it must be like for you. I haven't been honest with my feelings, I've kept them buried because of this man, if you want to call him that, who attacked me and made me a slave to him.

"Isabella, what are you saying?"

Scooting in a little closer, I took his hand in mine. "I realized after all this time, I have still been his slave." Shaking my head, I watched him intently for his reaction, but I could see his breathing become shallow. "Not anymore, I won't allow him to be part of my life any longer. With the help of God, he won't be." Carter sat stone still. "Carter, breathe, I'm not leaving. I gave my life over to God. I know it isn't going to be perfect and I don't understand all of it, but God was there waiting for me and I accepted it."

Slowly, a smile appeared, and without warning, he hugged me tight against him. "You won't believe what God can do for you if you let him. I'm so happy for you. It's time to heal, Bella. Thank you, God, for giving me my wife." Releasing me, he still had that breathtaking smile on his face. "Isabella that has got to be the best news I have ever heard."

"I'm very happy. I've been given a new start, and I intend on taking it."

Standing in the shower, I let the warm water wash away the care and worries of the day. Somehow, with the day as bad as it had been, it turned out to be one of the best. I was relieved, I felt light and carefree, and all was now right with the world. Of course, my problems had not dissolved, but it didn't seem to matter. I could see Carter in my mind as I stood with my eyes closed. The water pounded against me, and the sweet smell of my shampoo now filled the enclosure. The tropical smell of flowers was rising on the steam as I finished my shower.

Carter, no matter what had happened, stood by me, never wavering, never a complaint, never accusing. He was there for me and had never made demands. It was simple that the love I had for him was pure and unconditional. It was clearer to me that he was not only the same way, but he had gone above that. He had taken care of me and loved me through so many horrific things, and he was always the one to sacrifice. He was the one that stepped aside for someone else, me.

We both had a lot to learn about each other. In the short time we had known each other, he knew me better sometimes than I knew myself. That was really an accomplishment when I didn't know myself. It was easy to see the love he had for others. Why had it taken me so long to see he had that kind of love for me?

Stepping out of the shower, I wandered over to the mirror and wiped the condensation from it. Looking at the reflection, I could truly see a person who was no longer the shattered girl but a woman, healing and triumphant, not of her own accord but of God's. He had given me a precious gift, a family.

Thinking of my husband, I dried my hair into long waves, and it fell over my shoulders. This evening, I was going to take the time to get to know my husband. Not sure where it was going to lead me, but I wanted to spend it with him without any fear. I smiled back at the reflection, an idea had just come to mind. Walking to the closet, I picked up a memorable shirt, one that brought back the memory of the man I first met and fell in love with. Taking the blue shirt from the closet, I could smell his cologne mixed with his own scent. I fluffed my hair as I stood in front of the mirror, seeing my legs as they dangled beneath his shirt. Perfect.

Before leaving the room, I lit what candles that remained on the dresser.

The soft glow gave just enough light that the room wasn't totally dark, casting shadows on the wall as I walked to the door.

Walking into the dimly lit room, my vision had tunneled on the man sitting on the couch. The shirt I'd made into my gown smelled of him, rich woodsy cologne, and his own scent, well-seasoned.

He had enveloped me without ever touching me. Sitting at the end of the couch, he cradled a coffee cup and reading his newspaper, as he often did.

His beautiful eyes were riffling through the obituaries or reading last night's sports page.

Looking at him set my mind to the thoughts of spending a night with him, loving him as married couples should do and what I had feared for so long. There were times unfortunately I looked at the act of being with any man after what I had been through was that I would rather have faced the devil.

His unruly dark hair was askew from him running his fingers through it.

He sat perfectly poised, unknowing for the moment I was watching him and what I was thinking. My body ached for his touch. The need was there, and I had fought it way too long. The flame that had been ignited in me now had become a steady burn and had become white-hot.

The thoughts I was having were sinful. I wanted him. I wanted him to take me in his arms and wrap himself around me, to touch me in places that no one had touched me since, since the attack of that monster. I had to put that from my mind. Could it be possible to have those kinds of thoughts, was it sinful if it was one's own husband? In a little over the month we had been married, he had barely touched me because of the incident that came to light on our wedding night. I was still sorry for that.

Feeling my eyes on him, he looked over his paper. The look on his face was priceless as he saw me standing there dressed only in his shirt, a familiar one. My legs dangled below the hem, making me feel sultry. My hair tumbled over my shoulders in waves with the first two buttons open, my hair resting above the opening of the shirt, giving the masculine shirt a womanly sex appeal.

He lay the paper down on the table beside him. As I walked toward him, he never said a word but kept his eyes locked on me and watched my every move. His look was relaxed as he sat there with one ankle crossed at the opposite knee, giving him the look of confidence, a king of his dominion.

Watching him like prey as I closed in on him and removed the cup from his hand and placed it on the table behind me. He had captivated me. The man that sat before me was my husband and I loved him, my mind played it over and over. Keeping my eyes on him had deterred me from thinking of other thoughts that could ruin the moment. I refused to let that happen.

Placing my knee on the couch, I crawled toward him inch by inch. Finally reaching him, I rested my hands on his jean-covered knees. His square jaw, his lips parted softly in surprise, his unruly dark hair swept softly across his forehead, and his piercing blue eyes that I truly could get lost in were focused on me and me only.

Blinking after what seemed to be a stare off, he grinned that wonderful boyish grin. "Mrs. Blake, are you trying to seduce me?" His voice was low and hopeful, but he remained restrained and calm. He hadn't made an effort to move or touch me. His expression remained unreadable, and mine was set in a no-nonsense manner. I felt a little out of my element as I let him know in no uncertain terms what

I had in mind.

"I don't know. Is it working?" My voice I didn't recognize, it's soft and timid, even though my actions didn't reflect it.

Pulling me into his lap gently, he wrapped his arms around me and looked down over my shoulder and smiled. "You don't have to seduce me. I'm your husband, I'm always here for you."

Remembering what he had said to me months earlier, I gave him his own words back to him. "I want your heart, all of it."

"Isabella, you ha—" Then he got it, the whole scene. This was him just a few months ago. "I get it, yes, I remember and I love you for it." Kissing me on the temple, he gave me a squeeze.

Turning to look at him, I saw him, truly saw him. "I do love you." I beamed at him, and I felt my face flush. "This isn't just a trip down memory lane. I have something else in mind."

His puzzled look was evident, and he cocked his head to the side.

"Isabella, you're blushing. I haven't seen you do that for a while. Just what's on your mind?"

I could feel my body react, all my muscles became tense and my mind was fixated on him. I wanted to be totally his, but my mind and body was fighting me. My heart told me there's more than fear, there's love and affection between two people who are committed to each other. Prayerfully in my mind, I was begging for God to take away my fear. I loved him, the feelings I had was frightening. I could lose myself in him and there would be nothing left of me. "I want you," I heard these words escape me in a most uncharacteristic manner.

"Angel, you have me, anytime you feel like you are ready."

"I'm ready, I want you. I want to be totally yours. I

think it's time that you were introduced to your wife."

His eyes became dark and his jaw clenched as he thought about what I had said. "This is a big step for you." He traced my cheek delicately. "You sure this is what you want?"

Awkwardly I shook my head yes and gave him an anxious grin. Clasping my face gently, I felt his breath on me as he leaned in to kiss me and I closed my eyes. His lips were soft against mine as he brushed against them, my thoughts of anything other than this moment had vanished. What he must think of me, of what we are about to do and who I am. That could be a little disturbing. Maybe I didn't know who I was.

"Bella." Tracing his fingers down my cheek, his eyes were fixed on me.

"You're distracted, focus on me."

I was here with him, and my thoughts of what and who I was had dissipated. *Concentrate,* Bella, my everloving conscious taunted. Returning his kiss feverishly, he stopped me momentarily. Picking me up in a one long sweep, he walked purposefully to the bedroom door, allowing me to slide down his body at the threshold. Standing behind me, he swept my hair from my neck and ran his fingers across my shoulder. Standing still under his touch, he watched me for my reaction. My eyes closed as I savored the warm kisses. My heart started to pound heavily, feeling my heart in my throat.

"Calm down, I know what you're thinking. I've been where you are. I'm going to stand with you. The storm will pass, the safety is in these four walls."

Stepping in closer to me, he wrapped his arms around my waist. "You're my wife, I'll always protect you." I leaned into his body as the heat from his chest radiated through my back, sending me comfort. He kissed me behind the ear and down the curve of my neck, and I shuddered. My troubled mind stirred, and I fought it furiously. Picking me up, he deposited me on the bed and I sat on my feet with my knees bent under me, watching my husband as he stood at the foot of the bed. I'd seen that look before, it's one of acceptance, one of asking permission. Tilting my head to the side, I smiled at him and he mirrored me. Waiting in the center of our bed, I watched him.

He's contemplating the situation. Running his fingers through his hair, he ruffled it and I laughed at him nervously. I'd thrown him off guard, and he's stunned.

"Honestly, Bella, you fascinate me. I never know what to expect." Placing a knee on the bed, it sank under his weight. Two moves and he sat in front of me. He didn't touch me, he just sat and gazed at me. His look was soft and his eyes shined. Scooting in slightly, he's close enough that our knees touched together. He sat very still and never blinked. "You okay?"

"Yes," I whispered. How could he make me feel the way I did without ever touching me? My breath caught as he placed his hand against my face.

Leaning my face into it, I kissed the palm of his hand, feeling the softness and the heat from it.

"You're so beautiful. I still can't believe how lucky I am to have you." I couldn't say a thing. I felt like every breath I had ever had in me had left. His long, deft fingers traced the curve in my neck and down my arm.

"I'm scared." My voice shook as the electrified tingles traveled through me under his touch. "I'm scared of what I feel for you. I'm scared of what you will see or feel about me if I make myself vulnerable. My heart is yours, I trust you with it."

"Bella, fear is normal, letting it control you isn't." His voice trailed off but his gaze didn't. He had waited for so long for this, and I didn't want to disappoint him. "I'm a little nervous myself." He never looked more in control, but his eyes told another story. He was as vulnerable now as I was.

"No one could love you more than I do. I promise I will guard your heart."

Seeing the tension, he cupped my face. "Take a couple of deep breaths, and don't take your eyes off me."

Taking a couple of breaths, I felt the tension ease. Carter had placed his hands down on his knees, not touching me, allowing me to recover.

The candlelight flickered off his face and made a shadow on the wall of his silhouette. My fear diminished, I reached for him timidly, unbuttoning his shirt and trying not to be too clumsy. He watched me swallowing hard as I pushed his shirt away from his shoulders and slide it down his arms.

He deposited the shirt on the floor as he kissed me softly on the cheek.

Straightening, he looked at me, studying me as he did. I unbuttoned the next button on my shirt just above my breast, and he clasped, it stopping me.

"Slow down, we have all night. I just want to admire you, Mrs. Blake, you take my breath away." Placing my hands on the bed on either side of my legs, I allowed him to look at me. I was in awe of him, his touch was loving, and I was enjoying it. My emotions were shattered under his gaze. Pulling me gently against him, he held me close and laid me down. He covered me with the quilt from the bed and smiled, "For your comfort, Mrs. Blake." He slid in beside me as the softness of the cotton sheets slid against my skin.

The covering gave me the comfort and protection that I needed. I was not totally exposed. He looked down at me with those beautiful blue eyes, and I couldn't resist him. He ran his hands from my thighs up my sides and gently pulled the shirt I was wearing up and over my head leaving me in my bra and panties. His eyes were down turned, looking me up and down. Coming closer, he traced my body from the dip in my throat down the middle of my chest to my belly with soft, gentle kisses, his hair fluttering against my skin.

"We're going to take it slow, Bella." His fingers ran down the strap of my bra, and I took an exaggerated breath, not in fear but for the emotion that it had brought. My hands rested above my head as he ran his hands down me so light that they glided over me.

His fingers traced the length of my bra and over the top of my breast.

"Breathe, angel," he coaxed as he unfastened my bra and removed it. He followed with my panties, running his hand down to my hip and lovingly caressing it. His bare chest met mine as he bent down and kissed me passionately, and I had lost myself to him. My body shook under him, his blue eyes hypnotized me. "Put your arms around my neck," he whispered gently, smiling. "Stay with me, don't close your eyes."

"I'm not afraid," I whispered. "I'm with you, I'm not afraid," I whispered.

My hands rested against his back, and I could feel his muscles flex under them. I was now vulnerable before him and he before me, there was no fear in it, no shame, no anger, just the love and affection of the man I fell in love with months ago. His body was wrapped around me, and I was so comforted by him. The hurt and the pain was gone, the fear was leaving.

"Don't think, angel." He breathed softly next to my ear. "Let yourself go, enjoy the time we have here together." There was never another word said between us. My heart melted under his touch, I could smell the cologne and the soft smell of shampoo where he had showered earlier in the evening. His touch was soft and delicate, nothing like what I had experienced before under the protest by a man who was evil and cruel. It's the kind of love I had hoped for, and now I had it. It would take a long time to get the image of the man that had been so cruel to me and the way he used my body, but there was no reason to fear my husband.

The early-morning dawn broke through the window softly under the cover of the drapes, leaving a shadowed room. Turning, I saw my husband lying on his side, watching and smiling down at me. "Good morning, angel.

Sleep well?" The look on his face was sweet and satisfied.

"Yes, after sharing myself with you, I slept very well."

"Me too." He grinned. "You and I have some things to talk about, but we aren't going to ruin this moment by talking about things of the past. I want to spend what time we have before Molly gets up together, just being here and enjoying it."

Kissing him gently, I assured him I was in complete agreement. Putting his arm around me, he pulled me close to him. Taking my hand and kissing the back of it, turning it so that my palm was exposed, he kissed the center of it delicately. "No regrets after last night, Isabella?"

The question startled me. Why would he ask such a thing? I had loved him without a doubt for months. I might have been in love with him from the time I first saw him. "Of course not." I smiled at him sweetly. "I can't think of a better time in my life than to be here with you. You have no idea how much you coming into my life has changed me. I never thought I would ever." Stopping for a moment, I collected my thoughts and feelings for him.

They remained so scattered after last night that I was unable to think. I would have thought by now he would have known what he had meant to me. Why was he suddenly so vulnerable, he hadn't been. He had always been my rock, he'd been the one I had depended on to be sturdy and strong. "I never thought I would fall in love, or so completely, nor did I think I would find anyone that would love me for who I am. It almost pains me to think I spent so much of our time on someone that hurt me and wasn't worth it."

Running my fingers through his unruly dark hair, I watched his beautiful face as a small smile appeared slowly. "You treated me like a lady." My face turned hot, and I felt flushed at the thought as I continued. After all, he wanted me to be honest. "Regardless of what happened to me before, in all accounts, last night was my first time. I couldn't have had a more thoughtful, loving, and gentle partner. Thank you for being so patient with me. You're some kind of a man. I'm very much in love with you, I love being your wife, and no, I have no regrets for loving you."

Carter sighed with relief, for what reason, I was not sure. He was content, and his body relaxed. I hadn't noticed the tension in his body from what was in my own. "It isn't going to be long before we have to get up and get going.

I have to be at work at nine this morning. They're looking into the deaths of three teens. I don't know the story, but it sounds like it's twisted. I'm not sure how long I'll be tonight. I could break off early if I can, but I'm not sure, if I can't it could be late before I get home. You sure you'll be okay until I get home?"

I knew exactly what he was talking about, but I couldn't say a word about it. He was looking into the deaths of Bailey, Jack, and Curtis. "You think they were killed?"

"It's not positive, but the girls involved had been missing for a month at least and the boys happened to find them when the police couldn't. It doesn't sound right. Besides, the police is also looking into a prostitution ring. It isn't typical, the girls and boys are more like slaves. What's believed at this time is that these young adults are being sold. The Portland PD seems to think all of this is connected. They found a young girl outside of town approximately sixteen years old. She was pregnant. She and her baby were found dead by a jogger that was out for an early-morning run. The teens had taken the same route out. I'm not liking the feel of this at all."

I hadn't heard about the other girl, but I knew Paige was one of the girls from the accident. She should be able to identify this man or someone connected. If that was the case, her life was in danger, and so was mine.

"What if I told you something that may be along the lines of what you are talking about? I'm trying to be ethical here, and I'm trying to protect my patient and myself."

Carter's face turned pale and became hard as flint. "What do you know?

If you know something, Bella, your life is in danger and so is your patient's and Molly's."

"I can't tell you the patient's name, but I think she needs police protection if this is a possible homicide investigation. You need to get with the hospital administration. You and the PD. If it is what you say, that girl is a sitting duck."

"I'm not near as worried about her as I am for you." Frustrated, he sat up in the bed and ran his fingers through his hair. "We need someone to watch you and Molly."

"Carter, I'm not afraid. It may have nothing to do with me. Her story was close to mine, but I'm sure it can't be the same guy."

"What makes you so sure? Give me one good reason as to why it couldn't be?"

I couldn't give him an explanation. "Yeah, I thought so." He got up and put on his jeans. "Get dressed. I'm calling the department, I have to see about getting you a bodyguard."

"But . . ."

"Isabella, listen to me. If this is connected, you're in danger and I'm not going to leave my guard down when it comes to my family." He never said a word and walked out the door.

Dear God, what's *next?* I couldn't go to work with an officer following me around 24-7. One turmoil after another had left me mentally tired and weak.

Walking down the hall, I could see Carter standing in his faded jeans and shirtless on his cell. He's involved and wasn't paying attention at the moment.

I looked in on Molly, and she was still sound asleep, hopefully dreaming of something sweet and less frightening than real life. She was my priority, keeping her safe was my objective.

"That's right . . . I want you to follow my wife . . . Look, I don't care what it takes, just do it . . . My daughter will be with her too. I expect this to go off without a hitch, you understand? . . . Well, get in contact with the commander for God's sake . . . I won't be in until someone is here. Just see that it is done."

Hanging up the phone, I watched him slip it in the back pocket of his jeans.

I had seen him upset before, but I had never seen him this commanding. This was the most controlled I had ever seen him. Taking a step back, I saw him in a position I had never seen him: manipulative, intriguing, and authoritative.

Some characteristics were a given for me, but I had never seen him this stern with anyone. This was what fear could do to people. I enjoyed the thought that he wanted Molly and me to be protected, but I didn't like the idea of feeling trapped.

Walking over to me, he placed his hands on my shoulders and, in a very authoritative voice, warned me to stay put. "Listen to me, if you have never listened to anything I have said to you before, make sure you listen to this and follow it to the letter. It could mean the difference of life and death for either or both of you. If this is the same man, he will come after you. If he knows the connection, he will come after Paige or Molly. I intend on keeping you all alive." Running his fingers through his hair, I could see he was tense but in total control. "Pierce is going to be your security from now on. He will be with you and Molly when I'm at work or when I can't be here. Do not go anywhere without him, don't go to work or out to pick up groceries, not even to the mailbox, without him. It's important that you listen to me."

"I can't have him at work, what am I going to tell my boss? Gee, I have a raving lunatic out there somewhere that could come into the place and kill me or maybe take my daughter? Where is Molly going to be when I'm at work, I can't just leave her?"

Carter shook his head. "Don't worry about it, I'll see to Molly. If it were up to me, you wouldn't be going to work while this is going on. It isn't like I can't take care of you." Removing his grip from my shoulders, he paced the floor a moment then rubbed the back of his neck. "Isabella, why don't you take family medical leave? It would be easier, and Pierce could watch you both without any trouble."

"Look, I know you're trying to protect me, but I can't live in a bubble forever. It may be months before they find this guy. Do you really want Molly to live in fear? Eventually, you will have to explain to her why there is a strange person with us that carries a gun no matter where we are. We have to be realistic here."

"Bella, I'm not asking, I'm telling you, take Pierce with you. If he is there, I know you're protected. I'll clear it with the hospital if you must work, Molly can stay in the daycare facility at the department." He really acted like he was unnerved. Trying to move around the subject wasn't going to be easy. I was not going to win here, I could see that.

"Carter, I know you're concerned, but really, there isn't any reason for me to be under guard at work."

Looking at me, he almost had fire come from him,

and his voice raised.

"Isabella, you will do what I say. I'm a patient man when it comes to most things, this isn't one of them. Your life could be in danger. Now you either do this my way or I will see that you are put under house arrest."

I could feel the fury rising in me, and my voice dropped an octave. "Just what do you think you're going to put me under arrest for?"

"I have ways of getting what I want, and if it means that's what it comes to, I will do it."

"You are a stubborn man. How could you? I'm your wife, not a fugitive."

Raising his voice to the point it shook me, he bellowed out why he was being so cool and ruthless. "I can't live through the loss of a second wife. I won't let it happen when I can stop it." And there it was, the very reason he was so rattled. He did have fear, he had a weakness, and his family was definitely it. My stomach tightened at the thought, that's it. He really thought that this maniac was coming after me. *Pull it together,* Blake, you're *in for a bumpy ride.* I felt remorse for what emotional turmoil I had put him through. I should have just listened to him and left it at that. Walking to him he had his back to me and his head was bowed with his hands resting on his waist. I couldn't stand that he was this stressed. I'd made the difference in his demeanor, his reaction to the situation. Stepping in slowly behind him, I wrapped my arms around his waist and rested my head against the firmness of his back. "I'm sorry, I shouldn't have questioned you. You know what you're doing, and I'm only making things difficult. I'll do whatever you want me to,"

I murmured.

Turning slowly, he hugged me tightly to him. "I'm sorry too, I shouldn't have raised my voice. That isn't like me." His voice had softened, and he ran his fingers through my hair, soothing me. "I don't know what I would do if something happened to you. I love you, Isabella. All I want to do is keep you safe."

Days had passed and nothing in particular had happened, pretty boring really. Our normal daily routine had been altered somewhat, and it was a little strange to be escorted by a bodyguard, even more strange was when my husband escorted me to work and stayed. Molly was well protected by the force when she wasn't with us, and she made a lot of friends in the daycare center run by the department.

Carter sat outside a trauma room in one of the lounge chairs for guests of patients. When I was more than three rooms away, he followed close behind.

After a while, I got used to having someone on my heels. Going for meals and to the bathroom was a little awkward when it wasn't Carter. I didn't exactly feel comfortable with a male officer standing outside the door of a lounge, bathroom or going to supper with me.

Thank goodness this shift was over, and I would soon be home with my husband where I could unwind and feel at least partially normal again. Carter would be home waiting, and I would be rid of my watchdog for a while.

Peirce walked me to the door and opened it. Seeing Carter standing in the middle of the room, he made his departure. "Thank you, Peirce."

"Ma'am." Peirce bowed out gracefully and returned to his car.

Molly had fallen asleep in the chair beside the television and was curled up tightly in a ball covered with her blanket. Carter seemed to be a bit on edge, but he had been for several weeks now. The thought of this guy was disrupting everything: my job, Carter's job, and our home life. It had driven us all to fear. At one point Carter had even thought of sending Molly and me to his parents to stay until they could find this man. I refused to leave him, I wanted to be home. If it took me to have a little inconvenience to do so, then so be it. I wasn't going to let this man run my life again.

He looked tired, and his hair was in disarray. He was unshaven and still wearing his gun. This was not my husband, in the few short weeks that this had all started, he rarely slept and took little time to himself. He was at the office most of the time, only home when he knew I was coming home for the night. The rest of the time I was either followed by Peirce or my husband, but it was all business. He carried his work with him along with a laptop and a radio. Landon had tried to take his place on occasion so that he could take a break, but in his stubborn Blake fashion, he refused. I was beginning to worry about him. He barely ate, and he sat watching and waiting most of the time.

All the doors and windows had alarms; it was like we lived in Fort Knox.

He rarely spoke to me. He would just sit as if he were in deep thought.

There was no emotion that appeared on his face. He heard everything, saw everything. I was in half a mind to drug him and call Landon for assistance.

This was getting out of hand, and I knew it.

Looking at him, I took a deep breath and noticed the glass in his hand. It wasn't anything typical of him. Getting closer, I could smell it. It was evident he had a drink or maybe two. Reaching, I took the glass from him. "I think you've had enough."

"Just how do you know if I have had enough?" His speech was off and so was his gait.

"How many of these have you drank?"

"I don't know, what does it matter?"

"Because you don't drink. I know this has been difficult, but you need to get some sleep and start acting like my husband again."

He looked at me like he could have put daggers through my heart. I had never seen him like this. He had never been this out of control. He swaggered to me, very unlike him. His attitude was that of superiority, and it frightened me.

"I am your husband," he huffed and grabbed me firmly by the arms.

"Don't think I'm not watching you when you're at work."

"What is that supposed to mean?"

"I see how you look at Reed, and he watches you. Every twist of your body, he watches you."

"Carter, you're drunk."

"You and Reed have been together, haven't you?" Taking me by the arms, he shook me. I couldn't believe what had come out of his mouth. As much time as it had taken him to touch me and now he thought that I was having an affair with one of the doctors I worked with, this was absurd. What happened to the sweet, gentle, loving man I married. "Answer me, Bella."

"Please stop, you're hurting me."

"Answer me!" His voice awoke Molly, and she screamed.

"Carter, please let go of me. Your daughter is watching, she has never seen you like this." He let go forcefully and walked off. Molly ran to me crying softly. Wiping her tears from her face, I waited until Carter was in the other room and I walked off with Molly to her room. Shutting the door behind me, I took Molly and sat her down on the bed. "Molly, it's okay. Daddy's just tired. He needs to sleep. You know how tired you get?" She shook her head trying to sniff back tears. "It's okay, baby girl. I'll call Uncle Landon and get some help for Daddy. Don't worry, it's big-people stuff, he's going to be okay.

Just sleep Tink, he won't yell anymore." Tucking her in, I covered her and sat in her room for a moment, hoping that Carter wouldn't come in. If he was mad, he would be worse if he heard me calling his brother-in-law.

Landon was the only other one I knew that could handle him.

Dialing the telephone, I tried to keep my breathing under control. The telephone rang three times before anyone picked up, and I was relieved to hear Landon's voice on the other end.

"Hello." Landon's voice sounded like I had woke him.

"Landon, it's Bella. I hate to call you like this, but I have a problem."

"Sure, what is it?"

"Landon, I need help."

"Help? What's wrong? Isn't Carter with you?" His voice was more on alarm now.

"Yes, he's with me, but, Landon, he's been drinking. He hasn't been sleeping, and now he's accusing me of having an affair with one of the doctors I work with. He scared Molly to death because he was yelling. Landon, I thought he was going to hit me. I have never seen him like this. It scares me."

"Okay, just sit tight, I'll be there soon."

"Landon, please don't let him know I called. He's already mad at me, I don't want to make it worse."

"Where is he?" Landon laid his coat down on the chair by the door and walked in. His voice was quiet and calm. A growl came from the bedroom.

"If you are referring to me, I'm right here." He pointed to himself and barely stumbled into the room.

Landon looked over at me as he took in the scene. "I swear he could a ant sneeze in hailstorm."

He raised yet another glass of what appeared to be liquor and plopped it down on the couch. "I heard that," he announced. "Did she call you, or is this a social call? If it's a social call, then you need to get social. Bottle's on the counter."

Landon walked over and sat in the chair beside him,

and I made an excuse to leave the room and placed myself in our bedroom. I could still hear what was going on, but I was conveniently out of fire. Sitting on the end of the bed, I wrung my hands and offered a simple prayer for my husband. Lord knew we both needed help right about now. Sitting there, I realized this was the first fight we had ever had. I didn't like the feeling I had from it, he's cold.

If it were any colder, I would have to build a fire in the floor. I felt like I had ice running through me after tonight's events. I looked forward to coming home and being home with him, now I wished I were somewhere else. Voices came from the other room that are too low to hear at first then I could hear Carter raise his voice.

"She's been with that Reed guy. You should see how he watches her, every move she makes, he's right there."

"Carter, you don't know what you're saying. You know Bella would never do that, she loves you and has since she first met you. You're tired, and you are pushing yourself way too hard. You need to sleep and to eat. I know enough that you haven't been eating at work when you are there. Have you been eating when you're with Bella?'

"I'm not hungry."

"No, but you sure have been thirsty."

"You don't know anything, why don't you leave?"

"Because we're family, because we're friends. Isabella is worried about you, and so am I. I haven't seen you like this for years. What happened? You've always been able to deal with things before, what's changed?"

Carter's voice cracked momentarily. "My wife," he choked. "I can't lose my wife. I can't sit and watch her die."

The innocence of his statement broke my heart.

"Then why did you do this to yourself? You're all she has. If you lose it, your chances increase. Not from the man on the street, you. You need to put the alcohol away, apologize to your wife, and get back with God."

Walking slowly back into the room, Carter sat with his head in his hands.

I could hear the faint echo of sobs below them. Landon noticed me but didn't say anything, he just nodded his head. Standing in front of him, I laid my hand on his shoulder. "Amore." I didn't have to say another word, he wrapped his arms around my hips from where I stood and laid his head against my stomach and wept like a child.

"I'm sorry, Bella, I'm so sorry." I stood and ran my fingers through his hair, attempting to soothe him.

CHAPTER 19

After getting Molly ready for the day, I sat in the tub as she played in her room. Carter remained asleep. After all the days he had gone without sleep, it had caught up to him. The steam rose from the water that now soothed the sore muscles of my arms. Not intending to hurt me, Carter had left his mark behind. It was evident to me why he had done what he had in some respect, although I didn't understand. Why would he think I had been with Dr. Reed?

That was baffling to me, I had not given any reason for him to think anything was going on or had ever happened. Thank goodness for Landon, he was able to defuse the situation. Carter was so different from the person that I had married.

The doorknob turned and the door opened, strangely my by body tensed and my breath left me. "Bella," a sleepy, gravelly voice called. His voice broke the silence, and I relaxed when he walked in the room. I hadn't noticed that I was ready to fight until the relief of his voice was heard. Walking inside the room slower than usual, he looked down at me. Taking the towel from the rack, I stood and wrapped it around me and stepped out. He didn't say a word for a moment, he just looked at me as I stood there. My heart sank as I remembered the night before. Reaching his hand out toward me, I jumped, letting out a small gasp. It was unexpected to him and to me. Dropping his hands, he made one step closer. "I won't hurt you," his voice reassuring me.

"I know I've given you every reason not to trust me, just give me a chance to make it up to you." Seeing I was not moving from him, he reached out to get my hand and then examined my arms. His face was filled with hurt and pain.

"Dear God, did I do this to you?" He grimaced as he

looked at the bruises on my arms where he had hold of them last night. It had left fingerprint marks on both upper arms from the strength he had enforced.

I shook beneath his touch, remembering being held down by the monster that had attacked me. Tears came easy from him, but I felt numb. "Isabella,

I'm so sorry, this should have never happened." Turning, he ran both hands through his hair and walked into the bedroom and sat down on the edge of the bed. He's hurt from what had happened along with me and Molly. There was no question if I had forgiven him, I had. The problem was what caused all of this to start with. After drying just enough to slip my gown back on, I went into the bedroom where he sat. He had never moved. Sitting down beside him, I laid my hand down over his. His arms found me, and he drew me into him so gently it was if he was afraid he would break me if he held to me any tighter.

My hand cupped the side of his face, and I wiped the remaining tears from it. It killed me to see him this way. "We need to talk," I whispered to him. He shook his head in acknowledgment. He clung to me, and my heart broke as I saw my husband this vulnerable.

I longed for his touch, his affection after last night's dealings. It had seemed that my husband had returned from war, he was back. My gentle, loving husband had made a brief detour, but he was here now and I needed to help him. I needed to find out what had happened that caused all of this.

Sitting back and looking at me, he studied me. His eyes fixed into a pained stare, and was visibly sweating. "I'm sorry." Rubbing the back of his neck, he looked down. "I promise you if you stay, you'll never see that man ever again."

Shocked at the idea that he thought I would even consider leaving had floored me. "Why would you ever think I would leave you?"'

"You have every right to. I promised you I would never hurt you."

Running fingers over the bruises on my arms, his expression was deeply pained. His voice is uncharacteristically soft after last night's boisterous outburst, it's chilling to see his reaction.

"I'm not going anywhere. I promised you on our wedding day to love you for the rest of my life. I intend on honoring my wedding vows, my feelings haven't changed. I'm just concerned at the thought of you thinking I could ever go as far as having an affair. Have I ever given you a reason to think I would ever do something like that?"

He shook his head but didn't offer anymore. "Carter, I was hurt that you could even have the thought I would do such a thing, especially after it took me so long to trust you enough for you to touch me for the first time."

Thinking back, it had taken almost two months for me to allow him to touch me, for me to allow him to love me the way a husband and wife should. It's still difficult at times. "I have never had an affair with Dr. Reed, nor would I want to. I'm perfectly happy with you, I love you. I gave my heart to you, and no one else will ever have the place you have in it."

After a short period, he looked up at me as I ran my fingers through his hair. "You mean that, don't you?" Did he doubt that? The time we spent physically apart had caused him to doubt. It wasn't the fact he had thought I had been with someone else, he doubted what I felt.

"I meant it the first time I told you I loved you, I meant it when I vowed before God that I loved you, and I mean it now. You silly, controlling, cynical man. You should have known that all along. I fell in love with you the first time I saw you, why do you think I couldn't leave? It wasn't because I was married to my job. I wanted to be there. I wanted to be there with you, and nothing was going to pull me away. I had issues and I still do, I don't know when I will get rid of some of the baggage I have, but I don't intend on carrying it around all my life."

Leaning slowly into me, he took me gently into his arms. His breaths were short, almost gasping for air. "I love you, Bella, don't ever leave me. My weakness is in you. I could never survive if you left."

"Just try to get rid of me, Blake, and see how far you get." I squeezed him tightly to me, and his heartbeat could be felt on my chest through the thin silk gown I had on. I could tell there was more going on than the fear of me leaving, but I left it at that. We sat holding on to each other for some time until I heard the pitter-patter of tiny feet headed to the door. Still holding on to him, I didn't want to let go. It didn't matter that Molly was up, she needed to see that her parents still loved each other. There was nothing wrong with her seeing us together. After last night, that's what we all needed.

She climbed upon the bed, dragging herself up by grabbing on to the comforter and was soon sitting behind her father. Carter never moved from my embrace. I didn't think he even realized she was there. Sticking her thumb in her mouth for comfort, she sat on her knees and tapped her father on the back. That's all she needed to do. Carter withdrew his hold and turned to find his daughter looking up at him. She looked up at him despondently, questioning him.

"Daddy, you mad?" Smiling down at her, he scooped her up and sat her down on his lap, hugging her up close to him.

"No, Tink, Daddy's not mad."

"Why you mad at Mommy?"

"I'm not mad at Mommy, Tink. It's hard to tell you so you can understand, but Daddy isn't mad. It doesn't matter anymore, okay? Daddy's okay and so is Mommy."

We were sitting on the bed, and it rocked and swayed a little, and it suddenly had made me a little queasy. After taking a few breaths, it had passed. After last night's happenings and not sleeping well, I passed it off as not getting enough sleep and watched my husband as he snuggled his daughter up into his arms. This was the picture I wanted to see, this was my family. The one I remembered and loved. I didn't have much time with them often. I was sure that Carter would prepare himself for work, and I would be set up with the watchdog for the day. I didn't mind Peirce. I just wanted to spend time with my husband. I needed it, craved it. Over the last few weeks, we had seen each other in the passing. Even though Carter had been with me most days, he had been more like a zombie.

Carter laughed as he tickled Molly, and she giggled in delight of her father playing with her. Carter's cell rang right on cue as usual. More than likely, it was the office calling him in to work early, no less.

"Hello," he answered in a short tone. "Yeah, I'm fine . . . She's fine . . .

We're fine, Landon . . . We're spending some time with Molly before work . . ." His lips pressed into a thin line, and he rubbed the back of his neck. "What do you mean? . . . Sure, okay . . . No . . . That's fine, I could use some time to be with my family . . . Dad had something set up for us for a couple of days. They wanted to take Molly for a few days and let us spend some time together, a honeymoon of sorts I guess . . . I think we could use it . . . Okay . . . You did? . . . I'm sure she will be glad to hear that . . . Okay, later." Hanging up the phone, he laid it back down on the table next to the bed. He gave me a little smirk. Oh good, at least it's something that wasn't a reflection of what had been happening of late.

"Mrs. Blake, how would you like to take a couple of days off with your husband all to yourself?"

Thinking it was a lovely thought, I knew I couldn't get time off that quickly. "I would love to, but I can't get the time off."

That boyish grin appeared once more, and I knew he had cooked up something. "You can and you have. Landon and my parents set it up, It wasn't my doing. This way I get to spend some much-deserved time with my wife and I know you're safe." He had relaxed was himself at last, what a relief.

"But how did I get the time off?"

"Landon pulled a few strings with the administrator."

"He knows hardnosed Lockley? She doesn't have a drop of sympathy in her."

Raising his hand and waving it, he kept that beautiful grin. "Yeah, but Lockley was one of his old flames, and if she thinks that he is still in the loop, he can get what he wants. He's still single you know even though he's promised to my sister. Not everyone knows that."

"Oh, that's just mean."

"Hey, she's the one that walked away from the altar."

"He was going to marry her?"

"He's not proud of it, but when Beth got married, he got involved with her and they were together for a couple of years. He asked her to get married, she said yes. And when it came time to walk down the aisle, she made it to the altar and turned around and left. After of course she made a little speech as to she knew he didn't love her. She refused to marry him and be second to Beth, so the rest they say is history."

"That's unbelievable, I wouldn't have even thought he would have been interested in someone like her." I couldn't help but laugh. I couldn't see Landon with her that was so unreal. She was his complete opposite. She was extremely controlling, selfish, and could be downright ruthless at times. Being attractive was a deterrent to what she really was.

"So, Isabella, aren't you interested to where we are

going?"

"Sure." I beamed at him as I sat there like a child at Christmas. Nothing would have prepared me for what he was going to tell me.

"We . . . are headed to one of the most romantic places that I know and one of which I'm sure you will like as well."

"Oh, I can't stand it. Where are we going? What have you cooked up?"

"Not me, angel, my parents set it up for their daughter-in-law. Guess they wanted to say thank-you for taking their son off their hands." He chuckled as he placed Molly on the bed and stood up. "First, we are going to drop Molly off with her grandparents, then we, my lady, are going to stay a couple of days in a secluded cabin, with no cell phones, computers, or anything that can distract us from each other. So get packed. Soon, as everyone is packed and ready, we're leaving."

What a wonderful view. I stood admiring it from the deck of the cabin, taking in the mountain air. What a wonderful calm and peace it gave knowing that now we were alone and on our own. There was not one person to worry about following or finding us here. Molly was safe at her grandparents, and I had a few days alone with my husband. I had to say it was a challenge getting here, seeing as the roads were snow covered. We are out in the middle of nowhere, but there were other cabins about. There didn't seem to be a lot of activity around at the moment, so that added to the romantic venue. The chill of the air seemed to hide from me as I admired the tree-lined mountains and the lined road that led here. There was magic here, this was going to be a particularly good time for us, I could feel it, one that was going to bring us closer together.

"Do you like this place?" he whispered as he wrapped himself around me.

"Yes, it's beautiful here. I can't imagine a better

place to be. I don't even mind the snow, it looks like a blanket lying across the trees and mountains."

"I like it here too. I used to come here when I was in college, it was an easy place to get away to. It gave me time to do something by myself, and if I wanted, I could go into the main part of town and see the sights, or I could hike. A winter or two, I would come and ski with Landon and some of the guys from the academy. Last time I was here, I broke my collarbone skiing."

"Well, let's not repeat that. I want you healthy and in one piece if you don't mind."

"Got plans, do you, Mrs. Blake?" he chuckled.

"Yes, I guess you could say I have plans, and they all include you and depend on you being in good health and in one piece, so don't break something."

"Yes, angel, whatever you say." Leaning against him, he kissed me gently on the cheek. I couldn't believe how much a few hours had made in him. He's back to his normal loveable self, and I was enjoying every minute of it until I felt the hardness of his holster against my side.

Why would he be wearing his gun? This was supposed to be a vacation, a honeymoon. I know I was going to hate myself if I asked. Why should I have even had the idea that we were perfectly safe? He shifted so that he was looking down at me. "This is our place anytime we want, the cabin belongs to us. It's a wedding gift from my parents, I couldn't think of a better place to be for Valentines week. Maybe we can ski while we're here. There's a nice resort at the top of the mountain that has lifts. I haven't been skiing in years."

"I hate to put a damper on things, but why are you carrying your gun?

You don't normally carry one when you're not working."

"Don't worry about that, angel. It's just me, I've been a bit on edge. I just want to make sure that you're safe."

"There's no reason to think otherwise, is there?"

"No, like I said, I just want to make sure that you stay safe. I've been a little jumpy since they found that young girl. I'm not sure there is a connection, but just in case there is, I want to be prepared."

"So they do think the kids weren't just running, they think they were killed?"

"Isabella, let's not talk about my job now. I want to spend time with you as my wife. I could care less about work right now. After hours of driving here, I want to relax and enjoy this time with one of the women in my life that I haven't been able to spend much time with as late." Turning me toward him and looking directly into my eyes, he absolutely mesmerized me. "We haven't had a honeymoon you know. I want to spend every minute, every second with you. I don't care if we spend it in front of a fire with a bag of marshmallows the whole time, but I want to spend it alone here, in this cabin with you."

My body shook under the chill of the mountain air and the thought of just being alone with him. I didn't think we had been totally alone since our wedding night. His blue eyes remained cast upon me, and that boyish smirk was slowly coming to light. My heart felt like it was sinking to my feet. "You know I can't resist you, don't you?" He chuckled in response. "It's just a pretty face, angel."

"You are handsome, but that's not what I'm talking about. You have that way about you that make women swoon over you and I'm just one of them."

"Come on, Bella, since when have I ever attracted anyone other than you?"

"You have got to be kidding. What about Marilyn?"

"Yeah, well, what about her?"

"She's all over you like hot butter. She made it so that you would have to catch her or she would have fallen. She knew you wouldn't allow her to fall.

She's not the only one. I see many others that I work with, they follow your every move when you're with me. They have since the first day you came into my life. I've seen them at the play, the different restaurants, and events we have attended. Surely you have noticed them?"

"Frankly, Bella, I don't care about any of the others, and no, I haven't noticed. I have always had eyes for one person." Tipping my chin with his cupped hand, he made sure that I was watching him, "It's you, only you."

"But . . ."

Placing a finger to my lips, he grinned sheepishly. "No, Bella, I don't want to talk about anything else. I have you here in this beautiful place and we're alone, the last thing I want to do is talk. Now we can stand here, or take this inside where it's a lot warmer. One way or the other, my intent is the same.

Now are you going inside, or are we staying here?"

Oh, I knew that look. This wasn't one of invitation, this was one of "I want you, and *no* is not going to be the word." Intimacy still was a problem, and we approached it cautiously, but it was no longer a no at any time. After the last few days, I needed to feel him close to me, as close as I could possibly get him. Never saying a word, I couldn't take my eyes off him. I could see every feeling, every struggle he had.

Letting his hand slide down my shoulder and down to my hand, he led me into the house. The scene had been set, it had been predetermined before we had arrived. The rustic feel of the cabin was softened by the scent of flowers and flickering candles that set the theme for the evening. I thought we were stopping in the living area, but he never stopped and continued down the hall turning out the lights as we went. The only lit room was at the end of the hall. It was dim but alluring. With each step I made with him, my heart picked up in rate. Carter hadn't said a word, he just squeezed my hand our fingers perfectly laced to each other.

404

The anticipation increased, and so did my breathing.

Standing at the door, I saw the flower-strewn bed. A thin layer of rose petals covered it, and the scent had filled the room. The corner fireplace flickered in red and orange sparks, fighting for attention in its glow. The mantel and the dresser were lit with hurricane candles that lit the room in a soft hue of gold.

"For you, angel, nothing but the best."

Sinking to my knees overcome by the feelings I had for him. It amazed me at what depths he would go to just to see me happy. To think it was just a few short hours ago that I thought we were at an impasse, never being able to get back to what we were before. It took a moment to realize that he was sitting in front of me. His thumbs pushed the tears from my cheeks that I hadn't known were there. "Bella, I love you," he whispered and held me by the hand. "I love you. I know things have been tense between us, but I want to change that. Give me a chance to let you see the man you fell in love with, I'm still here." Helping me to my feet, he held me close to him and kissed me passionately. His hands were soft and gentle against my body. His breath was warm against my ear, and I could hardly breathe. There was no one here but us, and it's a relief just to have him to myself. I didn't have to worry about the phone, the door, Molly walking in, or either of us going to work. This was our time, and we were deserving of it.

"You okay?" He smiled down at me and waited for his response. "You seem very comfortable, that's good."

"I'm with the person I love, how could I be any different?"

"Bella, you do something to astound me every day."

Picking me up off my feet, he sat me among the many rose petals that showered our bed. I heard the clunk of his shoes hit the floor as he made his way closer to me. Thinking about the first time we sat in his home alone, I remembered when we sat on his couch. My feelings had taken over me. I wasn't free to do so then, but now I was. It seemed so long ago, and yet it wasn't but a few months.

Tracing my cheek and pushing my hair back from my face, he smirked at me. "Isabella, what are you thinking? I can see the wheels turning, what's on your mind?"

"You, Mr. Blake. I was thinking of our first time in your home. I was a little to bold for my own good. I'm not sure where that came from, but it seemed to shake you a little."

"Yes, I remember," he smiled at the thought. "Being a bachelor for so long, I'm not sure what I had expected. A pretty girl, alone in a candlelit room was probably not my best choice. I wasn't as in control as you think. I wanted you as much as you did me, the difference was I knew if I let it go, I would never get to know the person you really were."

"And just what did you find?"

"A beautiful girl with an even more beautiful heart. Someone I could never live without."

There was not a smile, there was no grin, he was deadly serious. The words he had spoken had come from the heart. His soul was totally laid open to me. "Carter Blake, how can you come up with such beautiful things to say?"

"All true, angel, all of it. You need to be told daily if not more often what you mean to me, every second of every day wouldn't be enough. I'm madly in love with you. I hope that I have shown that to you."

I melted as I watched him. His eyes glowed against the flicker of the fireplace, a warmth flooded me as I looked into those endless pools of blue.

He never failed to captivate me. What a wonderful, intense feeling he gave me just sitting there next to him. "Every day of my life." He pushed off my coat and laid it on the chair beside the bed. Kicking my shoes in the floor, I met him in the center of the bed on my knees, looking directly into his soul.

The bed sank under our weight, bringing us closer to each other.

Slowly I unbuttoned his shirt and traced it up to his shoulders and pushed it away, trailing it with short kisses, ending in the bend of his neck.

He gasped as I kissed his jawline and then his lips. I knew how much he wanted me, I wanted him. Slow and controlled, that was what I wanted, to savor him. One more touch from him left me trembling, and he knew exactly what to buttons to push. He examined me with his eyes, every inch, as he pulled my sweater over my head. The palm of his hand rested against my belly as he kissed the bend of my neck. Tilting my head to the side, I allowed him a better access to his target. My breathing became ragged, making it difficult to get a deep breath. Placing his hand at the small of my back, he glided me down to the bed and looked down at me.

"You're so beautiful, Bella." His fingers floated over my skin, following the contour of my arms and down my sides. Covering me with the comforter, he slid in beside me. "I don't want you to fear me, I don't want you to ever be uncomfortable." Pushing my hair back behind my ears, he finally managed a grin.

"What?" I grinned.

"You aren't flinching, your body isn't tense. This is the first time I can remember that you have approached me without fear." His fingers ran through my hair, leaving chills running down my back.

"My heart belongs to you. Why should I ever be fearful of allowing myself to be vulnerable in front of you?"

Pulling him down to me, I kissed him fiercely, running my fingers through his hair. It's so soft, and it ran in layers between my fingers. He sighed, letting me know his feelings were on the surface, raw, reciprocating the passionate kisses I had given. His gentleness still overwhelmed me. I felt the heat from his body warming my bare skin, the smell of his cologne mixed with his own scent making me drunk. "I need you, Bella," his voice was low and distressed. The feel of his hands on me was enough to call me to him as I lost myself in his gaze. Tears flowed in small streams and ran down the corner of my eyes, hitting the pillow. Looking down on me, his expression was of grief as he cupped my cheek. "What's wrong, angel, am I hurting you?"

I grinned at him slowly, and the distress slowly disappeared from his beautiful face. "Nothing, I just love you so much."

His lips brushed against my cheek then my lips gently. "I love you," he breathed. "I've waited for this." He trailed soft, subtle kisses from the bend of my neck to my shoulder. His hands trembled as he ran them down my body.

I hadn't noticed him doing that before. His breath warm on my skin, I stilled under it, anticipating his next move. Feeling more like I was in a movie than in a mountain cabin in Tennessee. My hand laid against his chest as he kissed me, feeling his heartbeat racing against my own. His breaths were harsh as he attempted to control each of his movements.

"Carter?" He continued to kiss me. He was very controlled, and I felt the power behind him. The urgency behind each one. There was more than just love in the room, it was pain and anguish from the night before looking for redemption.

"What?" he stated breathlessly as he kissed my fingers, each one in turn.

He didn't look up, he just continued as he then changed to kissing me along my bra strap and sliding it to the side and cupping my shoulder to him.

"Honey, it's okay. Let it go."

He looked up briefly. "What?"

"I know you're thinking of last night. I'm fine, let it go."

"Just heal me, Bella. I need it. I need to be with you, I want to know you still love me." Each sentence was in short breaks.

"I do love you." My heart broke at what I was hearing. It ached to the very core.

"Don't let me go. Don't ever let go." His voice shook as he spoke.

The tenderness of his touch and his words consumed me. "I'll never let you go." My reassurance only added fuel to the flame and burned white-hot. For the first time since we were married, I was his and he belonged to me. It had sunk in that he loved me endlessly, I loved my husband with my entire being.

Clutching me to his chest, his eyes burned into mine. "I'll never let anyone hurt you ever again. I swear on my own life, I'd die for you."

My eyes opened on a brand-new day. The early-morning sun beamed across the floor as the sun rose over the mountain. Carter lay quietly, his eyes closed with his lashes fanned across his cheeks. His body entwined with my own, I felt like a brick wall weaved with ivy. My head lay on his shoulder with my hand splayed against his chest. I could feel the rhythmic fall and rise of his breathing. His arms encircled me as he slept. We had finally arrived to the point that the fear of what had happened had left, or so I thought.

Hating to move from his embrace, I didn't have much choice. I needed to go to the bathroom badly, and it didn't seem I could stand it a second more.

Standing on my feet, my head began to spin, and I suddenly felt very sick.

It didn't take long to find my way there. I lay down on the tile floor with a cold rag, and the rumbling of my stomach passed. What in the world was going on? I did this in a similar form yesterday, just not as severe. Oh well, it had passed, that was the main thing. Brushing my teeth wasn't exactly a treat either. It left a metal taste in my mouth that I couldn't seem to get rid of.

Sitting on the edge of the tub, I started to put things together. Oh no, it couldn't be. The doctors told me this could never happen. It was virtually impossible, yet some of the symptoms fit. I was just jumping the gun. It wasn't long before I was joined in the bathroom by my husband, and he was looking a little green himself.

"You okay, you look a little pale?"

Rubbing his eyes, he looked in the mirror over the sink. "Come to think of it, my stomach is kind of messed up. Did you bring anything with you?"

Now there was a shock, maybe it was something we ate, and it wasn't what I had in mind at all.

"Yeah, it's in the bag on the sink."

"You're up early."

"I wasn't feeling so well, so I got up and thought I'd take a bath to see if it would help."

"You too," he managed as he swallowed the medication. "Must have been something we ate last night."

"I thought that too, but we didn't eat the same thing on the way here."

"Maybe it's just coincidence. You feeling better?"

Twirling my hair nervously, I watched him as he went through the movements of getting his shaving gear from the overnight bag. "I guess so."

I sat watching him rinse his face then lather it. Noticing I was watching, he looked over and grinned. "Entertaining, Mrs. Blake?"

"What can I say, I always find you wildly attractive."

"Must not take much to entertain you." He chuckled.

Standing from my perch, I walked toward him and wrapped my arms around his waist. "I thought you were going to take a bath?"

"I was," I sighed looking into those breathtaking eyes. "Maybe I can assist you, and then if you're lucky, I will let you assist me."

"You drive a hard bargain. Just what would I be doing for you, Bella?"

"Whatever you like, Mr. Blake, but I'm partial to being pampered by you."

"Oh, so would you like a repeat of what happened when you were sick before? You weren't fond of it then."

"I think it would be more appreciated this time around." Pointing to the stool in the bathroom, he understood what I was saying.

"Are you going to do what I think you're going to do?"

Draping the towel over his shoulder, I took the razor in hand and slid it against it. "Pampering you is what I like best. Are you game, Mr. Blake? I do this often."

Nodding his head, I rinsed the blade and made smooth strokes and watched as it removed the shaving cream from his face in thick puffs.

Reaching and pulling me close to him so that I could feel his breath on me, he taunted me as he ran his hands up and down my legs. "Carter, if you don't hold still, this is tricky, and I really don't want you missing an ear." Grinning, he rested his hands at my waist. I finished the job and wiped his face with a cool rag and patted it dry. Running my hand against his face, I found it amazingly soft. "There, smooth as a baby's butt," I whispered. Did I say that?

"At least you left my ears and nose."

"What? Didn't you think I could do this?" I joked

with him.

"Of course, I just never thought that you would. I enjoy you pampering me, just having your hands on me is enough, I must confess."

"Rather bold, aren't you, Mr. Blake?"

"Only with certain young ladies that happen to wear my ring and have my last name."

"So I'm privileged."

"It's your turn. What would you like, Mrs. Blake? A nice warm bath with the trimmings, massage, foot massage?"

"That could prove to be a difficult choice."

"Hey, I'm a man of many talents. I can take care of more than one."

Kissing the rim of my hand and then the palm, he looked exotic. Standing, he walked to the tub and ran the water and tested it like he's giving a child a bath. He filled it with essential oils and pushed the water back and forth until the scent mixed with the heated water.

"Um, peppermint. That smells so good."

"Glad you like it."

Standing in front of him, he quickly undressed me and helped me step into the bath. The hot water washed over me, and it wasn't long before I was joined by my god of a husband. The water slapped over the side as he sat down and pulled me toward him. "Turn around," he directed so that I was facing him. "Feeling better?"

"Yes, you?"

"Yes, much."

Taking my foot, he started to rub my feet one by one. "Feel good?"

"Mmm, very."

Every touch left me more relaxed than before. I was calm, unbelievably calm. The nausea had left, and I lay against the rim of the tub.

"Bella, you awake?"

Turning my head, I could see him standing over me. "I must have drifted off."

"Come on, let's get you out." Holding out a towel, he gave me his hand and helped me to stand. Wrapping me, he picked me up and placed me back on the bed where I went quickly to sleep.

"Where is she?" I heard the gruff angry voice call from a room away.

"She is where she has been all along, where did you think?"

"I don't have time for this." The man's voice was so angry that it shook me, and I could feel the ground vibrate at the slam of a chair on the floor. "I have a group of young men that are going to be here, and I don't intend on disappointing them. Their coach is paying a hefty sum for these boys to be satisfied. I want her ready for business now!"

"Okay, okay. Get a grip, Arnell, geez. It isn't like we haven't managed this before. The Panthers come here every season. The coach knows what to expect. I promise you she will be ready. We do have others you know."

"I want her, don't you understand? She deserves everything she gets.

Punishing her in turn punishes the witch that left me. You do what I tell you."

"Arnell, don't you think you should go a little easier on her? She is pregnant."

"That's not my concern. When that brat is delivered, it will fetch a price, a good one. If it's a girl, I may consider keeping her for my own benefit. It wouldn't be an infant for long."

"Why don't you let her go? She isn't going to be of any use to us in a few months."

"You listen to me, Gage, my brother and her mother has done nothing but cause me trouble. I intend on taking every advantage of her along with her pain in the rear, brother."

His footsteps grew heavy as they beat against the hardwood floor. I lay lifeless on the broken-down bed. So tired that I couldn't move and I felt dreadfully sick. Looking around the room, it was just turning dusk and the room had become cold. Reaching to place my hand on my stomach, I felt the small mound below it. It was true, I was pregnant, and I was feeling it, just far enough to feel a bump at my belly button.

A tall, slender man entered the room, bearded and appeared well kept.

Not like the one that had been there before. Coming over to where I lay, he closed what light was coming in the room with a pull of the old paper blind.

"Sorry, I tried. He just isn't going to listen to reason. You need to get up and get ready, they will be here soon."

"I can't, I'm so tired. I can't."

"Look, you don't have a choice. I'm surprised that he has left you alive.

He's had others that he has killed. If you don't, you know he will punish you either by not feeding you, taking it out in favors, or beating you. It's your choice."

Taking hold of his shirt sleeve, he looked down at me. "You have to get me out of here, please."

"I'm sorry, but I don't have any control. Your brother is still alive. If you want him kept that way you will do as he says."

"How?"

"Look, I don't know the answers, but if you don't do what he says, Lee loses privileges and will eventually be killed."

He turned and left the room, and it settled into darkness as I got out of bed slowly and dressed in the usual that he had placed in the dresser, which was little. At least it wasn't just underclothes anymore. The lace teddies I

414

despised along with the garters and heels that I hated. Something that would have made a normal woman feel feminine made me feel dirty, trashy. Sitting before the vanity, I literally painted my lips with bright lipstick, the only one that he would allow me to have, and brushed my hair until it looked like a ball of waves falling across my breast. The old cracked mirror made me look older than my years. I looked like a woman of thirty years and how old was I?

It didn't matter, the days had turned to months and maybe years, I was no longer sure. The door swung open, and there standing in the door was Lee.

Shutting the door behind him, he walked quickly to me.

"Sis, I'm working on getting you out of here. I have to get you out of here before that baby is born, or they are going to take it and sell it or worse."

"Lee, you can't do any more about getting us out of here than I can. We're stuck here, face it. I waited for months for Dad to find us, and he still hasn't and isn't going to unless he goes looking for a sex slave."

He placed his hands on my arms, getting my attention. "I will get us out of here. I promise you. I just need to get on his good side, and he will eventually make a mistake."

"Lee, he has assaulted us both, he has done everything but kill us, and right now, that would be a relief."

"Don't say that. You can't mean that? You have a baby to think about."

Directing him to the door, I opened it. "You need to get out of here before he catches you here. If he does, it means trouble for us both."

He reluctantly turned to leave. "Regardless of what you think of me, I do love you. You're my sister, and I will find a way of getting you out." As he walked out the door, I shut it behind him and returned to sitting on the bed waiting for God only knew what.

"Your clients are here," a booming voice announced. The room filled with teenage boys of varying ages. "I'm sure you know how to treat them nicely." The man with the emerald green eyes and his scruffy appearance were among them. "Coach Turner has asked that you show these boys some extra attention, they are preparing for a championship playoff. You wouldn't want them to go into battle without a woman's affection, would you?" He laughed wickedly as he walked from the room, and the click of the lock let me know there was no way out.

One of the boys backed off slightly and the others with him, except one. Number 68 was reflected on his stadium jacket. He growled a little and turned to the team of boys behind him. "You guys backin' out?"

"No, it's just you're the captain, don't you think you should go first?" the young man stuttered slightly as he answered the captain of the team.

"Jennson, you're a genius, if we do this right, we can all have a turn."

This kid had no fear of anything, and he took me roughly by the arm.

"Come on, she belongs to us for now, and we can do anything we wish."

It was then I recognized one of them. Ryan Bentley was the center for the team. He was the one to back off first. He could have had any girl he wanted. He was more of the blonde surfer type that the girls were head over heels for. His brown eyes were set perfectly to his high cheekbones. "Hey, Bentley, why don't you go first?" The team captain had stood behind me and held my arms together with one of his hands and attempted to undress me with the other. Ryan walked toward me and whispered into my ear so no one else could hear him.

"I'm sorry, Isabella, I didn't know it was you. I'll

get you out of here somehow. Play along for now."

Salvation at last, my high school sweetheart of all people, had found me by accident. "What's the problem, Bentley, need some help?"

"No," he had very firmly answered. "I work better alone. Just go, leave her to me. I'll take care of her."

CHAPTER 20

"Bella, wake up."

I could hear a distant voice calling me as I looked into the eyes of Ryan Bentley, and they slowly faded.

"Come on, angel, wake up."

Sitting straight up in the bed, I gasped for a breath. My heart was racing, and I felt cold as ice. Arms wrapped around me, and I knew I was safe. Carter was here, and it's the safety of his arms that broke the nightmare.

"You okay? You were pretty restless."

"Yeah." Pushing my hair away from my face with both hands, I got a grip on what had just come to me. Ryan, he was there. I was in a room with a group of high school football players.

"Carter, the group of kids that was in the car accident, the boys, they were part of the Panthers football team?"

"Yes, why do you ask?"

"The girls, they were cheerleaders for the team?"

"Yes. Where are you going with this?"

"Before I met you, I dated a Panthers football player, he was the center for the team."

"Okay, so what does that have to do with anything?"

"Carter, Ryan Bentley was that player. He and a group of players came to where I was." My skin crawled as I remembered the events. "I know the name of some of the players that were there. I was a cheerleader my freshman year of high school for the Panthers."

"Ryan Bentley took care of you, he's the one that got you out of that mess."

"Yes, I know, he told me he would get me out that night. He told me to play along and he would get me out. That's not all I remember, I remember the first names of the men.

Carter paled as he listened. "Isabella, if you know the names, we can shut them down. We can put them away."

"I just remember the first names."

"That's a start. What are they?"

"Arnell and Gage."

"Are you sure of that?"

"I'm sure."

"Arnell is the one that beat me and caused me to lose Jenna. He's the one that . . . that . . ." My words caught in my throat.

Holding me tight to him, he rocked me, comforting me. "It's okay, you don't have to say another word, I'll take care of it. In the meantime, try to eat something. I brought you some soup. It's on the table beside you. I won't be long."

He started to get up, and I grasped him by the arm. "Please don't leave."

"It's okay, I'll be back. I just want to text Landon so he can get the department working on it."

"You said you didn't have your cell."

"Okay, so I lied. I needed it so that if we need something in an emergency, I would have a way of getting help."

"Help? Why would we need help?"

"Isabella, you ask too many questions. I'm going to the next room and get the cell, and I'll be right back. I promise."

Sitting there trying to analyze what I had said as I watched him leave the room, it left me feeling cold and empty. Why had this come to me now?

I had spent months maybe years leaving it behind, and now it's coming back.

Okay, if I was going to remember, I might as well try to stir it all up. Why was I there? What were the men's last names and why did they come after me? Carter said Ryan was the one that took me to the hospital when I lost Jenna. How did he get me out? And Lee, Lee was my brother? I didn't have a brother. Where did that come from? I was the only child my parents had, wasn't I? I had a brother? If so, where was he? Who was he?

"Carter!" Getting out of bed, I slipped a robe on and started to walk to the next room. "Carter!"

Before I could leave the door, he met me there.

"Isabella, what's wrong?"

He's breathing a little harder than normal and running his hands through his hair. "Your cell, can I use it?"

"Sure, why?"

"I need to talk to my mother."

"Bella, why don't you let it wait until we get home, it can't be that important.

Besides I want to spend what time we have alone with no distractions."

"Please, if I don't, I won't be able to get this out of my head."

"Something you remembered?"

"Yes, and it's driving me crazy. It could be just something my mind has made up, and I hope that's all it is. If not, it just got more complicated."

"Can you tell me?"

"Just hang around and you'll find out." After he handed me the cell reluctantly, I dialed my mother's number. My hands shook. I already knew the answer before I asked. My stomach started churning, and I wasn't sure I was going to be able to sit there until she answered. The phone rang for the fifth time, and I had almost hung up when I heard her on the other end.

"Hello."

"Momma, I need to ask you something," my voice hurried.

"Isabella, honey, aren't you supposed to be on your honeymoon? You shouldn't be calling me, you should be spending it with Carter."

"Momma, listen to me. I need to ask you something, it's important."

"Of course, what is it?"

"Momma, I don't know how to ask without just coming out and saying this."

"Whatever it is, dear, I'm sure it isn't that serious."

"Do I have a brother?"

The line was dead silent. She had given me her answer by her silence, but I needed to hear it from her.

"Lee, Momma, is Lee my brother?"

Her voice cleared. Taking a deep breath, I heard her anxiety without a word. "Yes."

"Why didn't you tell me? Where is he, and why have you kept it from me?"

"You were just a little girl." She choked. "It was a long time ago, and you couldn't understand."

"Momma, where is he? What happened to him?"

She was choking back tears now. I could hear each sob.

"I don't know, Bella. I haven't seen him in years. It's a long story, and one we shouldn't discuss over the phone."

"When were you going to tell me?" Tears came readily down my cheeks as I remembered an earlier memory of a man that had forced us together.

"Oh my god, Daddy, he's not Lee's father. I remember the man calling him his son."

"We'll talk when you get home. I can't talk now."

"Momma, he forced us together, you knew, didn't you? You knew?" Being unable to talk any longer, Carter took the cell from me and spoke to my mother.

"Anita, I'll take care of her . . . No, it's okay, I can take care of it . . . Yes, I'll see what I can do . . . Me too . . .

421

We'll see you soon."

My jaws clenched at the thought that my mother had been keeping this from me all this time. What else had been hidden from me, what other things had I forgotten? Where was Lee now? Was he dead, did this monster of a man kill him? Why couldn't I remember growing up with him?

"Bella, turn it off. I know what you're doing, and it's just going to make it worse. Shut it down, let go of it." Carter caressed my face as I tried to leave the now-known truth behind. I couldn't do anything with what I knew here.

"I'll put in a call to the office about Lee, but you need to promise me you won't worry about what you remember. It's in the past. You can't change any of it."

Shaking my head in agreement, I sat down on the bed and Carter paced the room as he dialed the cell, finally making contact with the Portland police department. He was talking to Landon or maybe it was J.C. I wasn't sure.

I started to feel nauseous again and dizzy, and it didn't take long before I found myself in the bathroom praying to the porcelain throne. I hadn't had anything to eat that would do this to me, but then again, Carter had been ill this morning too.

Thinking back, it struck me. When was my last cycle? No, that couldn't be right. I was told I could never conceive. There was way too much damage from repeated infections and all of the tortuous things that Arnell had done.

I had problems delivering Jenna, and that had not helped the cause. My tubes were badly scarred, and I had all matter of surgical scars from delivery, and it was hard to tell what other damage that had been inflicted.

How could that even be a possibility? Looking through my purse, I found the calendar that I carried and marked each cycle. This was February 14, and my last cycle was when? My fingers traced back each date coming to rest on a day in December. No, that couldn't be right. Looking again, there was no mistake that was my last cycle. *It's just the stress and pressure you have been under,* Bella. *Get hold of yourself, it isn't possible and you know it.* Putting the calendar away, I dismissed it and remained sitting in the floor with a cold wash rag in reach. I was starting to feel better, but to keep from rocking the boat, I sat there.

"Bella, you okay?" I could hear him calling, but I couldn't seem to get up the energy to answer him. I could hear the rhythm of his footsteps against the floor as he approached the bathroom door. He knocked at the door. "You okay?" His voice was unwavering. What was I going to do if it were true? He already had in mind that I had an affair, what would he think now? I had only been with him a handful of times, and the first time was almost the end of January. I could have counted the times we had been together on one hand.

"Bella, are you okay?"

"Yes, come in, I'm okay." That was putting it mildly. I sat there wrapped in the robe I had thrown on. The tile on the floor was cold, but it was soothing to the nausea that was now hitting in waves. Looking up he walked in, I could see the concern etched in his face. Stooping down beside me, he laid his hand against my face. "Feeling sick again?"

"A little," I lied. The room was spinning, and I felt large waves coming at me, but there was nothing more to come up.

"You don't seem to be fevered." Offering me his hand, he helped me up from the tiny space from where I sat. Walking me back to the bed, he motioned to it. "Why don't you lie down for a minute?" I watched him in distress, and I knew I had to play it cool. He still motioned for me to lie down. "I won't leave you." Climbing in the bed, he covered me and then lay down beside me, pulling me into him. "It's upset from everything you have on your mind. You have to let it go. If you don't, it's going to get worse." He had no idea, not even a thought of this, might be a child we we're talking about.

I snuggled in close to him. I wanted him close to me; I needed that. I could see now in my mind some of the images from my past. Flashes of what Arnell had forced us to do. He had forced Lee at gunpoint, and I could see Lee plead with him and asking me to forgive him because if he didn't do what he wanted, he would kill us both. It choked me at the idea that he could do his own child that way. He was a mean, evil man capable of anything. I had wished this man dead thousands of times now. I had wished that he was alive so I had the opportunity to kill him myself.

"Feeling better," Carter's voice broke me from my thoughts. Assessing the way I felt, I shook my head yes. Not wanting to elaborate on what I had in mind, there was too much going on and way too fast. "Good, we'll just stay here for a while. Later we can do something if you're still okay. I don't want you to get sick again."

It wasn't going to be easy to hide from him what most assuredly was going on for long. A month or two at the most would be all I had. What would he say or do if I found out it were true? I had enough to worry about now to kill me.

"You sure you're okay? You're so quiet, I'm a little worried. Are you angry with me for what happened?"

My heart lurched when he brought it up. He really thought that was what was bothering me. He was far from what had been on my mind. I have a brother out there somewhere if he were still alive. I could be pregnant with a child that belonged to him, but with the outburst he had experienced, would he believe the new life belonged to him? It could potentially destroy everything we had built. Why was it with every turn it meant disaster for us? If Lee were alive, what else went on with my brother I don't remember?

It was so painful to think that we were forced together. He was forced to do what he did to protect us both. Was he the one? Did he get me out of the hell I was in, or was it Ryan? Did they work together?

Turning me gently to him, he looked down at me in great pain. "Angel, I'm sorry. I will never do or say anything like that again. It kills me that I did this to you. Forgive me."

Looking up at him, I could see the stress and tension on him. My dear sweet husband had blamed himself for what was going on. It really wasn't his fault, it was my own. Smiling up at him, I tried to reassure him. "Carter Blake, you are an amazing man. I love you so much, don't blame yourself. It isn't you at all. Nothing could be further from the truth, it has nothing to do with what happened, it's over and buried."

The days passed quickly while we spent time in the small cabin, and I was grateful for the time we had spent there. We had one more night there, and with all the other things that we needed to concentrate on and to get back to, I just wanted to stay there with him and never leave. I was comfortable lying in his arms. The couch before the fire was cracking and popping as the bright orange, yellows, and reds sparked along with the white flames against the hearth. No sounds but the night and the rhythmic sounds of his breathing.

The week had brought many things to mind, one of being, what did he think of having children? This was the chance to talk to him, a chance to feel him out and see what his thoughts were. Better here than anywhere, he was relaxed and he was focused on me. There was no job, no house to worry about, and no one to arrest or to investigate. Bringing it up, I had to do it subtly or he would suspect. The last two days, the nausea had eased, not that it had left, but it was easier to keep hidden. Carter had only had the few times where he had felt a little off, but I had pushed it off as not enough sleep or eating what he should. He had spent weeks not eating or sleeping, and that was my explanation.

Sitting there leaning into him, he wrapped his arms around me, bringing the cherry red throw over us both as we sat gazing into the fire. "Sad to go," he murmured as he ran his fingers through my hair. His breath fell on my cheek, and the scent of his cologne filled me.

"Yes." I smiled as I sat there loving every minute spent with him, trying to hide the anxiety I felt. "This has been the best week I can remember. How could I not enjoy a snow-covered mountain in a cabin out in the middle of nowhere, with the most adorable man I could ever hope to be stranded with?"

It was met with a chuckle freely from him. "Mrs. Blake, you do have a way with words." Kissing my cheek, he tightened his hold. "Did you stop to think maybe I wanted to get stranded with you?"

"What about Molly?"

I felt him smirk. "I love our daughter dearly, but she is in good hands and I'm enjoying some much-deserved time with my wife."

Here it goes, Bella, it's *now or never.* "What would you think about children? We never talked about it before. Would you want more?"

Bringing his hand to his brow, he rubbed his forehead and grinned.

"Where did this come from?"

I grinned nervously as I watched his flawless face. He wasn't angry, that was a start. The sudden prickles of anxiety washed over me, I was sure he could see through me. It was an unsettling moment, but I tried to act as if it were a for instance.

"Just asking, like I said, we had never discussed the possibility of children.

426

I just wondered what you thought."

He ran his finger over his bottom lip, his slight grin remained. "I don't know, I just assumed that you weren't able to have any more from what Lily had told me." As he sat there contemplating an answer, he ran his finger across my shoulder and up and down my arm. "I guess it would be okay if you weren't in danger. I really don't want to raise a second child alone. For now, I would prefer time with my wife. I know Molly is there, but she is a little older and she does still need care, at least she sleeps through the night. I can manage to spend some time with you, and we're still a family most of the time."

It wasn't exactly the answer I was looking for, but he was honest. "Does that answer your question?"

"Yes, I guess so."

"If it were a girl, I would want her to look as lovely and have the wonderful spirit her mother has. A boy would be wonderful too. I could take him to the ball games, teach him how to fish, ski, the things dads do with their sons." He turned a little more so that he could see me, examining me. I knew eventually he was going to figure out why I had asked. Even if I were pregnant, there was nothing I could do now. He continued to smile and traced his long finger down my cheek. "If for some reason, when we decide that's what we want, and if for some reason we can't have children naturally, we can adopt. I have no objection to that since my sister and I were adopted. I love my family, and I know if it comes to that, you will be a wonderful mother no matter what. You're so good with Molly. I watch you with her, and I know Andrea would be very pleased with the love and affection that you give her."

"I didn't know that you were adopted. You look and act so much like your father I would have never guessed. As for Molly, she's easy to love. She's a lot like her father, a kind, gentle, and loving person. She loved me from the time she met me, unconditionally."

"She is more of a reflection of her mother than me. Andrea never met a stranger, she looked for the good in everyone even when I thought there was nothing good about them. She always gave everyone the benefit of a doubt.

And as for my parents, they brought me out of a very dark period of my life.

I love them as if they were my birth parents. Just because someone gives you life at birth doesn't mean they are going to be good at raising a child. My birth parents however were very king and loving people, and I do still miss them at times, but it's the little boy that misses them. Grayson and Iris took Beth and me in and loved and cared for us the majority of our lives. I just wish they had gotten us sooner."

"What changed? I mean when you met me, you didn't know me, but yet you treated me like you had known me all my life. You accepted me."

"You learn eventually that life is short. You live your daily life like it's going to be your last, believe me, it puts things in perspective."

"I can imagine how it would change things."

"Hey, angel, wake up, we're almost home." My eyes were still heavy from sleep when I heard the soft chatter of Molly's voice in the back singing

"Wheels on the Bus." Looking out of the slightly fogged window, I saw pines still covered in a light snow with a distant view of the ocean. We were home.

I wasn't sure if I liked the idea. I had enjoyed my time away with my husband, being alone without disturbance. It wouldn't be long before we were thrown back into the reality of work and the daily worries. I had enough to deal with here, and it seemed to be mounting. At least I hadn't been sick at my stomach today, couldn't say so much for Carter. We had stopped at a local restaurant for lunch, and even though he was hungry, he hadn't eaten half

428

of it. He had said his stomach seemed to be upset, but he had since improved. I hope he isn't coming down with something. He had too many things going on right now to take time to be sick. I know he would push himself even if he was.

Molly continued in her little song as we pulled into the drive. Home, we're home. The dusk of the evening was closing into darkness as he had turned the key in the door. Carter walked into the house, more cautious than usual, setting me a little uneasy. Molly ran over to her dollhouse and began to play as if nothing was different from normal. As I sat down on the couch, I felt my stomach churn, but it's under control. Carter walked from room to room, and I knew he was looking for someone to be there or something to be out of place.

"Hey, honey, why don't you come sit with me, it's been a long day." He turned to see me on the couch, and he knew that I was on to him. Turning around, he grinned and walked slowly over and sat down beside me. "Relax, no one's here."

"You know me too well, don't you?"

"I'm catching on."

"Just protecting my family." Picking up my hand, he kissed it and gave it a gentle squeeze.

"There isn't any reason for you to be so jumpy, is there?"

I could see he really didn't want to answer the question. "Of course not."

I smiled back at him to ease the tension, and then the atmosphere calmed. "I had a wonderful time at the cabin this week, I hated to leave."

"So did I." His eyes danced as he looked into mine. My heart leapt within me, and my stomach fluttered furiously. What a wonderful feeling, the feeling of being loved. The love for my husband grew every day.

"What's going on in your pretty little head?" He

grinned. "I can see you're thinking of something wonderful, you always blush."

Leaning into him, I ran my fingers through his thick dark hair just to be able to touch him. Unlike me, he never flinched when I touched him.

"Mrs. Blake, are you thinking of a wild weekend in a secluded cabin?"

His smile brightened, and his blue eyes gleamed as he toyed with me.

"Thinking about you."

"Oh, I see." His voice was soft, and he ran his finger along his bottom lip.

"I suppose we could do a little recreation here." His boyish grin was slowly building.

"We do have a little company you know." I pointed out that Molly was here with us and awake.

Gathering me to him, he whispered softly in my ear. "She won't be up much longer." The heat from his breath only intensified the emotions left from our trip.

"All you have to do is say yes," he prompted and ran his finger along my cheek. My body shook at the thought, no longer in fear but in anticipation of feeling him next to me.

"Yes," I answered weakly in a whisper against his ear. I sank into him, and he clutched me tighter.

"Soon, very soon, meet me in our room. I won't be long."

Awaking during the quiet dawn, I found him holding me next to him, relaxed with his opposite arm resting behind his head. He had a way of blocking out the rest of the world, making me feel like we were the only couple in love. I could never get enough of him. I was treasured by him, and he handled me like a fine china doll.

My fingers played across his cheek, savoring him, and the stubble of his unshaven face prickled beneath my touch. The warmth filled my heart.

430

Lying beside him, my head lay on his chest with his arm wrapped around my shoulder. Awaking slowly, he smiled, apparently contented as his fingers stroked my arm in a rhythmic unhurried manner.

"You look peaceful, Mrs. Blake," he murmured in a low voice. "You're positively glowing."

"All because I have you." Yes, I was peaceful and contented to stay where I was among the rumpled sheets next to him. My hand rested on his chest and remained there, undisturbed, until he reached for it, taking it to his lips and brushing against my skin, sending tiny charges through me.

"I love every inch of you." He breathed, kissing each finger.

"Can you stay home today, just for a while?" I asked, knowing full well the answer I would get.

He sighed and looked over at me and flashed a chaste smile. "Isabella, you know I have to work."

Feeling a little disappointed, I looked down, remaining where I was feeling the comfort in his arms. If this was all I could have for now, it was enough.

"Hey, look at me." He tilted my face to him. "Do you really want me to?"

He turned, propping himself on his elbow. His deep blue eyes fixed on me.

He always looked sexy no matter if he was dressed in a suit, his favorite jeans, or next to me, skin to skin. He never had a bad day.

"If you do, I'll stay a while longer, but you may not make it out of the bedroom for a while," he teased.

I didn't have to answer, all I had to do was smile.

"Okay." He gestured like it was a horrific thing to do and then laughed.

"Just for a while longer, but I have to be at the office by ten. I have some comp time I can use, and this seems to be like a good-enough excuse."

Reaching over to the nightstand, he was unable to get to the cell, so he stood on his feet and immediately ran to the bathroom.

"Carter, are you okay?"

He didn't answer immediately. Soon I heard the water running. Pulling on his T-shirt, I walked to the bathroom. Standing at the sink dressed in his jeans, his head was bowed. His skin was pale and wet where he had splashed his face.

"What's wrong?"

He looked at me through the mirror.

"I don't know. I was fine until I set my feet on the floor. I thought whatever this was, was passing. I'm not so sure."

"Why don't you go lie back down for a while." Rubbing his head, he walked out and lay down across the bed. I had no doubt now; I know what's going on. I was going to have to confirm it soon. I'd heard of things like this, but I had never seen it before. Today, before I started to work, I was going to see my doctor. I wasn't going to be able to keep it quiet much longer. Carter was smart, and it wouldn't take long for him to figure it out.

Going to a doctor is hard enough but sitting on a table with nothing on, but a sheet in a cold room is worse. There is nothing glamorous about going to an OB-GYN. Waiting impatiently for this to be over, I sat and wondered if it were true. If I was pregnant, how was I going to tell Carter? We hadn't been married two months, not to mention I was told it was virtually impossible.

The room was covered with pictures of mothers and babies, and I looked at them imagining what it would have been like to have raised Jenna. I didn't even know how old she would have been had she lived. I knew nothing about what all the damage that had occurred. Either I had never asked or it was such a shock they told me and I no longer remembered.

432

Carter wouldn't be happy, I was sure of it. He wanted the time to get to know one another before we talked about children. Yet he didn't seem to be upset when I brought it up over our honeymoon. My nerves were on edge, and I fidgeted with the sheet that covered me. There wasn't anything I could do if I were.

There was a knock on the door, and soon a young woman with long straight blond hair appeared. Dressed neatly in a gray skirt, white shirt, and equally white coat, she came into the room gracefully.

"Mrs. Blake, I'm Dr. Eisenberger. Most of my patients call me Dr. Carley, it's easier to remember." She extended her hand to me then took a seat at the desk in the corner.

She started with the normal battery of questions, medications, and such, then got into the questions that ate into my brain. "Have you been pregnant before, any miscarriages?"

"Yes, I've had one pregnancy."

"Did you have any complications?"

"She died at birth. I don't know the details."

"When was your last period?"

"In December, but they aren't regular. They haven't been for some time."

"Okay, well, shall we take a look?"

She assisted me to lay back and did a full exam and then did an ultrasound.

"This is an internal ultrasound," she explained. "It will tell us a little more than a regular ultrasound, you can see a little more and it gives us a better time frame. From what you have told me, we may be too early to hear a heartbeat, but we'll see." After inserting the wand, she turned the screen so that I could watch with her. She clicked the keys on the panel, and soon I could see a gray haze of what appeared to be multiple tiny pencil dots. The sound was like ocean crashes as it washed in an out.

Pointing to the screen, she smiled widely. "Can you see it? That little tiny area that looks like a bean, that's your baby. Congratulations, Mommy, it looks like you are approximately eight weeks along. Your due date should be around October 26. Have you been having any morning sickness?"

"Yes, some," I hesitated and told her about Carter. "My husband seems to be having it more than I."

She laughed in sympathy. "Yes, that does happen sometimes. They call it Couvade syndrome or phantom pregnancy. Most doctors don't recognize it, but there are men that experience all the pregnancy symptoms their partner has, and sometimes they are the only ones to experience them." Finishing the measurements, she gave me instructions. "I want you to take some prenatal vitamins once a day, do your exercise just as you always have although most mommies enjoy a walk, and it's the best, just don't overdo. Let me know if there are any problems at any time. I will get you in."

I was in shock even though I suspected that I was pregnant.

"Is Daddy happy?" she prompted.

"What?"

"Your husband, is he happy about this baby?"

"I don't know, he doesn't know yet." I trembled a little at the thought of telling him, and he would have to be the first to find out, that was important.

"I'm sure he will be. I don't think you will have any difficulty, but we will keep an eye on you. There is some scarring from a previous surgery from what I could see in the chart and some other issues. If anything is of concern, let me know and we will go from there. Go home and celebrate. It was nice to meet you. I'll have the nurse set up your next appointment. Take care." She extended her hand and left the room. I quickly dressed and went to the desk where the nurse had my paperwork and prescriptions ready.

I collected them and tucked them into my purse. How was I going to tell him? Would I go to his office and tell him, or would I wait until I got home? The hospital had called and had given me the evening off. It appeared that there were too many on staff, and they needed to cut back. Maybe it was for the best, it would give me the chance to tell Carter what was going on.

Pulling up into the drive of the police department homicide division, my knees started to get weak. My stomach rumbled and fluttered, so I was sure I was going to be sick. Stepping out of the car, I walked into the building and watched as there were multiple people walking back and forth between the mazes of hallways. There was no way I would be able to find him on my own.

A young woman that was an obvious detective stepped out of an office.

Tall and slender in her build with delicate features. Her gun holster strapped to her body, she walked with purpose and confidence. "Can I help you?"

"Yes, I'm . . ."

The conversation was cut short when Landon saw me making his way down the hall. "Bella." He looked at me in surprise. "What are you doing here? Are you okay?"

The other detective walked away and left me with him.

"Yes, I'm okay. Do you know where Carter is? I need to talk to him."

"I think he's in his office. He's not been out of it much since he came in today. A little under the weather it seems."

"Yes, I know." *There's a reason for that*, I was thinking as he was explaining.

"I'm sure he'd be glad to see you." He paused then looked at me again.

"Aren't you supposed to be at work?"

"Yes, but they gave me the night off, too many

435

Indians for the night I guess."

He walked me down the hall to Carter's office, the click of my heels made a high-pitched sound against the tile.

"It must be something pretty big if you came down here to talk to him."

"You could say that."

He grinned at me, and I knew he suspected. If he did, so did Carter. "Are you feeling okay?" He paused a moment for me to answer, but I didn't say a word. "You don't have to hide it from me. I know an expectant mother when I see one. I went through all of it with Beth." He made an attempt to comfort me. "He has no idea, but don't worry, it'll be fine. Trust me, he loves you."

Stopping in front of an unopened door, he reached and turned the knob and opened it. "It's okay." He said as he smiled down at me. "You will make a wonderful mother."

Looking across the room, I saw Carter sitting at his desk with his elbows propped and holding his head in his hands.

"Hey, bro, I found something in the hall I think you might want to see."

He didn't move. "Yeah, what?"

He walked me in a little closer and showed me the chair in front of

Carter's desk.

"Your beautiful wife." Patting me on the back, he turned and walked away as Carter looked up from his desk.

"Isabella? What are you doing here, angel?" He got up and walked around to the front of his desk and leaned against it, standing before me like he already knew the answer. His arms were crossed at his chest, his legs crossed at the ankles as he looked at me expectantly. I squirmed uncomfortably in the chair in front of him.

"Okay, let's start with an easy one. Why aren't you

at work?"

"There were too many working tonight, so they gave me the evening off."

"Okay, easy enough answer. You don't normally come here, where's

Peirce?"

"In the car, I guess he thought since I was coming here, he didn't need to walk me in?"

"Well, since you aren't offering much information, I'll start." He looked down on me, never cracking a smile. "I haven't been feeling well, you knew that. So I went to the precinct's doctor. I told him about the symptoms, so he ran some test. Every test he ran came back negative. He looked at me and told me he couldn't find a thing." He looked down at me and started to grin at me a little, and it grew a little bigger. "I'm yanking your chain, Bella. Now, I'm a relatively healthy guy, I can't imagine why all of a sudden I would be sick." He prompted me to speak, but I sat silently, not knowing what to say.

He knew, I was certain of it. I couldn't tell if the smile he had on his face was hiding anger or if he was happy. "One more time, do you have something that you want to tell me?"

His stance changed, and he crouched down in front of me with his hands clasped in front of him. "I really don't want to pry it out of you, but you are going to have to say something within the next nine months."

My voice cracked as I tried to speak. "You knew?"

"Not until I saw the doctor. He told me to go home, there was nothing wrong with me other than my wife was pregnant, go home and celebrate."

"Are you angry?"

"No, angel, I'm not." He helped me to stand, and I looked at his face. He was happy, his smile was wide, I had never seen this side of him. All I could see was the love pouring from him. Placing his hand over my stomach, he

437

looked down. "I can't believe it, I'm going to be a father again. We created a brand-new life together. I didn't think it was possible, not with the medical history. I'm thrilled. I want you to have the child you wanted so badly. Didn't you think I knew?" Looking at me, I was stunned at his reaction, tears streamed down his cheeks, and my heart broke.

"I love you so much, I wanted a child with you, but I wasn't sure if it was what you wanted. I didn't think I could conceive, and you told me you wanted to wait. I was so afraid of what you would think."

"Angel, I could never be angry over something like this. It's a gift." He ran his cupped hand down his face and wiped the tears from it, and I finally realized that he was okay and threw my arms around his neck. "I don't care if I have to go through this every day as long as you're all right."

Pulling away, he smiled. "When?"

"October 26."

"And everything is okay? No problems?"

"I'm fine, everything is fine. In a couple of weeks, we should be able to hear the heartbeat. I want you with me."

"Angel, I wouldn't miss it."

A few weeks had gone by, and I wanted to talk to my mother. I still didn't know the details about my brother. Before I called or tried to get in contact with her, I needed to get ready for work. Standing in front of the bathroom mirror, I looked at the reflection in front of me. I couldn't say it was stunning, but I looked better than I had thought. I hadn't slept much lately from having to make multiple trips to the bathroom during the night, but somehow I managed a little extra last night.

I was dressed for work, but I was having difficulty with my hair. Every time I raised my hands above my head to curl it, I was sick and had to lie down. It wasn't pleasant, but I soon finished and stood looking into the mirror trying to decide whether to pull it back into a ponytail.

From a room away, I could hear Carter's voice faintly. He was obviously on the cell with the department. I was making out bits and pieces, but the conversation didn't make sense so I lost interest.

Pulling my hair back into a ponytail, I walked back into the bedroom to put on my shoes.

"I can't do that, not now...I know that." His voice was angry, and it was evident he was upset. "Look, something else has come up, and...Can't you get someone else...Yes, I understand...You know the situation...I can't talk anymore now ... We can discuss this later..."

From the bedroom door, I could see him pacing the floor and rubbing the back of his neck just as he did when something was bugging him. He slipped his cell in his back pocket. Walking into the living room, I saw him standing in front of the sliding doors looking out onto the back deck. He's tense, his arms were crossed, and his eyes were staring out into nothingness. Walking up behind him, I put my arms around him.

"You okay, you seem a little tense."

He unfolded his arms and put one around me. "Yeah, I'm fine, just a disagreement with the captain, nothing for you to worry about."

Standing there for a moment, I knew something was wrong, I could feel it. Turning to me, he walked me over to the couch. "Come sit with me." I could tell he wasn't happy, but he's trying to hide it. Sitting down next to me, he took my hands in his. "Isabella, I have an assignment. I'm not happy about doing it, but I don't think I've have a choice. I want you to promise me something. I want you to promise me no matter what happens that you take care of yourself and the two children. It's very important that you do that for me. Peirce will look after you, and Landon will be around, but I want you take extra care about where you go and who you talk to."

"Carter, what's going on? You're really scaring me."

"It's okay, I don't want you upset. There is always a risk on an assignment.

I just want to know that you are going to be okay. Promise me that you will take care of yourself, Molly, and that little baby."

"Sure, I will, but I don't understand."

"Angel, I can't tell you anything more."

Molly ran into the room as usual and jumped into her father's lap. He grabbed him and held to him tight. "Mmmm. What a hug, Tink, something special for Daddy?"

"Daddy, pease not go."

"Tink, Daddy has to go to work."

"No, Daddy, not go."

This was worse. For some reason, this wasn't fitting.

Stroking her hair and pushing back, I could see she was crying. "Tink, why don't you want Daddy to go to work?"

"Cause he not come back."

That was it. The words hit me so hard it took my breath. I walked back to the bedroom to the desk drawer. Answers, I needed them, and I knew if there were something brewing, I would find it there. Carter's and Molly's health records were there, Carter's and Andrea's burial plot, a living will, advance directive, healthcare insurance, house insurance, social security numbers, a life insurance policy, and a will. Just as I thought, he had this changed one week ago, it included our unborn child. He knew something, and he wasn't going to share it. Picking it up, I carried it with me back into the living room now ravaged with emotional pain. "You knew something was going to happen, didn't you? That's why you changed the will! You knew you were going on this assignment."

"Isabella."

"Carter, how could you do this? You knew I was pregnant, and there could be issues why would you do this?"

"Angel, it isn't my choice. I don't want to do this. Just because I'm going doesn't mean anything is going to happen."

"You knew enough that what you would be doing is dangerous, enough that you changed this will."

"I just want to make sure that you're taken care of."

I was so angry at him that I couldn't even cry. "Carter, please, for God's sake, don't do this."

He wrapped his arms around me and held me close to his chest, his lips next to my ear. "I don't want to go. Trust me, I'll be back."

He had Peirce follow us to the hospital that evening so that he could have time alone with me before he went back on shift. He had taken a break away to be able to do that, and I was grateful. Walking me in, he followed me to the break room. Placing my things on the floor, I turned to see Peirce waiting outside the door. Carter shut the door and walked to me slowly. "This is it, angel, I'll keep in contact somehow. Don't worry okay?" He smiled down at me as he cupped my face. "Everything will be all right, I promise you."

Leaning in, he kissed me passionately. "I love you," he whispered and walked away. My heart sank as he walked down the corridor away from me, it left me bitter inside. His words were assuring, but it hurt me so badly I wasn't sure that I was going to be able to finish my shift. I had to get control of myself. My shift started in less than fifteen minutes, and I had to be ready.

This wasn't going to be easy. I wasn't sure when he was coming home, he hadn't said. All I knew was that whatever he was doing was dangerous, I felt it from the time I found the changed will, and what made it worse was the scene with Molly. She had begged her father not to leave. That wasn't our little girl, she never had done that.

Sitting in the break room, I prayed. *God, please, whatever it takes, protect him. I can't do this alone. He's all I have. I can't raise this baby alone without him.*

We worked so hard to get where we are, please *don't take him from me.* My heart clenched at the very idea that he wouldn't return.

The evening wore on as it often did on some slow evenings, and it was like a crawl. This was one night, I wished that it had been busy, anything to take what was happening off my mind. The bays had few patients, and I was left doing some pickup work and supplies. It was nearing the end of the shift when I saw a crew crash through the door. It wasn't good. A flood of patrols followed, and that was always a bad sign. "Officer down," I had heard from a fellow officer. Looking up, I knew I recognized the voice. Landon was running close behind the cot that carried a lifeless body of a fellow officer.

They took the officer to bay 4 and were quickly working with them. Landon stopped me as I ran toward the room.

His voice shaking, he took me from the door forcibly. "Don't go in there.

You need to come with me."

"No, I have to help them."

"You can't go in there. Bella, listen to me." He clung to me tighter than he had to. "Let them take care of it."

"What is it? What is it you're not telling me?"

J.C. ran through the back door toward us. His clothes rumpled with blood covering him. "Landon! Where is he?" His voice panicked as he closed in on us. Landon's grip became stronger than before, holding me in place.

Immediately, I felt ice run through my veins and my

442

knees fell from under me.

"No! . . . God . . . No! . . . Carter!" I reached to get to him, and Landon clasped me to him.

"Isabella, please sit down with me. Listen to me, Carter was after Arnell, he got caught in the fire."

"No! He can't, he's supposed to come back to me. We were supposed to go next week to the doctor to hear our baby's heartbeat for the first time.

Dear God, this can't be happening."

Sitting in the chair between Landon and J.C. assured I wasn't going into that room. I rocked back and forth to the point I couldn't sit any longer.

Starting to stand up, I was held in place.

"Bella, no," Landon insisted. "Don't go in there."

"Why not, I need to see him. I need to be with my husband."

"Bella, you don't understand."

"Please!" I was enraged by him.

"Bella, you don't need to see that."

Breaking away from them, I was met by one of the interns with Landon and J.C. behind me.

"Mrs. Blake?"

"Yes," I answered hoarsely.

"I'm sorry, we've done all we can. There was a lot of damage to the face and chest. I did everything I could."

I sank to my knees, thinking I would never recover.

Please see the sequel to in the next book of the series
Stilling the Thunder.